Cedar Mill & Bethany
Community Libraries
library.cedarmill.org
WITHDRAWN
CEDAR MILL LIBRARY
OCT 2020

Praise for *The Curse of Misty Wayfair*

"Wright creates an inspirational mystery with thrilling finesse, blending chilling supernatural elements with the raw interiority of mental illness, and taking readers on Heidi's haunting search for identity, which is sure to keep them up at night."

—*Booklist*

"The past and present collide in this time-slip suspense, weaving the lives of two women together in a high-intensity thriller. . . . Prepare for a mystery transpiring through time that will stimulate the senses."

—*Hope by the Book*

"With a masterful dual narrative, subtle romance and spine-tingling suspense, Jaime Jo Wright navigates the lives of two young women seeking a sense of identity."

—*BookPage*

"In this thought-provoking novel, the contemporary story and the 1910 threads intertwine to explore the consequences of past sins and the way light can break through the dark. . . . With depth and intelligence, Wright explores the role of faith in life."

—*Christian Retailing*

"A pitch-perfect gothic that highlights the extraordinary talent of Jaime Jo Wright. I stayed up past midnight gobbling up this mesmerizing tale and was sorry to see it end."

—Colleen Coble, author of the Rock Harbor series

"Stellar writing combined with stellar storytelling are rare. Wright brings both in abundance to *The Curse of Misty Wayfair*. The intrigue starts immediately and doesn't let up until the final pages."

—James L. Rubart, author of *The Man He Never Was*

"Two tales twist together into a story that draws the reader in and won't let go. *The Curse of Misty Wayfair* is deliciously thrilling, with a resolution steeped in light and hope."

—Jocelyn Green, author of *Between Two Shores*

D0980667

The Reckoning at Gossamer Pond

"The movements between time periods are perfectly done to heighten the intrigue of each unraveling mystery. . . . A complex story with sympathetic characters and many surprises."

—*Historical Novels Review*

"Brilliantly atmospheric and underscored by a harrowing romance, *The Reckoning at Gossamer Pond* pairs danger with redemption and features not only two heroines of great agency but one of the most compelling, unlikely, and memorable heroes I have met in an age."

—Rachel McMillan, author of *Murder at the Flamingo*

"Intoxicating and wonderfully authentic . . . delightfully shadowed with mystery that will keep readers poring over the story, but what makes it memorable is the powerful light that burst through every darkened corner in this novel—*hope*."

—Joanna Davidson Politano, author of *Lady Jane Disappears*

"*The Reckoning at Gossamer Pond* is true to Wright's unique style and voice. Multilayered characters who intrigue the reader and a story the threads of which are unpredictable and well woven together make this a must-read for anyone who enjoys suspense."

—Sarah Varland, author of *Mountain Refuge*

The House on Foster Hill

"Jaime Jo Wright's *The House on Foster Hill* blends the past and present in a gripping mystery that explores faith and the sins of ancestors."

—*Foreword Reviews*

"Headed by two strong female protagonists, Wright's debut is a lushly detailed time-slip novel that transitions seamlessly between past and present. . . . Readers who enjoy Colleen Coble and Dani Pettrey will be intrigued by this suspenseful mystery."

—*Library Journal*

"With one mystery encased in another and a century between the two, Wright has written a spellbinding novel."

—*Christian Market*

"Jaime Jo Wright is an amazing storyteller who had me on the edge of my seat. . . . *The House on Foster Hill* is a masterfully told story with layers and layers of mystery and intrigue, with a little romance thrown in for good measure."

—Tracie Peterson, author of the GOLDEN GATE SECRETS series

THE
HAUNTING
★ _AT_ ★
BONAVENTURE
CIRCUS

THE HAUNTING AT BONAVENTURE CIRCUS

JAIME JO WRIGHT

BETHANYHOUSE
a division of Baker Publishing Group
Minneapolis, Minnesota

© 2020 by Jaime Sundsmo

Published by Bethany House Publishers
11400 Hampshire Avenue South
Bloomington, Minnesota 55438
www.bethanyhouse.com

Bethany House Publishers is a division of
Baker Publishing Group, Grand Rapids, Michigan

Printed in the United States of America

All rights reserved. No part of this publication may be reproduced, stored in
a retrieval system, or transmitted in any form or by any means—for example,
electronic, photocopy, recording—without the prior written permission of the
publisher. The only exception is brief quotations in printed reviews.

ISBN 978-0-7642-3389-0 (trade paper)
ISBN 978-0-7642-3776-8 (cloth)

Scripture quotations are from the King James Version of the Bible.

This is a work of fiction. Names, characters, incidents, and dialogues are products
of the author's imagination and are not to be construed as real. Any resemblance
to actual events or persons, living or dead, is entirely coincidental.

Cover design by Jennifer Parker

Author is represented by Books & Such Literary Agency.

20 21 22 23 24 25 26   7 6 5 4 3 2 1

To my Buddy Boy

Oh, to always be Wendy to your Peter Pan.
Let's never grow up.
Let's always snuggle and laugh, wrestle and karate-chop.
Let's always make up our own Pokémon names.
Let's be superheroes and believe we can fly.

My little man.
You will always be Momma's.
Chase after greatness of heart,
faithfulness of spirit,
and courage of the mind.

Never be afraid to be who God created you to be.
You are not hidden.
He will fight for you.

CHAPTER ONE

PIPPA RIPLEY

**BLUFF RIVER, WISCONSIN
AUGUST 1928**

L ife was not unlike the wisp of fog that curled around the base of a grave marker, softly caressing the marble before dissolving into the violet shadows of the night. There was a sweetness in its bitter that left an aftertaste, a vision, a moment of wonderment. Too often it floated away before one could grasp it, retrieve it, hold on to it, savor it, and then bid it farewell with a tear and a reminiscent smile. Instead, the race to capture life was ended before it ever really began, leaving behind the dewdrops of questions, the footprints of unmet needs, and the spirits hovering just out of reach—voices lost to the annals of unwritten histories.

It wasn't Pippa Ripley's preference, then, to be padding across the damp, leaf-covered earth of the graveyard. Her deformed leg created a lesser footprint impression in the ground as she bore much of her weight on her good leg. She would never have come had it been night or even dusk. She wasn't brave, she wasn't assertive, and she would never be disobedient—unless she had to be. This was a had-to-be moment. In the early dawn, whose warmth began to seep through the chilled autumn air as the sun tipped the trees and made their colorful branches glow, Pippa questioned whether any other young women her age still sought to be obedient. Women had, after all, won the vote eight years before and, on occasion, could even be spotted wearing men's trousers. Short hair bobbed and curled close to their faces. Strands of pearls, dresses that dared to show the knees when these girls spun in a scandalous fox-trot . . . they even imbibed alcohol. Secretly, of course, because Prohibition was very strongly enforced in Bluff River. Still, Pippa knew the rumors. The places where the carefree gathered. Quietly whispered meet-ups. She'd heard the whispers. They swirled around her the entirety of her growing-up years.

Maybe Pippa was just old-fashioned enough. Traditional. Or perhaps it was fear that latched her to her father and created an ingrained sense of respect for his authority. Regardless of its cause, it was why Pippa's stomach knotted with guilt as her brown pumps sank into the earth that stretched in straight, unending lines between the rows of graves. She wasn't supposed to be here. She wasn't supposed to be curious or ask questions. She wasn't supposed to leave the manor unless her father knew her whereabouts or her mother had stamped her approval on the outing. She was an only child. Alone. She walked in the shadows of an elder brother who had died at age three from polio, and another brother who would have been two years older than she had he not died during childbirth, stillborn and perfect. The Ripleys were not keen on the slightest risk of losing their only surviving child—even if she was a girl, and even if she had been left on their doorstep as an infant, with a twisted leg and a note that clearly defined she was a castoff from the local circus troupe. Too much of a misfit for even their circles.

Now, at the tender age of nineteen, her life was carefully commandeered. She was submissive and dutiful, just as she'd been reared to be.

Yet, here she was. Alone, in a cemetery, in the wee hours of the morning, all because *he* had summoned her. He had always been there, it seemed, along with the other questions that lingered in the shadows forever following her. Pippa had sensed him as a child, though she hadn't been able to define the feeling. The feeling of being watched, guarded, looked over.

In past years, Pippa had seen him only a few times. Just a form, a silhouette really. But, when she'd asked if anyone else had seen the man watching her, no one had. At the onset of her sightings—once she'd finally admitted them aloud—her parents worried something was dreadfully wrong with her. That Pippa saw someone when no one else did. Still, Pippa insisted he was there, until her father's firm command had silenced her. Silenced her out of fear, perhaps, that she was losing her mind. *"Possession,"* she'd heard her mother mumble worriedly to her father—although Pippa wasn't entirely certain what she'd meant. A visit from the local priest and a long, dreary interview ended with a swift shake of his head and a shrug of his shoulders. Pippa never saw him again in their home, which made sense, for they weren't Catholic. She also learned, after that, to keep to herself the things she saw or felt. They were meant for her, after all, and no one else.

Pippa reached with a gloved hand and caressed the cool surface of a grave marker as she passed it. Ahead, in the distance, stood a large crypt, its marbled form impressive and outstanding in the middle of the other markers. A generous plot of earth surrounded it and a black iron fence. From there the graveyard resumed its pattern and rows of stones, some pillars, some flat and facing upward, some carved cherubs, and one, a cross. But it was the crypt her eyes fixated on. The name *Ripley* was etched along its arched doorframe. The family crypt where her grandparents, her brothers, Uncle Theo and Aunt Ramona lay, and where Father and Mother would someday be interred. Perhaps even she would lie at peace there, if she didn't marry, which was a fate neither of her parents seemed fond of and had already made moves to rectify.

But *he* had been more open in the last year. It was here at the family crypt that Pippa found many of his messages. Here or at the circus grounds. Hidden in secret places only she and he knew of. A habit formed after the first summoning a few months ago, cryptically hand-delivered by a messenger.

It created guilt within her. A churning and awful sickening feeling of guilt that she had acted in disobedience and secrecy against her parents. Still, Pippa assuaged that guilt by focusing on the delight she found in meeting dear friends at the circus. Friends she imagined might have been like those ones she would have grown up with had she been acceptable enough to keep as an infant. Clive the dwarf, Benard the smithy, Ernie the elephant trainer, and even the brooding Jake Chapman who worked with the menagerie and refused to speak of his past as a bare-knuckled ring fighter from the wharfs out east.

Yes, the messages were intoxicating. *He* had connected Pippa to the world she'd been born into and then rejected from. *He* was the one whose vowed allegiance to her was something Pippa had no desire to share with anyone. She kept his missives tied with a blue ribbon and tucked into a neat pile in a secret place in her room. Short letters that told her nothing and everything all at the same time. Nothing about her past, and everything about her future.

He would always be there.

Watching.

Watching her.

He was her Watchman. But more than that, she belonged to him.

CHAPTER TWO

BLUFF RIVER, WISCONSIN
PRESENT DAY

The transition from life to death was a metamorphosis of the soul. A conjuring up of courage to release your last breath and allow your spirit to drift away into new life. Unless, one could argue, it was taken from you. Strangled from you. Your eyes drilling into your killer's as their fingers bruised the delicate skin of your neck, as their breath painted your face with the last scent you would ever smell, as your heels kicked the wooden floorboards in an effort to sustain life. There was no beautiful metamorphosis in murder. It was simply that. Murder. A deliberate, heinous act that catapulted you into the afterlife, your destiny be damned.

No one had told Chandler Faulk before she'd recommended the purchase that the abandoned train depot her uncle had invested in was likely the site of an old murder. No one had suggested that local lore claimed a woman's body had once hung from a rope where the depot's chandelier used to light the main ticket room. Or maybe she hadn't hung there, the realtor finally admitted after the purchase had been completed. No one knew for sure. Some stated the woman—a circus seamstress by day and prostitute by night—had been found in one of the now-dilapidated circus buildings. The zebra house, or maybe the tack

13

building, the blacksmith's shop, the wagon barn? It was all a muddled story of many opinions, and as it grew, so did Chandler's concern that she might have made a poor recommendation to her uncle. She bore the sole responsibility of this massive financial investment—to flip the historic building into something lucrative or else demolish it in exchange for the standard housing that was guaranteed to bring in revenue.

Chandler jammed the padlock key into her jeans' pocket and unwrapped the chain from its intertwined tangle through the iron door latch. When she tugged on the heavy door, the air, like a finally released breath that had been held in for decades, assaulted her senses. The old circus train depot was musty and unused. Over twenty years of silence entombed behind padlocks, cement-filled windows, and rumors of spirits no one locally born and raised wished to tangle with.

The two-story, rectangular brick building had once been home to a bustling hub of traveling and mayhem. Business mixed with pleasure, mingling with the tempting smattering of colorful humanity. Al Capone, they said, had been no stranger, lingering nearby in a local inn that was more of an underground brewery and brothel than it was a place to sleep for the night. But then there were the more unknowns but no less magnanimous, which graced the train station platform and left old echoes of footsteps across its marbled floor. They were the acrobats and costume makers of the circus. Lion handlers and blacksmiths. Tattooed men and elephant trainers. Both the mob and the circus had ridden these rails and, in their wake, left the ancient echoes of laughter and charade.

"Hello." Chandler's murmured voice echoed through the aged air, bounced off the elaborate wood walls she could barely make out in the darkness of the night, and dissipated as the remaining tones floated upward into the vaulted ceiling. She greeted the old ghosts as one might a friend. Chandler hoped, if such a thing really existed, that they would be friendly spirits. Like Casper the Ghost. Cute. Almost cuddly. Avoiding poltergeists would be preferred.

Arriving at the depot at eleven at night wasn't Chandler's preference for a first real tour since she'd visited the site a month prior. It had been daytime then. The depot was impressive and unimpressive at the same time. Just an old brick shell of had-beens. But now? Only thirty minutes ago, Chandler was readying for bed when she'd received the phone call. Whispered. Warning. A nighttime call of goodwill mixed with suspicion.

"I think someone is in your building," Lottie Dobson had hissed. Lottie was a local real-estate agent turned paranormal groupie. "I see a light."

Why Lottie was outside the train depot hadn't been important. She was Lottie. Chandler had already deduced that Lottie was very fascinated with the other world but also respectfully aware that others were not. It was probably why she'd withheld the information of the supposed hauntings of the old depot. It made the building's sale less palatable. Few people wished to purchase haunted grounds unless they were either nonbelievers or purely unconcerned. Now Lottie was acting as the depot's Good Samaritan bodyguard, of sorts. Or maybe Chandler's bodyguard.

Regardless, it was Lottie's call announcing a potential trespasser that reminded Chandler that this entire project—this historic restoration—rested on *her* shoulders. Chandler Neale Faulk's very determined and very exhausted shoulders.

Chandler had dialed 911 as she ducked from her rented cottage.

"I'll be back soon," she called to the high-school babysitter, who had just been readying to leave after a day of watching Chandler's son. The sitter accepted the opportunity to make an extra ten bucks and stay longer. So, in spite of the pang of regret as Chandler wished she could crawl in beside the curled-up form of her precious seven-year-old son, she left. To confront a trespasser.

"Or a ghost," Lottie had whispered just before she hung up. "It might be *the* ghost!"

Now, stepping inside, Chandler fumbled for her flashlight, irritated she'd beat the cops to the building. Small towns. They probably didn't have a squad car at every corner, did they? This wasn't exactly the ghetto. It was just the run-down, historic south side of a small town, population eight thousand.

"Don't touch anything."

Chandler screamed, falling onto her backside and casting a panicked expression in the direction of the depot door she'd unlocked less than two minutes before. She could barely make out the outline of the door. The moon was dark, and now her flashlight flicked off as it rolled away from her across the wood floor.

"You don't want to disturb anything." Instruction came from a monstrous man in the doorway behind her.

Chandler berated herself for not waiting for the police as her mind scrambled to come up with some method of self-defense. Pepper spray—in her back pocket—a quick burst of it and he'd be temporarily blinded—or shot through with adrenaline and therefore becoming more dangerous. She'd heard of that. Men in the throes of violence reacting to pain as a stimulant. She listened to the audiobook biographies of serial killers. They were fiends of another breed entirely.

"I'm not going to kill you." The man moved toward her.

Chandler backed away, her rear end scraping against gritty floorboards that probably hadn't been walked on in decades. She couldn't see much of his features, though she could make out the longish hair, scraggly and unkempt, which waved away from a broad forehead.

His hand shot out.

Chandler bit back a second scream, opting instead for a feminine growl that sounded more like a strangled yelp.

"Knock it off. I'm trying to help." He barked and gripped her wrist, pulling her up from the floor. Corded muscles in his forearms boasted the type of veins that jutted out after a solid pumping of iron in the gym. She could feel them against her skin. Glancing down, Chandler caught a glimpse of a tattoo that ran a diagonal coil around his skin. A crucifix with an inked rosary wrapped around it that disappeared beneath the rolled cuff of his shirtsleeve.

"Let go!" Chandler twisted her arm from his grip, and he released her easily. She rubbed her wrist but noted vaguely it wasn't sore. He'd handled her rather gently. She swiped the back of her jeans, casting off dust and debris from the floor, then straightened her glasses that were tilted on her face.

"Who are you?" Chandler demanded, feeling everything foolish and stupid for coming here alone. Like she was going to be some sort of aggressor and shoo away a trespasser. But heck. She'd expected a kid maybe. Some prankster. Not a Sasquatch hiding in the darkness.

She raised an eyebrow and hoped she looked stern. She'd always been described as "too pretty to be ugly" and learned that, sometimes, ugly earned a woman a lot more respect in a male-dominated world. But it didn't matter. If she could barely make out his features, her casting him a stern eye was going to have minimal impact.

The man ignored her and stalked in a wide circle around her. His eyes were narrowed, his dark brows pulled into such a deep valley that he reminded her of a wolf stalking its prey.

"Did you see the light too?" he questioned, even as he held his massive hand toward her, palm up, arm outstretched. "Don't move."

Sirens howled in the distance.

Chandler snapped her head around to glance at the door, then shot a suspicious look back at the man.

"It's the police." She stated it like a threat. Chandler didn't miss the quiet snort from the man as he stood in the middle of the large ticket room, staring up into the cavernous darkness toward the roofline.

"Do I look like I care?" His shirt was unbuttoned at the top few buttons. A wrinkled, nondescript button-up shirt with no

17

logo or distinct pattern to it. At least that Chandler could make out through squinted eyes.

The sirens grew more pronounced.

He moved past Chandler and strode toward a doorway across the room, which was the width of a rolling barn door. The room beyond was even darker. A woodsy scent of balsam or pine mixed with citrus wafted from the man and teased Chandler's senses. He clung to the doorframe and seemed to assess the blackness.

"Do you want my flashlight?" Chandler couldn't hide the edge of aggravation to her voice. He'd barged in. Scared the life out of her. Now he was tromping around the place as if there were ghouls lurking in the corners and he were some vampire hunter.

Chandler opened her mouth to demand—well, she didn't know what—when he spun on his heel and charged toward her. Without a moment to collect her wits, his arm shot around her midsection, pulling her against him as he pressed his back against the wall, just to the right of the open main door.

"What are you—?" Chandler felt his chin on the top of her head.

"Shh!" His silencing echoed deep in her ear, his breath warm at her lobe as he curled around her, glaring through the inky blackness of the depot.

Everything in Chandler's senses awakened. From the vacant stale room with its vaulted ceiling to the hard torso at her back and the feeling of the man's breath rising and falling in controlled silence.

She wasn't safe. No more than the woman who had supposedly died here when the trains still blew their whistles as they entered Bluff River.

The arm tightened until Chandler found it hard to breathe.

The sirens were close now.

A pigeon fluttered as it flew across the room, chortling its frantic irritation at being disturbed in this antique deathtrap.

Chandler dared not speak.

She didn't even try to struggle.

"Someone was here. I swear I heard someone." His mouth moved against her jaw, his baritone vibrating against her. His lips outlined the seriousness of his declaration against her skin.

"I didn't hear anyone—"

"*Someone* was in here," he whispered again, not offering any evidence to support his claim. His arm tightened against her in a quick squeeze to emphasize his point. "Don't come here alone ever again. Not at night."

When she nodded—what else could she do?—he released her, setting off an emotional controversy in Chandler. With the bulk of the man gone, she was both relieved and bereft. She was in danger, but she was safe. She was terrified, but she was intrigued. She was—

Alone.

The red-and-blue lights of the police car illuminated the interior of the old building. The glow revealed nothing but emptiness. The man was gone and the depot, a shell, once bustling with travelers, now dead. Its secrets forever silenced.

CHAPTER THREE

PIPPA

Some secrets should never be told. This was the mantra of the circus. They were a proud, exclusive family who held the rapt attention of their audience with the gift of scandalizing, horrifying, and monopolizing on daredevilish acts. Yet they were more than performers, more than humans battling oddities and deformities. They were also wagon masters, trainers, blacksmiths, handymen, costume makers, and more. These were the people who made the circus run. The nuts and bolts, so to speak. These were the private people, the small city of workers and performers who never quite fit into society, who fine ladies whispered behind gloved hands were heathens, gypsies, and ill-bred. Still, they fascinated the general public. A magnetic draw of demonized, underprivileged, hardworking men and questionably moral ladies. Delightful to behold . . . from a respectable distance.

"And they're perfect." Richard Ripley leaned against the wheel of his Duesenberg Model A, its shiny dark metal frame receiving an absent stroke of fondness under his hand. The white-rimmed tires almost sparkled, and Pippa knew one of their handymen had more likely than not washed them down with soap and water before her father took it out that morning. The car was the flashy exclamation point at the end of the Ripley name. *BONAVENTURE CIRCUS* were the capital letters that began their story.

"Have you seen them?" Richard cast a proud grin toward Pippa, who smiled obediently in response. An instinct. Always agree with her father. Always. "They're a well-working machine!"

And I should have been one of them. But Pippa didn't voice her thought. She wasn't. She was a Ripley, no matter what she felt deep inside her soul.

The car was parked at the top of the hill overlooking the circus grounds, the river that split it into two, and the railroad tracks that forged their iron path toward the train depot whose roof could be seen a few blocks to the west. In the foreground stood the row of circus buildings. The bright yellow octagonal elephant house, the green menagerie barn, the brick two-story costume house with its white clapboard siding, and on the corner a three-story brick boardinghouse for the circus staff.

They were spectators this morning. The autumn breeze blew through the thin silk of Pippa's stockings and pressed the navy pleats of her skirt against her legs. She drew in a breath, taking in the familiar and nostalgic scent of fall, the leaves that fluttered across the street, the damp air that teased of the rain to come and reminded of the rain the night before.

Richard swiped his hat from his head and slapped it against his leg in satisfaction, drawing not only Pippa's attention but also that of Forrest. Forrest Landstrom. Her father's protégé, and her parentally chosen fiancé.

"A well-working machine in a mud pit." Forrest's dark brows were drawn, emphasizing his deep-set brown eyes and winsome features.

Pippa said nothing, instead turning her attention back to the scene down the hill. The rain had created havoc on the grounds. Wagons were stuck a quarter of the way up their rims. She noticed a man trying to shove a wheelbarrow through the muck, and it might as well have been filled with a hippopotamus for the way he pushed and strained to get it to move.

Shouts echoed through the valley, drifting to their ears. Cursing.

The neighing of horses as they were hitched to wagons and attempted to pull them through the mud that refused to give up their prisoners. One of the wagons had elephants hitched to the front. Four of them, with thick leather straps and harnesses. The beasts bore down, and the circus wagon groaned as mud sucked at its wheels. The vibrant red of the wagon, its gold trim, and the glorious profile of a golden lion's head were spattered with the evidence of mire.

It was not a beautiful sight. It was chaos. It was a mess. It was the muddied, sullied faces of men tired of a long season on the rails. The circus traveling from town to town, state to state, and finally ending up here. The wintering quarters of the Bonaventure Circus. Soon the performers who had arrived along with the circus train would all scatter, many of them heading south for the winter. But for now they were here in this little town in the middle of Wisconsin, where the circus's origins had been birthed by Pippa's father, a businessman, years before. It had been a fabulous part-nering with his entertainment-minded friend who was now dead but who had left behind his son, Forrest. The Ripleys and the Landstroms would be bonded by more than just the circus in the months to come. Pippa's intended was fully on board with the pairing. Business trumped romance, regardless of the passionate beauty the circus might have inspired.

"What a phenomenal year this has been!" Richard Ripley slapped his hat back on his head and nodded with vigorous assertion. "You've seen the financial reports. We've both seen the circus in action this summer. You agree, yes, Forrest?"

Forrest didn't bother to exchange any looks with Pippa. To both men, she was barely even there. "Yes, sir. A good year."

"And with the elephant calf arriving soon!" Ripley's grin might have well stretched off his face if that were possible. "Posters for spring have already been printed, and what with all the hype we've been able to muster over the past season, our attendance will more than double. Who in America gets the opportunity to see a baby elephant? Not many!"

"Definitely, it will be only a continued boon, sir." While Forrest's reply was agreeable, there was an underlying edge of steel that communicated very clearly to both Pippa and her father that Forrest saw himself as the forty-percent partner that he was. "I would like to spend more time with the train next summer." Forrest's comment seemed innocent enough, yet it reeked of insinuation. He had, more often than not, been left behind in the offices this year. Richard Ripley had been the one to travel and meet the circus throughout the summer. To oversee it, Ripley had explained. For he was, after all, the father of the circus. Forrest was merely a son.

Pippa braced herself for her father's reaction to Forrest's barely veiled suggestion that he was wiling his way deeper into the management of the circus.

But Ripley only nodded. "Of course, of course." He gave Forrest a sideways glance and smile. "You did enjoy your visit to St. Louis, did you not?"

Forrest didn't answer.

The circus was at the pinnacle of popularity. With the war over now, the States were returning to a lucrative economy. Even the poorest of the poor could muster up a penny, a nickel, or a dime for admission, and if not, the boys would find ways to sneak beneath the canvases of the tents for a peep at the weird and never-before-seen. Granted, it meant the loss of some ticket sales, but those "whelps"—as Pippa's father called them—were word-of-mouth advertising. A nickel a shout. And the boys' mouths flapped, and word spread, and Bonaventure Circus was fast becoming one of the most popular circus trains to cross the Midwest and South.

It might be more unassuming, here in Bluff River, but the very essence of the circus permeated the air of Bonaventure's birthplace. It was magic. It was a fairy tale of Mother Goose proportions. It had stolen from Pippa every sense of individuality she could have ever hoped to have. And yet, even as she stood next to her father and folded her gloved hands in front of her, very aware that she was frail-looking and waif-like in appearance, a part of her drew strength from the sight of the elephants below. Their lunging bodies, rippling muscles, and broad foreheads. The power they exuded. Harnessed into submission, the power hidden inside an elephant could kill a man if he weren't careful. Yet, the animals worked meekly, without argument, a deep soulful longing reflected in their long-lashed eyes. A longing to be free, perhaps, or maybe just to have a quiet night at home, in the straw, resting and away from the screams and laughter and repetitive pipes of the calliope's musical diatribe.

Pippa could relate. She empathized with the elephants. They were there to perform and, when needed, bear the burden of the circus family. But they weren't loved so much as treasured. And there was a difference between the two. Love sacrificed, whereas a treasure was hoarded.

Forrest's hand rested on her shoulder. A light touch. As if he read her thoughts. Read the thin line of rebellion in them that made Pippa wish to run willy-nilly down the hillside, slide in the mud, and throw her arms around the trunk of an elephant and let it swing her onto its back like one of the scantily clad ladies under the Big Top.

Pippa didn't cringe or shrink beneath Forrest's touch. He was a good man. A strong man. He was like her father. She would be treasured. But, she wondered, would she be loved?

It was a stuffy dinner party. The beauty of candles and crystal aside, claustrophobia drove Pippa outside. She gripped the railing of the wide front porch, her long strand of pearls tapping against the whitewashed wood. Drawing in a quiet breath, the night air entered her lungs like a refreshing dip in cool water. Oak trees lined the street, and beyond them she saw the twinkle of lights in the smaller homes that sat just a little lower than the sun-yellow Ripley Manor with its white-painted trim. Pippa noticed a few lanterns hanging from carriages that maneuvered down the street and in between a couple of motorcars that rumbled their arrogant exhausts in the announcement of the new, modern era. It didn't seem that long ago when Pippa was a small child and her father was the only one in town who owned an automobile. But with more and more of them in the streets— honking their horns and disturbing the peace—this seemed to be the way of things now.

A small whine pulled Pippa's attention away from the town that sprawled across the valley. It brought her gaze downward to meet deep gray eyes set in a furry face.

"Penn." Pippa's smile was genuine this time. She knelt to greet her dog and run her fingers over Penn's short steel-gray fur. The pit bull terrier had been her caretaker since Pippa was fourteen. Her nanny dog. She'd been inconsolable when her original nanny dog had passed away. Father had been fast to replace her with Penn. A few of her other somewhat wealthy friends also had nanny dogs, but typically moved on once they passed. Pippa was different. Though it went unspoken, there were times when her leg deformity caused her pain, when it would simply give out, and she took comfort from the guarded nature of Penn. The dog sensed her every mood and nosed her way into the privilege of sleeping against Pippa's back at night. A habit neither of Pippa's parents had ever discovered, and one that, even at nineteen and betrothed, Pippa had no intention of sharing. God help Forrest after they were married. Pippa wasn't certain Penn would give up her place in the bed.

Warmth crawled up Pippa's neck at the thought.

The dog nuzzled Pippa's chin and gave it a short slap of a wet tongue.

"Now, now." Pippa tilted her head away from the offending moisture. "I'm all pretty for the party. You mustn't mess my cosmetics."

Pippa's attempt at silly humor fell flat even to her own ears.

There was nothing entertaining about her. She was mousy. An afterthought. A figurine to be placed on a mantel. She could be content with that too, if it wasn't for . . .

A tiny envelope, tucked into Penn's collar, snagged Pippa's attention. Almost with a frantic flurry, Pippa fumbled with the collar, snatching the envelope and staring down at its blankness. No name. No handwriting. Nothing. Pippa turned the missive over and tore open the flap, pulling a small card from inside. A pressed violet was glued to the front of it, and the card was so miniature that the violet was perfectly centered with maybe an inch to spare on either side. She lifted it to her nose. As usual, there was no scent. It was void of anything familiar, other than the randomness with which these sporadic communications came. That the Watchman had been able to approach Penn and find the dog trusting of him spoke volumes.

With a slight frown, Pippa opened the card and tipped it toward the electric lights that shined from the front windows onto the porch. Though the handwriting was small and difficult to read, she recognized it all the same.

"Pippa?"

She yelped, crumpling the card in her palm and tripping into the porch rail. Penn sniffed the air as Forrest approached from the shadows.

"Let me help you." Forrest reached down and extended his hands to assist her from her awkward lean against the railing. Pippa hesitated, then reached out with her left hand to avoid revealing the card in her right.

His skin was smooth, but his grip strong. Forrest steadied her with his other hand around her forearm, and when she straightened, there were mere inches between them. He cleared his throat and stepped back. Pippa smoothed the front of her silk sheath, making pretense that it had somehow been soiled. Forrest's proximity unnerved her, and she wasn't certain whether she liked it or whether she didn't.

"My apologies, Pippa. I didn't mean to startle you."

Ever polite.

Pippa smiled. She also was always polite.

It was a relationship that reminded her of her paper dolls. Stiff but pretty. Fake but full of imaginary potential.

"Why did you leave the party?"

The door to the porch was open, the sounds of laughter and chatter drifting out behind Forrest's tall frame. His deep eyes studied her, and the intensity in them caused Pippa to move her hand behind her back. The card poked into her skin as her fist wrapped tighter around it.

I was suffocating, she responded mentally.

"I desired some fresh air." She answered with enough of a twist of the truth that it wouldn't offend nor would it leave her feeling guilty, like a liar.

"Ahh." Forrest gave her shoulder a light pat. "Don't be too long. You're a good egg, Pippa. The world shouldn't be kept from your charm."

With a grin that made Pippa's insides melt just a bit, Forrest gave her temporary freedom and left her alone. A good egg. Yes. She was someone who lived a wealthy, enviable lifestyle—at least from the outside looking in.

Reassuring herself that she was once again alone—apart from Penn, who had stuck her nose between the porch rails and peered out over the yard—Pippa brought the card out to read it. These messages enhanced the tiny seeds of rebellious adventure that grew in her soul. She had something no one else knew. She had *someone* no one else knew.

The words, though small, jumped off the page with a brilliant flash of challenge. She snagged her bottom lip between her teeth.

Come.

Elephant Alley.

11 pm.

He wanted to meet. Face-to-face. Her. The Watchman. In the inky blackness of a moonless night.

Pippa folded the card and tucked it back into its envelope.

She shouldn't dare.

But, dare she would. Just this once. For him.

CHAPTER FOUR

CHANDLER

The cops had been understanding. Maybe a little on edge, if she was being honest. Chandler got the sense they didn't really *want* to be at the old depot. That any nighttime excursions near the town's local haunted relic were preferred to be avoided.

Let them know if it happened again.

Do you want to file a report?

It wasn't really trespassing when no trespasser was found, was it? But then there was Sasquatch Man, who had moved off to the side and talked in low tones to an officer. Chandler had wanted to say "no duh" to his earlier declaration that someone had been in the depot. But then it really wasn't that simple. If the door had been padlocked, how had someone gotten inside to even have a light on? And, if the majority of the windows were cemented over, that meant the room Sasquatch had been investigating had to be the room where the light was seen. It was the only wing of the depot where windows were still intact. Yet no one had been inside. Still, he'd heard footsteps, or so he'd claimed.

The cops seemed to know the Sasquatch Man. He shook hands and strode away long before they'd finished with Chandler. In the end, the police helped her re-chain and padlock the door and then they'd offered to drop her off at her rented cottage.

She hadn't declined. She'd been exhausted. She missed her son. And, God help her, if Lottie hadn't texted to make sure everything was all right, further setting Chandler on edge. She didn't need the realtor peering over her shoulder. The purchase was complete.

Walk away, Lottie, walk away.

Chandler prayed that last night was the end of it. That Lottie would cease hunting ghosts on the property. That the picturesque town she'd imagined really did exist. A safe home. For her and Peter, her son. Where she could prove herself, maintain her independence, and yet relax a little in the anonymity of a small town. Just a little. Enough, perhaps, to breathe. She'd traveled quite a bit with Peter the last few years. Cities mostly. Big projects. Successful ones. One would think Chandler had more than proven her capability, but here, in Bluff River? She hoped to hide her biggest weakness.

Walking at a steady pace along the river walk, Chandler scanned the area, collecting a picture of the historic side of Bluff River. She'd traded in last night's babysitter for a replacement today. Something else Chandler would need to figure out—and fast. Peter couldn't be tossed between caregivers. He was just a kid. He needed consistency and guidance, routine, and well, he needed his mom. More than anything. Just like Chandler needed Peter.

The river cut between the banks, the sidewalk paralleling the railroad tracks on the other side. Tracks that wove between run-down buildings with faded yellow, blue, and green paint. Once vibrant but now dulled with age and weather. In the distance, the distinct triangular circus flag of red blew at the pinnacle of the Big Top. A tent erected for the summer months on the historic circus grounds. A memorial of sorts. A museum that lived in the shadows of the unused buildings and depot, trying to keep alive yesteryear, its vivacious entertainment, its exotic aura, and its tumbling success. The calliope's reedy tremor floated across the riffles of the river, a present-day echo of the past.

30

It was early September, and Chandler was growing warm underneath the cable-knit sweater she wore. It was oversized and yet skimmed her generous curves on her average-height body. And, it was black. Chandler often wore black. It was her safe color. It preserved and bolstered her confidence and, of all days, she needed it today.

She nodded at a few passersby—tourists who probably hadn't realized the museum's Big Top performance was closed for the season, the animals having been sent to the warm climate of Florida to wait out the impending winter.

The peal of her phone jerked Chandler out of her thoughts. She dug into her pocket, "The Phantom of the Opera" theme song lending its unwelcome eeriness to the late morning. Chandler leapt out of the way of a couple of college students speeding along the walk on their bikes, wishing, not for the last time, she could be back at the cottage with Peter, building their own little precious world of imagination. Just the two of them. Pretending all was right with the world—with *their* world. But she couldn't afford another hitch.

"Hello?" Chandler eased off the sidewalk and onto an iron bench bolted to the concrete. It was shiny green with a bronze memorial plaque to some otherwise unremembered community member.

"Hey, Champ."

Chandler closed her eyes and willed her heart to stop beating so fast. Her breathing was too short. Quick little breaths she needed to control. Chandler drew in a deep breath.

One, two, three, four, five, six, seven, eight.

And blew it out through her nose.

One, two, three, four—

"You there or did you evaporate?"

"No, I didn't *evaporate*, Jackson." Chandler winced. She'd fallen for her co-worker's patronizing bait within three seconds. She knew better. But every nerve was on fire. Guarded. He could twist her thoughts into a garbled mess if she wasn't careful, and she'd end up not even knowing what she really thought or felt. "What do you want?"

Best to stick to straight points. No chitchat or attempts at kindness.

She could hear in his voice his smile filled with tolerance for her. "The report from this morning. What did you find? What do you think?"

Jackson knew she didn't have time to draw up a detailed project plan. That would have been irrational. But, of course, he'd want her initial assessment. Quick and skilled, Jackson would expect her to already have a mental manila folder of specs, tests that needed to be run, a generalized estimate of square footage of the depot, and a projection of the town of Bluff River itself. Tourism specs, demographics interested in historic sites, and even the potential for the town's cooperation in the project. It was what Jackson would have already done. It was what had already been included in her proposal before they'd ever purchased the property. Yet he'd want to see if she could repeat it, if she had a handle on her latest project. Since her last one had needed—no, *required*—Jackson's assistance to offset a few of her miscalculations. Chandler never miscalculated, but now? Her mind, her memory . . . some days were as foggy as those days in Jack the Ripper's London.

Worse, Jackson's genius was impressive, his skill set off the charts. And he knew it. He'd been hired as her uncle's project coordinator, but he wanted more. He wanted to be Uncle Neal's right hand. A position Chandler had tenuously held for the past seven years. Since graduating from college. Since being pegged for brilliance of her own. Since becoming a single mother and inheriting the unending supply of capability question marks that came along with that title. Apparently, to succeed, she not only needed to *be* a man but also needed to *have* a man. Otherwise her career expertise would always be under a microscope. And as she'd overheard a lady in church mutter behind her hand, "A single mother raising a little boy? He won't even know how to grow up to be a proper man or father without a masculine influence as his authority."

"It's nice." Even Chandler stuck out her tongue at her belated and elementary answer.

"Nice?" A short laugh was followed by a sniff. "Okay, Chandler. Gonna need more than *nice*."

"I know. I just got here Thursday, it's only been two days, and—" She stopped herself. She didn't owe Jackson an explanation, and if she used the reasoning of getting Peter settled in a stable environment before she launched into work, Jackson would simply be jotting that fact down in his little black book of Chandler Inadequacies. She didn't have proof of said book, but it existed regardless. She knew it did. Either in his brain, on a spreadsheet, or typed into the notes app on his phone.

Chandler blinked rapidly, fighting back the unexpected tears of frustration and exhaustion. "I'm working with Neal on this project." She infused firmness into her voice. "I'll discuss any adjustments to what was originally proposed with Neal."

A sparrow hopped along the sidewalk in front of her. It tapped at something in a crack, then jerked its head to look at her before flapping its wings in a fluttering escape from her observation.

"A project *I'll* be a part of managing." Jackson had a point.

"And we'll include you as we always do." She hated sounding bossy. Or—well, there was another word that a few co-workers said Jackson called her. But she hadn't a choice really. She had to hold her ground. Chandler sought to divert him from the technical details, something less impacting. "We may have had a trespasser last night. I might need you to look into a security system for the place."

Silence.

Chandler slung her leg over her knee and bounced her foot. "We didn't actually find anyone, so I don't want to act irrationally, but precautions make sense. I filed a report with the police. They said they'll have an officer drive by occasionally—"

"Tell me the property wasn't vandalized." Jackson's tone was low.

"No, and I'm fine, thank you," Chandler quipped back.

"You know as well as I do, if we're going to flip this property, we need to move as fast as possible. Any vandalism will just cost more money, not to mention the last thing we need is some criminal act to turn the place into a crime scene and tie it up for eons."

"We're discussing a potential trespassing, Jackson, not a murder scene. And, I don't see why you keep saying 'if we flip' the property. I proposed that we *restore* it, and Uncle Neal signed off." Images of ghosts and murdered circus prostitutes drifted through Chandler's mind. She pushed the vision away.

"*If* we flip it," Jackson repeated. "Stats can change as you really dig into the project, Champ, and you know that."

Reason number 598 for not having Jackson as Uncle Neal's right hand and for fighting to maintain her position. He was a bulldoze-rebuild-and-sell type of guy. He could see the prospects with historical sites, but restoration was far more laborious and often more of an investment at the outset, requiring a long-term vision. It needed quality research, a quest for authentic materials to restore it properly, a specific clientele, and even documentation and certifications with state affiliations to make it a legitimate historic landmark and thus increase its value.

Jackson was annoyed. Chandler could hear him tapping a pen against his desk. He cleared his throat. "Listen, I gotta run. I'm meeting with Neal in a few minutes to look over a potential property in Cincinnati."

"Keep me in the loop." Chandler grimaced. She hated it when Uncle Neal embarked on another potential buy without consulting her. She was cautious and savvy. She'd look at the angles he couldn't see with his natural optimism. But then so would Jackson.

"Sure, Champ, I'll keep you in the loop."

Jackson hung up.

Chandler engaged in her breathing exercise again. How could it only be eleven in the morning and she already felt exhausted? Her mind felt thick, the morning's adrenaline wearing off and leaving her shaky. She knew why. It wasn't a conundrum anymore, not since her last medical appointment a few weeks ago. It was a huge reason why Chandler had escaped Detroit to do an on-site proposal under the argument that a circus train depot might be a potential pot of gold, if they handled the project with kid gloves.

She wasn't dying. No. But her body was rebelling, and there was no going back to the days when she was without a health concern. No going back to the days when her joints didn't throb, or her mind didn't lapse, or she didn't feel like a weighted rock of fatigue had settled on her head. She had a career to think about, to maintain, but more than that, she had a little boy.

Tears sprang to her eyes, and Chandler bit the inside of her lip to hold them back. She had her Buddy Boy, her little man. With his ginormous brown eyes that were just like hers. His surfer-blond shaggy hair with a million tints of gold and brown woven through the waves. He was her mischievous cohort, the little boy who took her to their own personal Neverland every day, where they flew on their imaginations, and where he would never grow up. He was her own Peter Pan, and she his Wendy.

No, she wasn't dying, but if she lost him, if they took her son, it would be worse than dying. She couldn't lose him. She couldn't lose her son at the hands of family who already thought she'd be lucky to succeed saddled with her biggest mistake in college. A big *F* on her scorecard of life. People had a way of trying to help, of looking out for another's best interests, when in reality they caused a slow bleed in the very one they hoped to rescue.

Well, Chandler wasn't looking to be rescued by anyone. She

would rescue herself, and in doing so she'd rescue her relationship with her little boy. No autoimmune disease would steal that from her, would disable or maim her enough to take from her the title of caregiver and sole provider.

If that happened, it would be its own sort of violent death.

CHAPTER FIVE

PIPPA

He was here. She could sense him, even though she couldn't see him. A dark hollow in the darkness, illuminated only by the pale light of her black-and-chrome flashlight. Pippa's hand wrapped around the Eveready light, thankful that it wouldn't dim as quickly as the one her father still used from his college days, the light having to be flashed off after a bit in order to be used again. Her shoes crunched on the pebbles that lined the walkway between structures, her dress sticking to her stockings. She quivered, inside and out, anticipation warring with caution.

"Hello?" Pippa whispered.

She touched the side of her wool cloche, the gesture a nervous one. The dinner party at home had dissipated, her parents retiring to bed. Pippa had changed from her evening dress into a practical cotton one. Dark and unassuming. She had locked Penn in her bedroom, trying to ignore the pathetic whines that vibrated in the dog's throat. She would be wise to bring Penn along with her, yet she wasn't keen on the idea of what might happen if Penn took a disliking to the Watchman—or worse, awakened her parents. Nothing could disrupt this meeting. It mustn't. Pippa was intent on keeping in order what she could, even as she eyed the alley that stretched between the elephant house and the ring barn. What appeared so welcoming during daytime visits was now eerily silent, shrouded in a black translucence that promised the presence of wandering spirits, of riffraff, and of—

Gravel disturbed at the opposite end of the narrow building-length alleyway. A footstep crunching, even as Pippa froze in response. Squinting, she peered into the deep, lifting the flashlight that was growing warm in her grip. The torch didn't stretch to the end of the alley, but she heard it again. That evident sound of someone approaching.

"Hello?" There was a tremor in Pippa's voice. She could feel it as well as hear it. A weight of trepidation settled on her chest, suffocating deep breaths and increasing the rate at which Pippa drew short, quick ones.

Quiet. She must be quiet.

The Watchman was like a ghost. He would spook and flee at too much sound. She could feel it, sense it. He was as spooked as she was, perhaps more. Maybe even the light from her flashlight . . . Pippa flicked it off, allowing the moonless sky to wash her in its ominous insinuation.

When the moon slept, evil awoke.

Pippa's superstitious mother had taught her that throughout childhood. Be fearful of the night. God had turned to cast His grace on the other side of the world, and it was on nights such as these that wickedness ran rampant, that dangers were not thwarted, and evil found its voice.

A hiss drifted through the stillness, like breath being muffled as it was expelled. A stone skipped down the path toward Pippa. She could hear its tripping journey, though she couldn't see it in the blackness. Reaching out, Pippa touched the siding of the elephant house, her gloved fingertips catching on the rough wood.

She dared not say hello again. The Watchman had not shown himself. He'd not spoken. But he was there. She heard a deep, shuddering breath sucked in, and then—

"You came."

The voice was unfamiliar. A raspy and reedy tenor like sandpaper, which only aggravated her raw nerves, sending another shiver through Pippa's body.

She nodded. And then, because she realized he could not see her, Pippa answered, "I did."

Silence.

Breathing. A heavier breathing now. One that indicated the Watchman was as nervous as she—or perhaps it was something else.

"W-will you show yourself?" Pippa ventured, and with her brave question she took another hesitant step, tendering her twisted leg and dragging her fingers along the side of the building.

He didn't answer.

She stilled.

The sacred yet menacing silence was shattered as a ferocious crash vibrated the wall of the elephant house. Pippa squelched a scream, and the flashlight she held flew from her grasp, her body jarring away from the building. Another enormous bang shattered something inside, followed by an earsplitting trumpet pushed through the trunk of a circus pachyderm.

"All hands! All hands!" The shout from behind her caused Pippa to spin in place toward the street and the lamplit walkway.

Cold fingers touched her neck. A scream clawed from Pippa's throat, and she fought away the frigid feel of flesh against her skin. Callused fingertips dragging along the back of her neck where her hairline wisped into loose curls.

"Noooo." It was the Watchman's hissed whisper. Urgent. Demanding.

Pippa ran. As best as she could, she ran toward the street. Away from the Watchman. Away from the question of whether the marriage of darkness and evil was true. She plunged toward the sound of humanity. Toward the urgent shouts from the doorway of the elephant house. Seeking security in the crashing fray and shrieks from inside and fleeing the very one she had so desperately wanted to see.

She stumbled, her weak leg giving out as her foot twisted over something. Whether a rock or a wayward brick, Pippa didn't know. Tripping forward to gather her balance, she cast a glance over her shoulder. Back toward the shadows.

There the Watchman stood. A silhouette braving the brush of light that now washed through the windows of the elephant house as the electric lamps were turned up. A burlap sack covered his head, black holes where his eyes should have been. Holes that were ragged and frayed, lessening the distance between them as the empty void became a frightening traverse.

In that moment, Pippa was bound to him. More so than she had been before. But it was a binding that imprisoned her, not freed her. The Watchman held captive all her secrets, held prisoner her soul, and she began to drown in the hollowness of his eyes.

The screaming trumpet pushed through the elephant's trunk, ricocheted off the house's walls, and pummeled the street outside with its vibrations. Pippa noted a few lights coming on in two small houses across the street. Houses that had only a muddy road to separate them from the wildness of the circus that spanned blocks in both directions. But in the darkness, Pippa could see little, and even the small electric lamps that flicked on cast only tiny shafts of light. The primary beacon came from inside the elephant house, whose double doors were rolled back to reveal the octagonal ring where the elephants were exercised and trained in the cold winter months. A menagerie laborer sprinted past Pippa, his shoulder brushing hers as she stood dazed in the opening.

"Outta the way, miss!" he shouted.

Pippa leapt to the side, just in time to avoid being run over by Ernie Phelps, the elephant trainer. The man stumbled in his sprint into the elephant house. His brown eyes collided with Pippa's and widened in stunned surprise. He shot a glance of confusion toward the doors opened on the far end of the house leading to the boarding stalls for the elephants, then back to Pippa.

"Miss Ripley!" His expression clearly indicated she shouldn't be here, and he waved her off with dismissal.

Ernie hurried toward the elephant stalls as another frantic trumpet threatened to shatter the roof. Pippa followed. Curiosity mingled with fear urged her toward the ruckus. Whatever animal emergency had awakened the circus menagerie crew also brought awakened life into a world that had turned very dark, very quickly. She was resistant to finding her way home through the blackened alleys of Bluff River, the walkways of the downtown square that were no place for a lady at night, and up the hill to the stately yellow mansion that overlooked its kingdom. She had been foolish. Reckless. There would be no way to explain any of this to her father.

Chains linked around the elephant's feet clanked against the cement as she was led into the ring. Her eyes were rolled back in fury, the whites of them bulging with a ferocity that made Pippa scurry to the wall and press herself against it. A few men fought to soothe the elephant, who seemed to have been calmed into some sort of obedience. Ernie, whip in hand but gentleness in his voice, murmured to the great creature. The branch of a tail flipped back and forth at the elephant's hindquarters, her trunk extended, like a weapon preceding the breadth of a body so large that, if she tried, she could surely trample them all. Yet the elephant had a healthy respect for the whip in Ernie's hand. A whip he didn't brandish but merely tapped firmly against the elephant's shoulder.

"Hook the rings," he commanded over his own shoulder.

One of the workers tugged the end of one of the ankle chains, latching it to a metal ring bolted to the floor. The elephant's ears branched wide on either side of her head. Whatever had enraged her was now the focal point of the other workers in the massive room of elephant stalls beyond.

Unnoticed, Pippa edged around the wall, her hands and back pressed against its cold stone. She made her way to the entrance of the barn addition, catching the sleeve of her dress on a splintering piece of bright yellow wood that framed the doorway. Lights illuminated the inside, lone bulbs dangling from wires. A lantern at the first stall hung from an iron hook, adding more specific light to the large enclosed area. Straw was strewn about. Bloodied straw. An unfamiliar scent assaulted Pippa's nose, and she lifted a gloved finger to hold beneath her nostrils. Slipping forward, she peered around the thick wooden framework of the stall, desperate to see and dreading to know all at the same time.

An animal doctor knelt in the straw, his hands running gently down the back of a prostrate, newly birthed elephant calf. The animal was stocky, with large padded feet and skin covered with patches of afterbirth. Its ears looked like limp, oversized lily pads, and its eyes were shut. The calf's trunk lay still, resting in the dirtied straw. It was difficult to tell whether all the blood was from its birth or from something worse.

Another man knelt beside the doctor, who held a stethoscope to the elephant. Both of their backs were to Pippa, and she gripped the frame of the stall opening for support. She recognized the doctor. Dr. Thurston, whom she thought she'd heard her father mention recently. He was a necessary and relatively new expense for the circus, and an attempt to relieve the trainers of the full onslaught of the animals' medical care.

This. This must be the long-awaited birth of the elephant calf. The one Forrest and her father had heralded as the next major focal point of profit. Pippa winced. If they knew their investment lay in the straw, unmoving and covered in blood, would they be so thrilled?

"How could you leave her unattended?" Dr. Thurston's growl was directed at the man kneeling beside him. Jake Chapman. Pippa had met the retired ring fighter a few times, but mostly she had stayed clear of him. He was a scrappy muscle-bound man, his face half covered with whiskers and an ever-present cigar hanging from the corner of his mouth. It wasn't always lit, but his eyes were usually squinting as though he found it disagreeable—found the world disagreeable. He had never acknowledged her. Even when they'd met. His eyes looked through her as if to confirm how invisible she truly was.

Jake Chapman didn't bother replying to the doctor. Instead he ran a large hand over the calf's forehead.

"We'll be lucky if the calf survives," Dr. Thurston continued. "There's got to be massive internal injuries."

The echoes of Ernie and the men in the ring almost drowned out the grumbling of the doctor.

"Without her matriarchal herd, Agnes panicked." Dr. Thurston shot his companion a dark look. "A terrified elephant will stomp her newborn to death by sheer fear of the unfamiliar. She wasn't to be left alone. She must have been spooked. Completely spooked."

No excuse was offered, but Jake must have heard Pippa's intake of shocked breath. He darted a sharp look over his shoulder even as she clapped a hand over her mouth. Their eyes connected. His were questioning, then quickly shifted to irritated. They were gray, like the color of Penn's fur.

"Get out," he growled.

Surprised, Dr. Thurston turned toward Pippa. The doctor's expression held the distinct glare of disapproval. "Miss Ripley!" How he recognized her, she wasn't sure. "This is *not* the place for you."

The calf was motionless.

"We'll have to put her down." The words were blunt. Jake had no sensitivity to her female delicacies. His candor caused another gasp to escape uncontrolled from Pippa's lips. Worse, Dr. Thurston gave an abbreviated nod. A regretful and clearly frustrated agreement.

"No!" The protest didn't even have to fight its way from Pippa's normally nonconfrontational self. "No, you can't do that!" She stepped into the stall.

It wasn't a wise choice, she realized instantly. She shouldn't insert herself into circus business. Into *men's* business. The world of blood and killing wasn't meant for femininity. Mother had taught her that. It would taint her. Mark her, even subtly, as too experienced, and the loss of such innocence would mar her future. She must be above reproach.

Yet, Pippa realized, she wasn't. She hadn't even been born above reproach. The circus was in her blood. The same color red that stained the straw beneath the elephant calf.

"Miss Ripley, you've no say in this." Ernie's voice sounded behind her right shoulder. He was overseer of the elephants, long-time employee of the Ripleys' circus, and someone Pippa had grown up in the shadows of. The older man's thinning gray hair was askew, his clothes disheveled, and his small frame stiff with resolve. "You need to take yourself away from here."

"This isn't a place for a woman," Jake said, affirming Pippa's unspoken thoughts.

"You. Quiet," Ernie snapped at the man.

Pippa swallowed back her nerves, frayed at all ends. The Watchman had brought her here, and now she was drowning in the muck of circus life. The tragic reality that not all animals survived in the circus, and that without the wildness of their habitations, being confined sparked in them an instinctual fear to protect and defend. Even against their own offspring.

"D-did I spook her?" Pippa's voice trembled as she asked Ernie. She cast a desperate glance to Dr. Thurston. "Did my presence outside set the mother off?"

"No."

"Yes."

"We won't talk about it."

The simultaneous answer came from all three men. Ernie with reticence to involve Pippa in any way, the daughter of the circus owner, and a liability just by being there. Dr. Thurston seemed to have little wish to place guilt on her shoulders and therefore barked his denial of her responsibility with swift reassurance.

It was Jake's blunt "yes" that shut them all up.

Pippa bit the inside of her lip.

He was brutal, but he was honest.

"I did? I spooked her?"

"Impossible," Ernie said. "It's not uncommon for a mother to reject her calf shortly after its birth. She'd have no way of knowing you were outside the house tonight. None at all."

"She could have sensed it," Jake muttered, never taking his eyes off Pippa, who stared back at him. She was lost in his unguarded animosity.

Dr. Thurston shook his head. "Unlikely."

"You don't know elephants," Jake snarled at the animal doctor. "You take care of cows and horses. They aren't anywhere near the same."

"Jake," Ernie said, his tone one of warning.

Whoever was telling the truth, or whoever was nearest to being right, didn't matter. That she might have even played a part in alarming the mother into trampling her calf made Pippa's stomach turn. She eyed Jake cautiously while taking a few more steps toward the baby elephant.

Kneeling, she ignored the moisture from the soiled straw that seeped through the material of her dress and onto her stockings. Pippa reached out tentatively. Cautious and unsure, she again met Jake's eyes. She needn't get permission from him to touch the calf. She needed it instead from Ernie. He was in charge. He was the boss here. Yet, Pippa couldn't help but seek permission— unspoken and perhaps begrudging permission—from the man named Jake. The man whose broad shoulders and thick arms nearly busted the seams of his shirt, which was unbuttoned indecently down to the middle of his chest. A bare chest.

Jake gave a short nod, and Pippa brought her hand to rest on the calf. Its hide was warm, leathery, with tiny little hairs that prickled her palm. She trailed her fingers down the back of the infant, grieving the loss of such a beautiful animal.

"Please," Pippa whispered. "You can't put her down."

Dr. Thurston cleared his throat.

Jake's jaw was firmly set. "We've no choice. She'll suffer."

Ernie drew in a deep breath. Consternation laced every syllable in his words. "We'll lose a fortune."

Yes. Yes, they would. As Pippa ran her hand down the animal's back once more, she could almost see her father's face. A face that would be lined with darkened fury. They had advertised that there would be a baby elephant for next spring's Big Top. A major attraction once the circus took to the rails and traveled across the country. The huge pachyderms were magnificent, and in comparison the baby would be the main draw. Especially for women. Women who might otherwise scorn the circus atmosphere, the oddities, the violence of the roaring lions and raging tigers. They would be drawn by their own maternal instincts. The instinct to love and to nurture the long-lashed infant with the curled trunk and innocent eyes.

Her father stood to lose thousands.

Pippa wasn't sure where her courage came from. Courage or maybe foolhardiness. But she reached in front of Jake and laid her palm on the calf's forehead. As she did, she felt the warmth radiating from the man's body, for he was stubborn and refused to move away. Everything in Pippa willed the calf to live, to breathe, to fight for its life, and when its eyelid opened and it lifted the tip of its trunk in response, Pippa took heart.

"See? See, she's alive!" Pippa breathed with hope.

"For now," Jake said and terminated that hope.

"We can watch her—tend her best as we can in hopes she makes it," Dr. Thurston offered.

"Yes!" Pippa nodded vehemently, tenderly stroking the baby's face.

"The skin will already be flayed off my back," Ernie growled. "Ripley's gonna have my hide. Do what you want." He was resigned, aware that Richard Ripley would be a force to contend with regardless of the outcome.

Jake stood, his leg brushing against Pippa's. Her face flooded with heat, and she leaned away from him, causing her to lean into the calf. A whimper gurgled in the animal's throat.

Jake's hands fisted, and he spun on his heel. "I'll go get my gun."

CHAPTER SIX

CHANDLER

The day had been grueling. Grueling and exhausting. Chandler's stomach growled its irritation at not having had breakfast, and with the lunch hour already on her, it was a warning she needed to heed. Her blood sugar would be running low. Her body needed protein and oxygen, but she needed her son.

Chandler yanked open the screen door on the small Cape Cod–style house set just off Broadway Street.

"Peter!" Yelling for her son, Chandler attempted to squelch the undertone of helicopter-mom panic. She'd tried calling the new sitter—the one she'd hired off Nanny-Nine-to-Five.com—but they hadn't answered. That unanswered call was close to unhinging Chandler. The idea of giving a stranger complete control over her most precious treasure made Chandler nauseous the moment she'd dialed the number. Yet Margie Robertson came with five-star references. A whole two of them.

"The last nanny in St. Louis came with gobs of stars." Chandler hadn't meant to whine to Uncle Neal, who'd patiently listened to her, knowing that her best way of figuring out a problem was to spew her thoughts without censure.

"That was also St. Louis. When you relocate for projects such as these, you've never chosen to relocate to a small town." Uncle Neal's observation was true. Typically, Chandler chose to work remotely with contractors and project managers in smaller towns such as these. Occasional visits to drop in for on-site observance. But places like St. Louis? There had always been some adventure in packing up Peter, not to mention, in the bigger cities, the projects typically took far longer.

"But, how do I know I can trust her?" Chandler had argued, feeling inadequate and foolish.

Uncle Neal's reassurance that it was a small town with small-town values hadn't really assuaged her nervous nature. It was a new decade, after all. Morals and ethics were disappearing faster than the Arctic ice. But then, Uncle Neal's dismissive attitude toward the care of Peter was nothing new. For him, it was Old Village Management, Inc. His business. His pride and joy. His life. Heck, it was his child, and if Chandler hadn't bit her tongue, she would have reminded her uncle that he never left his baby to the hands of another. Not completely.

"Peter!" Chandler's voice echoed back at her in the small entryway, bouncing off the scarred hardwood floors. Chandler's ballet flats were soundless as she hurried into the hall, looking to the left under the arched doorway that led into the tiny living room.

No one.

She scanned the crowded dining area to the right. It'd been the allotted four-hour stint she'd hired Margie for. She wasn't late in returning home. The silence in the rental cottage was eerie. It was unnerving.

"Peter!" Chandler rushed into the living room, glancing out the large picture window with its antique lace curtains and velvet sofa perched in front. An ancient willow tree draped over the yard, its feathery branches swaying in the autumn breeze. But there was nothing soothing about it. Nothing peaceful or welcoming.

"Peter!" Her voice was a bit strangled.

A foam bullet spiraled through the air, clocking Chandler in the middle of her forehead and bouncing off.

She screamed.

Peals of laughter ousted Peter's position from behind the corner sofa.

"Nitro Steel attacks!" Chandler's scrawny son flipped himself over the back of the chair onto its cushioned seat, a blue toy gun in his hands. He cocked the plastic weapon. "Watch out, Momma!"

Chandler held up a palm just in time to deflect the second bullet that rocketed toward her face. "Peter, stop. Please." Her tending toward tears was now teetering toward a smile and indulgent acceptance of his sneak attack.

Peter lowered the gun, his smile top row toothless, and his enormous eyes like two giant questioning Tootsie Rolls of softness staring back at her. She'd always told Peter she wanted to eat him, from the moment he was born. He was delicious and delectable, and the echo of her mother's voice rang in her ears.

He's a baby, not a Twinkie, honey.

Chandler wasn't sure Mom had ever really understood the bond between her and Peter. But then she'd never really given Mom the chance either.

Pushing that thought out of her mind, Chandler tried to ignore the memories of her mom's nurturing soul and the disappointment etched in the once-proud eyes.

"Oh, there you are, Ms. Faulk!" The pleasant and very cheery voice of Margie collided with the end of Chandler's frayed nerves. She sucked in a breath to steady herself as she reassessed the buxom woman whose cotton shirt barely concealed her overabundance of cleavage and whose face was hometown friendly. Margie's naturally curly red hair striped with gray-and-white strands was pulled back into a messy knot that revealed how thick Margie's hair was. She was flushed, with sweat beads dotting her forehead. The only evidence that something might still be off in what remained in the day.

"Margie, I tried calling you." There was more insistent interrogation running through Chandler's mind, but she didn't have the guts to voice it now that Peter was perched safely on the sofa, his toy gun still ready to go on the attack under his superhero made-up pseudonym Nitro Steel.

Margie drew her hand across her brow and wiped it on the side of her chest as though her natural-made shelf was also a ready-made towel.

"I know. I'm so sorry!" She was breathless. Her hand extended in a haphazard manner and pointed behind her. "The kitchen. It flooded. I've been mopping up water all morning and it just keeps coming. I don't know why."

"What?" Chandler skirted Margie and hurried to the kitchen. Sure enough, water was still spraying in a slow but steady stream from the pipes underneath the kitchen sink. The cupboard doors stood open, and a pile of soggy towels were mounded beneath it and wrapped around an ice cream bucket, a poor attempt at catching as much of the leak as possible.

Chandler noted the mounds of paper towels in the garbage can. Wet ones. And the mop leaning against the wall.

"Did you call a plumber? The landlord?"

"Noooo." Margie winced. She was honestly apologetic and frantic at the same time. "I looked for a number for the landlord and I didn't see one posted. Usually a rental would have one, but . . . well, and then I tried to call a plumber, but the lady said her guys were all out on calls."

"Did you try another plumber?" Chandler squatted in front of the pipes, eyeing them.

"There's only one plumber in Bluff River" was Margie's explanation. "Well, unless you call Bob's Benders, but I wouldn't recommend that."

Chandler squeezed her eyes shut, trying to ignore the raging headache that had sprung up since ending her phone call with Jackson. "The landlord's number is inside the pantry door."

"Oh!" Margie rushed to the door and flung it open. "There it is!" She whipped out her phone and dialed without waiting for instruction from Chandler. "Well, gosh, I didn't know this was one of Denny's rentals!"

"Momma?" Her son's voice drew her attention away from the spurting water.

"What is it, Peter Pan?" Chandler tempered her frustration. Her son was seven. *Seven.* And he was shooting up in height. A full inch in the last four months. All his size 6–7's were too short, but she'd be darned if she bought him size 8. The idea was unbearable. Her baby boy. It'd been just them. Just the two of them, for so long.

"You okay? You look weird." Peter scrunched his nose and eyed her.

"Oh, sure." She ruffled Peter's shaggy hair. "I'm just tired."

Chandler tried to downplay the exhaustion that was biting into her muscles and handicapping her mental capabilities. She wanted to collapse onto the couch, succumb to a deep sleep, and pray that God would bless her with regeneration when she woke. But life didn't afford time for naps.

"But you're all shaky." Peter's fingers touched her arm. "Are you having an episode?" He was so tender, so trusting and tender. So observant too. He'd seen her, those nights in the past few months, shaking on the couch, her hands and arms in tremors, trying to will away the onslaught of another seizure. "Non-epileptic," the doctor had declared, as if that was somehow a small victory. Maybe it was. She wasn't sure yet.

Chandler crouched and pulled the scrawny boy into her embrace. She whispered into his ear, "No, Buddy. No episode. Shhh. I haven't had my coffee yet." She'd no intention of explaining the stress of last night's trespass scare and her anything-but-reassuring conversation with Jackson.

"Ohhhhhhh!" Peter's toothless grin stretched on his face. "That's sorta—dumb!"

She noticed his attempt to avoid the banned word *stupid* and didn't bother to correct any remote vibe of disrespect. Yes. Blame it on lack of caffeine. A little white lie, but necessary—at least it felt necessary. The one thing Chandler would never do was impose her own limitations on to Peter or expose him too early to a world touched by evil. He wasn't responsible to care for her, and his innocence was too precious to her to see it tarnished before it needed to be.

"The landlord is on his way." Margie reached for the coffeepot. "I heard you say you hadn't had any coffee yet. That is completely unacceptable."

Margie took control of the moment. With the faucet already leaking and spitting water over everything, she disappeared into the small powder room just off the kitchen.

"I never start a day without some sort of hot goodness. My aunt used to run a diner downtown, and every morning on my way to school I'd stop by and she'd give me three sips and half a spoon of sugar. Of course, my momma would have had her sister's hide had she known, but . . ."

Chandler could hear Margie filling the coffeepot with water.

"Of course, then I had to zip by Ned's Drugstore there on the corner, and by the time I made it to junior high, I was all hyped up on sugar and caffeine." Coming back into the kitchen, Margie tossed Chandler a smile. "Comes with small-town living, you know? A kid ends up having more than one parent by the time they're six. Everyone knows everyone, and everyone else's kids too."

Margie started rummaging through cupboard doors. "What do you have for coffee?"

"I haven't been grocery shopping yet," Chandler responded lamely. Today sucked.

Margie tossed her a look of disbelief. "Do you need me to hang on here a bit yet today, honey? Seems like you could use some help getting settled."

She could. Chandler hesitated. She had the money to pay for

help, but she resisted it. Too proud, her dad would've said. Capable and not wanting to impose was more of Chandler's reasoning.

"No, I'll—I've got it covered."

Margie scanned Chandler's face, and a super-thin eyebrow rose over her gray eye. "Mm-hmm. Sure you do. Well, canned coffee grounds it is, then." She pulled a can of coffee from an otherwise empty cupboard. "I've got nothing planned this afternoon, so I'll just hang here anyway. You'll need help cleaning up, and otherwise I just go home to an empty house. My husband left me two years ago and took our kids with him, all the way to Georgia. Blasted man."

Chandler grimaced. She instantly related to being left alone but shuddered at the idea of her ex taking Peter. Of course, he'd never shown an interest. If she were even sure he was the father. Her cheeks warmed at the memories. College had been . . . fun. For a while.

"Goes to show you shouldn't marry your high-school sweetheart. You change too much as you grow up." Margie scooped grounds into the built-in filter. "And no, just 'cause I don't have full custody doesn't mean I was an unfit mother." She smiled as if she was used to explaining it, although the thought hadn't crossed Chandler's mind. "We just made an agreement that he'd get the kids for the summers. They'll be back in mid-August to get ready for school. Until then"—Margie shoved the filter into place and hit the on button—"I do in-home childcare, and on the weekends I work at the memory-care center. It pays the bills. I could be working in a factory, but I'd go nuts doing the same thing over and over and over again."

A pounding on the front door broke into their rather one-sided and chatty get-to-know-you's. Chandler shoved away from the counter she was leaning against. "I'll get it."

It was a good excuse to get away from Margie's kind and welcoming visage. The kind that hinted she might relate to Chandler, might actually understand what it was to be a single mom, to have to fight to prove herself and make a living. It was disconcerting, the knowing look in Margie's eyes. She had read Chandler silently, in a way that Chandler's family hadn't noticed even when she'd screamed for attention.

He was not what she'd expected for a landlord. Denny Pike's wiry gray beard hung like Santa's to the top of his rounded belly. A black leather vest hung over a gray T-shirt emblazoned with an American eagle and a beer logo. His blue jeans were held up with a belt, his paunch hanging over. A red bandanna was tied around his forehead.

Chandler glanced beyond him and noted his Harley leaning on its stand, chrome exhaust pipes on the back and, curiously, a fluffy pink stuffed rabbit tied to the front of the handlebars. It was either sentimental, a joke, or perhaps a bug catcher in lieu of a windshield.

She brought her attention back to the older man with the friendly eyes and the distinct smell of cigarettes.

"Mr. Pike?" Chandler couldn't help the question in her voice. In her experience—which was pretty vast—landlords or landowners were, at a minimum, casually dressed in jeans and a polo shirt. At a maximum, like Uncle Neal, they wore tailored suits and ran large companies.

"Denny." He grinned, exposing a row of teeth stained by coffee but otherwise clean. His blue eyes were small in his face, though they sparked with energy and confidence. "Like bikes?" He pointed over his shoulder, having noted her survey of his Harley.

"No." Chandler shook her head, then stuttered to lessen the bluntness. "I mean, I don't ride. I don't know much about them."

Denny laughed. A deep, chesty laugh that was a bit congested. She caught another whiff of the cigarette smoke clinging to him. Maybe that was the cause of the chest rattle?

"Didn't figure. You're a cute-'un but ain't no biker chick." He winked. "S'okay. I got your back anyway. So, what's this Margie said about a leaky sink?"

"It's in the kitchen." Chandler started to lead the way, even though, she realized, he knew it well enough. She attempted to make small talk, feeling awkward and uncomfortable. "Margie says you're friends?"

Denny's boots clomped on the wood floor as he followed her. "We go back a ways, yep. Was about ten years ahead of her, but she went to high school with my little sister. Ohhhhh, I think that was back in the eighties?" They paused in the kitchen doorway, where Denny edged by Chandler, who was still struggling with feeling completely inept. She needed to eat. She needed a nap. She needed . . . something.

"Let me check out that sink." Denny grunted as he squatted down by the open cupboard doors. "I might need to run for parts, and I've got a meet-up with my nephew in about thirty minutes."

Denny and Margie exchanged hellos, laughs, friendly banter, then Denny asked, "You try turning off the water supply valve?"

"The what?" Margie raised her brows.

"Oh duh!" Chandler exclaimed. It was the first thing she should have thought of if she hadn't been coming off a call with Jackson, which had ruffled her nerves like rubbing a cat's fur backward, and worse, the jarring circumstances of last night.

"S'okay." Denny eased onto his knees from his awkward squat. "I got ya." He grunted again as he reached under the sink to shut off the water. Once done, he tinkered around a bit, muttering under his breath.

Chandler noted that Peter had disappeared.

Margie read her mind. "He went upstairs to play Nitro Steel." A sparkle in Margie's eyes proved she'd been introduced to Peter's imaginary persona and was more than up to the challenge of chasing around a seven-year-old superhero.

"Yeeeeeup, looks like a bad seal." Denny gripped the edge of the sink, his knees cracking as he straightened. "I'll have to run to the hardware store. I can be back later this afternoon to get it fixed. Meanwhiles, if you're okay just cleaning up? Leave the water shut off till I get back."

"Thank you." Chandler managed a smile as Denny faced her.

But he was looking at Margie as he wiped his wet hands on a dish towel. "You hear about the scuffle at the old train depot last night?" he asked.

Chandler stilled. It wasn't that she had anything to hide. Nothing had really happened outside of her interaction with Sasquatch Man and Lottie's claim that she'd seen lights inside.

Margie shook her head. "No, I didn't. What happened?"

Denny tossed the towel on the counter. "Nothin' much, I guess. Except Lottie is swearing up and down about the supernatural."

"That Lottie." Margie's voice went up a few chords and she laughed. "That place has been boarded up since *I* was in school. If it's haunted, like they like to say, only Lottie *would* see it. No one cares."

Denny wrapped his hand around his beard and dragged it down. "Yeah, I know. And you know how the town goes. Somethin' appetizing about our history, everyone wants a taste of it." His eyes flickered with shadows for a moment, then they vanished and the sparkle returned.

Margie clicked her tongue and patted his arm. "Everyone always likes to gossip, hun." Her bosom rose and fell as she heaved a sigh, the sequined purple flower on the front of her T-shirt glittering a reflection onto the watery floor. "Besides, all that haunted nonsense started eons ago. It's nothing new."

Denny shrugged. "Lottie said she got the sense there was another presence there last night."

Chandler frowned. There *had* been another presence. A very male, very *human* presence.

Margie let out a quick shout of laughter, complete with a musical giggle at the end of it. "She's a French fry short of a Happy Meal, God love her."

"Ehhh, maybe." Denny rubbed his nose and then tugged at the bandanna on his forehead. "But you can't argue she knows stuff. Sees stuff."

"You believe Lottie?" Chandler tested them. She was curious how much clout the woman had in Bluff River. Or, for that matter, how many rumors of hauntings and ghosts circulated in this small historic town.

Margie squished her lips together and rolled her eyes. "I went to school with Lottie. She's a lovely lady. Really, she is. And, she's our local, well, *she'd* say she's our local medium. But *we* just say she's our ghost chaser. She and her son, Cru. They lead the ghost tours in the old section downtown, and I think that depot's always been on the tour trail, right?" She glanced at Denny, who nodded his affirmation. "Yep. It's a good gig for the tourism we get here 'cause of the circus museum. Sort of goes hand in hand with history. What's better than ghosts and creepy old clowns? But sometimes Lottie takes it past a story and thinks she's actually in the know, ya know?"

Chandler didn't.

"Sees things," Margie supplied.

"Dead people," Denny added.

"Ah." Chandler raised her brows.

"That's what she says anyways." Denny sniffed and slapped his palm on his leg. "Welp, I'd better head out. My nephew and I are grabbing a late lunch, and then I'll be back after I hit up the hardware store."

Chandler and Margie both led Denny Pike out of the kitchen, their shoes leaving wet footprints on the floor in the hallway. Denny paused at the door, his light-blue eyes raking Chandler's face. He must have seen something there—she wasn't sure what—but he offered her a warm smile tainted with something she couldn't interpret.

"Don't you worry. Bluff River ain't known for people getting murdered nowadays. That's all old history. Leastways by ghosts."

Margie gave a nervous laugh.

Chandler met her eyes. There was hesitation in them. The kind that insinuated Denny Pike wasn't telling the whole truth and that Margie had no intention of bringing up the past . . . or the dead.

CHAPTER SEVEN

PIPPA

The elephant trainer's exasperation at her was palpable, yet she'd always liked Ernie—always gotten along with him. The times she had visited the circus grounds without her father or Forrest leading the way, Ernie had allowed her to wander the barns and gander at the menagerie as long as she maintained her distance. But Pippa could tell he wasn't happy with her presence now. *Displeased* was probably the best description. No. She caught herself swallowing nervous energy. Annoyed? Maybe both. She couldn't blame him. Not really. She was the daughter of Richard Ripley, and her presence could only add pressure to the man and the decision before him.

Ernie sat back on his heels, obviously well aware that Jake Chapman had charged from the barn on a mission to retrieve the weapon that would end the calf's already-horrifying start to life. The baby elephant blinked, but it was her only movement. Still, Pippa noticed emotion shift Ernie's face. There was a weakness in the man. A good sentimental kind of weakness. The kind that Jake Chapman didn't appear to have.

"We've got to try to get Lily on her feet." Ernie's statement was more a mutter than anything.

"Lily?" Pippa's quiet insertion was ignored. Far more than just the life of an animal was at stake. Her father was never quick to give grace to others.

Dr. Thurston ran his hands over the calf. Massaging its legs, bending each one, and doing other ministrations as if trying to see past the thick elephant hide to the skeleton beneath. The internal organs. To every part of it hidden from the naked eye that could bring about the baby elephant's termination. He pushed his palm across the calf's back. "I don't think she has broken ribs as I'd originally thought. But she's bruised. No telling what internal injuries she may have."

"Can't you just leave her to rest? Just to see if she improves?" Pippa pleaded. She tried not to disturb the calf while shooting a desperate glance at the darkness beyond the elephant row where Jake Chapman had disappeared to fetch his rifle.

Ernie shook his head. "I do that and she'll waste away for certain. Injured or not, Lily at least has to get in a position where she can eat. She needs nourishment." He reached for a three-legged footstool behind him and pulled it close so he could sit on it.

"May I?" Pippa extended her hand toward the animal but directed her question to Ernie.

He gave a curt nod.

The luminescent glow in the elephant's black eyes drew her as they connected gazes. It blinked. The ache behind Lily's stare was palpable. Her mouth was closed and the corner tipped downward, uncharacteristic of an elephant's more typical upturned mouth. The kind that gave the impression of a permanent smile. Her wide, leather-like ear lay flat on her head. She blinked again.

"Baby," Pippa crooned and stretched her fingertips toward Lily. If God could hear her prayers, now would be the time. He was so distant, so militant like her father, but God had been known to do good things. He'd saved animals on the Ark, hadn't He? Perhaps He would extend a favor of healing to Lily. Preferably before Jake returned on his mission of death.

Pippa brushed her hand over Lily's forehead and down the base of her trunk. She leaned over the elephant and noticed Lily's eye following her movement.

"You need to fight, sweet one." Pippa leaned down, and her lips grazed the elephant's ear, its skin coarse. The smell of the new-born was almost overpowering, but Pippa continued to whisper encouragement. "We need you here. We've waited a long time for you to be born."

Ernie muttered a shocked oath as Lily lifted her trunk and curled it around the back of Pippa's neck. An embrace. The first recognition that she might respond.

Ernie shifted, his movement anticipatory. "Keep talking to her, Miss Ripley."

Pippa did as directed, this time in cooperation with Ernie, who carefully rounded the babe and approached her shoulders. Her heart had risen into her throat at the feel of the trunk encompassing her neck. The embrace was intimate, trusting, and she had locked eyes with Lily. In that moment they were both somehow connected by the reality they were more than just belongings of the Ripleys, of Bonaventure Circus. They had emotion, need, and a desire to belong.

"I'm going to try to coax her to rise," Ernie explained. "Keep soothing her, Miss Ripley."

Her whispers were for Lily's ears only. Pippa reassured the elephant that she wasn't alone, that she knew what it was to be left behind but that others were here to care for her. Pippa caught Ernie's quick glance as she whispered, "I won't leave you, Lily. We deserve more than our mothers abandoning us."

She hadn't meant for Ernie to overhear. Pippa met Ernie's eyes over Lily's head. He dropped his stare. It wasn't a secret that she was a castoff child of the circus, yet no one ever spoke of it, certainly not the circus members. That the Ripleys had taken her in and branded Pippa less one of the circus family and instead one of the circus royalties cemented the fact that Pippa would never quite belong in either world.

Ernie shifted his attention to urging the calf into a sitting position. A futile effort considering the calf far outweighed Ernie's strength. Dr. Thurston positioned himself at the elephant's hindquarters. They counted together, then urged Lily to rise, risking the possibility that Lily was injured in places they could not see.

Pippa caught her breath as Lily extended a leg and pawed at the straw. She jumped back to avoid being clubbed by the calf's foot. Lily struggled to rise, a guttural moan escaping her. One of pain and protest. Her trunk swung in the air before bracing against the floor. Ernie urged his shoulder against the calf to assist her, and she repositioned, her body rolling upright onto her knees, her stomach still flat on the floor. She looked much like a dog did when the dog lay upright but not quite ready to spring into a stand.

Lily groaned again and reached with her trunk to lay it against Pippa's soiled dress.

Ernie swore. "She thinks you're her mother."

Commotion outside the pen drew their attention. Jake entered the stall as abruptly as he left, a rifle held loose in his left hand. A twinge of guilt nicked at Pippa as she took no small delight in the surprise that fluttered across Jake's face.

Another moan pulled from deep in the calf's stomach.

"She's in pain." Jake held out the rifle that was clutched in his hands as if he expected Ernie to take it.

Ernie extended his palms. "No."

A curse escaped Jake.

Dr. Thurston eyed the gun with hesitancy, as if the doctor in him agreed with Jake, the human in him with Pippa, and the business in him with Ernie. The business side responded. "Mr. Ripley would never condone it. There's too much of a financial investment at stake."

"Mr. Ripley can go to—" Jake shot a glance at Pippa, whose eyes widened. He tightened his mouth and bit back his words. "Be human, Thurston. It isn't right to make the animal suffer."

"Maybe not," Ernie interjected, "but there's such a thing as being too hasty." He tipped his head at the calf. "I know for a fact that Lily was offered as collateral to the bank for the expansion of the elephant show. Mr. Ripley might well be able to recover, but do you really want to be the one to tell him of the loss?"

"You're not going to even think about—" Jake's voice pinched off in desperation as Ernie rose to his feet.

Pippa held her breath.

"Take care of it." Ernie's directive sliced the silent tension.

"No!" Pippa cried.

Jake edged past the elephant trainer, but Ernie's hand shot out and latched like a vise on to the barrel of the rifle. He stared up at Jake, his eyes hard. Jake's were like gray steel drilling back at his boss. Both men had the same desire—to see the animal live and not suffer—but both had a different necessary end in mind.

"That's not what I meant." Ernie gave the rifle a shove at Jake.

Jake adjusted his grip on the firearm. His jaw tightened, and the scar that ran under his left eye puckered white as his face reddened with intensity. "Ernie . . ." There was warning in his voice.

Pippa looked into Lily's eyes. There was still pain, physical pain, etched in the recesses of that gaze. Yes, she was victorious in rising from the straw and her prostrate position, but would she— could she—eat? Heal? Jake seemed familiar with the suffering of animals, and perhaps his willingness to take its life was, after all, the more merciful path.

Ernie jabbed his finger toward Jake. "*You* put us in this situation, Chapman. Sloughing off your post. It all could've been avoided if you hadn't been off"—Ernie waved at the door, seeming to have forgotten Pippa's presence—"drinking bootleg whiskey with Patty and Benard."

Jake's expression darkened. "I was coming back."

"Unacceptable," Ernie spat. "Now, *you* need to try to get food into Lily. Get rid of that thing," he said, pointing at the gun, "and get the large bottles from the storeroom, milk, and a lot of it."

"Don't do it, Ernie," Jake urged. While his tone was firm, his expression held a hint of desperation. "I've seen animals suffer. It's not worth it—not just to save Ripley's dime. It's inhumane."

Pippa looked between the two men. There was so much she wanted to argue and say—shout, really—but she'd learned long ago to remain silent. Not to speak. She wouldn't be listened to anyway, and it was a miracle she'd even assisted in extending Lily's life this long.

"We need this elephant," Ernie said. Dr. Thurston nodded in the background, affirming the menagerie master's leadership. Ernie eyed Jake. "You're going to stay by this beast's side until it's on its feet, until it's reunited with its mother, and until that animal walks the ring come next summer."

Jake opened his mouth to speak, but then snapped it shut when Ernie concluded through gritted teeth, "Or *you* can answer to Ripley and pay back every cent this circus will lose."

Pippa couldn't identify the expression on her father's face, and the fact that he was unreadable was even more disconcerting than she had originally prepared herself for. Richard Ripley paced the solid wood floors of the entrance hall of their grand home, his two fingers squeezing the bridge of his nose. He stopped, dropped his hand, and crossed his arms over his chest. He stared at the hand-painted scene of sage-green maple saplings on the wallpapered top half of the wall, split into two by a piece of wood trim and painted solid green on the bottom.

Her father's silence was more nerve-wracking than if he shouted his fury—which, admittedly, she was more accustomed to. She noticed dust particles dance in the ray of light that streamed through the window and land on his shoulder. Dawn had broken over Bluff River and with it came her arrival home. An arrival she'd hoped to keep covert, sneaking in the back door and up the stairway to her bedroom before anyone had awakened. It was not to be. Her father was already moving at the morning hour of four a.m. Penn had been apparently yipping and scratching behind her closed bedroom door. Upon rescuing the distressed dog, Ripley had discovered Pippa's absence. He'd been surprised, then incredulous, and now . . . horribly unpredictable.

Forrest had been summoned. Summoned as if he was somehow responsible to keep his mouse of a fiancée from turning into a rebellious woman. He'd just arrived at Ripley Manor, and Pippa, having changed into a fresh drop-waisted dress of deep purple, meekly followed her father to greet him. If it hadn't been for finishing the night watching Lily fumble with and finally suckle the gigantic nipple from the quart-sized bottle, Pippa knew she would have regretted every moment of her own wayward behavior. Regret tainted even more by the fact she'd run from the very person she so desperately wished to commune with.

Forrest cleared his throat.

Pippa waited, just as she was expected to. She picked at a fingernail. If only her father would say something and stop his infernal pacing!

Ripley turned on his heel. He looked through her to Forrest. "You say the calf might not survive?"

Business first. Pippa bit her lip. The concern she held for Lily's tenuous survival squeezed the breath from Pippa's chest, but it also held hands with the bitter pang of being ignored. Pity the Watchman hadn't run away with her, or maybe an elephant trampled *her* to death. Then her father might have noticed or at least been disappointed in her.

Forrest shook his head. "It doesn't look good. And Ernie put Jake Chapman, the one who abandoned the mother to begin with, in charge of its vigilant care."

Pippa's stomach tightened as she searched Forrest's face to find some motive behind his statement. Blame? Diversion of attention off of her and her actions? She wasn't sure.

Ripley's incredulous bark of a laugh echoed in the hall. "Are you saying the man responsible for this situation is also responsible for fixing it?"

"Yes." Forrest's nod of affirmation was met by frigid silence.

Jake Chapman was hardly to blame for it all. Pippa tightened her lips and bit her tongue. Maybe he had left his vigil by the elephant's side as she labored, but labor could be long. And no one had really given him opportunity to explain.

"What was Ernie thinking? Chapman should be run out of town. At a minimum he should be booted off the grounds immediately."

"Ernie told Jake that he will owe the bank if something happens to the calf." Forrest must have already had a long conversation with Ernie this morning. Somehow the details had made their way to him very quickly.

Riley gave a *tsk*, his eyes narrowing in rebuke of the idea. "His year's salary would be a pittance of what that elephant is to me. We need that calf alive, not being tended by some nincompoop who doesn't show the brains to focus on his responsibilities."

"You know Georgiana Farnsworth will be all over this." Forrest's warning sliced through Pippa. Her father stiffened.

"The young woman needs to mind her business and stay home where it's her place to be. Prancing around town like a suffragette. I predicted this would happen—giving women the vote. Now they think they can comment on everything!"

Forrest gave a short nod. "She'll try to get the press involved. Georgiana will do anything to shout animal abuse in order to further her cause."

Pippa could hear the stringent sounds of Miss Farnsworth's last outcry against the circus—when a camel had broken free and trampled across Mr. Gregory's front porch, only to be stopped by what Miss Farnsworth considered a "vicious tethering of the animal's freedom."

"Well, shut her up!" Richard shouted.

Pippa jumped.

Forrest had no reaction. He was used to Ripley's outbursts.

"And *you*."

Pippa squirmed now that her father had leveled his fiercely black gaze on her.

"Why were you on circus grounds in the dead of night? Alone, no less, and without my knowledge? I expect an explanation and in the presence of your fiancé, who you have also disrespected by making an unwanted spectacle of yourself."

Words, answers, she had them all, but could tell him none of them. Her father would demand to see the letters from the Watchman, rage about the outright audacity of a stranger claiming such hold over her, and insist Pippa cease all contact. She couldn't risk that. She needed to know. It was this man, Richard Ripley, whose overbearing paternity caused an insatiable hunger to find her roots.

He stepped nearer and lowered his face, his eyes commanding her own. "I asked you a question."

She was six years old again. Tongue-tied. Remorseful and yet horribly frustrated at the restraints over her. A noise captured her attention, and she glanced to the top of the long, winding staircase. Her mother stood there, elegant in her housedress, an expression on her face that, while she held sympathy for her daughter, she hadn't any more courage than Pippa did to stand in defiance of Richard Ripley.

"You're not going to answer me, are you?" He raked long fingers through his hair and then dropped his hand with a slap against his leg. "You're a fathomless pit of disappointment."

Pippa ducked her head, focusing on a swirling pattern in the marble floor, trying to avoid the soft sound of her mother's footsteps retreating to her suite.

Forrest cleared his throat. "Pippa did do some good last night."

Cheers for her fiancé. At least beneath his strictly business-focused manner beat a human heart.

"Really?"

Pippa could feel her father's censure as he emphasized the word with a raised eyebrow of scornful doubt.

"The elephant calf," Forrest offered. He took a step forward, which brought his arm within proximity of Pippa's, and his sleeve brushed hers. For reassurance, perhaps, or maybe to stake some of his claim as her future authority. "According to Ernie, the animal responded quite well to Pippa. It was Pippa who persuaded her to rise and eat."

Her father's tone grew low and very, very controlled. "We need to handle this affair before we allow *my* circus to be run into the ground by placing an inept idiot over the care of the very investment he almost killed. And, Pippa, there is to be no more circus for you at all."

Pippa's throat closed. Her own actions had sabotaged her best-laid intentions. Last night had ended abysmally. It was as if she had juggled fine china and let it slip from her hands to shatter. It was her fault. All of it. The Watchman spooking in the chaos, her own fears throttling her bravery, and their very presence creating havoc in the wake of the elephant's birth.

"The calf needs me." Pippa's voice quavered with the only words she could afford. There was so much more she wanted to say. Wanted to scream. But the words didn't come. They never did.

Ripley waved his hand over the length of Pippa's stature. "She's your intended, Forrest. What do you say?"

Her father was washing his hands of her.

Forrest shot her a quick glance and then gave her father a curt nod. "I agree. She needs to stay away. The circus isn't the place for—a proper lady."

Pippa didn't miss his hesitation. Of course, she wasn't a proper lady. Her origins were the first strike against her, her deformity the second, and now being seen on circus grounds in the middle of the night? These might be modern times for modern women, but tradition and perception sneered at that idea.

Forrest continued, his voice smooth and confident, bypassing her like the nothing that she was. "You'll need regular updates on the calf. I can continue to invest my time there. We can keep this quiet, and I'll be sure no one makes any rash decisions regarding the calf's welfare."

"And you'll make certain Pippa stays away from the circus?" Ripley pointed a finger in her direction as if she couldn't comprehend reason. "If it gets out that she was there alone and unaccounted for—and for that matter, with that riffraff Chapman—it will shatter the decency of your betrothal and future union, not to mention besmirch our name. Carousing and consorting with the rabble of his like . . . well, we both know his sort."

"I'll keep Pippa accountable."

Every nerve in Pippa's body screamed to fight back, to rise in her defense, but she didn't. The expression on Richard Ripley's face indicated he was not to be crossed in the matter. Maybe, if Pippa could see him through different eyes, she would be able to appreciate that he was trying to protect her honor—and maybe her welfare. But she couldn't. She couldn't look at the man who had been her father since she was a babe and see anything other than the replacement for someone else. Her real father.

CHAPTER EIGHT

CHANDLER

Nothing was as sweet as that moment she deposited a sleepy Peter Pan into her bed, his lanky arms and legs, bare chest, and basketball shorts transforming into a tightly curled ball. Eyes closed, Chandler's son edged his way toward the middle of the bed, and his hand reached out to pat her empty pillow.

"You're awful close to my side of the bed, Dude-face." Chandler launched into their nightly routine.

"It's so I can snuggle while I sleep, Momma." Peter might be seven, might be on the verge of no longer being a little boy, but for now he was still all hers. At night, he reverted to his toddler years when he gave up his little bed and sleeping solo to crawling in next to her. Truth be told, Chandler would never freely tell anyone that Peter slept beside her at night. Her parents already seemed doubtful of her parenting skills, and creating co-dependency, as they would put it, was unwise at best.

Chandler bent over and brushed back the damp, wavy hair, its ombré tones something a girl would kill for, but which Peter came by naturally. She pressed her lips to his temple, taking a second to draw in a deep breath of little-boy scent.

"Ni-night, Peter Pan."

"Ni-night, Wendy," he murmured, already almost asleep.

One more kiss and Chandler clicked off the lamp by the

bed. She cast a quick look upward at the night-light hologram splashed across the ceiling. Wolverine. One of Peter's favorite superheroes. Somehow, instead of being scary, the spread of Wolverine's claws across the ceiling brought him comfort. He was protected by an imaginary man with wolfish sideburns and a yellow suit.

Chandler smiled to herself and padded across the wood floor of the rented cottage. She needed sleep too, and a hairy super-hero wouldn't be all that bad, either. No. She would be her own superhero. Her body was begging for rest, yet her mind was still sharp and wary.

Making her way into the kitchen, Chandler stopped in the door-way and stared at the unrepaired sink. Denny Pike hadn't returned as he'd promised, and he hadn't called to give her any messages either. After a dinner of ramen noodles and some box-mix biscuits Margie had scrounged up, the nanny took her leave—but not before giving Chandler a cozy hug and a whispered "Tomorrow's gonna be fresh and new, hun."

Now her phone rang with the indicative ringer of a video call, and Chandler snagged it from her joggers' pocket. She glanced at the screen, biting back an oath as she dreaded the sight of Jackson's name. He'd call her any time of day. The man was always working, always devoted to proving himself as the more competent of the two. Instead it was a welcome name.

Chandler swiped to answer. "Nel?"

"Hey!" Her friend's voice was almost raspy on the other end. Nel was second only to Peter. Nel was . . . well, she grounded Chandler. "You didn't text today."

Chandler squeezed her eyes tight. "No, I'm sorry. I was—it was a—heckuva day."

"Aw, tell me what happened."

Chandler hardly noticed her friend's confinement to her wheel-chair from spina bifida. It wasn't Nel's defining feature. It was her eyes, so dark, so knowing. All knowing, it seemed, and framed by dark curls and olive skin. She should have a degree in counseling, but instead she worked at a local grocery store and relied on assistance to help get her from point A to point B. Someone had to pay for school, Nel always said with a chuckle while waving away Chandler's sympathy. Pity wasn't something Nel liked. She'd get through school, eventually, and as independently as possible.

Chandler exited the kitchen and entered the small living room, sinking into a cushiony couch of taupe faux leather with a top stitching that made it rustic and homey. She stared vacantly at the cold white-brick fireplace and the cast-iron pot on its hearth filled with kindling. Denny must have employed a designer's help in making this rental so cozy. He seemed more like the type to decorate with pyramids of beer cans and a few old flowerpots for ashtrays.

"It's just—tough." Chandler bit her tongue. Really she was just tired. Tired of keeping her health a secret, tired of maintaining through the stress, and tired of worrying that one of these days it was all somehow going to explode around her.

Nel laughed, her husky tone carrying through the phone. "Now, now. My tough isn't your tough, and I can see you checking your words and comparing the two. Knock it off, sister. You've a right to cry 'trouble!' now and then."

"You have no idea." Chandler had to admit something or she'd self-combust. She sank deeper into the sofa, pulling her feet off the floor and perching them on the edge of the cushion. "Do you believe in ghosts?"

She'd been contemplating it since Margie had gone on and on about Lottie over dinner. How the real estate agent was as professional as they come but a bit loony about the spirit world. How the ghost tours she ran on the side had fished up stories about the murdered depot prostitute, a poltergeist who busted mirrors in the old house on 10th Avenue, and the theory that other spirits from the old Native American burial grounds were none too pleased that their graves had been built upon eons ago. But Chandler couldn't shake the eerie sensations that had made the hairs stand up on her arms last night in the depot. If a light had been seen inside, there was no physical explanation for it. And Sasquatch Man seemed convinced someone had been inside too. If it wasn't a human, could it be a wandering spirit?

She could see Nel's black eyebrow raise, her inquisitive look and searching expression. "Do I believe in ghosts?" she repeated. "Um. No. Although my aunt saw my uncle standing over her in bed one night. She swears by it. He'd been dead for five years. And I know for sure he was dead 'cause I was a kid and touched his body in the coffin. It was sort of cold and spongy."

Chandler grimaced. "Thanks for that."

Nel just smiled.

Chandler continued, plowing ahead in spite of misgivings that she'd sound a bit crazy. "Some . . . *stuff* happened last night at the property I'm working on. And, I found out there's a local story about the long-ago murder of a woman that might have taken place there. I don't know if it will affect resale if we decide to flip the property, but people get superstitious about ghosts and such. Of course, there's no requirement that I can find here in Wisconsin that information like that be disclosed before a sale. So . . . *voilà*! I may have purchased a ghost! And Jackson is breathing down my neck just waiting for me to mess up so he can show himself to be god almighty of the company."

Nel gave her an empathetic smile. "You look like a train wreck." She grew more serious and tilted her head to stare down her nose at Chandler.

A desperate ache grew in Chandler's chest. It was familiar and dark. A sensation riddled with longing and a need to find a place— just one place—where she could stop fighting, stop *being*, and just rest. Wasn't rest supposed to hold hands with faith and marry itself to a person's belief that God had things handled? All those pretty memes that popped up on her Facebook feed, the little coloring book of inspirational quotes the lady at the women's outreach at church had given her, and even that T-shirt she'd bought on a whim online from a click-bait site. All those things printed with cursive and flowers promised a rest that was as elusive to Chandler as catching a falling star.

"You need to sleep," Nel advised. Not rest. She knew better. She knew better than to tell Chandler that. Rest was a completely different thing than sleep. Chandler hadn't rested since the day she found out she was pregnant with Peter and didn't know who the father was. Hadn't rested since her own parents said they'd be there to help if Peter needed them, but also made it clear that Chandler had made her own choices and needed to live with the consequences. They weren't going to bail her out like a privileged kid who didn't need to answer for herself. Even when Uncle Neal had recognized potential in her after she labored her way through her last year in college and offered her a job, she was immediately struck with the accusation of nepotism from co-workers. Maybe not spewed from their mouths directly, but it was in their eyes nonetheless. The challenge, the doubt, the disappointment.

"My sink is busted, and my landlord hasn't bothered to fix it yet," Chandler mumbled.

Nel opened her mouth and started to speak, but Chandler didn't hear her. A loud knock on the door startled her, and she twitched in surprise. A quick assessment through the cross-paned windows and the filmy curtain that covered it told her it was still dusk. Not completely dark outside, but the early autumn night most assuredly evolved quickly toward it. Another month, Daylight Saving Time, and it'd be well into nighttime by now.

"Nel, someone's at the door. I need to go."

Nel offered Chandler an understanding albeit tinged-with-concern smile. "Fine. But you call again if you need me. You know I'm here, day or night."

Blessed Nel.

"And," her friend finished, "I'll be praying for you."

Another knock at the door. Chandler nodded. "Thanks, Nel."

She hung up, wondering when Nel's prayers would bring the peace God had promised but didn't seem to care about seeing through.

And here was proof that God's peace that passes all understanding was more likely a myth than a reality.

Chandler had the bolt lock hooked as she stared through the open crack between the door and frame.

He glowered back.

Chandler couldn't resist darting a look over her shoulder at the ceiling toward the room where Peter slept. If the man tried anything—*anything*—he'd experience a far fiercer version of Chandler Neale Faulk than the one he'd encountered last night. A man knew no violence like that of a mother bear enraged on behalf of her cub.

"What do you want?" Be direct. Be firm. Chandler coached confidence into her voice, the same confidence she infused herself with when going into a corporate meeting where she had to lay out her proposals with the façade of professional expertise that was so critical to keep her footing as a woman in a roomful of contractors, investors, architects, and other sundry positions.

He didn't appear any friendlier than last night in the depot, only this time she could see his eyes were green as they drilled into hers with unsettling intensity. It was as though he was seeing through her and into her, attempting to translate who she was, assess her intelligence, her threat level, even her honesty. Or was he gauging her vulnerability? Chandler recognized he could snap the bolt lock from its anchor with one well-placed kick of his boot-clad foot.

Chandler's common sense took over. She had no obligation to entertain a stranger who'd butted into her business last night with the finesse of a bulldozer. She was moving to slam the door shut when the tip of his boot wedged into the crack.

"Don't." His word was a command. His voice gravelly.

"Tell me who you are." Command for a command, she determined, and she locked eyes with him.

He didn't grace her with an answer. Just a declaration. "My uncle sent me."

Confusion hampered Chandler's reasoning. "Your—*who*?"

"To fix your sink," he finished as though she'd never interrupted.

There was no way she was letting Sasquatch Man into the cottage. "I'll wait for Denny, thank you."

"Fine." The scruffy man with the long wavy hair that framed a broad, chiseled face gave a short nod and pulled back his toe from the door. He turned remarkably thick shoulders to her and started down the walk with intentional steps that held no regret at being thwarted from his purpose.

Chandler opened the door until the chain on the bolt was stretched to its max. She squinted into the fast-growing night. A Harley. Very similar to the one that Denny had rode earlier in the day.

"Wait!"

He turned.

Why had she stopped him? Uncertainty warred within her.

"I'm not going to hurt you. You saw me with the cops last night. We go way back. I'm harmless." Harmless. He looked like with a flick of his wrist he could break her into two pieces.

"How comforting," Chandler retorted. "What do you want? Who are you?"

His mouth curved slightly at the corner in a dry, tilted smile that offered no friendship and made her feel smaller than she already was. Maybe even a little playful teasing—mischievous. Definitely that.

"I'm your plumber."

"You're way more than that," Chandler shot back, remembering him strong-arming her into silence for fear the trespasser—or as Lottie would claim, the *ghost*—would spook. Ha! Spook. Even in her nervous fluster, Chandler noted her unintentional mental pun.

He shrugged. He didn't seem to care one way or the other if he fixed her sink.

"Just a second." Chandler shut the door and retrieved her phone from the couch. She was going to call Denny. She had no intention of letting a stranger into her house—or a Sasquatch. But intentions were sometimes thwarted by necessity, and she had a sink that needed fixing.

One thing was certain, the last twenty-four hours had almost proven to Chandler the foundations of her worst fear. She was growing inept. Inept and incapable of remaining stable and level-headed, of wearing her big-girl pants, of being Uncle Neal's right hand without question. She was floundering. And floundering made a person very, very vulnerable.

CHAPTER NINE

The sink was repaired. Denny had vouched for his nephew and even offered to come over and stand there with him if Chandler was that upset. She was torn and almost took him up on the offer, but then thought she had to be overreacting if the guy was Denny's nephew. Of course, she'd only met Denny once too, so what if he wasn't trustworthy? Still, last night the cops hadn't seemed worried about him. And so on and so forth went her circular thoughts until, before Chandler realized it, the sink was working again.

Darkness invaded every non-lit section of the tiny kitchen, made tinier by the grizzly who had silently worked his plumbing talents with no introductions and no further conversation.

Hank. Hank Titus. Denny had given Chandler his name and was adamant that Hank could do a better job of repairs than he could. What was she nervous for? Hank was just a younger version of himself. A softy.

Chandler eyed Hank from across the room, keeping her phone clutched in her hand. It brought her a false sense of security.

The clank of a pipe wrench being tossed on the linoleum floor startled Chandler from her swirling thoughts.

Hank eyed her and declared, "It's fixed." Then he wiped his hands on a dish towel.

"Thanks."

They examined each other wordlessly, the tension taut with the unspoken. He finally broke it by tossing the towel on the counter and bending to retrieve the wrench.

"So you didn't see anyone last night at the depot?" he asked.

Chandler scowled. "No one except you."

Hank cussed and kicked the cupboard door shut on the pipes.

"What *were* you doing at the depot last night?" Chandler didn't bother to try to sound nice.

He glanced at her and then back at his toolbox. Hank dropped the wrench into it without care or concern for the other tools or any semblance of organization. "What were *you* doing there?" he countered.

"I own it." Which wasn't exactly true, but it was a long, round-about story to try to explain her uncle's business of acquiring, restoring, and flipping old properties.

Hank's thick brows rose. He grunted as if he hadn't expected that response. He shut the lid on the toolbox. "I need to get back inside."

Chandler recalled Denny's descriptor of Hank. A softy? Nope. She didn't see it. "Why? No one was there. It was a trespassing false alarm."

Hank shrugged. He hefted the toolbox off the table as though it were made of lightweight foam. His hands were large and corded, his fingers strong.

"Someone *had* been inside before we got there." He gave her a look that clearly communicated he knew more of something than she did. That he had a mission of some unspoken sort and that getting it out of him—short of a waterboarding interrogation— was going to take skill.

Chandler bit the inside of her lip. He took a few steps toward her, and the closer he came the more imposing he was. Intimi-dating. His bulk towered over her five-foot-seven frame, and she vividly recalled the strength of his arm as he'd trapped her against him. It wasn't romantic or comforting or even intriguing. It was just shy of utterly frightening.

"N-no one could have been inside. *I* unlocked the padlock and unchained the door. That's the only entrance."

Hank's lips thinned, and he raised his brows as if to insinuate he'd let her believe whatever she wanted but that she was also wrong.

"I never saw a light inside either. That came from Lottie. Lottie is the one who called me." Now she was chattering. Peppering Hank Titus with all the information she had and receiving none in return.

"Not everyone uses doors to enter an abandoned building." His growl was ominous. His hair waved around his shoulders like a Neanderthal's, or a Viking's, or . . . no. She'd stick with Sasquatch.

Chandler squeezed her eyes shut against the image of otherworldly trespassers and against the vision of Hank Titus in her kitchen. She drew in a slow, stabilizing breath, but still reached out and grasped the back of the kitchen table chair to steady herself.

"I don't believe in ghosts." She might as well declare it now for herself as much as for Hank and Lottie and the rest of Bluff River.

A tiny smile toyed at the corner of Hank's mouth. Chandler was finished with his brooding mockery and cocky confidence.

She pointed at the front door. "Thanks for taking care of the sink. Good night."

A sideways, taunting smile tipped his carved lips. "Getting rid of me?"

"Gladly." Chandler winced. She hadn't meant to say it out loud.

He chuckled, and his craggy features softened. Only for a moment, though. "Be careful."

Hank brushed by her, and Chandler made a concerted effort to close her open mouth as his shoulder touched her still-extended hand.

"Be careful?" The thought of Peter asleep upstairs and waiting for his momma to crawl in and snuggle beside him fluttered through her overprotective imagination. "Be careful of what?"

Hank turned and locked eyes with her. "Haven't looked up Bluff River history, have you?"

"I know enough." The murdered prostitute of the 1920s. It was gory.

He tipped his head but continued staring down his nose at her.

"It doesn't have anything to do with me." She wanted to convince herself of that, yet she was becoming increasingly aware that the train depot could not be purchased without bringing its baggage with it.

He assessed her as though she should know, or simply conclude, based on his miniscule explanation. Hank shrugged. "Sure, it does. You just bought the epicenter of a serial killer's string of crimes."

Chandler sensed the color had left her face. "No. No, Lottie said there was a woman who *may* have been murdered there years ago. She didn't say a word about a *serial killer*." It would be just her luck to learn something like Bluff River was the old stomping grounds of Ed Gein. She'd heard Gein *had* been from Wisconsin, after all.

A twinkle of satisfaction glimmered in Hank's eyes. He nodded. "See? Even a hundred years later, the Watchman haunts us."

"The Watchman," Chandler parroted, feeling like an idiot. That was a killer she'd not heard of—ever.

Hank smiled wryly, crow's-feet deepening at the edges of his eyes. "Careful he doesn't come after you. Some say they fried the wrong man for the crimes."

He opened the door and exited. The sound of the door shutting behind him resounded through the entryway, and Chandler stood dumbfounded, every nerve tingling. She hurried to the door and twisted the door lock, hooked the chain, and slid it through the bolt. For good measure and with probably little-to-no lasting effect, she pulled over the small table by the door and positioned it in front of it. Not to deter anyone so much as to make noise if an intruder attempted a forced entry. Of course, that wouldn't help with a dead spirit.

Her breaths short, a chill ran through her, covering her skin with goose bumps. Hank was gone. She was alone on the first floor of the small rental cottage. But she didn't feel alone. She could almost feel a presence. She'd heard once that the sensation of cold and the resulting evidence of bumps on one's arms was the result of a spirit passing through a person to make its presence known. The idea was ludicrous.

The idea was all too real at eleven o'clock at night.

Sleep had been restless, breakfast a quick protein shake with almond milk, followed by some fast paper work to take care of all the necessaries to enable her to homeschool Peter while on assignment for her job. Not that they would be doing a lot of regular schooling. Not this first month, anyway. Chandler tried not to think about it. Another failure. She could envision Mom either rolling her eyes or offering to teach Peter for her. Both were unwelcome visions. But, call her overprotective, she hadn't the heart to enroll him in public school only to yank him when the project was completed.

After Margie's arrival, Chandler gathered her thoughts and her laptop to head to the other portion of property Uncle Neal had bought that she'd hardly had time to consider yet. She'd spent most of the week getting Peter settled. Now the real work would start. Lottie had insisted she meet Chandler this morning at the two-story white house that had once been the costume house for the circus. Whirring machines, bolts of vivid materials, girls who sewed and beaded and sequined skimpy leotards and ringmasters' coats. While empty for now, Chandler had agreed with Lottie's original real-estate assessment of the property. A little fixing up with vintage circus décor, and when the depot project was finished, she could either flip the house with it having bed-and-breakfast potential or maybe just pitch it as office space for a law or accounting firm.

Now Chandler greeted the agent—or small-town medium—

outside the costume house. Lottie opened the wood-framed screen door and unlocked the inner front door.

"I'm so sorry if I overreacted the other night in calling you. I saw a light, and I'm the first to admit a ghost can be frightening or it can be intriguing." Lottie's voice rang with sincerity, as though she were chatting about something normal and routine. "But it's the trespassers I'm more concerned about. Ghosts don't graffiti walls and damage woodwork. Ghosts don't need a light."

Lottie wore capris, even though it was in the fifties outside. There was nothing about the older woman to indicate she was, well, off her rocker, and really her normality made Chandler want to relax, even while the topic at hand made her nerve endings spike.

Lottie led her through the front room with familiarity. Chandler noticed the desk and chair she'd bought online had been delivered and even set up. Probably thanks to Lottie's son, Cru, whom she had yet to meet. Chandler followed Lottie to a door that opened to a stairwell leading to the second floor.

"A ghost suspended between worlds is a lost soul, begging for freedom, but somehow that suspension affects their emotional state." Lottie's voice and her footsteps echoed as she climbed. "Some souls apparently don't like being in limbo, and they transform from wandering haunters into torturous poltergeists that seek to destroy. Which"—Lottie swung open another door at the top of the stairs and shot Chandler a wince—"is why I asked to meet you here. You can't be angry at a ghost—it won't accomplish anything."

Chandler frowned, then stepped past Lottie to look beyond her into the upstairs room. It opened to an expanse that ran the length of the building. The far end of the second floor was cluttered with cardboard boxes, old trunks and crates, their tops frosted like a cake with years of dust. They looked to have been tossed about haphazardly, like a tornado had ripped through the room. Some were tipped over, others ripped into shreds. Unexplainably.

"Spirits can be temperamental," Lottie finished as if her explanation would excuse a misbehaving ghost who acted like a child and pitched a tantrum in the upstairs room. Lottie positioned her manicured fingers in a steeple over her wrinkled lips and watched Chandler closely, waiting for her reaction.

Chandler took a few steps toward one of the demolished boxes. "What happened?" Ignoring Lottie's opinion, Chandler scowled. There wasn't anything of value. Old magazines and books were in most of the boxes. Now even they were strewn about. "This is vandalism without a purpose. Blatant vandalism." She bit her bottom lip to stifle her temper.

"She's temperamental." Lottie's eyes were the color of aquamarine, and they widened with apology.

"Who's temperamental?" Chandler didn't want to know. Well, she did *and* she didn't.

"Patty," Lottie supplied.

"Patty?" Chandler raised a brow and bent over to pick up one of the larger pieces of torn cardboard.

"Patty Luchent," Lottie reaffirmed. "You know, the woman found murdered?"

"The one in the depot?" Chandler struggled to piece everything together in a way that would yield a more reasonable explanation.

Lottie nodded and moved to right a box. "She was a seamstress, but also a frequenter of the Bluff River Inn—if you know what I mean." Lottie cleared her throat meaningfully, a veiled reference to a bordello. She continued, "They found her dead, and most say it was at the depot. However, some say it was right here in the costume house."

Chandler didn't honor the spirit with acknowledgment. Instead she took out her phone to call the police. "I need to report this."

Lottie glanced at the window and the depot beyond. "You

can, but the police won't do much. Patty's always been unsettled. I've seen her. So has Cru. She will do things like this—upend objects, even break glass—when she's disturbed. Although I didn't imagine she would be so upset at the sale of the depot and this place."

Chandler paused on dialing. Since the urgency was nowhere near pressing, instead she picked her way through the wreckage. *Patty Luchent.* The name resonated in her mind and collided with Hank's mention of the Bluff River Killer.

"Was she murdered by the Watchman?" Chandler asked as she squatted to pick up an old circus pamphlet that was warped from water damage. The animal tamer on the front was dressed in 1970s bell-bottoms with sequins racing down the legs.

Lottie gave a tiny snort of surprise. "You've heard of him?"

Chandler nodded. "Briefly."

"The story goes that she *may* have been. But that's up for debate as well."

"So, no one really knows anything for a fact about Patty Luchent's murder?" Chandler tossed the pamphlet into an open box. She decided to test Lottie's theory. "Why would her spirit be so un-settled? Especially to do *this* to the room." She glanced around at the jumbled mess before them.

"Because you're here, dear." Lottie patted Chandler's arm ab-sently as she brushed past her to peer through one of the front windows to the street below. "This place has been unused for months. This upstairs uninhabited for decades, really. Now you're here and planning to use it regularly. Well, she won't be having any of that. This is *her* place."

"I thought the depot was her place," Chandler said, crossing her arms and wishing she were anywhere but here.

Lottie twisted and gave Chandler an earnest nod. "Oh, it is. She's a wanderer." Lottie batted a manicured hand at Chandler in dismissal and moved away from the window, walking back toward the stairs they'd used to get to the second story. "Patty Luchent isn't anything to worry about. She'll toss a plate or a pillow, a box or maybe a picture frame, but she's never hurt anyone."

"No?" Chandler pictured a snarling white-faced ghoul bending over her while she worked. She wasn't impressed by the self-proclaimed medium's comfort with the supernatural. A supernatural Chandler never believed in.

She gave the room another scan and shivered.

At least not until now.

CHAPTER TEN

PIPPA

She watched him from her vantage point on the front porch of the costume house. It was as close to the circus as Pippa could get without completely disregarding her father's instructions. Considering Forrest had allowed her to come along with him, she needed to show respect to her intended as well, even though every ounce of her spirit rebelled against the constraints.

Forrest had parked his Ford in front of the two-story white house where the circus costumes were mended, sewn, and created over the fall and winter months. Assuming a visit to the place filled with bolts of vibrantly colored materials, bins of sequins and faux jewels, and the whirring of sewing machines would somehow satiate Pippa's restless nature that had attached itself to the circus, Forrest had left her here. She was diminished to an accessory with predetermined dispositions not entirely her own. Although, Pippa did admit to appreciating the bright colors. They tugged at her spirit, at a place inside her no one could touch. Wild but imprisoned.

Pippa watched Forrest as he strode down the hard-packed dirt street toward the elephant house. The bright yellow octagonal building shone brilliant in today's sunlight. Brilliant and ominous both.

"Your fella is a sheik, if ever I saw one."

The silky voice drifted over Pippa's shoulder, and she spun, immediately sensing warmth in her cheeks. A woman, not much older than she, had come up the porch steps. In contrast to Pippa's deep-green cloche hat pulled down over a delicately rolled bun at the nape of her neck, this woman's hair was bobbed to her chin in the reckless, insubordinate way of women who were shunning a conservative upbringing. Her dress hung straight and shapeless, with a deep v that plunged down her flat chest. She probably bound her chest tightly, as so many of the fashionable set were wont to do.

"Anyone in there?" The woman waved her ungloved hand in front of Pippa's face.

Pippa blinked. "Oh. Forrest?"

"That his first name, huh?" Pippa's companion lifted a cigarette to her lips and took a long drag, staring past Pippa to Forrest. A smile tipped the corner of her mouth. "Like I said. A sheik. He's handsome, ya follow?"

Pippa glanced back at the tailored form of Forrest. She supposed he *was* handsome. Maybe she was simply too used to him. But in comparison to Jake Chapman, he was . . . Pippa halted her wayward and unexpected thought. She'd never really considered Jake Chapman before—at least not consciously.

"I'm Patty." The stranger's blue eyes sparkled.

She seemed nice. Lovely, actually. Pippa smiled.

A train whistle sounded in the distance, announcing the arrival of a locomotive at the depot blocks away. Patty shot a look westward, where the brick building tucked into the side of the bluff.

"Train's early," Patty observed. "Ever want to jump on and just get away from this place?"

Another long drag and then a spiral of smoke blown gently between red puckered lips.

Pippa bit hers. She nodded. It probably wasn't wise to admit that, especially to a stranger and a circus gypsy at that.

Patty dropped the cigarette to the porch and ground it with

the heel of her pump. "Me too. Of course, I ride it all spring and summer, so you'd think I'd be tired of it. But I'm not." A faraway look washed over her eyes. "Funny how no one's ever happy where they're meant to be."

"Meant to be?" Pippa raised a brow and fingered her lace collar tucked so modestly against her neck.

Patty offered up a tinkling laugh. "Aw, honey. We were all meant to be. My momma taught me that when I was a wee thing. But, I ain't never met a soul who liked where they landed. 'Providence,' Momma always said. Providence places you there. Who'm I to argue with Providence?" Patty shrugged. "Still, that don't mean I gotta like it."

"You don't like being part of the circus?" Pippa could almost taste her surprise. Surprise that Patty was discontent with the very place that drew Pippa like a magnet to metal.

Patty smiled again and tipped her head in the direction Forrest had gone. "When men like him show up, I don't mind. But a girl can get tired of the circus, same as she can get tired of—makin' a livin'." A knowing eye swept Pippa from head to foot.

A blush crept up Pippa's neck, warming her skin. "Do you ride the horses?" Pippa diverted, not completely sure as to what Patty had alluded to. She imagined Patty standing on the back of a white Lipizzan, wearing a tiny shining outfit, feathers arranged in a fan attached to the back of a headband that embraced her short dark hair.

"Me?" Patty's voice rose a bit. "No, honey. I just sew things, and I . . . I sew."

Pippa had been sure she was a performer. Sure that the glamour radiating from the beautiful face was honed by a profession of being in the circle. The lights, the booming voice of the ringmaster, the trumpet of an elephant and roar of a lion.

"Do you enjoy it?"

Patty gave Pippa a searching look, then a little smile. "You're cute." She tilted her head toward the door of the sewing house

90

and rolled her baby blues. "I sew till my fingers drop off. It's a job. Better than a lot of girls have, I guess. At least I'm independent and fancy-free. In my spare time, I like to have a little fun." She winked playfully and tugged open the screen door. A saucy smile was tossed Pippa's way. "Guess I was meant to be a costume artist. Who knew God had one of me up His sleeve!"

The door closed on Patty's laughter, and Pippa stared after her, a bit in awe and a bit in shame. Awed by Patty's flamboyant challenge for her life, and shamed that she suddenly wished she were like Patty. That she had the gumption to wear short hair, to bind her chest, to fling a strand of pearls around her neck and smoke a cigarette.

Pippa shrank against the porch rail, forcing her attention back to the elephant barn. She would wait for Forrest. The trumpet of an elephant echoed the whistle of the train as it approached the depot, announcing its arrival and soon-to-be departure. Pippa longed to open her mouth and cry out along with it. But she didn't. Ripleys didn't cry. They didn't argue or make a fuss. They just did . . . as they were told.

Forrest was not pleased, and the glower that settled between his dark eyes only emphasized the fact. That, and the pace he was setting as he led Pippa down the street toward the elephant barn. He'd returned to retrieve her with the exasperated instruction that they needed to see if the elephant calf would respond to her as it had a few nights ago. The calf wasn't eating, and the mother wouldn't respond to it.

"We're going to lose thousands!" Forrest muttered under his breath. The pinstripes on his trousers blurred together as he took fast steps. "This is asinine that I have to bring *you* to fix the problem."

An insult? Perhaps. But she preferred to believe it was frustration directed at Ernie's inability to get the calf to eat. Pippa hurried beside Forrest, her feet twisting on the little stones in the dirt road, making the pace even more challenging with her leg. She ignored catcalls from some of the circus hands they passed—apparently they didn't mind the hitch in her gait. She caught glimpses of the river in the alleyways between the buildings, and across it, circus supplies being off-loaded from a flatbed on the train, which had now pulled through on the tracks that ran perpendicular to the river.

"Forrest, please slow down," Pippa managed to say between puffs. While their pace was hurried, it was more the effort not to trip that made Pippa expend energy.

The autumn air was crisp, and the scent of the colorful leaves of the maples and oaks mixed with the tangy smell of animals wafting from the barns. The horse barn consisted of two levels, and Pippa caught a glimpse of a horse being led from its stall by a man in blue trousers. It was a draft horse, large and bred for work. They were probably taking the horse to help with the train's cargo.

"Come on, Pippa," Forrest urged, this time taking her lightly by her upper arm and steering her around a clump of mud that had fallen off a wagon. "Ernie has requested I allow you to see the calf. If she responds to you as she apparently did a few nights ago . . ." His voice dwindled as he cast a sidelong glance at her.

She couldn't deny the thrill in her stomach as she increased her pace. She was needed, and that invisible bond she sensed between herself and the calf reawakened.

A shadow stretched across their path. Pippa lifted her eyes, meeting the turbulent storm in Jake Chapman's. He glared at her, his mouth stretched in a thin line, his coarse beard short and rough-looking. Next to Forrest, Jake looked almost like a vagabond, albeit a tad cleaner. His hair was raked back from his forehead, and she couldn't tell if he'd attempted to use pomade to keep the long light-brown strands in place or if it was just shy of a few days from being washed. Pippa couldn't find her tongue to offer any sort of courteous greeting. He really was quite intimidating. A cigar hung from the corner of his mouth and emphasized the tough squint of his eyes. Disgusting habit. And the stench. He really should put it out. Actually, he shouldn't. It was attractive, in a brutish sort of way.

"Chapman." Forrest jerked his head toward Pippa. "I've brought her, but I expect congeniality and propriety."

"Go home." The cigar waved in Jake's mouth haphazardly. "You shouldn't be here."

"I *should* be here," Forrest said, his voice edged with steel. "It's in the financial best interests of the circus to have this animal on her feet as soon as possible. A circus isn't a circus without an elephant."

Jake's eyes narrowed. "You have elephants. A lot of them—"

"Not a calf," Forrest shot back.

Jake pivoted from Forrest, and his eyes roved Pippa's face lazily. The fact that his attention caused her nerves to flutter was insignificant. What mattered right now was Lily—that she was cared for. Loved and nurtured.

"That's foolhardy." Jake tossed his cigar down and ground it into the dirt. It left a black scar in the dust. The smoke wafted up and dissipated. Snuffed out. Like he seemed to want to snuff out their presence. Jake spun on his heel and entered the elephant barn.

Forrest was fast behind him, Pippa following unbidden yet knowing it was expected.

"Apologize to my fiancée," Forrest insisted.

Pippa winced. Forrest sounded downright petty.

Jake smiled wryly. "Nothing but the best for Her Highness." While there was a roughness in his tone, when he looked at her, Pippa thought she saw a glimmer of apology. That maybe his sarcasm was directed at Forrest and not her, and maybe there was kindness, even understanding beneath the rugged exterior. The tension between the two men was so thick it hung in the air stronger than the tangy-sweet scent of elephant dung.

The straw smelled fresh, however, and toyed with Pippa's nose, sending particles through the shaft of sunlight that highlighted the calf's slumber. "Is she . . . ?"

"She's alive," Jake said.

Pippa knelt in the hay beside the calf. The newborn wasn't very responsive. The tip of her trunk lifted a few inches off the hay and then rested back in its place. She heard Forrest sigh behind her. The kind of sigh that insinuated the direness of the situation. Pippa looked up at Jake and was surprised that he was watching her and not the elephant. There was mutual concern in his expression.

"Is she going to live?" Pippa tried again.

Jake squatted next to her. "Lily needs a lot of care."

Pippa was very aware of the breadth of his muscular frame. He was tense, taut, like a spring waiting to jump. Barely restrained, and dangerous if given free rein.

"What do you need me to do?" Pippa returned her attention to the four-hundred-plus-pound animal whose sad eyes blinked with lashes that curled like feathers over tough leathery skin. "Sweet one." Pippa leaned over the elephant and kissed Lily's temple, running her hand down the elephant's face onto the base of her trunk. "Shhh . . ." she crooned as if the calf were her own infant.

"Try to feed her." Forrest's direction broke through the intimate moment.

Silently, Jake handed Pippa a bottle, its nipple tugged over the glass neck, milk sloshing inside. His hand encompassed the large feeding instrument.

Pippa bit the inside of her lip as she tugged off her gloves. "I-I'm not sure what to do."

"We've tried just about every way we know how," Jake admitted. "Just see if Lily will respond to you, like she did the other night."

She eyed his fingers wrapped around the bottle. The hand was corded, the knuckles callused.

"Take it," he said, only this time his voice was soft. It seemed he comprehended Pippa's reticence. If she failed . . . if Lily didn't respond to her . . .

Pippa looked up at Forrest, who towered over them, refusing to crouch down in the straw with them. Yes. It was all over Forrest's face. If Lily didn't respond to her, she was Bonaventure's last hope. The calf would most likely die, along with all the profits plus a great loss in advertising of the upcoming spring train.

Even now, Pippa was a chess piece. Moved wherever the men in her life wanted her on their board. Still, she did as she was told—

"And here we have it!" The stringent voice jolted Pippa. Forrest spun around, and Jake pulled the bottle back. Pippa scrambled to her feet.

"Georgiana!" And now the afternoon was for sure and certain to get worse.

Georgiana Farnsworth stood in the doorway of the pen, a raised eyebrow of auburn clashing with the blaze red of her dress. She was tall, curvy but trim, with enormous brown eyes that diminished her otherwise striking beauty. A broad yellow sash ran across her chest like a suffragette. Only, she wasn't a suffragette. She peered past them at Lily. Pippa caught a flicker of sadness in Georgiana's expression before her face set in its usual irate glare.

"I've said it before, and again now"—she waved her hand at the calf whose wounds from its mother's attack were visible—"here's the evidence."

"Who are you?" Jake rose to his feet and used his presence to invade the woman's space.

Georgiana was not intimidated. "Miss Georgiana Farnsworth." She jabbed her hand out as if to shake hands like a man.

Jake ignored it.

Georgiana dropped her hand. She adjusted her sash as her eyes darted between Jake and Pippa. Then, turning to Forrest, she continued, "Well, Mr. Landstrom, it's obvious that my suspicions about this circus have been correct. The maltreatment and abuse of your animals, and now the outright disregard for the birth of this elephant? It's disgraceful. An abomination."

Forrest stiffened and straightened his necktie. His brows drew together in such a blatant look of disgust that Pippa was fearful he'd fly into a terrible outburst just as her father was prone to do. Instead, when he spoke, his voice was monotone. Politic yet vaguely patronizing.

"Miss Farnsworth, your methods of fact-finding leave much to be desired. That you've been influenced by the European newspapers shows little for your personal fortitude."

"My fortitude?" Georgiana drew back, her lips pinching together in an expression of distaste equal to Forrest's. "I am not easily influenced. If you read the papers, you'll note that many of the European circus animals are treated abominably. That we have our own pretentious form of entertainment here in Bluff River's own home grounds is shameful."

Jake glowered from the corner of the stall, the bottle gripped so tight in his fist that Pippa wondered if he might actually break it beneath the pressure. Forrest ignored them both, his attention focused solely on the misled activist who only last year had made it her mission to picket and form gatherings against the not-so-secretive basement speakeasy at the Bluff River Inn. That was a better mission, Pippa decided, than this one.

Forrest chose his words carefully. "Bonaventure Circus tends to the welfare of our animals. Our trainers are responsible."

Pippa saw the muscle in Forrest's jaw twitch.

Miss Farnsworth skewered him with a respectful but determined stare. "Then how would you explain the condition of this poor baby elephant?" She tugged at her glove as if remembering Jake's refusal to shake her hand. Georgiana craned her neck to see around them. Her eyes took in Lily's immobile body. They softened at the corners. She was genuinely concerned for the animal's welfare, Pippa could acknowledge that, yet she was severely unfounded in her accusations.

"This is downright grievous." The woman's chin lifted, her eyes ablaze. "Pippa Ripley, you must beseech your father to have this madness stopped at once."

"There's been a horrible accident, that's all," Jake inserted with a growl.

"An accident? This town has waited eons for this baby to be born. Twenty months, I believe. It should be a gift to all of us. But I knew this would happen. I did. This circus mars the grandeur. Its beauty, its magnificence beaten down by the entrapment of performance and caged disciplines."

"The baby was brutalized by its mother," Forrest attempted to explain.

Miss Farnsworth huffed. She crossed her arms. "That helps not your case, Mr. Landstrom. It only speaks of further negligence, and it's most abhorrent."

"Big words for someone with little knowledge," Jake muttered, his squinty eyes never wavering from the protestor's pretty face.

Georgiana tilted her head to the right. The black hat with the purple netting she wore slipped a tad, held in place by a crystal-topped hatpin. "Never accuse me of being an idiot, Mr. Chapman."

She knew his name. For some reason, it both surprised and bothered Pippa. Surprise that Georgiana would know someone so far below her station, and bothersome because . . . Pippa looked down at her feet. There was a definite connection between her and Jake Chapman. Tenuous and vague, perhaps, but there nonetheless. It was Lily. A mutual cause. A mutual reason to fight for what was right and good.

"I will bring justice to this place. To this suffering creature." Georgiana righted her hat and pushed the pin in farther. Her skirt flipped around her calves as she spun toward the door. She tugged on her sash, its brandy color bragging her cause.

"There is no justice to be sought." Forrest's firm protest rolled off the female rabble-rouser's shoulders.

The woman paused as if to reconsider her grand exit and looked over her shoulder. "I have it on good authority that the reason this happened in the first place is because your employees were imbibing in illegal substances at the Bluff River Inn."

"You've no proof of that." Forrest wasn't defending Jake, of that Pippa was certain. But, it would bode no good if Georgiana Farnsworth linked the circus's personnel to the rum-running resources of the inn.

Georgiana followed Forrest's declaration with a delicate snort. "No one will believe for a moment that a *mother* would do this to her babe. Once my case is made, the entire town—no, the entire state and Midwest—will stand against Bonaventure Circus, as well they should."

A gloved hand pointed at Pippa. "And you, Pippa Ripley?" Georgiana's words sliced through Pippa with the numbing smoothness of a sharp knife. "You're one of them. You always have been. One of these days your father will pull the blinders from his eyes and stop trying to protect his little empire with all its secrets. He'll be honest and will do what's right."

"Enough." Forrest's command silenced the protesting woman. But it didn't feel as though he did it in her defense. Pippa scanned his face for something—anything—that made her feel warm and assured by his protection. But she saw nothing there.

"Get out." Jake took a menacing step toward Georgiana, who only tilted her nose up at him.

"Gladly. This place reeks of indiscretions."

Indiscretions? Pippa realized she'd edged closer to the elephant calf during the heated exchange, until the backs of her heels brushed up against the bruised animal's leathery skin. Lily's trunk lifted and wrapped around her calf. *Indiscretion, abuse, neglect*—words that mimicked the many layers of the circus. The hidden layers. The parts no one wanted to acknowledge. The abandonment, the mockery, the misfits. Strange how someone like Georgiana wished to protect them from this place, while in so many ways it was here that they sought sanctuary. Those who were put on display, whether for entertainment or for a father's purpose.

Pippa's eyes met Jake's as Georgiana breezed into the corridor, Forrest not far behind, intent on making sure she took her leave.

His eyes squinted in some sort of consideration as he ran a hand over his beard, his sigh one of barely restrained tension.

He cursed, and it echoed the desperation in Pippa's soul. A soul that wanted to find fairness for them all, in a world where fairness was simply a fairy tale that would never reach a happy ending.

CHAPTER ELEVEN

W ell, well!" The musical laugh broke the tense atmosphere and echoed through the elephant house.

Jake's head snapped up from his brooding glower
at Pippa. One she hadn't quite yet determined was caused by the
verbal tussle just barely ended with Georgiana Farnsworth, or if he
was just that displeased with her own presence here in Lily's pen.

Patty Luchent swung around the doorway, her red nails flashing
with the jaunty wave of her hand. "So Miss Farnsworth has picked
us to pester now! What jolly fun. She's so cheeky, I just want to roll
my eyes at her and burn an imaginary hole right into her back."

Jake's bark of laughter startled Pippa, and she edged away, staring between the two of them. They seemed very comfortable in
each other's presence.

"Her backbone is so rigid you'd hit steel." Jake's gravelly quip
was accompanied by a genuine smile that reached his eyes and
creased their corners. It transformed his face. It transformed *him*.
For a moment, Pippa wished it was directed at her.

Patty swung her body lazily into a half-slouched position, her
back against the doorframe. "You got to admire her, ya know? She's
a fighter, and I like fighters." Her eye drooped in a slow wink, her
eyelash brushing her cheek.

Pippa blushed at the blatant flirtation.

Jake didn't seem to mind, nor did he seem inspired. Instead,
something crossed his face. It was subtle, however, and Pippa
didn't think Patty even noticed it.

"A woman around here better know how to fight," he grumbled. His words made Patty tilt her head, and she exchanged a look with Pippa.

"I know things can get a bit wild once the sun sets." This time Patty's attention was fixed on Pippa, searching her face for how she would react. "But a girl's gotta make a living, Jake. It's not like Bonaventure Circus pays enough to send home and still be able to afford my good looks." She still stared at Pippa, daring Pippa to rebuke her, even with a look. To insinuate that somehow she was better, more righteous than Patty, even though she'd been born of the circus herself.

Pippa wasn't ignorant. She might not be well versed with regard to relations between men and women, but she'd slowly deduced that Patty dabbled in another career far less respectable than sewing circus costumes. Now, meeting Patty's gaze, Pippa was careful to temper her expression. Whether she condoned Patty's actions or not, she did like her. There was something inspiring about her. Something honest.

"Anyway . . ." Patty shoved off the doorframe and moved to crouch next to the very still elephant calf, whose primary sign of life was the steady blinking of her eyes. "I don't got no worries with you around, Jake." She reached out and patted Lily's back, concern drifting across her face. It was fleeting, and she stood. "You'll be good for Lily, Pippa." Patty tossed a grin in her direction. It felt like the type of sunshine that inspired a person to be naughty and good all at the same time. "And for Jake too."

Jake scowled.

Patty waved him off. "Oh, shucks, Jake Chapman. I know you worry about me. Heck, if they all knew you were simply making sure I made it back to my room with no trouble the other night, you'd be a hero instead of the cause of all this." She swept her arm in an arc over Lily and nodded at Pippa. "Oh yes. Jake knows that some nights I get quite—well, we'll say I get a bit too happy for my own good." Another wink. "And he worries somethin' fierce about me. Don't you, Jake? Like in a protective-big-brother kind of way."

Jake's eyes were turbulent. His mouth twitched, and his hand reached up in a restless gesture to rub his whiskers with a fist. "Don't, Patty." His words were rife with meaning.

Patty's smile wavered, and her body lost some of its pep, her shoulders lowering a bit. For a moment, Pippa felt like an intruder. This was a moment between Jake and Patty. For them alone. A story they shared that no one else had read.

"I'm sorry," she whispered.

Jake coughed as though he was choking on something. He craned his neck left and right, then in a gruff motion shoved the bottle of milk he'd been holding toward Pippa.

Startled, Pippa grabbed for it. The minute her grip was secure, Jake charged from the stall, following the steps Forrest and Georgiana Farnsworth had taken only minutes before.

All turned silent for a while as Patty drew in a breath and released a shaky sigh. Then she turned, and with the movement a whiff of perfume teased Pippa's senses. Patty's eyes grew soft and a bit watery, if Pippa wasn't mistaken. Pippa adjusted her hold on the bottle, aware that her legs were still pressed against the elephant calf, with Lily's trunk still wrapped around her ankle.

"He coulda worked for Capone, ya know?" Patty shrugged as she informed Pippa of Jake's secret world. "But he told him no. Straight up told Al no." She gave a wry laugh. "People think Jake's here at Bonaventure 'cause he's good with the elephants. But it ain't that."

Pippa waited, giving Patty the space she needed to continue.

Patty's smile was sad, and she pressed her lips together in resignation. "He's gonna kill someone someday, I just know it. And you know what?"

Pippa's breath caught.

Patty leaned forward, her voice dropping as she spoke conspiratorially. "I ain't gonna say a thing when it happens either.

Jake knows what he's about, and he knows what he's gotta do."
She snapped her fingers, the sound bouncing off the wooden
walls. "It's what happens when someone messes with family, ya
know? That's what I love about Jake. He and I? We'll never be.
He's too good for me. But he'd kill for me. He'd probably even kill
for you, if you wile your way into gaining his loyalty." Patty ran
her finger under her bottom lip as if wiping away errant lipstick.
"When *she* was alive, he would've gone to hell and back for her.
Problem is—" Patty paused, making sure Pippa was listening and
not explaining who "she" was—"he *did* go to hell for her. And he
ain't never been able to leave."

The riverbank was a beautiful place to escape to, and escape
was Pippa's sole purpose now. Lily had not responded to Pippa,
nor had she suckled from the bottle. Jake hadn't returned, and
Patty had left almost as abruptly as she'd appeared. Forrest, for
the moment, seemed to have forgotten his charge over Pippa,
leaving her to herself, to her thoughts, and to the disturbance
deep in her soul.

Was no one truly happy? It was a question that plagued her
mind with the persistence of its basic entity. Patty's observations
about Jake left Pippa troubled—very troubled—and were an unsettling sequel to Georgiana's strident declarations of abuse and
accountability for such. Maybe this was why the Watchman was
so elusive? He was trying to guard her, to protect her from the
troubled secret world of this place. This vibrant, glorious, dark
place called Bonaventure Circus.

The meadow that stretched to the east of Pippa was in sharp
contrast to the circus grounds across the river, where a few tents
had been erected for training purposes, where ruts from wagons
marred the countryside, with groups of men busy working, preoccupied with one job or another. A corral boarded a small herd
of zebras, their black-and-white stripes like an exotic flag against

the hillside that rose beyond the circus headquarters. Once, two summers ago, Bonaventure Circus had erected its magnificent Big Top, with the intoxicating red-and-white stripes, flowing flags, golden cords, and massive tent pegs wrapped with heavy ropes. Bluff River had celebrated their own circus to end a successful year—the town had showered upon them their accolades. Now? Georgiana's voice was only one, but she was persistent and loud and completely uncaring what anyone thought of her. People were restless. The war and Depression had left them jaded, Prohibition had reinforced the concepts of morality, and women winning the vote threatened the moral fabric of the small town. It would be easy to find a reason to cast angst onto the circus.

Pippa sank to the ground and tucked her knees against her chest. The baby elephant was on the brink of death. The circus's welfare hung in the balance. Georgiana Farnsworth would capitalize on all of it and try to bring the circus to an end. Was it inevitable? An ending to an illustrious beginning. Perhaps it was because of all this that the Watchman had become more persistent of late. To protect her from the shrapnel when it all exploded into a final demise.

Movement beside her snagged Pippa's attention. She twisted to look over her shoulder. Warmth curled around her senses as Clive the dwarf approached her. They were eye to eye with her sitting and him standing. Wispy gray hair lifted in the soft breeze, and his brown eyes twinkled as they always did. His nose was too large for his face, according to humanity's arbitrary standards, and his ears winged from his head with thick lobes. Age spots dotted his face. The dark blue shirt he wore had been tailored to fit his short arms, which ended in thick hands and stubby fingers. He was both beautiful and kind.

The older man settled himself beside her. His eyes were sharp when he looked at her. "You've nothing to smile about today?"

Pippa attempted one, for Clive's sake. "I'm worried." About so many things.

"The calf will be fine." Clive stared out over the river as if he hadn't a concern in the world. It wasn't surprising he'd deduced a portion of her anxiety, yet it was the unspoken ones that stabbed at her. They all had question marks stuck at the ends of them. The unanswerable dilemmas, the unknowns of the future, and the equally unknowns of the past.

Clive's head turned, and he moved his hand to Pippa's shoulder. "Ernie is a good trainer. And Jake . . . he needs this calf."

It was a cryptic statement, especially after Patty's unsettling remarks. Pippa realized her unspoken question was written all over her face as Clive searched it with his eyes and nodded.

"We all have our secrets," Clive continued, "some worse than others. All require healing."

His eyes roamed the sparkling waters of Bluff River as it rippled over the rocks in its journey. It wasn't a large river—not like the Mississippi to the west of them—but was only the breadth of a few circus wagons side by side.

The snort of an elephant on the other side of the river grabbed their attention. Pippa watched as a line of three Asian elephants, with swinging ears and waving trunks, plodded toward the river. Jake led them, his short crop at hand to give gentle prods if needed.

Clive's voice was quiet, as though he didn't want it to carry to Jake's ears. "He's a troubled soul, Pippa, with much anger." Clive shifted his gaze to her. "While he is also good, revenge can blind that goodness. Be cautious."

Pippa watched Jake, the familiar cigar hanging from his mouth and the confident swagger of a man who fought his way through life. She picked at a blade of dying grass, the autumn breeze rustling her sleeve and reminding her of the impending winter.

"Revenge?" She questioned the dwarf, noting not for the first time how aged he really looked. The lines creasing his eyes, cheeks, and neck. Was it really age or was it perhaps the onslaught of life's required endurance?

Clive's nod was subtle, even as he kept his eyes fixed on the elephants, on the flapping of the large tentlike ears, and on Jake, who stood solitary and troubled on the riverbank.

"Revenge is an evil in and of itself." Clive finally tore his gaze from Jake and rested it on Pippa. "In it we seek to find ourselves, but more likely than not we become more lost than we ever were before."

CHAPTER TWELVE

CHANDLER

Chandler fingered the black-and-white postcard she held in her hand and lifted her eyes to compare it to the outside of the building. The depot had been an impressive place back in the early nineteen hundreds. By the time this photograph had been taken, it seemed its future decrease of necessity was prophesied by the presence of a Ford Model T parked just outside the canopy. A couple dressed in twenties garb loitered on the walk near the very entrance where Chandler now stood.

"That window there was the men's sitting room."

The voice over her shoulder startled her. She reared back, already uneasy being at the train depot alone, even though it was daytime and for some reason ghosts tended to prefer darkness. Chandler eyed the man.

"I'm Cru. Lottie's son." He extended a hand.

Of course he was. The same vibrant blue eyes. She took his hand and was pleased at his firm but polite grip, his eye contact, and the fact he seemed to have manners. Unlike Hank Titus.

"Chandler Faulk."

"Yes. I know. I was walking by and saw you. Figured I'd say hey." Cru stuffed his hands in the pockets of his jeans. His T-shirt was clean and emblazoned on the front with the logo of a local coffee shop. "Do you know much about this place?"

"Not really," she answered and noted the undisguised inter-est in Cru's eyes. Maybe if she threw out the single-mom card now, he'd run. They all did. She bit her tongue and opted instead to take advantage of his potential expertise. Jackson was leaving pestering voicemails on her phone, and she'd even had an email from Uncle Neal asking how long it'd be before she started her detailed assessment of the property. No time to get settled in for a few months. No grace to stay home with Peter and be a mom and make sure he was okay and set up his online schooling before she launched into the massive project. No. She was ejected into the job like a spitball launched from a rubber band.

Chandler handed Cru the postcard she'd obtained from the local historical society. "I know the depot was built just before the turn of the century for the Madison-Charleston Railway, but I'd be grateful for any information you could give me as well."

Cru smiled. It reached his eyes, elongated creases in his cheeks, and reminded her a bit of Jim from *The Office*. There was eagerness in his voice—eagerness for the history but also to please. "Yeah so, originally it was just going to be a stopping point, but then the Madison-Charleston Railway decided to move its headquarters here too." Cru pointed to the second story. "Their offices were up there, along with the telegraph center. They also rented out one or two to the circus higher-ups who preferred fancy office space over being in the trenches of the grounds. The first story was where the ticket agent was located, plus the men's and women's sitting rooms. Toward the far end there"—Cru swept his arm toward the west of the building—"is where the rooms were for luggage, unclaimed baggage, and the like."

Chandler studied the building, its brick darkened with age, its roof now tilting inward as if inhaling a breath and holding it. In the initial pre-purchase inspection, the building had been deemed structurally sound. But Chandler wasn't blind to the fact it was going to need a lot of work. Jackson was right in one regard. De-molishing a building and starting fresh was often less hassle and the least expensive way. Yet he didn't always have the foresight to envision the long-term attraction of a historic building like this one. It still called to people, years later, and with the circus museum just over the hill, and the old railroad tracks skirting the view of the river, it was far from a foolhardy notion. In Chandler's opinion, it was brilliant, and this wasn't the first historic site she'd brought back to life.

Chandler cleared her throat. "Did the circus train come through here too?" If it did, that was just another added draw. Restore the old depot, decorate it with vintage circus posters, build it out for small, unique shops inside. Maybe a coffee shop in the middle to greet visitors when they first walked in. A partnership with the museum would result in a little foretaste of what guests would find when they purchased a discounted ticket here to visit the nearby circus memorial.

Her mind was spinning with possibilities.

Cru nodded. "Yeah, it did. Only, they unloaded most of the cars over there." Again he pointed, this time toward the east. "The rail yards were down farther. The area was a lot more open than it is now. What you see over there is the county co-op building and the old feed mill. Even those are deserted now. The south side of Bluff River needs some TLC, now that we've revived the historic district downtown."

Time to uncover a bit more about Cru. Chandler tucked the postcard into her messenger bag slung across her chest. "So, your mom says you lead ghost tours?"

A low chuckle and she looked up in time to witness Cru's grin. He kicked a stone that went hopping into the burned-up patchy grass that grew untrimmed along the depot's foundation.

"My *mom's* ghost tours," he clarified. "We started them about five years ago. I've always been a bit of a history buff, and my mom, well"—Cru waggled his eyebrows—"you know she's more than a firm believer in the other side."

"Are you?" Chandler couldn't help but ask. A motorcycle rumbled toward them on the cracked asphalt street. It wasn't a highly used street, so she cast the bike a curious glance. Hank Titus. Their eyes locked as he rode by. Beefy arms and shoulders. Wild hair. A bit of Tarzan mashed together with a gorilla. His look was piercing and, in Chandler's opinion, rude.

"Maybe." Cru was answering her.

Chandler tore her gaze from the bike as it sped away.

"It's hard not to be sometimes," he went on. "I've seen things. They're unexplainable. Once, I was leading a tour down by the river, and we saw someone running through the woods. It was across the water, so it was impossible to get very close. But it matched up with the story of the girl who drowned in the river back in 1902. She was fishing with her brother and fell in. She couldn't swim and neither could he. It was just a sad story really, but seeing her ghost?" Cru gave a mock shudder. "Weird. Just weird."

Chandler couldn't help but raise her eyebrow. "And you're sure it wasn't an actual person running through the woods?"

Cru returned her skepticism with a smile. "What's the fun in believing that? Especially when you're leading a tour and people want to see a ghost."

Chandler laughed. Cru was coming more from the angle of tourist attraction than actual belief in the spirit world. She was okay with that. And yet reconciling such phenomena with her faith was something she still considered. There were many opinions on the subject, biblically and supernaturally, but Chandler preferred to handle these things with care, regardless of how they were interpreted by others.

"Anyway," Cru said and hefted a big breath, "Mom said you might need help with this old place today."

"How did she know I was coming?"

"She just knows," Cru replied with a shrug. Accepting. Not questioning.

Chandler wasn't sure she liked the creepy sensation that rattled through her, but then it wasn't exactly rocket science for anyone to figure out where Chandler was likely to be. Lottie only needed simple intuition really.

Chandler adjusted her messenger bag and dangled her keys in the air. "I was just about to unlock the door and go inside." Actually it was why she'd been hesitating and instead assessing the old photograph while standing outside the building. Going in meant going in alone. Something about this place. Its skeletal remains, hollow on the inside, with dusty memories embedded in the stale air . . . it gave her the heebie-jeebies unlike any other old building she'd been in before.

Unlocking the padlock, she and Cru stepped back in time. The echoes of their footsteps reverberated on the wood floors, and the image of their profiles reflected in the mottled floor-to-ceiling mirror that hung across the room by the door leading to another large space.

"The women's sitting area." Cru strode toward the tall mirror and its accompanying doorway.

A wave of dizziness disoriented Chandler for a second. She grabbed for the wall, planting her palm against it to steady herself. Thankfully, Cru hadn't noticed. He seemed too enthralled in the old building. She needed to sleep. Badly. But she hadn't been able to. Not since Hank had thoroughly creeped her out with his sadistic hints of some old serial killer called the Watchman, and Lottie's insistence that the spirit of a murdered woman haunted the upstairs of Chandler's new office.

Chandler squeezed her eyes shut to center herself. When she opened them again, Cru was studying her. She needed a conversational red herring and fast. "Have you ever heard of Patty Luchent?" she blurted.

Cru raised an eyebrow and then nodded, as if choosing to ignore whatever concern he might have had with seeing her hug the wall with her eyes closed. Chandler mentally chided herself and dug in her bag for her water bottle as she followed Cru into the women's lounge.

"Patty Luchent is quite the lady." Cru's voice echoed against the antique framework. He was standing in the middle of the floor, looking up. The ceiling was high, the walls marred with graffiti and layers of mold and dust that had permanently embedded into the gilded wood. Carved scrolling on the crown molding draped wooden flowers halfway down each of the room's four corners. But some of the wooden petals had been busted off, and the wood was blackened with moisture and rot in many places. Eyebrow windows, curved at the top and straight at the bottom, were made solid with brick and concrete.

"Do you know how she was murdered?" Chandler stepped around a gaping hole in the floorboards. Lottie had given her an assortment of rumors, and she was curious to learn what Cru would speculate about.

Cru swiped at a cobweb that blanketed a lone high-backed chair tipped over on its side. "The most popular of the stories say she was found strangled in the old costume shop—your office," he said with a quick glance. "Or that she was found hanging right here in the depot. History has left the exact whereabouts unclear. But, they say she was found with a necklace around her neck, twisted so tight it'd dug into her skin."

Chandler grimaced and bent over to right the antique chair. "I wonder why that little fact has been remembered."

Cru frowned. "I'm not sure." He stuffed his hands in his pockets again. "Patty's death was sort of the catapult to the discovery."

"Discovery of what?" Chandler had a feeling she already knew what it was going to be. She moved away from Cru and began to circle the room, sidestepping mouse droppings and swiping at cobwebs that hung in the air seemingly suspended from nothing.

Cru's voice followed her. "Bluff River's one claim to criminal fame. The Watchman. Ever heard of him?"

Chandler nodded. "Briefly." *Thanks to Hank Titus.*

"Legend says he was responsible not only for Patty's death but also several others along the rails. Always women. Always young

112

and with loose morals. Prohibition probably didn't make them too hard to find, as they all congregated in the speakeasies and underground bars."

Chandler wanted to lean against the wall again, but she held off. It was too filthy. "At least they caught him," she stated, recalling Hank's vague reference to the wrong man being executed for it.

Cru poked at a canvas tarp with the toe of his shoe. "A lot of people think the Watchman was a hobo, while others say he may have been associated with Bonaventure Circus. No one knows for sure. Regardless, the guy was vicious."

"Well, the good thing is, that was decades ago, and it's not like people turn up dead on a regular basis in Bluff River."

Cru widened his eyes in recognition of Chandler's thought process. "No, we're not a cesspool for murder, but . . . well, outside of Al Capone stopping in occasionally to drink in the basement of the old Bluff River Inn, the Watchman is the bad legend the town loves to wrap itself around."

Ghosts didn't murder. Besides, Chandler didn't believe in ghosts, in spirits, in poltergeists. But she did believe there were serial killers out there, and she also believed there were copycat killers. She'd heard of them many times. Wannabes who imitated their preferred killer's methods. Insane people, psychopaths, those who thought they could revive a lost art of inducing death.

She needed to stop watching crime shows.

She needed to focus on restoring this train depot and raising her son.

She didn't need to awaken any of the old souls—kind or evil— who had once walked across this wooden floor, their footsteps leaving behind the indelible mark of their presence. Never to leave, never to be erased. They had walked here. The good, the bad, and the wicked.

CHAPTER THIRTEEN

Chandler collapsed onto a porch chair—the plastic kind that cost all of fifteen bucks at Walmart. She was glad for the excuse to sit down. Her head felt as though it weighed fifty pounds, and the pressure that banded around the back of her head was an ever-present reminder that she had pushed too hard today. Exploring every room of the depot had been finished by midmorning, and then she'd allowed Cru to treat her to lunch at a diner in the downtown square. What used to be an old gas station had been converted into a hamburger joint like one would find back in the fifties. It was a good sign that Bluff River embraced the idea of historic properties being repurposed.

After lunch, she'd split ways with Cru and spent the afternoon alone in her office. Making phone calls, catching up on emails, making connections surrounding the revitalization of the train depot—all while sending covert glances at the ceiling and the very silent yet still upended second floor. It was lonely in the building. Now that she knew Patty Luchent had potentially been strangled and gargled her last breath in this place, Chandler swore she felt cold fingertips brushing the back of her neck.

Here I am was the inaudible whisper of Patty's spirit that flitted from corner to corner in the old sewing room that once housed tables with sewing stations and bolts of colored materials.

Chandler didn't want to find Patty. She didn't want to find any dead person—ghost or otherwise—ever.

Now, seated in the peaceful still of her front porch, Chandler didn't miss the irony that she was sewing. Much like Patty Luchent had done at the costume house, only Chandler was a few miles away at the opposite end of the small town.

She adjusted the silver material in her lap and bit off the end of a thread she'd just tied. Peter's superhero cape for Nitro Steel needed mending. It was second nature to her, since she'd excelled in sewing class in high school.

"Is it finished, Momma?" Peter bounded up the porch steps, his cheeks reddened from expended energy. His light-colored hair was flattened to his head with the sweat a little boy produced from merely existing and playing regardless of the outside temperature.

"Just a second," Chandler muttered around the thread in her teeth. She ground them together, picturing her sewing scissors in her travel kit upstairs. The thread snapped. She ran her fingers across the mended section, then flipped the silver cape out and up so it caught the small breeze and floated down around Peter's shoulders. "There you go."

"Epic!" Peter shouted. He liked to repeat big-kid words from the Disney Channel. "Nitro Steel can fly again!" He spread his arms and flew-jumped down the stairs, then twisted and took a knee, extending a closed fist in Chandler's direction. "Pew, pew, pew!" His high-pitched gunfire traveled across the porch.

"Steel darts again?" Chandler smiled. Gosh, how she loved this kid and his imagination!

"Steel *arrows*! Nitro Steel leveled up today! And I captured Rustman!"

"Rustman?" Chandler allowed an eyebrow to wing upward. This was a new twist on Peter's self-imagined superhero stories.

Big brown eyes widened and twinkled so bright that his enthusiasm was contagious. "Yep. He's the only one that could kill Nitro Steel. But since *I* am Nitro Steel, I ran super fast and shot out steel arrows from my fingertips and my eyeballs. It totally captured Rustman."

"Why is he called Rustman? Does he collect rusty nails for bullets?"

Peter tilted his head and scrunched his face in a bewildered expression. "Ummm, noooo. Rust. Steel rusts. He's like—the opposite of Nitro Steel!"

He darted off into the yard, his silver cape flowing behind him. Chandler was impressed how her son had somehow figured out that steel could rust.

The screen door slammed, and Margie stepped onto the porch, two mugs in her hands. She handed one to Chandler. The raspberry tea wafted to Chandler's nostrils, soothing and enticing. It was almost a perfect evening. Almost a night in Mayberry. If Andy Griffith had walked up the sidewalk whistling, she probably wouldn't have been surprised. But no. Bluff River wasn't Mayberry. Its history was shadowed and haunted.

Margie eased the bulk of her frame onto another plastic chair. She took a sip of her tea, and her hazel eyes smiled.

"Your son is a stitch. I'm having so much fun watching that boy."

Chandler observed Peter as he ran up and down the lawn. He was. He was a precious stitch. She squeezed her eyes tight to ward off the wave of dizziness that accompanied the painless migraine. Her doctor had explained there were different sorts of migraines. Some—the ones Chandler experienced—brought on severe pressure, like a blood-pressure cuff pumped to the tightest level and not releasing.

"Are you okay?" Margie leaned forward, and Chandler opened her eyes to meet the concerned study of her rent-a-nanny.

"I'm fine. Just—tired."

"I've got you topped by at least fifteen years, and I'm not acting like an old lady." As Margie sipped her tea, her expression told Chandler she was far savvier than one might first give her credit for. And caring. Chandler wasn't quite sure how to process the caring Margie exuded. She was used to going it alone.

"There's a lot of pressure with work, and . . ." Chandler halted. What could she say? She was hiding her autoimmune disease for fear her parents would weasel their way into adopting Peter's care. She was constantly worried the disease would inhibit her ability to travel, to do her job properly, and that Jackson would edge her out. These were admissions Chandler barely faced herself, let alone vocalized to someone she'd just recently met.

Margie tapped her foot on the porch. "It sucks being a single parent. I know. I'm there right now. Of course, my kids are with their dad for now, but once they get back it's like all hell breaks loose sometimes. My ex all but forgets the kids exist, and then I have to pick up the pieces after they just spent a summer with him being spoiled. He buys their forgiveness and then I'm the idiot mom who makes them pick up their clothes, do their homework, and actually has to say no to the two-hundred-dollar video game console."

"Do the kids hold their dad over you?" Chandler ventured. Their mutual single-parenthood-ness granted Chandler the confidence that it was okay to ask.

Margie kicked off her flip-flops and stretched her bare feet out in front of her, crossing them at the ankles, waggling her purple-painted toenails. "No. Well, maybe at first. But then it's more the abandonment that follows. The 'why doesn't Dad call?' The 'how come Dad doesn't want us to visit for Christmas?' I can't make sense of him, so I don't see why the kids would." Margie set her mug on the small table between their chairs. "But I keep fighting the good fight. One sign of weakness and I swear he'd be all over me for custody like a bee to honey. It's a game with him. Who will be the winner? It's not about the kids—not really."

Chandler hid her emotions in a long drink from her mug.

"You're a fighter, aren't you?" Margie crossed her arms over her chest.

Chandler smiled sadly and shrugged. "Maybe? I do what I need to for Peter's sake."

"We always do what we need to for our kids," Margie acknowledged.

Peter ran across the yard, hollering, waving a stick in the air, and yelling, "I've got you, Rustman!"

Chandler felt that sharp pang again, that fear which nagged at her. That someday she would lose her boy. That she would lose her very heartbeat, and then where would she be?

"I'd kill for my kid," she mumbled.

Margie chuckled and responded, "Wouldn't every mother?"

But Chandler wasn't sure that Margie realized she was never more serious than in this moment.

"Go long!" The very deep, very male voice caused Chandler to leap from her plastic chair, tipping it over. Margie jumped at Chandler's quick movement. A football—Peter's neon-green football—flew, and she saw her son put his arms straight out, completely lax in his ability to catch it.

She hurried down the porch steps to see what man had intruded uninvited into her son's life. Hank Titus was hulking toward her, his gray T-shirt loose on his muscular frame. His jeans were loose too, and it was apparent he didn't care much about looking particularly *GQ*, as his feet were shoved into leather sandals, his hair damp and hanging in waves.

"Hey! Good throw!" Peter ran in front of Chandler and skidded to a halt a few yards away from Hank, drawing his arm back to throw.

"Hold up, kid." Hank shot Chandler an unembellished glance, which stopped her mid-word as she was ready to call Peter's name. He crossed the sidewalk that split the yard and approached her son. Chandler stood and watched, sensing Margie's presence beside her.

An intake of breath.

A low whistle.

"Helllloooo, hottie," Margie muttered for Chandler's ears only.

Chandler's face turned warm, and she sent a *be quiet* glare in Margie's direction.

Hank ignored them both and came up alongside Peter. He bent, hair falling forward, his corded forearms in severe contrast to Peter's skinny, pale arms.

"Hold the ball like this." Hank adjusted Peter's hands on the football. "Draw back and use your shoulder when you throw. Move your waist." He directed Peter's body and arm to help the boy feel the motion.

Something tweaked in Chandler as she saw Peter's expression. Hero worship was already blatant on the boy's face. There was no nostalgia, no sentiment, no longing in Chandler. It wasn't a moment where she suddenly wished Peter's father were around—that she even knew who his father was. It was jealousy. Peter was supposed to adore her. Only her.

Wow. That was petty.

Chandler recognized it all in a split second and then justified her jealousy when she recalled Hank at the depot. Uninvited. Hank fixing her sink and all but threatening her with ghost stories.

"Peter, time to get ready for bed," she called.

It was a pathetic attempt to interrupt the special man-boy moment. But Hank Titus had less rights to her son's time than anyone else on the planet.

She debated about whether to be civil or hostile. To demand what Hank wanted of her, why he was here, and why he'd given her the stink eye when he'd ridden past the depot that morning on his bike while she was there with Cru. Chandler opted to remain on the porch and cross her arms while mustering the willpower not to rush inside after Margie and Peter. Hank positioned himself at the bottom of the porch steps, and for a moment they both eyed each other. His serpentine green eyes were sharp and wary as he assessed her with the perfect calm of the still air before a tornado.

"Nice kid." His peace offering made her bristle. She didn't trust him, didn't like him, and didn't want him anywhere near Peter.

"What do you need?" Chandler purposely inserted the word *need* instead of *want*. Somehow it seemed just shy of harsh while still maintaining a firm ground.

"We need to talk." He mimicked her stance and crossed his arms over his chest. His biceps were very noticeable.

Chandler averted her eyes from his arms and met his green stare. "Why?"

"The depot," he answered.

"What about the depot?" she countered and managed to remain steadfast in their war of the stares. Neither of them blinked.

"You have what I need," he said.

She didn't know why his words made her stomach tickle as if a thousand butterflies had been set loose inside. There was enough distance between them and yet his very presence filled the entire yard, climbed the stairs, and wrestled with her emotions.

"And what's that?" Chandler tried to steady her nerves by turning her back to him and going to retrieve the mug of now-cold tea she'd set on the windowsill. It was a nonchalant gesture, but when she faced him again, she could see he wasn't fooled.

A dry smile bent the corner of his mouth. He knew he unnerved her. He could tell she was floundering for confidence. It was obvious he liked that he had that effect on her.

"I need to get into the depot. Figured I'd ask or you'd probably call the cops on me, like you did on whoever broke in the other night."

"Brilliant idea." Chandler tossed him a fake smile. "And you're going to tell me why you're so confident someone was inside the very *locked* depot?"

"No."

Jerk. He wasn't going to offer her anything. Chandler plopped onto the plastic chair, irritated that her nerves had heightened her shakiness. She hid her trembling hands beneath her legs and chose not to say anything.

Hank put a foot on the bottom step and shot her a look that seemed to ask silent permission. When she didn't respond, he took the stairs in a single step and leaned against the porch rail, staring down at her.

"Are you okay?"

His soft inquiry jolted Chandler. She hadn't expected it. Not from him.

"Yeah, I'm fine. Why?"

Hank tipped his head toward her lap. "You're hiding your hands. They were shaking. And, you look like you're going to pass out."

"I'm fine." Chandler's repeated assurance didn't erase the doubt from Hank's face. But he was right. She did feel light-headed. Now was an awful time to start experiencing the early-onset symptoms of one of her seizures.

No, God. Not now.

Her prayer was more mental than anything else. Sometimes God listened and considered, other times He listened and promptly told her no. It felt like He rarely ever said yes. She hadn't figured out His purpose in all of this. If she was being honest, she usually felt hidden from Him, and not in a good way. Like she had been playing hide-and-seek all her life, and people—God—had simply stopped looking for her and moved on.

"Listen." Hank's deep baritone rumbled across the porch. "I just need to look around the depot. I'm trying to connect some family dots, and it took me there." He seemed to think through his next words. "There's too much unfinished crap that I need to figure out. As for someone being in the depot, if Lottie saw a light, then she saw a light. And the dust on the floor was disturbed and—"

"What unfinished crap?" Chandler felt her shoulder twitch as she interrupted him. His words were starting to sound distant. His voice like an echo.

"There was a woman murdered in Bluff River."

"I know. Patty Luchent was murdered by a serial killer back in the twenties." Chandler rolled her eyes. If she heard the story one more time . . .

"And there's the missing girl from 1983."

"What missing girl?" Chandler's shoulder twitched again, this time noticeably.

There was a flicker in Hank's eyes.

Chandler realized her words had slurred. She was sounding a bit tipsy.

"Linda Pike." Hank's reply was accompanied by a narrowing of his eyes.

Where had she heard that name before? Chandler's mind turned foggy, and she blinked quickly to clear her vision. Hank's form swam in front of her, and suddenly her head felt too heavy to hold up. But she tried—she really, really tried—to stay conscious and pretend all was fine.

"Pike. Pike." She fumbled for the words to pair with the memory. "Isn't Denny Pike your uncle?" she managed to ask.

Hank nodded. Or at least she thought he did.

"Linda was his sister. She went missing. They never found her—or a body. She was last seen outside the train depot the summer of 1983."

Chandler's shoulders jerked simultaneously, and the pressure in her head made her vision go black. "Oh," she slurred. "H-how nice . . ."

It was the last inept thing she could utter before she slumped in her chair.

CHAPTER FOURTEEN

PIPPA

Pippa took Forrest's hand and descended from the car. Her bad leg wavered on the step, and Forrest tightened his grip. "Are you all right?"

No, she wasn't all right. It was another day, another sign that Lily was slowly slipping away. Richard Ripley was on a wrathful rampage and had left the house early that morning to do God knew what. Pippa's mother had coerced her into a trip downtown to go shopping. Pippa would have much preferred to simply dial 15 on the phone and have the Hemshaw Department Store send their needed deliveries to the house via old Charlie Bucket and his delivery wagon. But no. Mother wanted to shop, and there was no way she was going to entrust Mrs. Hemshaw with picking out a new hat.

Maybe it was Providence that they'd met up with Forrest. Chance, perhaps, that Mother had happened upon Mrs. Braylin and the opportunity to take tea together. So, before Pippa knew it, once again her day had been arranged for her, and she was accompanying Forrest whether she wished to or not. Her drop-waisted, striped cotton dress was hardly suitable for a midday lunch, yet here they were at a restaurant in the town square. All Pippa wanted to do was find a way to be alone. Be by herself with Lily. To coax life back into the calf and at the same time soothe her own ruffled spirit. Maybe . . .

maybe even run into Jake Chapman. Though she hated to admit it, the way the man's thundercloud-gray eyes rolled through Pippa's mind, setting her nerves on fire like the snap from lightning, convinced her that maybe he shared her restlessness. It was a strange, unspoken kinship that, for some reason, Pippa ached to explore.

Her fingers trembled.

Forrest tightened his hold.

Pippa allowed herself to offer eye contact. Forrest's brown eyes could be gentle, and maybe he had a soft side to him, hidden way down deep inside. The Landstroms were a leading family in Bluff River, with Forrest's father having been aligned with the railroad before partnering in the circus. She would never forget the day her father announced he had seen fit to give Pippa's hand to Forrest. The announcement came over family dinner, no less. Even her mother had the graciousness to appear bewildered, as if the medieval tradition of joining clans had been revived. And it had made Pippa's food sour in her stomach. Words of protest were stolen from her with one look into her father's eyes. Her driving desire to please him had silenced her tongue.

She regretted it now.

Pippa removed her hand from Forrest's, thankful she'd remembered to wear gloves. Not that she was drawn by any physical enticement.

Forrest touched her elbow. "Shall we?"

Do I have a choice?

She dare not verbalize such a rebellious question. Pippa reached into the car and reassured Penn. The dog, leashed and secured inside the car, whined and licked her fingers. She wanted to come along, to be by Pippa's side where she belonged.

"I'll not have a pit bull terrier following us into a restaurant." Forrest eyed the dog with obvious distaste. For a circus man, he was hardly a fan of animals.

"She'll be no trouble." Pippa's protest sounded weak, and she realized it the second it escaped her lips.

Forrest gave her a patronizing smile. "Darling, I realize this breed has been the constant companion of many a child for many a year. However, you are neither a child nor are they nearly so preferred now."

"It's not Penn's fault that men have placed her breed into the pit to fight." Pippa's ire rose. It was one thing to diminish her opinion, but it was another thing entirely to criticize her dearest companion.

"Fine then." Forrest gripped her elbow and steered her away from the car and from Penn. "It's the mere fact that I won't have *any dog* following my footsteps like she's my nanny and I'm in a pram. It's ridiculous."

And parading camels and elephants around the city square on their weekly exercise routine isn't?

Again, Pippa held her tongue.

"You've outgrown the need for a dog," Forrest stated in conclusion. "You have me now."

"Do I?" It was a risky thing to mutter, yet mutter it Pippa did. Under her breath. Barely finding the courage to say it at all.

Forrest gave her a surprised look. "Pardon?"

"Must I?" Pippa's tongue tripped over her reinvented words.

"Leave the dog behind?" Forrest tightened his mouth in a thin line of disapproval. "Yes. You must."

She allowed Forrest to lead her to the small restaurant. She much preferred a soda from the fountain at the corner drugstore. She wasn't hungry. Forrest helped her take a seat at the table, and out of habit Pippa arranged the linen napkin on her lap.

"What would you like to eat?" Forrest tried to be amiable.

"Why don't you decide for me?" Pippa noted his pleased smile and nod. She'd made up for her snippy back talk earlier. He liked that. He liked being in control as much as she resisted being imprisoned. That gnawing panic rose in her chest, an anxious feeling that made her want to leap from the table and flee. Maybe it wasn't Forrest, after all. Maybe it was just that she knew she didn't belong here, with him, with the Ripleys, with *normal* people.

She looked out the window as Forrest ordered their food. She heard him say something about fish. She didn't like fish. Once, as a child, she had gone fishing with her uncle and cousins on a lake not far from Bluff River. It was the first time she'd seen a fish caught with a hook swallowed deep, and ever since then, Pippa's appetite for eating one had been lost. The poor, helpless creature had stared at her from unblinking eyes as her uncle worked to dislodge the hook from its innards. In the end, it was a gruesome slaughter.

Forrest was speaking.

"I'm sorry?" Pippa snapped herself back to the present.

Forrest's brow furrowed, and he glanced out the window where she'd been emptily staring. "Would you like a side of rice with that? Or potato?"

"Rice." *Neither* was hardly an appropriate response.

Forrest continued considering his meal as her gaze returned to outside the window.

Pippa's eyes locked with dark ones set in the face of a boy no older than eight or nine. The shadows under his eyes were emphasized by the disturbing fact that he did not blink. He stood across the street, arms at his sides, tattered britches torn at the pockets. He tilted his head to the right, his newsboy cap staying in place while his eyes became more expressionless by the moment.

Forrest's voice droned in Pippa's ears. She couldn't tear her attention away from the boy. He beckoned to her, eerily reminiscent of the hollow-eyed masked man who called to her from the shadows of the circus. The Watchman.

People strolled by the boy, stepped around him, and ignored him. To them, he was no more than a hitching post or similar inanimate object.

"Pippa." Forrest's sharp voice yanked her eyes back to him.

She didn't realize she had stood, her chair pushed back. Forrest heaved a sigh and set his napkin on the table.

"I was hoping for a leisurely meal with you. To discuss—" his pause was heavy with meaning—"us."

Pippa glanced back at the boy. He was gone. A strange desperation filled her. She couldn't lose him. Pippa knew it, could *feel* it. "Forrest, I . . ." Pippa bit her lip.

He wasn't pleased.

Somehow she found the gumption to resist Forrest's annoyance and the feeling of guilty obligation that held hands with it. "I'll be back. Please. I just spotted someone I think I know, and I really must see to it."

"Who?" Forrest wasn't gullible. Suspicion reflected in his eyes.

Confound it. Pippa glanced out the large picture window of the restaurant again. The boy had vanished.

"What are you carrying on about, Pippa?" Forrest didn't trust her. He doubted her. He was right to.

"Just one moment, please." Pippa edged away from the table. She would have to face the consequences for her actions later—and she would face them. But if there was one thing that gave her enough courage to be even a tad defiant, it was the Watchman—or her need to discover him and his ties to whoever she was. She had no reason to believe the boy was connected with him, and yet . . .

The thump of Forrest's hand slapping the table followed her out the door. Pippa exited the restaurant and looked both ways down Fourth Street. The saloon, the liquor and cigar store, the shoe store, the drugstore, and . . . There he was! The boy wove his way between automobiles and a few carriages and bent at the waist to retrieve something from the ground.

As fast as her leg would allow, Pippa hurried after him. She dodged a man exiting the drugstore and limped around a Stanley Steamer with its white-rimmed tires. There. The boy was crouched by the front wheel. In his hand he held a wayward coin that had

escaped from a richer man's pocket. In his eyes there was emptiness. No emotion. No recognition. Life had sucked the personality
from this child.

The bustle of the downtown square drifted away. For the moment, it was just Pippa and the boy. She was motionless, afraid
any movement might frighten him. The boy remained in a squat,
his fingers closed around the coin, and a hint of challenge touched
the corners of his eyes.

"I don't care about the coin." They were the first words she
could think to say to him.

A tiny flicker of life crossed the boy's expression. His lips were
pale, his cheeks even more so, and the shadows beneath his eyes
spoke of malnutrition. He was probably from the south side of
town, across the railroad tracks, where the poor and the delin-
quents lived. Oddly enough, not far from the circus grounds.

"Here." Pippa fumbled with her purse. Coins. She found a nickel.
Holding it toward him, Pippa waited.

The boy stood.

She extended her arm as far as she could.

The boy reached out and snatched it from her fingers. His voice
was hoarse and it squeaked, betraying the boy's journey to man-
hood. "He says to tell ya that ya broke his trust."

Once again, Pippa was at the mercy of someone else who held
claim to her secrets.

"Please tell him I'm sorry." Without thinking, Pippa reached
for the boy's shoulders to grab him in her urgency, to have her
sincere apology communicated. He shrugged away with a frown.
She quickly pulled back, not wanting to frighten him, and debated
her next words. She was begging, which was pathetic of her. "Tell
him it wasn't my fault. I didn't know how everything would dissolve into complete chaos with the elephant."

I didn't know how terrified he would make me.

She didn't voice her last thought. It was a betrayal of him, of
who she believed the Watchman to be.

The boy pocketed the coin. Her explanation didn't move him. Giving her the message was his only task, and with that done, Pippa knew she'd never see the boy again.

"He said you're to find the toy."

"The toy?" Pippa shifted her weight onto her good foot. Her movement spooked the boy, and he took a step back.

"The zebra toy. When you find it, he will come to you. You're to leave a message for him when you do."

"I don't know what you're talking about—what *he* is talking about." Desperation gripped her. "Please. Do you know who he is? Have you seen him?"

The boy retreated another step and ignored her questions. "He has shown his loyalty. You must show yours. Bring him the toy. It's what binds you."

The boy spun on his heel then and darted away.

"Wait!"

Pippa stared after his retreating form. The boy was merely a messenger. The Watchman had sent him, and she was at his mercy. She looked over her shoulder, toward the restaurant where Forrest waited still, probably growing in exasperation.

A toy. She would find it. Pippa had to believe the Watchman would meet her again. The man who could still reveal who she was. And if she could uncover her true identity, Pippa knew she'd find the courage to become whoever she was meant to be. And when she did, she would fly away. Forever.

Pippa mouthed the lemon drop she'd offered up a penny for at the corner drugstore. The sour-sweetness puckered her lips and matched her mood. Candy didn't help Pippa find any sense of peace. Neither did Forrest's sore reaction to her desertion at lunch, and his equally dour mood when her mother acquiesced to her request to remain downtown, chaperoned only by Penn. Forrest was begrudgingly accepting of his charge to escort her mother home with all her packages. The knitting of his dark brows matched the questioning mistrust in his eyes.

Pippa tucked away the niggling sense of guilt. Guilt for cajoling her mother into giving her some rare freedom. Guilt for using the opportunity to escape a lecture from Forrest. She tickled Penn's ear with her fingertips as she walked in the direction of the circus. Guilt for heading to the one place she'd been told she was not to go to anymore. She gave her sailor scarf a nervous yank, straightening it before letting it fall against the striped backdrop of her dress. Penn trotted alongside her, nose in the air, ears perked, and her mouth tipped up in a contented dog smile.

A lion's roar penetrated the otherwise calm autumn afternoon. The ringing of metal on metal echoed from the blacksmith's forge. Benard the smithy would be there, pounding away his own personal angst against his body's deformities. She didn't speak with him often, but Pippa knew that not unlike many members of the circus family, he'd been born with a deformity. His was facial, and it stretched from his forehead and wrapped down around his neck. She'd been told it was a birthmark, though its splotchy color—from dark brown to pasty white—had people dubbing him "Giraffe Man." Just a blacksmith, not even a performer, and he had been labeled and shelved as an oddity like so many of them.

Pippa noted her own limp and without looking could recall every twist and ugly wrinkle on her leg. Thin and turned, her foot's angle made running nearly impossible and walking a chore.

Welcome to the circus. A place where eccentrics came to hide and where, even here, they abandoned their own.

She paused in front of the elephant barn. Penn panted, for the day was unseasonably warm for September. Pippa glanced left and right, afraid she would be noticed by someone who mattered. But, it was hardly common for her father to be loitering around the grounds during the afternoon, and Forrest was with her mother. Still, the very fact her visit here alone was forbidden made her heart beat an irregular cadence as she slipped through the doors of the barn in a hurried fluster.

"Oh, criminy!" Pippa couldn't bite back her exclamation as she smacked face-first into Jake's chest. He was exiting the barn. Now he grabbed for her arms to steady her, even as Pippa's outburst echoed in the octagonal ring. While the place was empty of elephants, piles of dung still littered the cement floor.

Jake pierced her with his steely gray eyes, and immediately Pippa's stomach flip-flopped. She was a tad hesitant about his beard, though intrigued by his dingy striped shirt that stretched over a muscular chest. The shirt looked as if it might rip if he even raised an arm above his head . . .

"Miss Ripley?"

He'd caught her staring. She laid her palm on Penn's head to stabilize herself. She needed stabilization, and not because her leg was disabling her. Pippa was going weak in the knees, and for once it wasn't because she was trepid and shy. Jake was—he was a *man*. Well, so was Forrest, but then . . . no, Jake was *dangerous*. Perhaps? Or was it due to the fact that Clive had insinuated he was out for revenge? No. The cigar. It was the cigar that drooped from the corner of his mouth, a tendril of putrid smoke drifting upward, that repulsed her. Made her stare. Made her completely, inadequately able to speak a lick of sense.

"Pippa?" Jake stroked her with his cloudy gaze.

The use of her surname made Pippa blink, and she ripped her focus from his cigar. He had a nice nose. But it was crooked.

Penn edged her way between Jake and Pippa, her muzzle turned up at him and her body tensed. Pippa kneaded the dog's short fur with her hand. Penn's stiffened muscles responded to Pippa's unspoken anxiety. Yes. Jake Chapman was a threat. To her safety and to her sense of reason. Pippa couldn't find her tongue, and if she could, it was as twisted as her leg in this moment. He really was intimidating.

"Go home, Pippa." The cigar bobbed in a haphazard motion as he spoke. "You shouldn't be here."

"Gosh, you're behaving awfully familiar!" Pippa's criticism slipped out before she could stop it.

His mouth twitched. So did the cigar.

"What I mean to say is—"

"Don't edit your words, *Pippa*." Jake tossed his cigar down and ground it against the floor with his boot. The smoke wafted up and dissipated. Snuffed out. "Say what you mean."

She didn't. She didn't say anything. She wasn't sure how to respond to that.

Jake reached around her for a shovel leaning against the wall. He kept his eyes locked on hers, and she couldn't move.

Penn growled.

Jake smiled cynically. "A dog like that could rip a man to shreds."

"She's not a trained fighter." Pippa hated the reputation dogs like Penn seemed to be achieving through no fault of their own. Such a loyal, gentle breed trained to be killers. It was disgusting, the dog pits.

"She could be." Jake turned on his heel and walked in a lazy line toward a pile of dung.

Pippa noticed the wheelbarrow parked at the edge of the ring. "I suppose you would know." She bit her bottom lip. Drat, her words would be the death of her, and why they flowed so freely and uninhibited with a man like Jake Chapman thoroughly stumped her.

His chuckle was dry. The scrape of the shovel against the cement cut through the veiled tension. Pippa's insinuation in regard to his previous life wasn't veiled at all.

"You should go home now." Jake dumped the load into the wheelbarrow. "Hasn't your father told you what a bad influence I am?"

"Yes," Pippa replied honestly.

Jake outright laughed this time. "Of course. I can't blame him.

Your father doesn't want you near me. Neither does your man," Jake tossed over his shoulder as he neared another pile of elephant dung.

"Forrest isn't my—" Pippa bit off her argument. Forrest was stuck to her indelibly, like the glue children used in primary school. "Please, may I see Lily?"

She skirted an elephant pie as she moved across the ring toward the doorway on the far end that led to the high-ceilinged elephant shelter.

"Not a good idea. Ernie won't approve of that any more than your father." Jake's back was broad, but it was the way his shoulders strained against his shirt that captured Pippa's fascination.

"And does no one care about Lily? What she needs?" Pippa winced.

Jake stopped and planted his hands on his hips. Penn was diligent to her mission and positioned herself between them. Her tail didn't wag, and her eyes were sharp and focused on Jake. Jake's expression was unreadable.

Pippa hobbled up to him. "My father isn't pleased with me."

Jake chuckled and tipped his head to the side. "Fancy that."

She forged ahead. "But I care about the calf and her survival. I still want to help."

"Even after you've failed as miserably as the rest of us. You want to work alongside me?" There was a twinkle in his eye.

"No, not you." Curse the man, he'd turned her into a flibbertigibbet. "I didn't fail miserably. Lily *did* take the bottle for a bit when I offered aid. Please, I just want to help." To give the baby elephant a sense that someone cared, that she wasn't alone, that there was hope for her future. Or, more honestly, to be at the circus so she might find the Watchman and also sift through this new information about a toy. A zebra toy.

"There's nothing you can do." Jake's curt response snagged her attention away from the toy.

"But the calf responded to me. I can bring her comfort." Pippa grew braver with her insistence. Something in Jake's demeanor seemed to give her permission, and a part of Pippa couldn't resist it.

"She's dying, Miss Ripley. You're only here to report our failure back to your father."

"That's not true!"

"So, you're not a snitch? Here to bring home more tales of misdeeds and the circus's mishandling of the elephants?"

Pippa drew back. The man was goading her. She knew it. She knew it was also working. "I'm not a snitch!"

"Pippa . . ." His voice caressed her name, as if even the sound of it tasted good to him. Maybe being alongside him to minister to the injured elephant wasn't such a good idea after all.

"Go home," Jake repeated. His eyes squinted with an insistence that wasn't gruff but instead seemed to be laced with a protective warning. "I know you like being at the circus. I've seen you here before."

Pippa's breath caught. He'd noticed her.

"But this isn't—" Jake hesitated and looked to the ceiling as though offering a quick prayer—"this isn't the place for a lady."

Pippa reached for Penn as she always did when she was feeling anxious. The dog responded and pushed against her legs, sniffing her palm with its black nose. "I won't go home."

Because it wasn't home.

They locked eyes.

Jake blinked.

Pippa didn't.

Jake's left eye squinted even more as he curled his lip and half snarled in resignation. "Landstrom won't be pleased you're here without him. Your father will hunt me down if they know I'm anywhere near you."

Pippa shook her head. "I won't tell them." The words slipped from her lips with shocking ease.

Jake raised his brows in surprise, and then a lopsided smile tilted his mouth. "You won't tell them," he said with a vague tone of admiration.

Again, Pippa's stomach flip-flopped.

Jake rubbed a finger under his nose as if considering the ramifications of allowing her to see the calf. "Fine. Follow me around if you want." Then he gave her a wink. But it wasn't flirtatious; it was a challenge. It was an *if you dare* wink.

It was dangerous.

CHAPTER FIFTEEN

Before Lily, Pippa didn't know that elephants could cry. Could weep the same lonely tears she wet her own pillow with at night. Lily's round face was damp, a tear having trailed from the corner of her eye to the edge of her mouth. Pippa had lost track of time, and maybe, if she was being honest, she was okay with disregarding the clock. Disregarding her father and Forrest too.

She rested in the straw beside the gray bulk of wrinkled skin. Penn had sniffed every corner of the stall and ignored Jake's dark look, instead huffing to slump beside the calf, her nose tucked against the elephant's trunk. The animals stared at each other. Reading thoughts, sensing emotion. Companions and, maybe, kindred spirits.

"Lily won't feed because she wants her mother." Jake broke the silence. He'd cleaned out much of the stall around them. Spread new straw. Emptied the water and hauled buckets of fresh liquid.

Pippa ignored the way her dress was no longer a crisp white. She leaned into Lily and drew her hand across the rough hide, the little hairs prickling her palm.

"Maybe," Pippa responded.

"Maybe?" Jake set down the bucket and leaned against the door-frame of the stall.

Pippa felt her cheeks warm. She avoided Jake's curious stare. "I just meant that sometimes an infant senses more than we give them credit for."

"Such as?"

She had no authority on the subject. Just instinct. Personal experience. Pippa traced her hand down Lily's trunk and then rested it atop Penn's gray head. Her dog whined, deep in her throat. An understanding and a confirmation of Pippa's thoughts. "Sometimes an infant just knows when they're not wanted."

Silence.

Pippa found courage in her words and in the lack of rebuke from Jake. "She's crying. That's sadness, a deep pain."

"You're giving an animal human emotion."

"And you don't believe they have emotions?"

Jake shrugged. He toed the bucket in front of him. "I believe . . ." He paused, then shook his head. "I don't know what I believe."

Pippa observed his face for a long moment. He was fixed on Lily. He didn't seem nearly as imposing or intimidating now. There was a lost look in his expression.

She moved her hand from Penn's head to Lily again and stroked her trunk. The elephant calf stirred beneath her touch, raising its trunk from the straw and flopping it onto her lap.

"Jake," Pippa breathed.

"I'll get a bottle," he said.

As Jake turned to leave, Pippa noticed a piece of paper sticking up from his back pocket. It caught on a splinter of wood and pulled from the pocket, floating onto the hay. She opened her mouth to make him aware, but he was already gone on his mission to retrieve the elephant's bottle.

Pippa leaned over and stretched, reaching for the paper.

Average height. He wasn't very tall.

Average build.

His hands were rough.

The cursive writing seemed to become shakier, and some of the ink had smeared as though water—or tears—had dripped on it.

I couldn't see his hair.

His eyes were blue. Ice blue. Like a frozen lake.

He wore brown trousers, and his shirt was gray.

He smelled like the circus. Dirt, sweat, manure.

Alarm grew inside of Pippa as she read words she knew she was never supposed to read. It was feminine script. The words of a woman who had experienced something horrific. Coldness spread through Pippa. Coldness that accompanied the presence of evil, of violation and wrong done to another human being.

She flipped the stationery page over, and her body froze. Her breath stuck in her chest, and if someone had come up behind her and held a knife to her throat, she might have been in less shock than she was now. Horrified, Pippa ran her fingers over the page, as if they would erase the image, and in doing so erase the implications.

A hand snatched the paper from her grip. Pippa squealed as she jumped. Penn scampered to her feet, and even Lily's eyes widened, her long lashes sweeping upward at the outcry.

Jake dropped the large milk bottle onto the soft straw. He re-folded the paper and rammed it back into the pocket of his denim pants. "That's not for you to see."

"W-who wrote it?" Pippa tripped over her question.

"Never mind." Jake retrieved the bottle from the hay. "Try to feed Lily." He was dismissing her. Dismissing it.

Pippa reached over and wrapped her hand around his forearm and was taken aback by the warmth of his skin. She dropped her hand as he jerked his head around to stare at her. Incredulous. At her touch? Maybe. At her uncustomary boldness? Most definitely.

"What happened?" she whispered. The image was seared into her memory. It linked them. In unexplained ways, it tied them together, and she knew Jake wouldn't want that connection, nor the obligation that came with it.

Jake's jaw worked back and forth. Pippa could see the war being waged within him. A war he'd locked up and refused to share with anyone. A fighter's fight that only he could strike against, only he could battle.

"My sister." His answer was clipped. He transferred the bottle to his other hand. Fidgety. Irritated.

"Is she—all right?" Pippa hated that she knew the answer before even asking it. Hated that she'd already deduced the reason for the darkness that hovered around Jake Chapman, like a phantom refusing to release its prisoner.

Penn whined in her throat, nudging his knee as though sensing the taut moment, thick with memory.

"She's dead." Jake's response was disheartening at best. He shot her a disturbing glance, one that was open enough to reveal an emotional pain deep in his eyes. This time Pippa didn't look away.

"What happened?" She needed to know. Selfish but necessary. Seeing the image sketched on the paper . . . her body was shaking from the inside out. Enough that she hid her hands behind her back, clasping them to control the trembling.

Jake flicked the large rubber nipple on the equally large glass bottle meant for Lily. "She was murdered."

"I'm so sorry," Pippa whispered. She couldn't say more. Couldn't ask more. It would be disrespectful and abhorrent to do so.

Jake grunted. "Sorry resolves nothing." His jaw muscle twitched, and he sniffed.

Pippa could tell he was dismissing any emotion other than pure rage. He locked eyes with her. A searing look that shook Pippa more than she was willing to admit.

"Sorry doesn't take away the memory of cutting your own sister down from where she hung. From trying to understand her when she was frantically trying to breathe, to talk, to tell me something. The rope, the strangulation—she had no voice left." Jake swore. "Bridgette couldn't talk." He patted his back pocket where he'd slipped the paper. "But she lived long enough to give me this. And I *will* find him."

Pippa shivered at the coldness in his voice. Determined and bold.

Then he yanked the paper from his pocket and unfolded it so Pippa could once again see the now-familiar silhouette. Jake jabbed at the man's face with his forefinger—at the burlap sack with gaping holes for eyes—and gave a dry laugh. "At least I'm good at one thing. I'll kill the coward who hid behind that hood. I'll kill him for Bridgette."

The idea was chilling. That Jake's sister had weakly sketched the visage of the Watchman on that paper was telling. It told a far different story than the Watchman being Pippa's guardian in the shadows. It told of someone far more perilous, someone who had left behind a horrible trail of violence.

CHAPTER SIXTEEN

CHANDLER

Where's Peter?" Chandler struggled to sit up in the hospital bed. Denny Pike pushed her back down, his thick fingers gentle against her shoulder.

"Don't be moving, girlie," he instructed. "Your boy's fine. Margie's got him back at the house."

Chandler scanned the room. The monitor. The IV. The window with the black of night beyond it. The cross-armed Hank, who stared down at her from the foot of the bed.

"You shouldn't have brought me here." Chandler fumbled with the IV tape. "I don't need to be hospitalized."

"They're gonna run some tests," Denny explained.

Great. Chandler pulled at the tape, ignoring the sting of it against her skin. "I don't need tests."

"Girlie, you need to stop that." Denny gripped her hand and pulled it away from the IV.

Ignoring him, Chandler fumbled for the call remote. She hit the button to summon a nurse. "I already know what's wrong. I had a seizure. It's not unusual, and it's happened before."

"It has?" Denny's brows winged upward. His leather motorcycle vest creaked a little as he shifted to exchange surprised looks with his nephew.

"Do you have meds for it?" Hank asked bluntly.

"No," Chandler responded, equally as blunt. "I'm not epileptic. I already had an EEG a few months ago. They ruled it out, along with just about everything else that's serious."

"So then . . ." Denny's words trailed off.

"I have an autoimmune disease. The fancy acronym for it is PTLDS." Chandler blurted it out as she sagged back against the pillow and stared at the ceiling. Their silence indicated their lack of familiarity with the acronym. "Post-treatment Lyme disease syndrome. It's basically chronic Lyme disease."

"Chronic what?"

Chandler tried to control the watery sound to her voice, her frustrations overwhelming her. "It's caused by a tick bite. A lot of people have it—even celebrities. It acts like lupus or multiple sclerosis but with a side of arthritis. Once it settles in the brain, you're pretty much screwed. It's not going away."

"What's the treatment?" Hank asked. His deep voice resonated from his chest.

Chandler didn't meet his eyes. The ceiling was a good place to keep staring. "Well, medically there aren't a lot of options. Lyme isn't well recognized. My neurologist suggested my seizures are stress-induced from PTSD. He thinks I should see a therapist." She winced. It was more than she'd meant to share, but the words just tumbled out under Denny's grandfatherly-like gaze.

"Is that so?" he barked, but with no edge or bite to it.

"No. Of course not. I've not been traumatized or experienced any abuse." And she hadn't. "I just . . . stress can *influence* my seizures. But there's no reason for them really other than Lyme."

Denny patted her hand. "Poor gal. Gonna have to get you healthy. How's it you can drive?"

"The word *seizure* is a loose term in my case," Chandler went on to explain, wishing she didn't have to. Wishing this had happened when she was alone and could just wake up feeling like crud with no one being the wiser. "It's more like being drunk. I can feel it coming on long before the extreme happens. It's not like an epileptic seizure that comes out of nowhere and makes you lose control. So I'm not technically registered as having seizures per se. It's just an easier way to describe whatever's happening."

"Still probably should take an Uber," Denny said. He looked genuinely worried.

Something inside of her warmed—she hadn't expected Denny to be the one by her bedside. Granted, she hadn't expected to *be* in a hospital bed. Hank was most certainly not her preferred companion. And thank God for Margie. She was proving to be a lifesaver. A Peter-saver.

"Did the hospital call anyone?" Chandler ventured. With her luck, her parents were on their way in Uncle Neal's private plane.

"Nope." Denny shook his head. "We didn't know who to tell 'em to call. Figured you'd come out of it and then we'd just ask."

Relief washed over her. The kind of relief that was palpable. She could taste it. Maybe she was overreacting. Maybe Mom and Dad wouldn't go hyper-grandparent on her and insist something change. Insist that Peter be better taken care of. Throw in her face how irresponsible she'd been in college and now look at her. Not to mention Uncle Neal. Gosh, she loved her uncle, but he had a business to run too. If Jackson convinced him that she couldn't do this job . . .

"Hey, hey!" Denny read the anxiety in her body. His beard brushed her arm as he leaned forward. "You need to relax. Worrying isn't going to help matters."

Footsteps sounded, and the door cracked open. A nurse peeked in. Her black hair was parted on the side, her dark brows arched over beautiful brown Latina eyes. Or maybe Italian. Either way, for the moment, Chandler felt quite dowdy and pasty, and she didn't miss the appreciative glance Hank tossed in the nurse's direction.

"You needed something?" Her smile was warm as she eased into the room, her scrubs a vibrant teal.

"To go home?" Chandler pleaded.

The nurse, whose nametag read *Beth*, reached for Chandler's glasses that sat on a side table and handed them to her. "Well, the doctor will have to release you. He'll be here in about an hour, I think. He'll look you over, see if there are any tests we need to run. Do you have medical records I can ask for from your primary care provider?"

Chandler motioned for her purse and reached inside, pulling out her insurance ID and the business card of her doctor back in Michigan. "You can get the records from them. I have PTLDS."

"Ahh." Beth nodded her understanding, and the hope in her eyes dimmed a little. She knew. She knew there wasn't much to be done. Maybe adjust some medications and hope for the best. "Well, we'll still have Dr. Fellows check in with you. You weren't in great shape when you came in."

Chandler didn't remember much.

Beth poured Chandler more water, checked the IV, and asked her if she wanted Jell-O. Jell-O must be hospitals' go-to first line of defense against most diseases, Chandler decided. Regardless, she said yes and requested cherry.

She closed her eyes and conjured up images of Peter. He was her calming agent. It wasn't fair that she used Peter that way, and she'd never acknowledge it to him or put that honest-to-gosh pressure on a little boy. But just envisioning his face, the cross between little boy and young man. His lanky frame in his shiny, sleeveless blue soccer tank and his silver cape.

"Rustman!" Chandler exclaimed, her eyes popping open.

"What?" Hank gave her an incredulous look.

"I told Peter I'd help him make a costume for Rustman." Chandler closed her eyes. Crap. She'd planned to get started on it tonight after Peter went to bed.

"I'm not sure who that is," Denny chuckled, "but I wouldn't worry about it. Kid's gonna understand, if he even notices you're gone. Margie said he was sleepin'. Now. Since you're awake and kicking, I'm going to find somewhere to have a smoke. You staying with her, Hank?"

Hank nodded.

Chandler grimaced.

Denny bent and, to her surprise, pressed a kiss to her forehead. A prickly one, his mustache and beard tickling her cheek and neck. Whoever had tried to convince her that bikers were mean motorcycle gang members had been wrong—at least about Denny. She caught a whiff of cigarettes and beer that lingered on his clothes. On any other person it might have been off-putting, but for some reason, Chandler found it comforting. Familiar and warm.

She met Hank's searching stare.

That was also familiar, yet she wouldn't qualify the green eyes as warm. Suspicious with a softness hidden behind them that seemed to beg to get out, only something held it back. Life. Life appeared to have damaged Hank Titus. Damaged quite a few people in Bluff River, as Chandler recalled. She waited until Denny exited, then took a deep breath.

"So. Tell me about Linda Pike."

The dusk ghost tour hosted by Lottie Dobson was a walking one.

"Wear tennis shoes," Cru had recommended when he invited her. The ghost tour, he'd explained, would give her a feel for Bluff River's past and how it intertwined with the circus and the train depot.

Two days out of the hospital and Chandler was feeling okay. Probably due to stress, the doctor had said. Stress had a way of making any autoimmune disorder flare up and take control. She could have told him that. The IV of medication had helped her bounce back more quickly. She just wished she could wrap her hands around the recent series of events and tug them to a screeching halt. No more murder. No more angry poltergeists. No more Hank Titus, whose explanation of Linda Pike had been woefully lacking in details.

She'd disappeared at the age of eighteen.

She'd last been seen around the train depot.

A search had ensued. Search parties. Police personnel from three different counties. Dogs. Grid search areas.

Nothing.

No evidence.

Linda just vanished.

For over thirty-plus years.

"To the left," Lottie said, her smiling voice once again captivating Chandler's attention, "if you look up and take note of the third-story window, it's been reported that sometimes the silhouette of a man wearing a fedora can be seen staring out the window." Lottie waved her arm in an upward motion toward the front of Bluff River's civic center.

Chandler pressed her lips together, hoping when she looked up that Fedora Man wasn't staring back at her. She lifted her eyes. He wasn't.

"Who is this Fedora Man?" another tourist in their small tour group of eight inquired.

Cru, standing beside Chandler, took up the tale in the tag-team fashion of a seasoned guide. "No one knows for sure. In 1907, the original Bluff River High School burned down. The superintendent at the time was injured and died from the effects of smoke inhalation a day later. While the civic center today was the replacement high school back then, it stands in a different location entirely. But some consider that Mr. Ferguson's spirit was never willing to leave the school in the hands of another, so he traveled to the new school and still lingers."

"Yes." Lottie retrieved her story from her son, her earrings tinkling as they bobbed on her ears. "And after the new school was built, students reported sensations of feeling warned deep in their spirits right before they narrowly escaped an accident. For example, in 1967, Karen Meade was walking down the stairs in the school when she heard a distinct whisper of a man's voice.

'Take cover!' it demanded. Karen ducked under the stairway alcove just as a tree happened to break off and crash through the window at the top of the stairs. Karen would have been killed or seriously injured had she not listened to the voice. She credited Mr. Ferguson with saving her. At least his spirit, anyway. She was a firm believer after that."

"Believer in what?" A man wearing a button-up cotton shirt of a startling emerald green crossed his arms and shook his head. "In ghosts?"

Lottie offered him a patient and understanding smile. She gave a little shrug as if apologizing for not apologizing. "The afterlife, Mr. Ford. Those who are sometimes lost between this world and heaven."

"Sure." He chuckled. "Okay then. I'll play along."

"Dereck." Mr. Ford's wife slapped his arm playfully. He flicked her curly red ponytail. For a brief second, Chandler was envious of their apparent affection for each other. The camaraderie they shared. Dereck must have noticed her watching them because he gave Chandler a polite grin.

She averted her eyes.

Lottie was convincing, authentic, and her sincere belief gave Chandler the chills. She looked back up at the window. A few of the others in the group raised their phones and snapped pictures of the building.

"What's this white blob in the window?" a teenage girl asked.

Cru edged past Chandler and looked over the girl's shoulder at her phone's screen. "Huh." He nodded and shot a knowing glance at his mother before pointing his index finger at the phone. "The 'blob' is an orb."

"A what?" The teen curled her lip.

"A spirit orb," Lottie said while maintaining her pleasant expression, as though she knew not everyone would understand or believe.

"Or a speck of dust."

Dereck's jab wasn't missed by Lottie, who tilted her head and playfully responded, "It is the manifestation of a soul. For some reason, they've chosen to reveal themselves to you."

"Is it Mr. Ferguson?" The teen's eyes grew wide, and she ping-ponged looks between her dad and brother standing there beside her.

"Perhaps," Cru nodded. "He tends to show himself to younger people more often. We believe he has a soft spot for youth and attempts to reach out in order to warn or perhaps find fellowship with them."

This was a bad idea. Chandler had never bothered to fully reconcile what she believed in when it came to the concept of ghosts or the afterlife. Faith taught her that God didn't need souls suspended between worlds, nor was He aloof and uninterested enough to let them float around without some sort of resolution. Biblically speaking, Chandler had always been taught once dead, a person was reconciled immediately with their eternal fate.

Still, it didn't mean the idea of ghosts didn't influence her. Chandler pulled the edges of her plaid wool coat closer and buttoned it. Somehow the action made her feel as if she were shutting out the spirits by buttoning her coat and covering her heart.

Lottie noticed. She caught Chandler's eye and gave her a small grin. A knowing one that indicated she was very aware of Chandler's discomfort. She turned to face the group and brushed some lint from her scarf that draped around her neck.

"Sometimes you will see the manifestation of a spirit on these walks, while other times it is simply an opportunity to remember those who have passed away."

The idea should be a comforting one, but it wasn't. What of Linda Pike, or Patty Luchent, or—that serial killer Hank had mentioned? The Watchman? Now that would be a ghost she would prefer to stay far away from. The ghost of a serial killer had to bode evil.

Chandler wished the group would move on to the next site. She was learning about Bluff River's history, which would potentially lend itself toward the restoration project, but it wasn't helping her in the way she had hoped. That the small-town history would be so alive, so very tangible that it would bring with it stories of endearment, of memories one could build a visitor's attraction on. Instead, Lottie and Cru's stories were reawakening the struggle Chandler faced every day. That awful tug and pull with reconciling the living with the dead. With the solitary sequestering of her spirit while she lived now, breathed today, and had her heart beating moment by moment. Yet who had missed Linda Pike? Did Denny still ache for his sister? The close bond shared between siblings was something Chandler always wished she'd had. And who had grieved the loss of Patty Luchent? A mother, a father, maybe a grandparent?

It was natural for her to envy Dereck and his wife, here, as a part of the tour group, but it was creepy to be jealous of the dead. The ones whose lives had been cut short, their relationships abruptly severed. It was unnerving that people like Lottie sought to connect with their spirits. *A spirit.* Whatever it was.

The connection so many sought in the afterlife was the connection Chandler ached for with the living. Images of her mom and dad swam in her mind's eye. Of their structured life together, their successes and their pride in her when she'd earned the scholarships in high school that helped pay for her college education. Of their agonized expressions when Chandler broke the news to them that she was no longer the popular and ambitious student, but instead was a knocked-up young woman whose too many evenings of alcohol and collegiate fun had tanked her future. And Uncle Neal—he'd stepped forward, stepped up and offered Chandler a new start. A beginning. One she'd sworn not to squander and sworn to prove she could do—and be a wonderful single mom. She could rise from the disappointment and show them all how she could still shine.

Instead, the shadows seemed to grow, until soon they were

crowding her out. She was her own person, staring out a proverbial window, staring at those she loved and wishing she could reach out, she could touch, she could reconcile. But the void between them was silent, and they were not speaking. It seemed they'd all withdrawn and left Chandler hidden in the abandoned building that was the remains of her once-promising life.

CHAPTER SEVENTEEN

W hat are you doing here?" Chandler whispered out of the corner of her mouth as Hank's shoulder brushed hers. He'd slipped into the tour group silently, unobserved and unquestioned. The man moved like a ninja, regardless of his impressive size.

His hands were jammed into the pockets of his gray pants. The cuffs of his button-up shirt were rolled in a messy haphazard fashion. A leather cord wrapped around his neck, and a gold coin of some foreign exchange hung from it. He'd pulled his unruly dark hair back and tied it with a band.

"Keeping an eye on you," Hank replied. His voice was so low it sounded like a distant rumble of thunder.

"I don't need a caregiver," Chandler hissed between clenched teeth.

"Says the woman who was just in the hospital."

"The ER," she corrected.

"Same difference."

"All the same—" she started.

"You need my protection," Hank finished.

"Like heck I do!" Chandler's words were far louder than she'd planned.

Cru glanced up and looked between Chandler and Hank. His brows dipped with a concentrated question. Lottie paused mid-sentence. The others in the group stared.

Chandler cleared her throat. "I'm sorry. Please. Continue."

Lottie grinned an all-too-knowing grin that insinuated everything Chandler wished it didn't. Cru didn't appear particularly welcoming toward Hank's insertion—of course, Hank probably hadn't paid for the tour.

"Are you stalking me?" Chandler muttered as the tour moved on.

Hank cleared his throat as though coughing and then grunted out, "Hardly."

"Crashing my date with Cru Dobson?" she countered in a wicked whisper. Baiting him, though she didn't understand why.

An ironic smile tilted the corner of his mouth. "You're on a date?"

"No," Chandler admitted honestly. At least she didn't think she was. She glanced at Cru, who walked a bit ahead of her, contributing to the tour's narration with the skilled practice of someone who'd recited it many times before. Sure he'd invited her, but just to be nice. Right?

Hank smelled spicy. He wasn't supposed to smell this good, especially since they were outside where the air was crisp and energizing. The spice only added to the delectable warmth an evening like this one could create. Tall oak and maple trees lined the street, their leaves occasionally floating down like miniature orange-and-yellow ghosts haunting the air. On either side, old houses stood, some ill-kept, some restored, but most looking lonelier the more south they walked. South. Toward the train depot. Toward the old circus grounds.

A warmth encased her hand, and Chandler stumbled. She righted herself as they kept moving, but every sense in her was wide awake. Hank's calloused hand had encompassed hers, like he had a right to it. She tugged, but he didn't release her.

"On cold winter nights," Lottie was saying, "sightseers will spot the shadowy form of a wolf prancing on the riverbank. A memorial to the people who once settled here."

"Give me my hand back." Chandler was fast losing her patience with Hank. He was a presumptuous walking Bigfoot.

He didn't reply, only his fingers began to maneuver between hers, linking and toying as if to tease.

Chandler heard a stick crack beneath her tennis shoe. She glanced down, glad for a reason to be distracted as his fingers wove around hers. Her cheeks were red. She could feel them. The stick broke into three pieces, and one of them jammed between the concrete spacing on the sidewalk.

Something cold pressed against her palm. It was thin and long.

She jerked her head up to meet Hank's eyes. They were narrowed in caution, and he gave his head a slight shake. The uninvited, warm tumbling of her stomach fled as Chandler realized Hank's caress was mere subterfuge. His hand left hers, and Chandler gripped whatever he'd so subtly slipped into her palm.

Looking down, whatever warmth his touch had inspired in her quickly fled. A thin gold chain. A necklace? It made little sense. Hardly a romantic gesture, and yet . . .

Chandler was lifting her hand to study the necklace more closely when Hank leaned in and whispered in her ear, "Not now."

"But—"

"Shhh."

Chandler narrowed her eyes. Why press it into her hand if he didn't want questions? Moron.

The group paused in front of a house directly across the street from the back of the train depot. To the right, the old Bluff River Inn rose two stories, its white wooden trim cracked and weathered, its brick walls dull and the mortar a dingy gray.

"In 1897, William Denver commissioned this house to be built for his spinster daughter, Velma. She lived here for over forty years, running it as a guesthouse for travelers who needed to rent a room for a nap, or a night, or perhaps stop for tea." Cru paused then, and a sly smile dimpled his cheeks. He caught Chandler's eye, though she wasn't sure why he singled her out. Especially when he continued. "However, rumors abounded that Velma Denver was running something far more . . . er, lucrative than a mere guesthouse."

"Enter Patty Luchent." Lottie flared her arm wide and spread it toward the east and the costume house, whose green roof peeked just a bit above the roof of the elephant house beyond the hotel. "Patty Luchent is known as Bluff River's *first* recorded murder victim."

A ripple of interested surprise ran through the group, but Chandler couldn't ignore the necklace clenched in her palm. She tried to catch Hank's eye, question him with a stark stare. His attention was casually leveled on Lottie and her story about the fabled ghost that haunted Chandler's office.

"She worked by day for the circus, sewing costumes and other etceteras." Lottie winked at Dereck, who looked uncomfortable as he edged closer to his wife. "But by night it was said that Patty was engaged in . . . shall we say for the younger ears here, *other* pursuits. It was a perfect career to carry out on the side, considering she traveled with the circus on the train during the spring and summer. There were many opportunities to . . . branch out."

Lottie's laugh was charming. She knew they were all getting squirmy. She had the grace to move on to the part that better suited the ghost tour.

"But in 1928 it came to a screeching halt when Patty's body was discovered in the costume house. Which we shall see shortly."

They would? Chandler eyed Lottie. She'd not been told that her office was a part of the ghost tour. No one had asked her permission. But then it was a sidewalk tour, and sidewalks were public.

The necklace chain bit into her skin as Chandler squeezed her hand tighter. Cru skirted the group and led the way across the street toward the train depot. If she were superstitious, Chandler would have sworn the necklace in her palm grew warmer. Alive. Singeing her senses as if the piece of jewelry were nearing a place that meant something to it.

A distant scream rent the air.

"No! Oh dear God! Stop—noooo!"

The atmosphere flipped from a lulling ghost story to instant panic. Dereck's wife grabbed at his arm even as he tried to free himself to run toward the scream. Hank sprang forward, charging up the hill toward the brick monstrosity of the train depot with its cemented windows and tilting chimneys. A few of the kids in the company instantly hurled themselves into their parents' arms.

"No one do anything!" Cru shouted, fast on Hank's heels.

Dusk setting in made it difficult to see, but the entire group moved at various paces up the hill. A streetlight flickered, buzzed, then flickered again. A bat swooped in its shadow, and the teenage girl from earlier screamed.

"Shhh!" her father barked.

Chandler tried to gain speed and get out ahead of the others. Wicked imagery of the murdered Patty Luchent's corpse flashed like a black-and-white silent film in her mind. Staccato and jerky. Slow motion yet hyperspeed.

They rounded the corner of the depot. The street was deserted, now serving the town only as a ramshackle side road toward the abandoned rail yards and the farmers' old feed mill. Chandler could make out the forms of Cru and Hank. They'd both stopped at the depot's main entrance.

"Does anyone have a flashlight?" hissed Dereck's wife, her voice quavering with undisguised fear.

"I do." Dereck fumbled for his phone.

"No, no." Lottie waved it away. "Wait."

"Shouldn't we call the cops?" The teenager was probably the most sensible of them all.

Cru waved them over, his arm a black silhouette against the navy-blue sky. Stars were beginning to pop out and twinkle in a mocking merriness. Chandler couldn't make out his expression, but he didn't seem as urgent as before. Hank was tense still, she could tell by his body posture. She guessed if she could see his face, it would look menacing and severe, like the day she'd first met him.

"Was it her?" Lottie's shoulders were hunched a bit as she half tiptoed toward the men.

"Who?" Dereck inserted.

"Shh!" Cru waved at them again.

The group huddled together, like a horror-filled audience should while on a ghost tour. The door to the depot stood wide open. The innards of the building as dark as night, with whispers of echoes coming from its interior. Fluttering. A chortle. A pigeon flapped its wings in a frantic escape from the inside tomb of memories and long-dead voices.

Chandler felt for her keys in her pocket. They were there. She vividly recalled having chained and locked the padlock on the depot door.

"This is crazy. I'm callin' the cops." Dereck lifted his phone, and the LED illuminated his face. His eyes were wide and stern. He'd had enough of whatever messing around was happening.

Hank held up his hand. In that one motion, his imposing figure somehow silenced them all. He crept stealthily toward the open door, tugging at something hooked to his pocket. It must have been a flashlight, for he flicked it on just before entering the cavernous building.

Chandler searched her memory in case somehow she had forgotten to lock up. But no. She knew the door had been closed. She'd locked it. There was no easy way inside without busting the locks, and she'd given a key only to the contractor's office who had said they wanted to stop by again early tomorrow morning to assess the roof from the inside.

Everything was still. Eerily so.

Chandler pushed through the group and approached Cru. He held his arm out to stop her from following Hank.

"I don't see anything." Hank's growl came from inside the building.

"Man . . ." Cru shook his head, almost in awe. He tugged on the brim of his baseball cap and shot them all an incredulous smile. "I—I—*wow*."

"Momma, I'm scared." The little voice of a child made Chandler irritated that they were all standing here like idiots, unprotected, and annoyed that a parent would bring a young child on a ghost tour to begin with. She thought of Peter and suddenly ached to be with him.

The necklace in her hand slipped. She forgot she'd been holding it.

"Dang," Chandler muttered under her breath. She squatted to feel the grass in hopes of finding it.

Hank exited the depot just as Chandler's fingers met with the delicate chain buried among the blades of grass.

"Well, folks," Lottie said, finally taking charge, "I believe you have all witnessed a phenomenon tonight."

"A phenomenon?" The frightened child's mother didn't sound impressed.

Lottie nodded and glanced at Hank, who drew near again to the group. "In 1928, when Patty Luchent was murdered, there was also the beginning of an investigation into a serial killer who was reported to have followed the circus on the rails, ending here when the train stopped for the winter. Some believe Patty was one of his victims, while others . . . well, no one truly knows whether the Watchman actually existed or not."

"What does that have to do with tonight?" Chandler finally spoke up. Lottie had about ten more seconds to explain or she was calling the police herself.

Lottie lowered her head, almost as one would at a funeral. That slight nod of sympathy, of recognition. Her voice dropped until they had to strain to hear her.

"The Watchman was merely the whisper of a rumor. But the killer was, in truth, real. As Patty was killed that night, stories have since circulated that shortly after she was last seen at the guesthouse across the street, she indicated she was meeting someone at the depot. Which was odd, since it was already past midnight. No one saw her, but one account says someone heard screaming coming from the depot. A woman, begging for her life. The next morning, some say Patty was found in the costume house, only no one could confirm whether she was killed there—" Lottie stopped abruptly, a pause that was irritatingly and unnervingly dramatic—"or here."

"Are you saying what we just heard was Patty Luchent's ghost?" Dereck's voice rose in question.

Cru nodded behind his mother.

Hank remained motionless.

Lottie also nodded. "People have reported hearing screaming from inside the depot. Personally I never have—until tonight. But the Watchman's ghost may like to resurrect the cries of his victims. As sobering remembrances."

"That was no ghost screaming," another group member argued. "I heard a woman plain as day."

"I called the police." Dereck's wife waved her lit phone in the air. "This is ridiculous, to just stand here and do nothing."

The sirens in the distance emphasized her point.

Chandler felt Hank brush up against her. "Pocket it." His whisper was harsh in her ear.

"What?" she asked just as she realized he meant the necklace. Wondering why, Chandler did so.

"There were only two certainties about Patty Luchent and the night she was murdered," Lottie continued, as though she'd fully expected the cops to have been called and wasn't bothered by the action. "One, wherever they found her body, the fact she was violently murdered was never disputed."

"And what else?" The teenager was thoroughly enthralled by the tale now, the shock and terror wearing off in exchange for a spine-tingling story.

"Well . . ." Cru stepped up next to his mother, and Chandler could tell he was once again looking straight at her. "They say she was found wearing a gold necklace with a unique charm of a mermaid with a tiny red ruby for her eye. Twisted into her neck like the angry signature of a violent killer."

"And," Lottie picked up, "it was. It was the handiwork of the Watchman. Patty was his last victim. As the story goes, the necklace went missing shortly after her body was discovered. The Watchman came back for the necklace. Or someone stole it from the crime scene. No one knows why it was important to someone. But it was. Just another mystery in the larger scheme of things."

Chandler gaped at Lottie.

Hank gripped her arm tight, until she was sure her skin would have red marks from his fingers.

She couldn't believe it. The story. It was too outrageous. Too supernatural. Too . . . awful to justify as real. That the necklace had been taken from Patty's cold, dead body . . .

And now burned a very real hole in Chandler's pocket.

CHAPTER EIGHTEEN

Pippa."

Her mother's voice had an edge to it. The shaking, barely controlled sort of edge that demanded Pippa's full attention. She froze, her hand poised just inside the open door of her mother's wardrobe. Silk sheaths, linen suits, and voile afternoon dresses pushed aside, Pippa was reaching toward the back of the wardrobe. A place where many women stored private articles. Sometimes in hatboxes or other storage containers. Nothing valuable like jewels or coins, but keepsakes and sentimental items.

"Whatever are you doing in my things?" Victoria Ripley was a regal woman. Her poise seemed to emphasize the slouch to Pippa's delicate shoulders as her body compensated for the twist in her leg. Her mother's raven-black hair and vibrant blue eyes were a stunning canvas of created artistry and proof that God existed. For unlike the rather popular opinion of the day, one would have a difficult time reconciling with the idea that beauty such as Pippa's mother possessed could simply evolve over time.

Pippa drew her hand back. She had been caught, and sadly she was not quick to come up with a satisfactory reply. The truth was, she'd been ready to search her mother's things for the Watchman's elusive toy. The vague item that linked them, bonded them, and was the next step in uniting them. So far, Pippa had scoured the

160

attic, tiptoed through her father's study, and even rifled through a trunk in one of the spare bedrooms she'd always been told held linens. It was true. Linens were all she'd found—embroidered dresser scarves, tatted pillowcases, crocheted doilies, and even a tablecloth threaded with gold silk. Beautiful things that smelled fresh with a hint of lemongrass and lavender. But they were not the zebra toy.

"I asked what you're doing in my things," Victoria Ripley repeated, and this time an eyebrow shot upward.

Pippa closed the wardrobe door in a submissive motion, waiting until she heard the click of the latch. She ran her hand across the scrolled woodwork and the tiny hand-carved wood roses that adorned the door's front panel.

"I . . ." The look she sent her mother must have been desperate, and maybe because Pippa had never been one to cause much trouble, it led her mother to have sympathy on her.

"Oh, never mind." Victoria waved her hand. Gold bracelets slid down her wrist and clinked together in the gesture. "I need you to accompany me to the parlor. *Georgiana Farnsworth* has dropped in for a visit. I abhor that young woman."

"What am *I* to do?" Pippa shrank against the wardrobe. Facing Georgiana might be worse than if Jake made Pippa help feed a lion. She'd be ripped to shreds.

"You stand beside me as a Ripley woman." Victoria motioned for Pippa to follow. Pippa did, and as she hurried behind the clicking of her mother's shoes against the polished cherrywood floor, she cast an anxious glance behind her toward her mother's room. She had been anxious since the afternoon a few days ago when she'd seen the sketch of the Watchman, the sketch Jake's murdered sister had drawn. Finding the zebra toy—assuming it existed, and the Watchman wasn't simply leading her on—felt more critical than ever. To exonerate him? She didn't know how it could, but Pippa wanted to hold on to the belief that the Watchman couldn't have done something so abominable. That it was someone else. He was too important to Pippa, and her link to who she was meant to be. He simply couldn't be a cold-blooded—

". . . she's quite the pot-stirrer." Victoria was still whispering over her shoulder at Pippa as they moved through the upper level of their large house. "Georgiana has indicated that Velma Denver has formed an alliance with Georgiana's little band of merry women campaigning for the welfare of your father's circus animals."

Velma Denver. She owned the guesthouse that serviced many of the train passengers disembarking from their journeys. There were other rumors too . . . Pippa touched her warm cheek. She wasn't so naïve as not to understand what the rumors were about.

The raucous lifestyle and vices of dancing and liquor.

That had been Victoria's explanation as to why such a place might or might not exist. Ever since women had won the vote and the Nineteenth Amendment had been written, a new sort of freedom was being tested.

Pippa was told it was sinful. Certainly, if the rumors were true, a place like Velma Denver's was just that. Debauchery of a vile sort. Still, there were elements of the "raucous lifestyle" that appealed to Pippa. Not the least of which was the idea of freedom. Freedom to just *be* and to be seen as a person, with a mind and a spirit.

"How lovely of you to join us," Victoria acknowledged Georgiana as they entered the parlor, a tiny quirk to her mouth. Pippa recognized that tip of her lips. It was filled with disguised disapproval.

"Yes. Yes. We can dispense with the polite chitchat." Georgiana bullied through all proper etiquette, and while they most likely all shared her sentiment, it was quite startling for her to speak it out loud.

"Very well." Victoria didn't bother to motion for Georgiana to sit. The inference was not lost on Pippa's equal in both age and height, but certainly not in passion and intent. "I'd prefer you get right to the point of your visit."

"That's berries to me!" Georgiana sat down anyway. "We see eye to eye."

"Hardly." Victoria lowered herself to a stiff high-backed chair in order to level their gazes. She gestured to Pippa, who obediently sat as well, her fingers interlocked and resting in her lap.

"I'm pleased to let you know that your niece, Franny, has been engaged to join my crusade against the travesty that is Bonaventure Circus. I feel that your family should be quite proud of her endeavors."

Pippa could see no reason why Georgiana would have dropped by to announce such a thing about her cousin, daughter of Victoria's sister, other than to rub their faces in it.

"What you *feel*, Miss Farnsworth, and what *is* are two entirely different things." Victoria Ripley's voice could pierce glass, but there was a tremor in it that Pippa heard. The tremor that matched those in her hands when she was forcing herself to be brave when, really, she wasn't.

"Do you disagree, Mrs. Ripley, that the animal abuse is appalling?" Georgiana tipped her head and crossed her arms. Her thick auburn hair was carefully waved against her face, framing it in a way that made her eyes seem large and luminescent.

"I do not believe there is any evidence of mishandling the animals whatsoever," Victoria stated. "Needless to say, you are better suited to discuss this with my sister, Franny's *mother*, rather than myself. I fail to see what purpose has brought you here other than utter vindictiveness."

"Mrs. Ripley, I don't mean to be spiteful. I merely wish to sway your opinion. Yours and Pippa's." Georgiana's eyes swung in Pippa's direction. Pippa shrank against the back of her chair. "You hold the primary influence on Mr. Ripley's affections. Should you come to see the reality of the concern for animal welfare, then you both will be exceptional hope for turning the future course of Bonaventure Circus. We all know the circus in Great Britain has long been under criticism for their disregard for the care of the animals and the outright infliction of pain and undue harm."

"We are not in Great Britain, Miss Farnsworth. I would remind you of that." Victoria curled her fingers on the arms of her chair, then flattened them.

Georgiana plowed ahead. "Evidence shows that animal abuse within circus confines is as prevalent in the United States. Perhaps more so. And I demand that—"

"You demand?" Victoria's voice trembled more as her mouth thinned into a barely tolerant smile. "*I* demand you leave my home, Miss Farnsworth. *And* you leave my niece out of your little brouhaha. I'll be speaking with my sister, yes, you may be assured of that. Franny will not be continuing in your little debacle. It's a shame, and your mother should be the one who is appalled."

Georgiana blanched. Straightened. Adjusted the cuffs of her flaming-red dress. "Well." Georgiana pulled on her gloves and gave Pippa a little smile, coyly glossing over Victoria Ripley's hospitality given out of etiquette's necessity. "I appreciate your time. I've no intention to upstage and flaunt anything. I merely believe that since Franny is seeing reason and the necessity for reform in these shows of freaks and damaged animals, you may also be so inclined. I find the circus utterly repulsive." She rose, grasping her beaded purse and smoothing out her dress, which fell in a straight line on her figure. "Our first organized display of opposition is tomorrow afternoon at two. I'm to assume, then, I shall *not* be seeing you there?"

Her outright defiance impressed Pippa at the same time it offended.

Any protest Victoria Ripley might have offered was cut short by the entrance of the butler. He hesitated and cleared his throat nervously. "Er, pardon me, madam."

So formal. So British. So old-fashioned. It was how Victoria Ripley preferred her household to be run. Or maybe it was how

Richard Ripley wanted it run and Victoria merely played the part of the mistress, her chin held high.

Pippa faltered when the butler's gaze settled on her.

"Excuse me, Mrs. Ripley, ladies," he nodded, "but I've a missive here for Miss Pippa."

Anticipation mixed with clammy cold rippled over Pippa's skin. He'd never been this bold before.

"Thank you, Grimson," Victoria responded, yanking Pippa's attention back to the butler, who extended the missive to her in a gloved hand. "And please," Victoria continued, "show Miss Farnsworth to the door."

Georgiana brushed past her, leaving behind a whiff of vanilla and sandalwood. She paused at the doorway and looked over her shoulder. "Tomorrow. Two o'clock. If you're so inclined." The audacious woman left them with the emotional remnants of her challenging smile.

Victoria *tsk*ed as she stared at the now-empty doorway. Her shoulders drooped as if in relief, then rose again as she seemed to muster strength. "I will be ringing my sister immediately. If Franny thinks she's going to gallivant around Bluff River with Georgiana Farnsworth and subject herself and our family to the shame of marching like a silly suffragette, Franny is sorely mistaken."

Pippa heard her mother like a hollow echo in her ear. She stared at the letter she half pulled from the envelope. Despite its missing a signature, the familiar scrawling, etched words curled around her, squeezing with the ominous feeling of being trapped and helpless. She'd seen these words before, knew them from somewhere. And yet Pippa couldn't quite place them.

To know much and taste nothing—of what use is that?

"Who is it from?" Victoria's inquiry was needlessly sharp. Probably because she was shaken by the recent exchange.

Pippa clutched the letter to her chest. "No one important."

Victoria's brow rose, and she swiftly snatched the missive from

Pippa's hand. Her eyes skimmed it. She frowned. "Who is this from?"

"I-I don't know." It was the truth.

Victoria sniffed. "They quote one of the saints—it's no coincidence."

"Saints?" That they weren't Catholic was not lost on Pippa. However, she knew of her mother's superstitious nature, of the way she'd consulted a priest on Pippa's behalf years before.

"You're not—*seeing him* again, are you? You've said nothing . . . for so long, I'd hoped . . ." Victoria sank onto a chair, her face ashen. She clutched the Watchman's note in her hand. Pippa eyed it. Wishing she had her mother's skill at snatching things from another's hand.

"What saint?" Pippa deflected.

Victoria stared at the paper. Her spirit and her fight drained from her, with Georgiana a forgotten moment. "Saint Bonaventure. He was a seeker of truth, they say."

Seeker of truth.

"But—"

"I know." Victoria waved the message in the air. "Bonaventure Circus. Curious, yes? Where did this come from, child? Who sent it to you?"

Pippa hated lying. But then it wasn't really a lie, was it? And she didn't need her mother fearing that she was seeing spirits, or was possessed, or, God forbid, losing her mind. Of course, it was a very real note, delivered in the physical realm. There was more than superstition behind it.

"I really don't know who sent it, Mother."

She was certain her mother would read her face, would know she wasn't being completely truthful.

"It's an ill wind that bodes no good." Victoria stood and handed the message to Pippa. Pippa reached to take it, but her mother held on to the opposite end, begging her attention. "To know much and taste nothing leaves a person very dissatisfied. Precariously so."

"Yes, Mother." Pippa nodded.

Victoria still did not release the note. "The pursuit of truth often leaves one wanting. It's best sometimes not to seek it, but rather to be content with one's lot." With that, her mother released it and stepped around Pippa. She paused before exiting the room. "The truth has always left me wanting," she muttered, a sad, almost desperate tone lacing her observation. "It can be remarkably horrid, and horrors are best kept tucked away."

Pippa's sleep that night was fitful. She'd caressed the note from the Watchman with her thumb as she tucked it safely atop the growing stack of messages and tied the red ribbon around them, hiding them in the far back drawer of her bureau. But tonight it had not been a fond, wistful caress as it had in the past. Now, as she lay in bed, even with Penn's weight lying over her legs, Pippa couldn't elude the uneasiness as she massaged the muscles in the thigh of her bad leg.

Leave the truth alone, her mother had implied. A warning? Did she know more than she was willing to say? Or was there only personal angst and life wrapped in her words, which had nothing whatsoever to do with Pippa and from where Pippa had come? One could easily argue that Pippa should be grateful, even feel treasured that the Ripleys had taken her in—an abandoned baby in a basket on their doorstep. That the note identifying her as offspring of circus folk hadn't turned the Ripleys away from her or made them shun her. That they hadn't handed her back to the circus they owned and insisted someone there care for the poor, deformed orphan. No. They had taken her in. Raised her. Safeguarded her. It was, one could argue, Pippa's own fault that she was ostracized and alone in her world.

Penn shifted, licked her chops as though she'd just finished a steak, then dropped her head with a flop on the blankets and returned to snoring. Pippa's thoughts took a more sinister turn as she stared through the darkness at her bedroom ceiling.

If the Watchman had been the one who attacked Jake's sister, it didn't fit. It wasn't consistent with what Pippa knew of him—what little she knew of him. His missives were sentimental in nature, almost gentle. True, they had turned pressing of late. More insistent. And she couldn't discount the burlap sack she'd seen over his face, with those gaping eyes that threatened to swallow her soul and drag it to a dark place. The visions of winged demons fluttered through Pippa's mind, and she twisted to her side in a swift motion, startling Penn as she buried her face in her pillow.

She curled her fingers around the crisp sheet that covered her body with its cool embrace. It had been cleaned and pressed into a geometric and tidy bed before she had retired. Now it was tossed and torn from its tucks as Pippa fought with the hunter that lived inside of her, stalking her peace like its prey, devouring her confidence as though it were merely an appetizer before the main course that would be her value and worth.

Clive had told her once that one didn't need to be recognized by humanity in order to creep out of the shadows and expose themselves to life. The dwarf insisted that life was meant to be lived in full vibrance of being recognized by the One who had created them.

"If I waited to live—to truly, really live—until my fellow man saw me as a whole person, even viewed me as human, then I would die a lonely and broken man."

"But you work in a circus," Pippa had argued. She was the most honest with Clive. He inspired it in her, that honesty that removed all shielding of words, all worry of offense. "People *do* see you, but they mock or laugh. Don't you encourage that by your own participation?"

Clive had smiled, a few stubbly whiskers on his chin and upper lip proving he could try to grow a beard but would never really succeed at it. "Perhaps. But there's little opportunity for a man like me, Pippa. The world doesn't recognize me as someone capable.

Some don't even believe I have emotion. They don't know the truth. But I do, and it's all right. I know who I am."

"Who are you?" she'd asked.

Clive had reached out and patted her hand, allowing for a long moment of silence. His answer had pierced her and plagued her ever since. "I am Clive. I am seen and loved by God. I was created for a purpose. I need no other truth."

Pippa threw back the sheet and sat up. The house was deathly quiet, and truth had never seemed so threatening as it did right now. A conundrum. A swirling vortex of confusion. How could truth be to one, like Clive, a comfort, to another, like the Watch-man or herself, a torment, and to someone like her mother something to be feared? Was it possible that truth could wield itself like an unpredictable weapon, healing some and scarring others?

The Watchman could tell her who she was. He could pull her from the recesses of life into the fresh air of knowing—really knowing—who she was and where she belonged. She knew it. In her deepest heart. Clive might credit his peace with that of a spiritual nature, yet hadn't God made mistakes? He'd skimped on generosity when He'd created Clive so little. He'd turned his back to her when she came out of her mother's womb deformed, and then He'd discarded her mother and father to the grave. Those were errors God could have corrected had He wanted to. But He hadn't. He hadn't spared Jake's sister the violence of an attack. An attack by a man Jake now hunted with a vengeance.

Swinging her legs over the side of the bed, Pippa drew in a long breath. Her mother was wrong. She had to be. Truth must be known, seen, and understood. Only then could a person walk forward, no longer blind and ignorant. But educated, even if the truth was, as her mother predicted, so full of horror it threatened a soul's peace.

The Watchman was Pippa's only pinpoint of light in the distance. Her only hope of finding her truth.

Pippa's bare feet padded across the wool rug that covered the cold wood floor. A floorboard squeaked beneath her slight weight, but she ignored it as she reached for the switch on the lamp at her dressing table. The electric glow filled her bedroom with a softness that warred against the wild pounding of her heart. Frustration roiled her stomach and caused Pippa to chew on the inside of her lip. She wanted to be seen. To be *seen*! Not just be Pippa Ripley the orphan, the nobody, but Pippa Ripley the *somebody*. Like Georgiana Farnsworth. Well, maybe not quite like her, but bold and vibrant all the same. Confident and passionate. If God wouldn't take her life into His hands, then Pippa must do it herself. She must be like Jake and fight. Fight until she became like Clive and found peace—however elusive it might be.

Her fingers were shaking as she slid open the drawer of her table. She pulled out a small pair of gold scissors, then slipped onto the stool facing her mirror. The metal of the scissors glistened in the lamplight. Pippa held them up, looking at her reflection in the mirror. At her delicate features, her eyes that turned up slightly at the corners, her nose that tilted just a bit to the left, and her lips that had a defined bow in the center and a little dimple at the corner. Her strawberry-blond hair spilled over her shoulders. Hair she twisted and curled and pinned every morning in traditional ladylike fashion.

"Who knew God had one of me up His sleeve?"

The words of Patty Luchent from the circus costume house resonated in Pippa's memory. Yes. Who knew indeed? She lifted a lock of her hair in one hand, the scissors in the other, and with a decisive *snip* she determined to fight her way out of the shadows of insignificance and be exposed by the rawness of truth. However horrible it might be.

CHAPTER NINETEEN

M y, my, my!" Patty Luchent slouched against the corner of the costume house, a cigarette balanced at the end of her sticklike holder. Her red lips tilted up in a friendly smile, and a knowing twinkle sparkled in her eye like the reflection of lights in a dance hall. "Ain't you a doll?"

Confidence. Confidence. Confidence.

She had very little. Pippa fought the urge to duck her head, turn heel, and hurry back home. Back to the manor on the hill where she could slink up the back stairs to her room and wait for her impulse to grow back. Added to last night's blatant act, she had also left home this morning to check on Lily the elephant calf's welfare. Without Forrest. Without her father. Worst of all, without their permission. Her mother hadn't stopped her. She'd stared vacantly into a corner, her arms wrapped around her as if trying to protect herself from something. She had hardly spoken since the Watchman's message had been delivered yesterday.

Patty pushed off the wall of the house and swayed in Pippa's direction. Her eyes glanced over Penn, who wagged her gray tail and sniffed the air as Patty approached. A mixture of tobacco scent and jasmine perfume clouded around the woman, her cotton dress fancied up with a scooped neckline and a strand of fake pearls landing at her waist.

Patty walked a slow, studious circle around Pippa, her smile growing wider. Then, without warning, she plucked the navy hat from Pippa's head and stepped back. Pippa grabbed for her covering. A special kind of panic grew in her. She felt naked. Naked without her heavy curtain of hair rolled into a proper cluster of curls.

"Please." Pippa stretched farther for her hat as Patty held it behind her back.

"Not at all," Patty laughed. Even her laugh was pretty. Infectious. "I say, honey, you are gonna turn some heads today. And with that dress?" She waved her hand with the cigarette holder up and down the length of Pippa. "You look smashing in jade green. Like a fairy princess who dances in the leaves."

Pippa paused.

Patty's eyes narrowed and she drew in pencil-thin brows. "Your hair is quite straight, though. Which is fine," she quickly added. "But I could teach you how to wave it with an iron. Or better yet, we should get you to the barber and have him even this out." Patty flipped the bluntly cut hair that rested in line with Pippa's chin. "Add some bangs. Yes. We must."

Pippa drew back, reaching instinctively for the comfort of Penn's short gray fur. She dug her fingers into it, and Penn must have sensed Pippa's anxiety. Her tongue lapped Pippa's hand in comfort. "I-I can't go to a barber. That's—shameful."

"Not shameful." Patty tossed Pippa's hat onto the costume house's porch. "Just not done by most women. You're a brave sort, Pippa Ripley, to cut your own hair."

"How do you know I cut it myself?"

Patty bit her upper lip to squelch a smile. "Welllll, as I said, it needs some evening out."

Pippa let her shoulders sag. This was ridiculous! A moment of brazen insanity caused by the pompous dark night that had the audacity to mess with her mind and allow the ghosts of bravery to tempt Pippa's sinful nature.

"I should never have done it." Anxiousness threatened to close her throat. She'd joined the level of women who frequented dives and sipped bootleg liquor and smoked and swore and were promiscuous and—

"Stop." Patty flung her arm around Pippa's shoulder and pulled Pippa to her side in a gentle but firm embrace. "I can see your fears all over your face. You know, there are all these rules and standards in 'normal' society, everything black-and-white"— Patty tilted Pippa's chin up to look down the road—"but when you live here, you live in *color*." A line of elephants was trudging toward them, with Ernie and Jake leading the huge beasts. The men walked them like an owner would casually walk his dog for some afternoon exercise. "When you live here," Patty repeated, "your life is anything but normal. You see that God has a far bigger imagination than those stiff-backed ladies at your church."

Pippa swallowed. There was something about the elephants. Their majesty. Their regal heads and their billowing ears. They were kind, obedient even, and yet in their eyes they were wild. Wild and strong, brave and savvy. Could God possibly mix such reckless beauty with order and control? One must choose between the two, mustn't one?

Patty tugged on Pippa, pulling her toward the house. "Come. Bring that dog of yours too. If you're not gonna go to the barber, then let me help. There's no shortage of scissors in this place."

She'd done more than trim Pippa's uneven self-bobbed hair. Patty had taken rouge papers to Pippa's cheeks, a lip tracer to her mouth for that perfect plum pout, and even performed some sort of cosmetic magic around her eyes that resulted in a darker, more dramatic look. Without a curling iron and a bed of hot coals, Patty had taken it upon herself to slash a thick fringe across Pippa's forehead, and now her straight, strawberry-blond hair was a perfect frame for her delicate features.

"Good gosh, you're straight out of a magazine!"

Pippa couldn't help the little smile that tilted her lips as she peered into the handheld mirror Patty all but shoved toward her face.

"Yes, that's right, doll." Patty nodded. "You like what you see. There ain't anything wrong with that. Of course, your momma will probably go to an early grave, but it's about time someone shakes up those stiffs on the hill."

"Who?" Pippa thought she knew who Patty referred to, yet she was distracted as she ran her hand down the silky shortness of her hair.

"Sorry, love. It's what we call your parents. The 'stiffs.' You'd think people who owned a circus would have some sort of imagination and free spirit, but the Ripleys sure don't act like it. You, on the other hand . . ." Patty laid the mirror on the table. "You're a step up and don't they know it? You've got circus in your blood and a shine in your eyes that is going to dazzle everyone once you take off that bushel basket and be yourself."

"I was taught to be obedient." Pippa heard the tremor in her voice—and hated it.

"Sure." Patty plopped onto a stool, leaning against the sewing table, her elbow knocking into the sewing machine. The costume house was quiet today. A day off for the seamstresses. "Weren't we all? And we're supposed to be submissive and follow our men and all that. But how does that account for girls like me? I ain't got no father, sure as heck have no husband, and don't even have a brother. So, what am I to do, huh? But I do have a mind. And, I do have . . . well, I have my ways to support myself, I do, and I know I ain't perfect, and maybe I don't do everything to make God smile, but I still believe in Him. And I try to make good choices, when I can. We weren't all born with a silver spoon in our mouth."

"And I was." Pippa finished the obvious comparison.

Patty leaned forward, her own kohl-lined eyes mirroring Pippa's newly sculpted ones. "Does it matter? Don'tcha think that if God had enough creativity to throw red and blue and purple and green all together with a bunch of other colors and call it a rainbow, that He might have a way of making the thunder and rain meet the sun and create something beautiful? They got to work together, not apart. The sun doesn't follow the rain, and the thunder isn't in charge of the sun, but together they make color. A masterpiece. All playing a different part."

Patty leaned back and reached for her cigarette case. "That's what I think. I think we all play different parts. I don't think one dominates the other. We all bring something to the sky to make it beautiful."

"It's a lovely thought," Pippa murmured.

"Isn't that right, fella?" Patty shouted out the open window.

Pippa jumped, her arm knocking over a spool of thread. One quick look out the window and she caught sight of Jake Chapman. Jake, who stood patiently by Agnes, the elephant calf's mother, as she paused on the road. Her trunk reached for some leaves dangling from an oak tree, wrapped around the branch, and pulled.

Jake must not have seen Pippa. The grin he cast in Patty's direction was just shy of stunning. It transformed his masculine features from brooding to that of humor and even fun.

"Isn't what right?" he shouted back.

"Come." Patty tugged on Pippa's sleeve. Pippa resisted, but Patty yanked harder. Rather than tumble from her chair, Pippa followed unwillingly, not missing the small whine from Penn as the dog scampered to her feet to follow also.

The screen door of the costume house was flung open by an exuberant Patty Luchent. It banged against the side of the house as Patty pulled Pippa out from behind her. With a hand on both of Pippa's upper arms and her body directly behind Pippa, Patty responded to Jake.

"We all bring something to make this world beautiful, right?"

A nudge made Pippa stumble forward. Hotness crept up her throat. If Jake Chapman even said a word, one word, Pippa might faint dead away. As it was, he had gone remarkably still. Like in a dime novel romance. Only there was nothing romantic about this moment. It was sheer and unadulterated awkwardness.

Jake cleared his throat. Agnes chomped on leaves while her

trunk reached for another branch. Penn sat on her haunches and let her mouth drop open, tongue out, panting with a droopy smile on her furry face.

"Sure," Jake coughed out.

Patty's laughter sounded like tiny bells. She stepped out from behind Pippa and extended an arm toward her like the ringmaster announcing his next act. "Isn't she beautiful? She finally got herself all dolled up and out from under her fiancé's thumb and her father's finger!"

Not really.

Pippa opened her mouth to protest.

She really hadn't.

Pippa closed her mouth.

"Looks fine to me." Jake gave a swift nod. Polite. Distant. The fun drained from his gray eyes like the sunlight hidden behind a cloud.

"I've got an appointment!" Patty announced with a sudden flourish. She skipped down the porch steps and waggled her fingers at Pippa, then at Jake. "Ta-ta and toodle-doo, my lovelies!" A sparkling smile.

A train whistle could be heard in the distance, and Patty's eyes darted toward the depot. "Right on time," she said, then took off at a brisk pace toward the station. Whom she was meeting and why, Pippa had no idea. All she knew was that once more, it was just her and Jake. Staring at each other. Unsure of what to say or if anything should be said at all.

"Lily took another bottle."

"Have you found anything out about your sister?"

They spoke simultaneously, and Pippa winced. Jake's news was wonderful and platonic, but no, she had to dive right into his sister's assault and murder and claw at an already-open wound with the finesse of an angry caged tiger.

"No."

"Oh, good."

They tried again.

Jake's mouth tightened. Pippa noticed him biting down on his ever-present cigar, his jaw flexing against some unspoken emotion or word.

"I need to keep going."

Of course he did. Pippa nodded. Jake had an elephant to tend to. Down the street, Ernie was already leading the other two elephants back into the indoor octagonal ring for practice. Even though the season was officially over and the circus was settling down in Bluff River to prepare for winter, that didn't mean the animals were left unworked and unrehearsed.

"It's nice to see you." Pippa offered the proper statement.

Jake's eyes darkened as he palmed his bearded cheek. "Sure." He gave one of his customary short nods. "And you *do* look pretty."

Pippa stood there staring after him, even after he'd disappeared into the elephant house and, as if in closure, Agnes's tail gave a resounding *thwack* to the doorframe.

CHAPTER TWENTY

CHANDLER

Where did you find this?" Chandler all but shook the necklace in Hank's face. He was walking her home, the ghost tour ended, the police having taken statements from the onlookers, after which they interviewed her.

How had the doors been opened? Who else had keys? Had she heard the screaming too? Did anything look disturbed or missing?

She'd been every cop's worst witness. She didn't know. Only herself and the contractor. No, never. And finally, it's an abandoned train depot—everything looked disturbed, and there wasn't anything to miss.

"You want to explain this?" Chandler asked again in the darkness, their footsteps scraping on the sidewalk.

"Sure. I think it's the necklace that they say was on Patty Luchent." Hank's voice was deep and sliced through the night.

"You don't say?" Chandler tried not to allow so much sarcasm to infuse her words, but she couldn't help it. "And where did you find it?"

"The depot."

"And how did you get into *my* depot?"

Hank stopped and stared down at her, although he was probably lucky to make out any of her features under the moonless sky. "You gave me a key."

"No, I didn't." She hadn't, had she?

"Yes. You did."

"When?"

"When you were in the ER. Before we left. It's why I'd come to your place to begin with, remember? I wanted access to the train depot."

It bugged Chandler that she didn't remember. It was a ramification of her disease, specifically during her episodes. Lost memories. Lost conversations. Short-term amnesia almost.

"So, you have a key? That I gave you? Did you leave the doors open tonight?" Chandler crossed her arms.

A breeze picked up and brushed between them, like a ghost playing around two stubborn lovers refusing to move.

"No, I did not leave the doors open."

"Then how—?"

"Chandler." Because his voice was so baritone, it sounded sharp when Hank said her name. She pressed her lips together, irritated that he'd shut her up.

"I entered the depot with your permission—or so I thought. I found the necklace upstairs. It was wedged beneath an antique desk in one of the rooms. I wanted to show you tonight, but you were on that tour with Cru and his—"

"With Cru. Ah-hah! You're jealous." Chandler couldn't help but goad him, even though it was probably far from the truth and took a lot of guts to say to his face. But her annoyance had inspired her.

"Sure. I am." Hank didn't deny it, and Chandler couldn't tell if he was being patronizing or not. He tapped her arm to get her to follow him, and they started down the sidewalk again. "The fact is, that's twice now someone has tampered with the train depot. I figure the first time they got in through the window."

"They're all cemented in."

"Not the one at ground level. I couldn't fit through it, but someone your size could."

Chandler didn't respond. She hadn't noticed it. She didn't like that she hadn't noticed it. Those details were rather important to be aware of in her field of expertise.

"I've no theory for the doors being open tonight, though."

"Why? Why would anyone care to be inside the depot, and why now after my uncle bought the property? Lottie never mentioned anyone trespassing on the property before."

Hank didn't answer right away. Finally he broke the silence. "I think it has to do with Linda. Uncle Denny's sister. It's why I'm here. We're disrupting a story no one has cared about for years. That could be threatening someone."

Chandler sniffed and couldn't help but peer into a lighted window of a small house they walked past. The TV was flickering inside. It looked warm. A haven. Not at all a house that belonged in a town with a haunted circus.

"*I'm* not disrupting anything," she argued. "I'm not here to mess with ghosts or to find missing children from 1978."

"1983."

"Whatever. My point is, I just want to do my job. It's what I'm good at." Chandler fished in her pocket and pulled out Patty's necklace. She reached for Hank's hand, which, she noted, was very large, and she pressed the necklace into it. "Here. Take this—*thing*. You can have your fun investigating serial killers, and while I have the utmost sympathy for your uncle and your family never finding reconciliation with Linda's disappearance, it has nothing to do with me. Or with Patty Luchent, for that matter."

"Chandler." Hank's tone held an edge of caution.

"No." Chandler stepped away from him. They had arrived at her rental. The cottage lights were on, evidence that Margie had stayed true to her post watching Peter. Chandler held her palms toward Hank. The screams from the depot still echoed inside of her, restless and unexplained. The mess in the upstairs of the costume house also flashed across her memory—also unexplained unless she chose to believe Lottie. It was unsettling at best, and terrifying at worst.

180

"Please. Do whatever you need to find out about Denny's sister. I'll support that, but I-I can't be a part of it. This place is . . ." Truth be told, Chandler had considered leaving. Yet that would leave her a wide-open target for Jackson to prove his point that she was slipping at her job. Not to mention it would be difficult to explain she had skipped town because of a ghost story. "Just leave me out of it," she concluded.

Hank tipped his head, searching her face in the darkness. "I'm not sure you *can* be left out of it. Especially if you keep inserting yourself into it."

Chandler wanted to tell him it was inadvertent insertion. Unwilling. Accidental. Unintended. But she couldn't. She couldn't explain any of it. The only thing she could shed light on was why she'd transplanted herself and her son to a different state, to a small town, to a jobsite—even going so far as to pull Peter from school and attempt online homeschooling.

She was running. Plain and simple. From the truth that dogged her feet. One day soon, *she* would simply not be enough for Peter. Maybe even for herself. And the idea of asking for—let alone accepting—help was akin to giving up her rights. It was independence suicide, and she wasn't ready for that to die.

Her call with Uncle Neal this morning had been brief and concise. Her follow-up call with Jackson had been the damaging weed to her struggling patch of flowers. The flowers of hope that she could turn in a proposal to restore this place—this behemoth of a building.

Chandler sucked in deep lungsful of fresh air, allowing its crispness to infiltrate her system and jump-start it with oxygen. The roof alone would cost over a million in repairs. It wasn't the estimate she'd been hoping for. She wasn't ignorant, though, as Chandler had expected the amount to be rather exorbitant. But that positioning of the decimal point would make convincing Uncle Neal difficult—that it was a good idea to restore rather than demolish and rebuild. Uncle Neal hadn't gone apoplectic on her when she'd briefed him on the estimate, but neither had he responded with a rose-colored outlook.

"And we're still waiting for the quotes on the foundation?" His tone was thoughtful. He was calculating in his head.

"Yes. But I have a good feeling about that from what I can see. As we know from the initial pre-purchase assessment, it is sound. It just needs some bolstering. And all the window framing will need restoring, and the windows custom-ordered," she added. Might as well be up front with the truth.

"We knew that. What about the flooring?" Uncle Neal asked.

"It seems all right in most places. Rotted away in a couple of rooms, mostly in the corners where moisture's gotten in."

She wasn't going to say a peep about the place being haunted or mention its history.

"Well, keep at it. I trust you'll put as much thought and time into the alternative too. I know where your passions lie, but I'd appreciate an unbiased proposal."

Chandler assured him she would. She was already in communication with an architect, who was busy drafting plans in the event they demoed the depot and started from scratch.

Jackson had been another beast altogether. He was her dandelion.

"You're wasting time and funds on something that is obviously not worth repairing. If it were, someone would have snatched it up long ago and done just that."

"That takes capital, though," she'd argued.

"Far more capital than a smart man would front," Jackson countered back. "A restored historic building to house custom hobby shops? You'll never have any ROI."

Right. Return on investment. And it had all gone downhill after that. Jackson's urging to simply work with the architect and forgo collecting all the quotes rang heavy in her mind as she unlocked the main door of the train depot. She liked the building better in the daylight.

But once the tall windows were unblocked and restored, the sunlight streaming in, she could imagine the beauty of the interior. Once the carved woodwork was refinished, the floors polished— floors scuffed from shoes and trunks and luggage carts—and the benches facing the ticket gate brought back to their original state, she could imagine people being drawn once again to this place.

Now, however, it was nothing but a hollowed-out relic of lost memories.

"Hey."

"Gahhhhhhh!" Chandler screamed and whirled around, her moccasins scattering gravel at her feet as she slapped out instinctively, her hand connecting with a solid chest.

Hank's left eyebrow rose, and he looked down at Chandler's hand that she snatched back as fast as she'd hit him. She hadn't fazed him in the slightest.

"A bit jumpy?" He winked. There was something about a brawny man with shaggy hair pulled back by a leather strap that had never attracted Chandler before. She wasn't sure why suddenly she was all twitterpated like a middle-school girl.

"No. Not jumpy." *Liar*. Chandler looked over his shoulder as though she would find some sort of explanation for his presence. "Why are you here?"

Hank crossed his thick arms over his equally thick chest. Chandler noted the rosary that wound up his forearm, encircling a cross. What should be comforting, a symbol of closeness with God, just left her with more questions.

"*You* told me it was cool if I came by. Remember? Just to leave you out of it."

"Fine. Just—tell me where you need to go inside and I'll give you a bit." Chandler cut to the chase, hanging on to the olive-green strap of her messenger bag hung across her chest as if it were a lifeline to an instant 911. She'd wait outside. Let Hank do whatever digging around for ghosts and cold-case clues he wanted, and then when he left she'd go about her business.

"I'll show you." He bypassed her and stepped into the depot.

"No. You'll tell me." Chandler heard the wobble in her voice, even though she was trying to sound severe. Determined and confident.

"You don't trust me." Hank stated the obvious, his green eyes sparking.

"I . . ." She stopped. She really had no answer. It wasn't that she couldn't trust him—she just didn't know him. Didn't really *know* anyone here, for that matter.

Hank was deep inside the depot already, his head tipped back to eye the vaulted ceiling as though Leonardo da Vinci had painted on it. Chandler followed with caution, clinging to her bag like it was a weapon.

"Have you been upstairs yet?" he asked and shot her a look over his shoulder. "It's all part of the explanation. The upstairs."

"I don't need an explanation," Chandler lied. Actually she would rest easier knowing Hank was nosing around the depot, and yet she felt she needed more reasons as to *why*.

Linda Pike had last been seen at the depot in 1983. If she had vanished then, and the police hadn't found her, what made Hank believe that, decades later, he would have better luck?

"What's so important about upstairs?" she asked.

Hank gave her a knowing smile. She'd caved. Her curiosity was going to kill her—like the proverbial cat—and Hank Titus would probably stand there and watch, laughing the entire time at what a walking contradiction she was.

"What's so important about upstairs?" she repeated.

"So, you haven't been upstairs yet," he concluded.

"Can we not dance in circles?" Chandler's annoyance was getting the best of her. "I just spent last night half convinced this place is haunted! My co-worker is pressuring me to bulldoze the building, and if any more weird stuff takes place here, I just may do that. I didn't come to Bluff River to play games, and I've enough on my plate to balance—as you well know. So tell me what you think you can accomplish with a cold case that's older than we are. Not to mention that stupid necklace and that crazy ghost story!"

"Feel better?" Hank cocked his habitual eyebrow.

"Yes!" Chandler exclaimed. Took a breath. Squeezed her arms against her chest. "No." She managed a slight smile. Her attempt to appear more civil and less like a raging Cruella de Vil.

"Do you know what they used the second level of the depot for?" Hank inquired, choosing to let her outburst slide, apparently also deciding to ignore answering her very valid, very pointed questions.

"Yes. Offices and telegraph communications." Chandler tried to squelch her frustration, to calm herself, to enter back into the realm of the sane and reasonable.

"That's all you know?"

"Yes."

"I'd wager a bet there's a direct line of sight to the circus grounds from the windows upstairs."

Chandler gave Hank a *no-duh* look and impatiently tapped her shoe on the floor. "And that's important why?"

Hank motioned her with a wave. "Maybe if we ever left the main room, we could find out."

"Fine." Chandler rolled her wrist in a fancy wave in return. "Lead the way."

His boots clomped up the stairs, and Hank waved an arm in front of him, clearing the path of spider webs. Mouse droppings collected in piles in the corners of the steps. The walls were gray with dust and years of grime. Chandler hunched her shoulders to avoid touching anything. It was gross and filthy. The smell of must and dankness grew thicker as they climbed. Footprints on the steps reminded Chandler that the contractor had already been up here to inspect the roof. Good. At least she knew they wouldn't fall through rotten floorboards.

Hank reached the landing and waited for Chandler. She stopped beside him and looked right and left, momentarily in awe of the complexity of the building's architecture. Large rooms branched off on both sides of the hall, and to her right, a tall oval window—now filled with cinder blocks—had at one point allowed in natural light from floor to ceiling. To her left, the hallway ended abruptly to wrap around an open floor in a catwalk of sorts. A person could look all the way down to the ticket area.

For a minute, Chandler forgot the purpose of her interrogation. She squeezed past Hank, skirted the offices to the left and right of her, and stepped into the open walkway.

"Careful." Hank's baritone vibrated in her ears. He was right. Chandler decided not to lean on the thick cherrywood rail that edged the walkway. There was no way to know if it was sturdy, and she didn't relish the idea of falling to the floor below.

Lifting her eyes, she examined the large room to the right of the catwalk. "That must have been the communications room," she mumbled. She was drawn to it, checking her footing to make sure the flooring was intact. On either side of the large double doors, circus posters were pasted to the brick wall. Though they were ripped and worn, faded from the years, Chandler could make out the silhouette of an elephant, posed on an oval podium, its trunk curled in a wave. On the other, a vogue Gibson-Girl type in a trapeze suit of purple, a mass of hair balanced on top of her head, and a brilliant smile with lips painted a shiny apple-red.

She sensed Hank behind her as she entered the room. Two more large windows graced the opposite wall. These were also cemented in, the room left dark from lack of sunlight. Three more posters were pasted to the walls, so aged she could hardly make out anything other than the words *Bonaventure Circus* and *Clive the Small Man* and something about a baby elephant named Lily. A table was positioned under the windows, but only its right side was standing. The left legs had collapsed after years of neglect and rot.

Hank pointed toward the table. "That's where I found the necklace."

Chandler eyed him suspiciously. "It's weird that the necklace that strangled the fabled Patty Luchent was just *lying* in an empty room after years of people walking around, busy working here and there, and then closing the building for good?"

"I didn't say it was lying in the middle of the floor."

"Where was it, then?"

"Come, I'll show you." Hank crossed the room to the rotted table. He reached his hand beneath it and pulled on the edge. A small drawer slid open. It wasn't necessarily meant to be a hidden drawer, Chandler noted, yet it wasn't obvious a drawer was there unless a person put their hand beneath the table to feel for it on the hollowed underside. "I found it in here."

"Why didn't anyone else find it before—" Her question was cut short as Hank held up a hand. His eyes snapped with a green sharpness, and he turned his head toward the door.

"What?"

He held his finger to his lips to shush her.

Wariness blossomed in the pit of her stomach. It was daytime. There was no danger. There were no ghosts.

Hank was eyeing the doorway, the catwalk, and tipping up his chin like he could somehow see over the rail to the main-level floor. He crooked his finger at Chandler, and she approached him.

"Were you meeting anyone else here today?" he whispered in her ear.

Chandler gave him a wide-eyed shake of her head. She pushed her tortoiseshell glasses up her nose, as they'd slid down from the sudden motion. "Well, someone was coming to look at the foundation. I'm not sure if that was today yet. I was waiting for a callback." She took out her phone to see if she had any missed calls.

Hank's hand enveloped hers and stilled it.

Then Chandler heard it. A low moan. It was so soft, so vague, she wasn't sure she would have ever heard it had Hank not stilled her.

"What is that?" she whispered. She stepped instinctively closer to the man's muscled frame.

He held his fingers against his lips again.

Another moan. Almost a hum.

"In there." Hank tugged on Chandler's arm. He reached for a door adjacent to the table and opened it.

"What—?"

"Shh."

It was a small closet. Hank pulled the door shut and it clicked softly into place. Chandler's back was pressed against Hank's chest. The closet was pitch-black and the dust thick. It tickled her nose and reached up into her sinuses.

"Why are we hiding?" Chandler whispered.

Hank's hands came up to grasp her arms. Chandler shivered at his touch. His breath moved the hair at her ear as he whispered, "Don't trust anyone, Chandler."

"What are you talking about?" She twisted, facing him now. It was a mistake. Now they were chest to chest, her nose almost touching the hollow of his neck.

"Shh."

"I'm not hiding from a ghost! Not in the daytime—!"

"Shhh!" He was insistent enough this time to put his fingers against Chandler's mouth. She blinked, staring up at him, trying to make out his features in the darkness.

She couldn't.

The floor outside the closet door creaked. Could ghosts make a floor creak?

A footstep.

The sound of the drawer in the table being pushed back into place.

A moan filtered through the crack at the bottom of the closet door. The kind of moan that either a male or a female might make, deep in the throat, in tired frustration.

More footsteps.

Hank's fingers were still against her lips.

The closet was stifling.

Chandler sucked in a deep breath of stale air. She leaned her forehead into Hank's chest. The spicy scent met her nose, a welcome reprieve. His fingers slipped from her mouth and trailed down her neck. Whether it was deliberate or not, Chandler couldn't help but shiver.

She froze.

Hank's fingers stopped at her collarbone.

The doorknob on the closet rattled.

A coolness overwhelmed Chandler. Cold. Bumps raised on her arms, and she shivered inadvertently. She could feel Hank's muscles tense.

Then it was gone. The cold air, the sensation that time had suddenly stood still, and the footsteps. All of it. Gone.

They stood in silence for a few long moments. Hank finally lifted his fingers from her skin and drew back his hand. He reached for the doorknob to open it.

He twisted.

Paused.

Twisted again.

"Open it," Chandler begged in a whisper. "Please."

"I can't."

"Why not?"

Hank tilted his head down until his nose touched her forehead. "We're locked in."

CHAPTER
TWENTY-ONE

C all someone," Chandler hissed. Claustrophobia might not be the worst thing she battled, but right now it was closing in fast, especially since she could hardly move without bumping against Hank—which was equally delightful and unnerving.

"I don't use a cellphone."

Chandler stilled. "Are you for real?"

Silence.

She dug around in her messenger bag and tugged out her phone. Now, like in any movie scene, this would be the time her phone died, or her battery was low, or there was no signal. Chandler pushed the side button, and light blinded them.

"Ha!" she exclaimed victoriously and waved it in Hank's face. "Welcome to the twenty-first century!"

"Don't get too excited." His voice was so deep that it rumbled his chest, and because she was so close to him, it rumbled in hers also.

"Why?" She dialed Margie's number. "I'll just call Margie. She can call someone to get us out of here."

"Mm-hmm" was Hank's only response.

Chandler held the phone to her ear as it started ringing. She heard Margie answer.

"Hey, Margie. I need your help . . ." Chandler heard Margie on the other end, but it was broken and robotic. "Margie, I—hello? Margie?"

The call dropped.

"Oh, you've got to be kidding me!" Chandler rammed the phone into Hank's chest.

He wrenched it from her grasp. "You're in an inside closet in a cemented-up and windowless brick building. Getting a signal will be sketchy."

"You're a gorilla. Bust down the door," Chandler said, her voice rising.

Hank's fingers squeezed her arm. "Hey, calm down. We don't know if we're alone yet."

Chandler flicked her phone light off. "What?" Her whisper was fierce. She wanted out. Out of this closet with Hank. Away from this haunted depot with creepy people and old necklaces from murder victims hidden in drawers.

"Just give it a bit more time."

"A bit?" Chandler dropped her phone back in her bag. "A bit?" she repeated.

"And be quiet," Hank advised.

Chandler bit her tongue.

Hank dropped his hand from her arm, and they stood at attention, chest to chest, face to neck. Breathing. Silent. Every nerve at attention.

"I've got to get out of here," Chandler whimpered.

The room was closing in even more. She could swear the closet's walls were compressing. Like that garbage disposal room on the Death Star in *Star Wars* that had threatened to crush Han Solo and Princess Leia and Luke Skywalker and—

Chandler launched for the doorknob, twisting and rattling it. "Break this thing down. I need out of here."

Hank's arms surrounded her, holding her back. Again, his mouth was against her ear. "Chandler. Stop."

She wriggled. "I don't care. Patty Luchent's ghost can eat me alive, I need out of this sweatbox." She was seeing stars. Ringing in her ears. The room was spinning.

"Chandler."

She jerked her arms up, apparently surprising Hank, and spun as if she were in a large room instead of a small closet. Her toe connected with the tip of Hank's boot and she tripped forward, her shoulder ramming against the back wall of the closet opposite the door. The wall gave beneath the impact.

Chandler heard the crack of the old wallboard. Dust puffed in her face as her temple hit the wall and her shoulder pushed through into the framework. She screamed, muffled because her face was against the wood, and she brought her other arm up to push herself out of the wall's interior but only succeeded in pushing in more of the deteriorating wall.

Something cold and damp fell against her, even as Chandler pulled back into Hank's body. It was hard and thin but with many pieces all tangling around her. Something soft brushed her neck. Like coarse hair. Long and stringy. Part of the object fell against her arm. It was long, like another arm, only fleshless, cold bone. Skeletal.

Hank must have found her phone in her bag as it swung to her other side. The light flooded the small closet, and Chandler blinked. Squeezed her eyes shut, then opened them. Deep pits stared back at her. The skeletal remains leaning into her like a corpse freed from its secret coffin. Patches of decaying hair brushed Chandler's neck.

Her scream would have awakened the dead—if the dead wasn't already staring at her with a vacant expression.

The room was blurry. Chandler lay flat on her back, the hard floor beneath her and the dark ceiling of the telegraph room staring down at her. She squeezed her eyes shut and then opened them, willing her vision to clear.

"Oh man, oh man, oh man," she muttered, scrambling into a sitting position as the memory of the skeleton's attack created an onslaught to her senses.

Hank must have broken through the door to the closet. It hung askew on its hinges. The debris from Chandler's stumble into the wall lay scattered on the floor, along with . . .

Chandler let out a half sob and half laugh. Hank turned from where he stood, hands on his waist, back to her, staring into the closet. He looked stunned, disbelief painting its way into every crevice of his face.

She peered beyond him, trying to avoid the shattered skeleton, dark gray with age, spread on the floor.

"Did you call the cops?" Chandler pushed out between the rapidly increasing tremors in her body.

"That's your answer to everything," Hank muttered and turned away from her. "You've got to see this."

Chandler pushed herself up and rose onto wobbling feet. She steadied herself, willing her weakness to take a backseat to the urgency of the moment. "I've already seen it."

"No. Not that." Hank motioned to the skeleton. "That." He pointed.

Chandler came up beside him and stared.

Neither of them spoke. The image before them was too astounding. Too shocking.

Finally, Chandler managed to push words from her mouth. "What—what is that?"

Hank shook his head and stepped closer.

The opposite wall was shattered from Chandler's fall. Boards had been busted and pulled away, and with the skeleton's careening embrace into Chandler, it had only taken more of the mess with it. Behind the wall, hidden between the old framework, were small torn sections of circus poster. The eye and ear of a zebra ripped and pasted onto the wall. The foot of what must have been a trapeze artist, based on the tilt of the slippered foot and the rope wrapped around the ankle. There was a section of poster with *Bona*-something printed on it, leaving to the imagination as to the completion of the word. On top of that was pasted another portion, of an elephant's trunk reaching up, a purple ball balanced on the end of its trunk.

Nails were hammered into the poster backdrops. Rough-looking nails, handmade, like they'd been forged on an anvil. From each nail, something hung. A remnant. A . . .

"Souvenir." Hank finished Chandler's thought.

"A-are those locks of *hair*?" she stammered. The locks, nine in total, were tied in the middle and the ribbon looped to hang off the nail. Brunette, a faded auburn, dark blond . . . dry and brittle with age.

Chandler gagged and whirled from the sight, covering her mouth with her hand. As she hustled away, Hank moved toward it. His voice offered commentary to what Chandler could no longer look at.

"There are necklaces here too. All of them women's. Gold, one is a locket. And then—crap—that's sick."

"What?" Chandler asked, muffled behind her hand.

"A circus token. Drilled out so they could slide a piece of ribbon through it."

"A circus token?" Chandler didn't know what Hank meant, but she didn't want to return to the gruesome sight to check it out.

"Yeah. Like a ticket to get into the circus, only it's a wooden token." He didn't touch them, instead raising Chandler's phone to shine the screen's light on them. "Yeah. 1922—Chicago. 1927—Des Moines. 1928—St. Louis."

"Is this a . . . ?" Chandler swallowed bile that rose in her throat. Burning, acidic bile that refused to go back down all the way. She struggled for breath and then managed to whisper, "Is this like a serial killer's stash? Did we just find the Watchman's lair?"

Hank didn't answer directly. He clicked off the phone light and stepped cautiously around the skeleton. "Chandler, go ahead."

"What?" She raised her brows.

"Do what you like to do. Call the police."

"For real?" *Oh, blessed relief!*

"Yeah." He eyed the skeleton. "I think we have more than one crime from one decade here."

Chandler stilled. "What do you mean?"

Hank locked eyes with her. "I think we just found Linda Pike."

CHAPTER
TWENTY-TWO

PIPPA

ousin Franny had already donned the yellow sash of Georgiana Farnsworth's cause and made quite the spectacle as she exited the manor to the protests of her mother and Victoria Ripley. With the scandal of Franny joining ranks with the protesters, it would only lend credence to Georgiana's accusations and implicate Father as a liar when he stood in the circus's defense. The circus *wasn't* a good place, the circus *did* harm the community, and if Richard Ripley's own niece was willing to stand against it, what part did the town have in supporting wickedness? The novelty of the circus was wearing off. People were tired of dodging the menagerie on the square. In what other town did you find yourself walking behind a row of zebras, have to skirt a four-ton elephant, or tip your hat to a camel before carrying on about your business? What was once a phenomenon was risking being relegated to worse than an annoyance. It was an offense.

What Pippa always took for granted was that Bluff River knew Bonaventure Circus as she did. As a place to hide, a place where the rest of the vast world diminished. Where curiosities became normal, and where normal became simply . . . a far-off place.

"You have to let me go with you." Pippa surprised herself by her grip on Forrest's wrist as he moved to swing himself into the car. He shook off her hand and looked at her with repulsion at her uncustomary defiance.

"You're not going anywhere near that place." His eyes smoldered, and not in a way that would cause a woman's heart to flutter. She felt him rake a distasteful glare at her bobbed hair.

Admit it. You like it. The rebellious thought crossed Pippa's mind but not her tongue. It was something Patty Luchent would say, not Pippa Ripley.

Penn nudged her leg, a high-pitched whine of question in her throat.

"I need to stop Franny," Pippa argued. "She'll listen to me. She is my cousin after all." Which really meant nothing, and Forrest knew that. No one listened to Pippa. Had that been true, Pippa could have stopped Franny before she ever headed downtown toward the circus and Georgiana's protest.

Forrest settled on the bench seat. "Let your father deal with Franny. You can't do anything."

It was painful to hear. Like a wax seal on an envelope to indicate the subject was closed. But she needed to stop Franny, to stop Georgiana, for reasons altogether different from Forrest's. If the Watchman noted her cousin's involvement against the circus, it might drive him further from Pippa. Further from trusting her. In turn, it would pit her more and more against the very place she longed to be. A place just out of reach.

Pippa hurried around to the other side of the motorcar. She snapped her fingers, and Penn scrambled up by Forrest's feet.

"What are you . . . ?" Forrest expelled an exasperated breath. He shook his head, and it was apparent he was unsure how to deal with Pippa's sudden act of obstinance. "Not the dog." His growl rivaled the dog's.

Pippa did Forrest the favor of ignoring him, more because her insides were quaking at her unforgivable defiance.

"No dog," Forrest demanded again.

Penn growled.

Pippa gripped the car frame and placed her good foot on the footboard. The car lurched forward.

"Forrest!" Pippa cried out as she struggled onto the seat, her weak leg no help in balancing.

Forrest applied the brake and shot her a sideways glare that grazed Penn with distaste. "Why won't you listen to reason? To me? This is highly unlike you, Pippa. It's not at all appealing."

Pippa's silence garnered her an additional scowl, but she remained silent because she didn't know what to say. She didn't care if she was appealing to him or not. But he was right. It was unlike her, and while there were reasons behind her actions, there were none that Forrest would comprehend, let alone understand.

Disapproval oozed from Forrest as the noisy vehicle surged forward. Penn wedged her body between Pippa's knees, her haunches swaying with the motion of the fast-paced car.

"My future wife doesn't need to create front-page news, and your own recent behavior . . ." He waved his hand wildly in the air while refusing to take his eyes off the street before him. "Your hair!"

Pippa reached up to finger the well-trimmed ends that boasted of Patty's finishing handiwork. "I-I like it."

Forrest eyed her. "You like it? Did you consider whether I would? I've no idea what's gotten into you recently!"

Pippa didn't respond. Any argument would broach further reprimand and questioning. She bounced on the seat, and her shoulder rammed into Forrest's. He ignored her.

With their rather swift descent down Ash Street, he guided the vehicle as they paralleled the river that bounced and riffled over large boulders and rock jams. The row of colorful circus houses was nowhere near as impressive as the line of thirty-some ladies marching with painted placards mounted to long poles.

End Animal Abuse

Animals Have Feelings Too
Circus Sins Must Cease!

That last one was the sign Franny lifted and lowered as she marched behind Georgiana. The happy little raven-haired apprentice was oblivious to the stir she created and the fact that a gangly news reporter had his camera ready to capture Franny for tomorrow's front-page headline.

"Blast it all! They're worse than the suffragettes." Forrest's scowl was focused on Georgiana, who taunted them with a smile as she hoisted her sign higher.

Somehow she had recruited quite a few women in a very short time. Bluff River seemed willing to forget the rich culture the circus brought to their town. The revenue they generated through wagon works, local farmers with a huge resource of fertilizer at their disposal, and certainly the boast of being the Midwest's only little circus town. Bonaventure Circus had put Bluff River on the map. One injured baby elephant had spun into a wild story of circus neglect by an overzealous activist, which had turned many against it in a space of a heartbeat.

The awful irony was that no one picketed against the verbal abuse in the form of mockery and laughter that Clive was subjected to. A dwarf who was as human as the next. Or Jolly the clown, whose own past was forever locked behind his face paint. Even Benard, who hid his mottled face from the world behind a forge, his talents lost to the outside.

Pippa caught Clive's eye as they rolled past. The dwarf hiked as fast as he could from the hotel on the corner to the line of women, who sang "Onward Christian Soldiers" so completely out of context—and tune—that she would have laughed if there were anything humorous to be found in it.

The car sputtered and jerked to a stop. Forrest alighted without a backward glance at Pippa. He targeted the newspaper photographer, his long strides eating up the ground between them. Clive hurried to the car as Pippa set a tentative foot on the ground and gained balance on her bad leg. Penn hopped down, her breaths coming in short, nervous pants.

"You need to stop your cousin." Clive gave Penn an absent-minded scratch over the left ear, oblivious to the inadvertent pressure he'd heaped on Pippa's shoulders.

"I don't know what to say to her." Pippa matched Clive's steps as they headed toward the foray, appreciative of the dwarf's shorter legs and that she was able to keep up with him. "She's headstrong and has no thought for anything but her own whims and fancies."

"So I see." Clive raised his eyebrows and heaved a breath through his nose. His arms swung at his sides.

Penn trotted between them, her head at the height of Clive's shoulder. They were their own miniature army against Georgiana's growing campaign. A crowd of onlookers grew across the street. Children, women with their hands raised over their eyes to shield them from the afternoon sun and perhaps the question of whether they should join, and men who seemed a bit dazed at the effect a group of strong, vocal women could have.

Clive raised his voice as the noise of the women's singing grew. "Your cousin's presence just increased the number of crusaders. There were only five to start with. Once your cousin arrived, they came like a swarm of bees. Her being here implies truth to Miss Farnsworth's claims."

"I thought you weren't worried about Georgiana Farnsworth's cause?" Pippa couldn't help but question Clive.

Clive cast her a sideways glance. "Don't twist my words, Pet."

She was twisting them. Clive's faith remained resolute, but he was also a man of action. An old man. A short man. With a crippled nobody and a nanny dog.

The crowd of women was loud in their chorus and chants. Forrest darted in and out, and Pippa saw him lean his face close to Georgiana. He was shouting. Her chin lifted. He pointed down Water Street as if to motion in the direction of the downtown. She shrugged.

Pippa edged past Clive, Penn at her heels.

"Franny!" She raised her voice to be heard over the din. It was obvious the crowd was unnerving the circus animals. A lion's roar shattered any measures of pause between the women's hymn singing, and the monkeys were shrieking in the menagerie barn. Pippa noted Benard running down the street toward them, accompanied by Jolly the clown and—good heavens—her father. This was getting out of hand far too fast. There was no keeping this story out of the press.

"Franny!" Pippa limped into the chaos.

Franny cast her a vivid smile. She was ignorant of the damage she was doing. Or else she just didn't care. Pippa grabbed for her arm and attempted to pull her aside. Franny lowered her sign and wrenched her arm away from Pippa.

"Isn't this glorious?" Her voice was like music, even while causing trouble.

Pippa yelled over the din, "How can you say that? Please stop, Franny."

"Stop? Why would I stop?" Franny twirled as if she were a toddler, her dress swirling around her knees like she was doing the fox-trot. "I'm a part of something grand!"

"You have no evidence to support your cause. You're only hurting the family!" Pippa argued, trying to grab Franny's arm again. Someone bumped into Pippa's shoulder and she stumbled. Righting herself, Pippa hurried a few steps after her cousin, who continued to twirl like a dancer in a club with a glass of whiskey in her hand. She had lost her mind. Completely and utterly lost her mind.

"The baby elephant! Stop the circus! The poor, battered baby elephant!" Franny's chants were accompanied by the other women, and she was swallowed by the growing crowd.

Pippa scurried aside as the women pushed past her. She darted a look toward the elephant barn. Poor Lily. This noise would do nothing to aid in her peaceful recovery.

"Stop manhandling me!" Resolve and determination were

chiseled onto Georgiana Farnsworth's pretty face as Forrest dragged her over to them. She twisted out of his grasp. "You're out of line, Mr. Landstrom!"

"Cease this madness at once!" Forrest's command fell on deaf ears. He swiped at empty air to grab at Georgiana.

Georgiana glared at Pippa's betrothed with a vehement self-defense that Pippa could only admire. "You've no right to stop me and most certainly none to touch me."

Forrest restrained himself but seethed through clenched teeth, "You're acting out of complete ignorance."

Clive reached Pippa's side. She exchanged a doubtful glance with him, then saw her father's magnanimous and commanding form pushing through the crowd. Pippa ducked behind another woman, leaving Clive alone. Her father couldn't see her here. There was no conclusion he would draw that would be in Pippa's favor.

"Miss Ripley!" Another voice joined the chaos. Pippa strained to find where it was coming from. She couldn't see anyone. Being petite didn't help.

"*Pippa!*" The same voice switched to familiarity. She spun on her good foot and collided with Jake, who propped her back up with two hands around her upper arms. Urgency pulsed from his gray eyes, and his jaw clenched as if he grew in fury.

"I need you."

Pippa's heart quickened, then slowed, catching her off guard as she momentarily misinterpreted his meaning.

"Lily. The noise has her all in a twist, and there's no one to calm her. Ernie is away for the afternoon. She might respond to you. I can't get her to settle down."

"Absolutely not." Forrest's refusal startled Pippa. His sudden appearance behind her made her sway on her leg. "You're staying with me." Forrest gripped her hand. Tight. Unyielding.

"Let her go." Jake glared at Forrest's hold.

Pippa squirmed. The feel of Forrest's skin on hers wasn't unfamiliar, but it wasn't welcome either.

The protesters moved closer and sang at such a high-pitched vibrato it hurt Pippa's ears. The crowd from across the street began to walk toward them. Some of the women picked up the tune. A few of the men started yelling at the group. Heckling. This was all a game to them.

"Pippa is my fiancée. You have no need of her." Forrest stepped closer to Jake.

Jake stepped closer to Forrest. "She's needed to help with the calf."

Forrest's face reddened. "You'd be smart to stop making up stories so you can be with her just to suit your own carnal whims. It's no secret she's already been back here with you alone—in spite of her father's and *my* wishes."

"No!" Pippa's protest fell on deaf ears. The insinuation was ill-timed and uncalled for.

Jake propelled Forrest backward, the heels of his palms rammed into Forrest's shoulders. He shoved Forrest against the wall of the elephant house.

"Jake!" Clive yelled and darted between Pippa and the men.

Forrest wrestled against Jake, his hands pushing at Jake's arms. It was obvious that Forrest wasn't capable of matching Jake's skill with wrestling an opponent. Jake drew his arm back, his fingers forming a flat fist.

"Jake!" Clive jumped and hung off Jake's arm.

Penn released a series of barks. The protesters turned down the street in Georgiana's direction.

"What is going on?" Richard Ripley shouted, even as he hustled Franny away, his head bent and his mouth to her ear. Reprimands, no doubt. He hadn't noticed Pippa.

Benard squeezed into the mess and shoved the brawling men apart. Clive jumped out of the way as Jake surged forward, but Benard held him back. His arms bulged with the muscles of a seasoned blacksmith.

"What is the meaning of this? We need to stop those ridiculous women, not incur fights among our own!" Pippa's father stalked back toward them, having lost against Franny's wriggle to get away from her uncle. His outrage was palpable. The veins on his neck were raised, his cheeks a brilliant red above his mustache.

"I need Pippa to help with Lily." Jake shook off Benard.

Forrest spit on the ground, and Clive lifted his palm toward him in a sign to stand back.

"Lily is about to go into a fighting panic." Jake's voice rose, his hands still fisted at his sides.

Pippa was sure he'd turn on her father if given half the chance. It was probably why Benard wisely stood between them, his left eye partly closed from the skin deformity on that half of his face.

"Pippa can calm Lily down. She's done it before. At least let her try!"

"Balderdash!" Forrest launched himself toward Jake. Clive jammed his hands into Forrest's waist, slowing the taller man.

Jake twisted toward Forrest, and this time Benard couldn't stop him. Jake's fist cracked against Forrest's jaw in a swift uppercut. Forrest's head jerked back, and Benard leapt between the two men, his arms spread straight on either side of him.

"Go chase yourself!" Benard shouted over his shoulder at Jake. "Get out of here!"

Jake snarled.

Ripley's booming command showered around them. Pippa shrank against Penn, whose sharp barks joined chorus with the raucous voices of the protestors. "That is enough!"

Clive sidled next to Pippa and tugged at her arm. "Go. Go to Lily."

"But . . ." She wanted to. Wanted nothing more than to escape controversy and conflict, especially that which half centered around her.

"Just go."

It was a command. Instinctively, Pippa obeyed and hurried to the doorway of the elephant house, Penn pushing against her legs. She heard Clive tell Jake to follow. Her father shouted, and Clive returned the favor, matching wits with the much larger man, who had every right to terminate Clive's employment for speaking against him.

Pippa's heart clenched. A prayer touched her lips that God would settle her father's fury and protect Clive from taking the brunt of the blame for everything. The man had done nothing but try to bring peace to the circus, to bring them together.

The din faded as Pippa scrambled into the elephant house, away from the chaos and insanity of the moment. Jake charged after her, and with a guttural snarl he slammed the large doors shut to close out the commotion. He spun to face Pippa. His eyes snapped with rolling storm clouds of infuriated gray. Penn barked and jumped between them, her teeth bared.

"Why are you with that man?" Jake thundered and shoved his hand, finger pointed, toward the door. His shirt stretched taut against his muscular arm, but his gaze didn't follow where his finger aimed. Instead, he drilled her with a ferocious expression of disbelief.

It was as if someone had stolen her voice. Pippa swallowed. She was numb. The sound of her father shouting at other circus laborers outside the elephant barn seeped through the cracks of the door. They were trying to break up the crowd of onlookers who had witnessed every bit of scandal.

Jake planted his hands at his waist. "Why do you tolerate it? What woman would just let herself be handled by a man like that?"

"He's my intended." Pippa offered what she knew to be fact.

Jake shook his head. "So, he can do whatever he wants?"

"He's just trying to keep me—"

"Keep you in line?" Jake raked his hand through his already-unkempt hair. "A woman should know how to stand up for herself. Being a canceled stamp is getting old-fashioned."

"I'm not a canceled stamp." Pippa tried to squelch the ire rising in her. If Jake thought Forrest was forceful with her, what did he think he was doing? Defending her? Insulting her? "I try to honor those in authority over me."

Jake rolled his eyes and charged past her, his shoulder brushing hers. "Who determines who's in charge? Next thing you know you'll be singing the same song my sister did. Some Joe will have his way with you, and no one will believe you. No one will give a—" He cut off his curse and halted. Twisting at the waist, Jake drilled Pippa with a steely glare. "Don't you want to stand up for yourself, Pippa? Be your own person?"

Frustration welled in her throat. Frustration and desperation. Pippa opened her mouth to retort, but there were no words. She couldn't choke out a lifetime of struggle. There was nothing that could encapsulate all she felt, all she wanted, and the idea that Jake was urging her toward the very inward rebellion she fought against left her conflicted.

"I-I'm sorry." It was all she could think to say.

The look on Jake's face, the way his eyes darkened and the sad shake of his head, told her she'd chosen the wrong words.

CHAPTER
TWENTY-THREE

She wasn't any of Jake Chapman's business, and yet the look etched into his face stated he thought otherwise. Pippa could sense his eyes burning into her back as she escaped toward Lily's pen. There was no reason for him to have any sort of protective attachment toward her. None. Yet she heard his frustrated curse, coupled with a tone of regret, as though he'd overstepped and yet somehow failed at the same time. He'd equated her to his sister. Bridgette, she remembered him calling her in a previous conversation. But Forrest was far from a man who attacked a woman in the shadows, who left her for dead, who had murder on his hands. He was simply—a man. The head of their future household.

Still, Pippa couldn't deny that, for a brief and unfair moment, she had to battle away the twinge of jealousy toward the dead woman. Toward Jake's sister. It was obvious he had always defended Bridgette, and he still was. Intent on fighting for her, for justice, for wrongs to be righted as much as they possibly could be. What must it have been like to be Jake Chapman's sister? His spring-like body, ready to go to war for those he loved. He was a defender at heart. It lived in his eyes, seeped from the very marrow of his bones. Pippa wanted to tell Jake that she was none of his business, but for an irrationally clear moment, she realized she wanted to be.

"Pippa, wait." Jake's call echoed behind her.

She didn't. She pushed the door back on its rollers and entered Lily's place, Penn beside her. The dog's tail wagged but with caution, not friendship. Pippa knew the four-hundred-plus-pound baby pachyderm could crush her with one placement of its panicked foot. Yet her huge eyes merely lifted slightly at Pippa's entrance. A weak acknowledgment from a creature who in many ways paralleled exactly how Pippa felt. A resigned acceptance of their unwanted and uninvited fate.

"Pippa!"

Jake surged through the doorway of the stall and stopped short. Lily pressed her broad head that rivaled Pippa's petite frame against Pippa, who leaned into the calf, sprinkling kisses on the animal's coarse skin. She would ignore Jake. She would ignore her father, the raging storm inside of her, the ostracized loneliness that came with being the castaway child of the circus, and she would level all her might and her power on Lily. Loving a creature who demanded nothing in return, but whose eyes pierced Pippa's soul and stamped their acknowledgment on Pippa's heart. Penn stood vigil at the calf's feet, and Lily's trunk nosed Penn's muzzle. As if in slow motion, the dog's tongue licked the elephant's trunk, and then Lily tilted her head toward Pippa.

"Shh, baby girl," Pippa whispered. Another kiss to the wide expanse of Lily's forehead.

The three of them were a cohesive unit.

Pippa could feel Jake watching them, yet he didn't say a word. She could feel her strength oozing into Lily. Finally, completely, a family in the middle of a fray filled with threat, foreboding, and a tentative future.

"Pippa?" Jake broke the silence. She heard him draw a breath, one that shook with the attempt to tamp down his passion.

"Yes?" Her response was muffled as she leaned into Lily. She didn't look at him.

"Thank you for helping Lily." Though it was far from prolific, Pippa heard the sincerity in his voice.

She rewarded him with a sideways glance, then quickly looked away. Pippa could feel tears burning her eyes, and if she could feel them so strongly, she knew he could see them. She leaned back from a calmer Lily. There was nothing to say. Nothing she *could* say except, "Lily needs to eat."

"She needs to bond first." Jake moved beside them, but he didn't reach out to touch Lily and left a safe distance between himself and Pippa. "Until she bonds, she won't eat well. This has been the root problem all along. But if she will bond with you . . ." He let his sentence hang.

Pippa eyed him. She wanted to be able to see inside him—well, as much as he would let her—to understand the dark pain that lingered just underneath his tumultuous surface. Jake was an explosion waiting to erupt. He was wound tight, so tight, even now in his semi-relaxed form his jaw muscle twitched from clenching his teeth. She turned her face back into Lily's. The elephant's eyes closed, the cuts on her face from her mother's beating making her look that much more pathetic.

"I hate what is happening here," Pippa admitted, not wanting to confide in him, but not able to withdraw either. Circumstances of the worst kind had thrown them together.

Jake tipped his head and studied her.

She blinked away the betraying tears, but her chin quivered. His eyes deepened. He'd noticed it. He'd noticed the fierce emotion warring within her, the same as she'd noted his. But neither of them could speak empty words of hope.

They focused on the elephant calf instead. The one link between them.

Jake cleared his throat and broke the silent connection. "Lily may heal from her physical wounds, but with no nurturing from her mother to inspire her to eat and no inspiration to live, she could still die. She hasn't been eating near the right amount."

Pippa ran her hand down the leathery skin of Lily's back, the tiny hair bristling beneath her palm. "I've heard that elephants mourn loss much like a human. She misses her mother, doesn't she?"

Jake nodded and moved his foot, pushing away some straw from the wood floor. "It's why Ernie had assigned me to watch her. I was supposed to form that bond and become Lily's parent."

"She didn't want you." Then a small thread of realization entered Pippa's consciousness. Lily hadn't responded to Jake. Her birth, the traumatic rejection from Agnes her mother, and Jake whom she didn't fully trust. She lifted her eyes to Jake. "You weren't able to save Lily the same way you couldn't save your sister."

Jake looked away, running his hand under his nose and sniffing as if to dismiss her observation. "Doesn't matter." He must have meant to respond strongly, yet there was a hitch in his voice. An unguarded, painful admission behind his dismissal.

"If my arms were big enough, I would embrace Lily's entire circumference." Pippa intended her words to be soft, to be understanding, and to be a riddle Jake could unwind and apply to his sister. "But my arms are too small. I can give her only my strength and my affection, but in the end, it's up to her Creator whether she lives or . . . or dies." Pippa locked eyes with him. "Some battles we simply can't—we can't win. But maybe we can fight some things. We can fight—fight Georgiana Farnsworth."

Jake's silence gave fuel to Pippa's fledgling determination.

"We can prove we love Lily and she's not abused. We can try to convince Lily to eat and to live. I'll . . . I'll help. I will."

The desperation in her timid declaration sparked something in Jake's look. His eyes narrowed and he seemed to contemplate her. Maybe it was the fact that she had been born to the circus. Pippa knew he could see it on her face and hear it in the tremble of her words. The circus flowed through Pippa like vengeance flowed through him. That insatiable need to attach themselves to a cause, to justice, to protecting what they loved. To have someone fight for them. To be *seen*.

"Clive would say that God can move in mighty ways." Jake offered his own version of tentative faith.

Pippa bit her lip. Penn must have sensed her anguish, as the dog pressed against her legs. Terriers were loyal, fierce protectors. Fitting that Penn joined their circle.

"I can't see Him move. I never have." Pippa reached for Penn, and the dog whined, nudging her hip.

Jake raked his fingers through his hair, dragging them down the back of his neck, over his jaw, and on to his beard. He was agitated. He was—

Pippa jumped violently as Jake's fist slammed into the wall of Lily's pen.

Again.

And again.

He pulled his fist back for a third time, but Pippa launched to her feet and grabbed for his arm. It was foolhardy to wrestle with someone like Jake. But he froze, his muscles trembling beneath her hands, a trickle of blood from the torn skin of his knuckles, running down the back of his hand onto Pippa's.

"I know, I know . . ." Pippa could only whisper, could only relate with the words she longed someone would let her admit aloud without judgment. "It's awful to never see God change a person, to never see Him intervene. It's a horrible existence. I've cried to Him many a time and nothing changes. It all stays so silent. Does He even see us?"

Jake lowered his arm a bit, but Pippa kept her hands wrapped around his wrist. He stared ahead, into the wall, as if seeing another time, another place, another person.

"I've asked God 'why?'" Jake rasped. "Why would He allow Bridgette to be brutally attacked? But I get it now. I've been training for this. To make the man get the justice he deserves. To make him suffer as others have. I only hope God stands behind

211

me when my chance comes. And it will." Jake blinked a few times, breaking his stare. He looked down at Pippa as he lowered his arm, becoming aware that Pippa held his wrist with both hands. "I know it, Pippa. My chance will come. I can sense it in my gut."

She released her grip on him, very aware his blood was smeared on her fingertips. She wanted to say he deserved justice. That Bridgette deserved it. But it warred inside of her. Would that heal, though? Justice. Or would it only leave him unsatisfied?

Jake noticed his blood staining her skin and reached for his pocket, tugging out a handkerchief.

Pippa watched him take her fingers. He stepped closer, looking down at them and touching his handkerchief to them.

"If you find him—whoever hurt your sister—will you feel better once you've . . . once you've done whatever it is you need to do?" Her words tripped out as his warm skin brushed hers. Tenderly he wiped his blood from her hand.

His expression darkened. "I hope I will."

Pippa watched him dab the last of the blood away. Without pause, Pippa fluidly took the handkerchief from his hand and reached for him again. He let her take his hand in hers and turn it so the knuckles were visible. "Why did you go after Forrest? Outside? He was only trying to—"

"Control you?" Jake adjusted his footing in the straw, which drew him a step closer. Pippa held her breath as she wrapped Jake's kerchief around his bloodied knuckles.

"It's Forrest's right to—lead me." Even Pippa could hear the defeat in her voice.

"There's a difference between leading and dominating. What do *you* want, Pippa? That's what he should be asking. What are *your* dreams? What do *you* think?"

Pippa released Jake's hand, the makeshift bandage tied firmly. She couldn't fathom Forrest ever asking her those questions.

The pause was awkward. Penn eyed Jake with the suspicious

look of a guard dog. Jake didn't seem uncomfortable under the dog's assessment. He seemed familiar with it, respectful, and stepped far enough away from Pippa so he wasn't seen as a threat by Penn.

"I know you want to be here, Pippa," Jake acknowledged, "but it's not safe. Not here."

"Georgiana wants to ruin my father. She's no vendetta against me. I'm in no danger." The elephant's trunk lifted and batted at her dress.

"That's not what I'm talking about." Jake massaged his wrist with his good hand. "My sister—she wasn't the first, you know? It's happened before."

A coldness settled over Pippa. Foreboding. She shook it away and stroked Lily's trunk. "I need to be here. For Lily. To stop my cousin Franny from being ridiculous." She deflected.

"Your cousin?"

"Didn't you see her?" Pippa's brow furrowed. She tilted her head, confused. Franny had been rather obvious, even among the throng. Her silly floating and laughter as though she were at a carnival or a dance.

"I don't know." Jake frowned. "Who is she?"

"The young woman with the dark hair, wearing the dress of emerald green."

Jake's reaction was simply a shake of his head.

"She was twirling?" Pippa offered.

"Twirling?"

"Smiling and twirling." Pippa waited for Jake to search his memory. There had been young, old, middle-aged women. Signs. Circus staff. Her father. He had to have seen Franny during the chaos, dancing and trailing Georgiana like a rebellious ballerina.

Instead, Jake fixed his gaze on her. Pippa shifted. It seemed he was unintimidated by the silence between them. By the distance or by the closeness. It felt as if he would look at her all day. Sear her image into his brain. Pippa knew when he spoke, he would only be honest. That Jake Chapman didn't know how to make his words pretty, how to dance around the truth. He knew only straightforward honesty.

She was not mistaken, and his words branded her soul.

"I saw only you, Pippa."

CHAPTER
TWENTY-FOUR

aw only you."

Pippa couldn't look away from Jake Chapman, nor could she surmise if he was sincere or just being polite. No one had ever seen only *her*. Pippa swallowed back the hope that rose in her throat, the expectation that maybe, for the first time, someone had seen past everyone into her heart.

But no. He'd been focused on her because of Lily. Sweet Lily.

The elephant calf's trunk curled around her arm. The trunk's strong muscle and coarse hide helped bring Pippa back to reality. She turned away from Jake, from his gray eyes that reminded her of Penn's fur, warm and homey. She tried to squelch the image of his broad chest, tanned forearms, and light-brown hair. His beard, so rugged, defining his square jaw. He emanated strength, vitality, ferocity, and the conundrum of aching tenderness that didn't equate well with the temperament of a fighter.

"Where is she?" Her father's firm command matched the clomping of his feet on the elephant barn floorboards.

"Richard, hold up!" Forrest's voice chased him.

Pippa leapt back from Lily and clutched for Penn. She met Jake's eyes. He stepped into the aisle, his shoulders squared.

Ernie arrived first. The elephant trainer must have been summoned back from his afternoon off. He took in Lily's relaxed state, and surprise registered on his face when he saw her trunk curled around Pippa's waist. She melted into the elephant while Penn reaffirmed her presence by leaning against Pippa's leg.

"What are *you* doing here?" Her father's bark at Jake echoed, and an elephant down the row answered with a snort.

The reality of the circus turmoil shattered any respite she had found in the barn with Jake and the animals. Forrest reached Ripley's side just as Clive poked his head around the corner, chest heaving from chasing after the taller men.

Richard Ripley shoved Jake aside, and Jake jerked his shoulder away. His eyes grew hard. Pippa noticed his jaw clench, and she winced, silently begging him. No more fights. No more thrown fists. Especially not against her father.

"Pippa, come."

Pippa eyed her father's outstretched hand. She reached up absently and fingered her short hair that tickled her chin.

Penn whined.

Ernie's eyes darted between Pippa and her father, and then he held up his hand with a frantic gesture. "Wait, Mr. Ripley, please." Ernie hurried into the stall. "You need to consider this."

"Consider what?" Ripley snapped.

"You need to look at what's in front of you," Ernie insisted, swiping his hand across the top of his balding head, gesturing toward Pippa and Lily.

Richard leveled his black glare on Ernie but stretched his arm in the direction of Jake. "I *do* see what's in front of me! I see my niece outside acting like a wanton hussy. I see my daughter here carousing with that—that *man*. I see a complete lack of control over this place. And you know what? I am to blame. For not doing anything about it. For letting it get this far out of hand."

Ernie stilled.

Forrest leveled a stern eye on Pippa.

Jake stood stiff, controlled. Very, frighteningly controlled.

Richard Ripley crossed his arms, his suit coat, tailored for his trim frame. "You're dismissed." He leveled his declaration on Jake, as though Jake was to blame for the chaos of the day in its entirety.

"No!" Clive argued.

Penn whined and leaned into Pippa. "But, Father—" Then she snapped her mouth shut at Forrest's stern shake of his head.

Ernie intervened. "Sir, please. I trust Jake's ability to care for Lily. And not just her, but the other elephants. I need him."

"You trust that man? He attacked Mr. Landstrom instead of helping cease that nonsensical display of female poppycock. And he was seen at the speakeasy instead of seeing to Lily's birth! What foolish notion do you have that would give you reason to trust the man?" Richard Ripley's mustache bobbed as his words grew more direct, more pointed.

Pippa dared a look in Jake's direction. He was brewing. She could tell.

"That's not the full story. Jake isn't to blame for what happened to Lily. Not entirely. Some folks—someone needed assistance that night." Ernie held up a hand to deter the conversation further.

"Sure. Some spiflicated jack who couldn't walk straight enough to get home." Ripley crossed his arms over his chest. "Or rather, it was probably a whore. Don't shake your head at me! I know my onions. I know what's going on around here, and trust me, I'm not above calling the authorities on our own folks."

Pippa shot a glance at Jake. He remained tight-lipped. He wasn't going to out Patty as the one who'd needed his assistance that night. The night Jake had left the elephant mother in labor to go intervene on behalf of his friend.

"All that's past," Ernie declared, his small eyes sparking. "Do you see this?" He pointed at Pippa. Gestured with a sweep of his hand the length of Lily's trunk as it remained wrapped around Pippa's waist. Bringing attention to the blink of the long-lashed calf's eyes and the fact that Lily's mouth was tipped up. Just a bit. A small elephant smile.

And now they were all looking at her. Pippa cringed. She wasn't keen on being the center of attention, but Ernie was trailing his hand down Lily's trunk and stopping a discreet distance away from where it curled around Pippa in an embrace.

"We need your daughter." Ernie's statement was followed by silence. "Lily responds to her like she doesn't to me or Jake. Pippa's presence here might be the best thing toward ensuring Lily's survival. But she needs Jake here too. He can offer the focused care that I cannot possibly give Lily. I have the other elephants to care for."

"There are other menagerie workers in the employ of Bonaventure Circus." Forrest's observation was accurate.

Clive stepped forward, leaning back and forth on each foot. "Yes, but no one knows them like Jake."

"I need Jake. I especially need your daughter," Ernie said again.

Pippa glanced at Forrest, who was fixated on her father as if waiting for his reaction and direction on how to respond. Clive held his undeterred attention on Richard Ripley's face. Jake leaned back against the doorframe of the stall and crossed his arms over his chest.

Goodness. He winked at her. It was deliberate, not the tic of emotion she'd seen in some eyes before. Pippa swept her vision off him and back to Penn. She needed security and Penn offered such. The dog gave her fingers a reassuring lick, and Pippa patted Penn's head in response. Lily hadn't released her waist. It was as if the elephant calf had attached herself to her new matriarch and had no intention of letting go.

Ripley broke the stunned silence and gave a snort of derision. "My daughter is not an employee of this circus, and she never will be."

Ernie tugged on his tweed vest. The wiry man had nerve. He raised up to face the man who bankrolled his circus. "I think you owe me this."

"I think you push too far. You're an elephant trainer. That's it." Ripley's words had an edge to them.

"Not after today's ruckus," Ernie said. "That *was* your niece parading herself like a peacock with that Farnsworth lady, wasn't it?"

"How dare you!"

"I oversee the elephants, sir, and there is no abuse. But now your own kin are insinuating just that. It's a blot on my service to the circus, and if it's not erased, it could ruin my career."

Richard jabbed a finger in Ernie's direction. His face reddened. "You've nothing to hold over me. I couldn't care less about your *name* as an elephant trainer." He gave a small shout of laughter.

Ernie nodded. "But you care about *your* name. Bonaventure Circus is no small business, and your elephants are at its center. It stands to reason the man in charge of their care and training wields a lot of influence in this world."

A veiled threat. He would smear Ripley's name. *Could* smear his name.

"Father, I would like to stay." She could hear the words that seemed to emanate from Jake's eyes to hers. *What do you want?*

Ripley leveled his gaze on her, and she could feel his eyes drilling into her as if trying to read her intentions, hidden motives, or otherwise clandestine reasons.

"No." His response was emphatic.

"I can make a difference with Lily, and I—"

"I said no." Ripley lifted his hand, his signature gesture for her to be silent.

Pippa clamped her lips shut, her courage to defy wavering in the tradition of obedience.

"You already caused enough trouble." Forrest edged his way forward. It was evident he had found his voice and was determined to speak his mind. "As Pippa's future husband, I must support Mr. Ripley and insist myself that Pippa will not be returning to the circus." He ended his statement with a burning glare at Jake.

The tiny spark of rebellion long smoldering inside of Pippa burst into a small flame, fed by the oxygen of Forrest's authoritative decision.

"Listen to me," Ernie urged the circus owner to bypass his pride. Pippa whipped her head to the right to look at Ernie, who had unknowingly interrupted the argument balancing on the edge of her lips. "We need your daughter," he insisted. "*You* need your daughter. If she visits Lily, spends time touching her, helping feed her, Lily could respond far quicker and heal faster. Together, *with Jake*, I believe we can save Lily's life."

And a massive financial investment.

Those were the unspoken words hanging over the stall. The ultimate threat to Richard Ripley, and the one he would care the most about.

Ernie hurried to add for extra measure, "Elephant calves are the offspring in a matriarchal system. In the wild, the females will band together to protect the young. In captivity, the young need their mother. If they can't be reunited, then they're subject to human care. There is no organized herd, therefore no replacements *except* the human entity the calf bonds with. In this case, Miss Ripley."

"Ludicrous." Ripley paced the floorboards in front of the stall. It was apparent he was aggravated by the correctness of Ernie's statement and was willing to argue it, even if it made him appear irrational. "Find someone else."

"There is no one else." Jake turned to Pippa. She caught her breath. For a brief second, it was only them. He had entered this fight, not for Lily but for Pippa. She could see it. In his eyes, in his posture, in the way the muscle in his jaw twitched with determination.

Jake met her gaze and smiled, even as he addressed Forrest and her father. "Pippa has a gift."

She returned the smile, drawing even more confidence from the contagiousness of his.

"What gift?" Ripley spat.

"She cares." Another voice joined in. This one caused them all to shift their attention downward. Clive stared up at them with firm challenge etched on his face. "Your daughter has always loved this place, its people, and its animals."

Ripley's lips tightened, the color draining from his face. Clive seemed to tower over her father, even though his shorter frame wouldn't have risen above Ripley's head were Clive to stand on a chair.

"Let your daughter be who she was meant to be. This place is in her blood. I know it. You know it. Even Lily can sense it."

Forrest shot Pippa a look. Heat crept up her neck. No one, ever, had the courage to call her father out about her birth.

Ripley stalked a few steps from the stall, flipped his suit tails back, and rested his hands on his hips. "You cannot hold my daughter responsible for the life of that elephant. And I don't want her any-where near *that man*." He pointed at Jake.

"No one was implying it was Pippa's responsibility to keep Lily from dying. It is her gift to nurture. Let her use that ability in hopes of success." Clive stepped toward Mr. Ripley. "Your niece took part in a crusade against the circus and inflicted God knows what further harm to our existence. Lily's survival hinges on qual-ity care, and the circus hinges on Lily's survival."

Ripley opened his mouth to reply, but this time, this moment, Pippa found her voice.

"I am staying, Father."

Her pointed sentence shushed all the men into silence. She dared to look at Forrest, whose mouth was slightly ajar. Jake, a spark lit in his eyes. Clive gave her a silent nod, and Ernie crossed his arms. She finally looked at her father.

His expression was discomforting, with his narrowed eyes and the way he studied her. Assessing, as if trying to read her thoughts.

"Lily needs me," Pippa added and followed up her declaration with a nervous, shuddering intake of breath. "I-I have to help."

"Richard," Forrest started in protest.

Ripley held up a hand, then ran it across his nose and mouth, agitated.

"You've no good reason to deny your daughter this—or yourself. You stand to benefit most of all." Clive tipped his head and stared up at his employer. "*Is* there any other legitimacy that would argue against Pippa's presence here?"

It was a challenge. And it was evident that Richard Ripley recognized the truth of Clive's wisdom. Recognized and hated it all at the same time. Pippa watched him eye Clive, who continued to look at Ripley with a stare that could only be interpreted as convicting by anyone who witnessed it. God love dear Clive. He was fighting for her too.

"Very well." But the words were ground out between clenched teeth, and her father's dark glare did little to give Pippa reason to celebrate.

CHAPTER
TWENTY-FIVE

They hadn't touched anything. Outside of the skeleton that had careened forward, clawing its way into the light after years of being buried behind the closet wall. Hank had gone one way, Chandler the other. The authorities gave her water, a blanket around her shoulders, and asked her a million questions. The ensuing chaos brought with it curious onlookers. People coming to see the train depot they'd ignored before. The presence of multiple police cars, an ambulance, the cop cordoning off the depot with yellow crime scene tape. All of it was a horror movie gone bad. Chandler searched for Hank among the growing throng of authorities, EMTs, and gawkers. His bulky form would be hard to miss, his strong features and confident pose. But he was nowhere to be seen.

A car pulled up behind a squad car. The front door opened, and Lottie jumped out. Concern was etched on her face as she zoomed in on Chandler and hurried toward her.

"Honey! I just heard! Oh my gosh!" Lottie grabbed Chandler's hands. Chandler carefully withdrew them. It wasn't that she didn't like Lottie—she did—but the woman's fascination with the haunted gave Chandler the willies, if she was being honest.

It wasn't surprising that Lottie would be here. She would want to lend her insights, her expertise, so to speak.

Lottie didn't seem offended by Chandler's withdrawal. Instead, she gave Chandler a light pat on the shoulder as she stood beside the stool the officers had provided Chandler when her shaking legs had forced her to ask to sit down.

"You must be completely terrified." Lottie's observation was nailing the truth, and Chandler nodded. She sniffed and shot a fast look at the depot. The yellow tape around it had so many implications. From death, to murder, to the sudden ceasing of work on the depot project itself.

Chandler squeezed her eyes shut to clear her vision.

"You need to get home and get your feet up."

God bless Lottie. Suddenly, Chandler liked her more. Her emotions were waffling, which wasn't unusual in heavy moments of stress.

Lottie hollered in small-town fashion at a nearby officer. "Warren, can I take Ms. Faulk back to her place?"

The officer looked up from his phone and walked in their direction. He shook his head. "I don't know if she's cleared yet. They may want her down at the station for questioning."

How many more questions could she answer? Chandler grimaced and bit the inside of her lip. "I really—really need to go home. I don't feel good."

Warren's eyebrow rose. "I'll get an EMT."

"No." Chandler almost snapped and regretted the tone of her voice. "Sorry, I just . . . I have a chronic condition, and until I lie down and get some rest . . ." She let her words hang.

Lottie inserted herself into the conversation, her bracelets jangling as she pointed to a man in khakis and a polo shirt. "Go ask your boss, Warren. Detective Janson must have sympathy for Ms. Faulk here. Unless she's going to be hospitalized, it's obvious she needs to lie down."

"There's the ambulance—" Warren started.

"At home." Lottie pinched her lips together.

Warren cleared his throat, gave a short nod, and headed toward Detective Janson. Within minutes, Chandler noted that Detective Janson nodded, glanced in her direction, said something to Warren, and then strode toward the depot and ducked under the tape.

Warren returned and released Chandler to Lottie's care. "You'll probably be called in at some point," he added.

"I don't know anything more than what I told you all earlier," Chandler insisted.

"Just be available," Warren prompted.

Lottie intervened with a smile. "Of course she will. She's got nothing to hide."

Five minutes later, Chandler was sinking deeper into the soft cushion of Lottie's car, the bucket seat wrapping up and around her hips. She closed her eyes and willed herself to bring Peter's face into focus. A semblance of normalcy in the riotous circumstances of the day.

As the car approached a red light, Lottie applied the brake gently. Her hands gripped the steering wheel at ten and two as she stared ahead at the strip of quaint businesses that bordered the river—a row of brick buildings that used to be machine sheds for the circus in bygone days.

Chandler wasn't comfortable with Lottie's profession. Oh, not the real-estate business, but her connection with the other world. Still, it nagged at her. The footsteps outside the closet. The moaning. The fact that it ended as quickly as it'd begun, and then the discovery . . .

"Did you—*sense* anything at the depot just now?" Chandler asked the question before she chickened out. She wasn't summoning a tarot card reading, and she certainly wasn't trying to have Lottie read the energies around her for some sort of communication with a dead loved one, but she couldn't help but be curious. There were things—moments in life—that simply couldn't be explained. Chandler's grandmother would have claimed it was demonic.

Her pastor might have touted spiritual warfare. She wasn't sure what Nel would think—the thought of her wheelchair-bound friend made Chandler wish Nel were with her now. Grounding her. Advising her.

The light turned green.

"Do you *want* to know?" Lottie responded softly. She steered the car around a corner and headed east toward Chandler's cottage. Lottie managed a sideways glance at Chandler, her blue eyes connecting for an instant before returning to the road. "I try not to impose where my gifts aren't welcome. I can respect a person's skepticism—even their beliefs."

"I believe in God, in His Scripture. But I am curious." Chandler tried to hide her wince of regret. She probably shouldn't ask. Like playing with fire, the spirit world. Whether a real dead person, a demon, an energy, none of it sounded particularly comforting.

Lottie cleared her throat. "I understand that. To answer your question, I *did* sense some energies at the depot just now. But I couldn't focus. I couldn't get a read on who it might be. Or what."

"You don't believe it was a ghost trying to make contact?" Chandler inquired.

Lottie shrugged, and her shoulders nudged her long earrings. "I don't necessarily believe every energy is a person who's passed. Sometimes it's just energy itself. Positive or negative. In a place where violence has been committed, very often it is a troubling energy and difficult to pinpoint."

"But you *do* believe in ghosts?"

Lottie nodded. "Oh yes. I do. In fact, the other night when we heard Patty Luchent scream, even *I* almost peed my pants."

Chandler laughed.

Lottie joined her, then continued, "Conversing with a spirit isn't like having a conversation like we're having. Typically, if they make contact, then I must acknowledge them before they will communicate. When they do, it's typically images or concepts brought to mind, not words of dialogue."

"Do you believe it's actually the person's spirit who's passed on or . . . well, some believe it's part of the spiritual world but not actually the person."

"A *demon*?" Lottie asked outright.

Chandler squirmed. The word seemed so blunt, almost as outlandish as *ghost*.

"I suppose?" Lottie shrugged. "I didn't grow up in a Christian home. But I do believe there's a whole spiritual realm beyond explanation." She gave Chandler a quick glance. "Whether you believe it's a demon or a ghost, it's nothing to take lightly. We can agree on that, right?"

Chandler nodded. Yes. They could.

"What do you know about Linda Pike?" Chandler ventured. Hank's declaration before the police arrived at the depot had Chandler's mind reeling. At first she'd assumed the skeleton was Patty Luchent. After all, it was Patty who supposedly haunted the depot and the costume house. Yet Patty's body had been discovered decades before, in the twenties. Hank's supposition made horrible sense.

Lottie nodded and waved at someone strolling on the sidewalk as the car breezed by. "I grew up with Linda, but she was a loner. She didn't have many friends. Her brother, Denny, was older than us, and Linda adored him."

Chandler didn't respond, only looked out the car window at the passing trees and houses. Her hand rested limp in her lap, though every few minutes it jerked involuntarily. A sign of extreme stress. Chandler forced herself to draw in deep breaths. Oxygen. Oxygen was good.

"Why do you ask about Linda?" Lottie asked, halting at a stop sign and looking both ways before proceeding.

Chandler hesitated, then opted for honesty. "Hank made a comment about her. That maybe it was Linda's skeleton we found today."

Lottie's expression shifted, her curiosity piqued. "That could be. I hope it's so."

"You do?"

"For the Pikes' sake. How many years has it been? Forty? I mean, to not know what happened to your daughter, your sister . . . I just can't fathom the trauma. I really can't. All of them, even Linda, must be so unsettled."

Chandler digested Lottie's words. The empathy in them was genuine and deep. Whether she agreed with Lottie's abilities or not, there was no denying that the woman cared strongly for the human spirit.

"I suppose Linda's disappearance rocked Bluff River," Chandler concluded. This being a small town, everyone must've been one person removed from Linda. A child disappearing . . .

"Oh, it did." Lottie's face fell as she turned onto Chandler's street. Large oaks lined both sides, the houses separated by narrow yards. "That type of thing doesn't happen in Bluff River. Well, not since the 1920s when all that talk of the circus train killer—the Watchman—was rampant. But that was almost fifty years before Linda. I think . . . well, no one wants violence to be Bluff River's claim to fame." Lottie paused and gave a sigh. "There's always something a bit creepy about the circus, don't you think?"

"But Linda and the circus aren't related," Chandler observed as she caught sight of her cottage. Peter. Margie would be inside too. A cup of coffee, a blanket, maybe a video chat with Nel to soothe her nerves . . .

"Oh, they were related." Lottie's contradiction gripped Chandler's attention.

"They were?"

"Mm-hmm. The Pikes are circus folk. Roots go deep, deep, deep in the circus."

"How so?" Chandler's pulse increased. Denny was a motorcycle guy. Hank had never insinuated any connection to the circus, and yet . . .

Lottie side-eyed her. "You don't know, do you?"

228

"Know what?" A feeling of dread sent a shiver down Chandler's spine.

"The Watchman. The man who was executed for the string of murders back in the twenties? He was Denny's grandfather."

"What?" Chandler sat up, rigid, so fast the seat belt locked.

Lottie's regretful smile filled the car, along with her silent confirmation. It was in her eyes. Finally she smoothed her short blond hair and rubbed the corner of her eye as if to wipe away an invisible tear. "The Pikes have always claimed he wasn't the real killer. Maybe he wasn't. But Linda was—she was fascinated by it all. That's why we all thought she was a bit off, you know? Who studies serial killers and circuses?"

Yes. Who indeed? The image of Hank's deep-set green eyes, his rosary tattoo, and his limited information assaulted Chandler's intuition. Hank was Denny's nephew, which would make Denny's grandfather a distant uncle to Hank. None of it seemed to be enough motivation to seek out the Watchman a hundred years later. Not unless it would somehow explain what happened to Linda. But how did a man long dead slay his granddaughter and then hide her in a wall? If it was her . . .

"Do you believe a ghost can return to—" Chandler broke off her sentence. The question was ridiculous on multiple levels.

Lottie seemed to read her mind, giving Chandler another sideways glance as she pulled into the rental cottage's short drive and parked the car. "Can a spirit return to protect their secrets? Yes. They will certainly try."

"But they can't . . . kill?" Chandler bit her bottom lip. It was stupid, her line of questioning, yet she couldn't help herself.

Lottie seemed to skirt around the question as she turned off the engine. "This is why I wish the dead really did speak clearly and conversationally, like the Ghost of Christmas Past did." She sighed again. "Maybe we could help appease them before they become violent. Negative energies are . . . well, they require more bravery to face than most of us possess."

Chandler reveled in the warmth of Peter's body, his lanky form curled up into a ball of boyish sweetness and tucked against her side. His hair was damp from sleep-sweat, curling at his temples. He snuggled under the wine-colored chenille blanket that also covered her lap. Chandler hugged the arm of the overstuffed sofa, her right hand clutching her coffee mug like a lifeline. Margie leaned over the coffee table and set a plate of sugar cookies on the glossy wood top.

"Freshly baked." She kissed the back of Peter's head. Chandler caught a whiff of Margie's perfume, mixed with the smell of warm cookies.

"I can't eat sugar," Chandler whispered, apologetic.

Margie waved off her comment. "I made them with a natural sweetener. And they're gluten-free."

"And they taste good?" Chandler asked with a smile.

Margie returned it with a bright one of her own. "Well, *I* would say 'heck no,' but when your diet consists of meat and vegetables and the minimal amount of carbs you consume, I'm gonna say they're probably the best dessert you'll have all year." She snatched one off the plate and handed it to Chandler, who took it and bit off a section. The warmth and sweetness met her mouth. A slightly different sweet than real sugar, but Margie was right.

"Wow." Chandler's celebration of taste was muffled by the mouthful of deliciousness.

"I always wanted to own a bakery." Margie squeezed Chandler's shoulder. "But you know—men. They mess up a woman's dreams."

Margie laughed, while Chandler tried to hide the pang inside of her. Sure, men could be piggish, but then women could be foolish too. Settle for less than they were worth. It's what she had done. Allowed herself to feel valued, to be seen by the boys who merely toyed with her affections until they tired of her. None of them really cared about her, her life goals, who she was deep inside. But Chandler remembered a few of them. They weren't horrible people either. They were just . . . stupid. Like she had been.

Chandler looked down at Peter, his lashes against ruddy cheeks. She brushed his hair back from his forehead with her free hand. How could she raise him to be more than a fool? To be honorable, to respect a woman's individuality while cherishing her femininity? How did a single mom teach her son to be a true man? She thought of her father. She'd not had a brother, but her memories of her father were that he was doting, and loving, and wanted to spend time with her—at least when she was a child and before she'd screwed up her life.

Margie had left the room. The TV was playing a sitcom, but Chandler wasn't interested. She was hurting, and hurting meant she dived into the darkness that was so hard to find her way out of. Everything about today had sent her spiraling. She dialed Nel's number, avoiding video chat so she didn't wake Peter.

"*Hola, chica!*" Nel's voice was chipper, stable, comforting.

"Hey." Chandler wasted no time in filling Nel in on the day. Nel's rapt attention communicated through silence broke only when Chandler ended the story with, "Now I'm here, trying to be calm, and Peter's asleep on my lap."

"You need to leave Bluff River. You need to go home and be done with this business." Nel's advice was based on protective emotion. When that came to the fore in Nel, it was the rare times that Chandler wasn't certain she could trust Nel's judgment. Nel wanted to protect, and if she sensed danger, logic took a backseat to flight.

"I can't leave." Chandler could almost see Nel's stern tilt of her head and the stormy brown eyes. "I can't. Jackson will come and take my place, and for sure Uncle Neal won't give me another big project like this in the future. It's exactly the opportunity Jackson is just waiting to snatch up."

"Chandler . . ." Nel's voice sounded patronizingly patient.

"Let's be real. Is this what you want in life? You want to travel like this all through Peter's childhood? To work your behind off?"

"What choice do I have?" Chandler was taken aback by Nel's going straight for the jugular and not mincing her words. "I went to school for this. I've always intended to be in this very position, and people didn't think I could do it, Nel. I can. I will. I'm not a quitter."

"But what do you really want out of life?"

Nel's question pierced Chandler's turmoil. Chandler took a sip of her coffee to calm her nerves. Or at least to try.

"I want—I want people to believe in me. I want them to believe that I am not a failure. I don't want them to blame Peter for my inability to succeed."

"No one would do that, Chandler."

Nel couldn't understand.

"My parents would."

"Would they?" Nel countered.

"Yes!" Chandler gripped the phone tighter and glanced at Peter to make sure her raised voice hadn't stirred him.

"How do you know that?"

"Because. Because I'm here in Wisconsin, raising a seven-year-old boy by myself. If they cared, they wouldn't keep saying they'd take Peter and raise him, they would offer to help me. I don't want them to take Peter. He's mine. *My* kid, not theirs. And just because I've chosen to raise him myself . . . well, they didn't need to abandon me. What happened to helping? They just want to take control and fix my mistakes."

"Maybe they don't mean it that way." Nel sounded tentative and a bit cautious about contradicting Chandler. She obviously heard the vehemence in Chandler's voice.

"What are you talking about?" Chandler wasn't sure she could handle this conversation. Not now. Not after today.

"It's like me and my chair. A lot of people just avoid me. It feels like they do it because I'm not *normal* or they can't relate to me, so why try? But sometimes they avoid me because they just don't know what to say. They're afraid to just be honest and ask me questions. Why are you in a chair? What's spina bifida? I don't mind if they're asking genuinely, but people just—they just don't feel comfortable. I can either interpret it as they don't care, or I can choose to interpret it as though they're afraid and fumbling. And I can have grace for that."

"So, you believe my parents are *fumbling*?" Chandler scowled at the TV.

Nel's voice filled her ear. "I'm just not sure any of you really came together after you got pregnant with Peter. You all just drew your own conclusions. Sometimes . . . well, I know your parents—they're good people, Chandler. I think sometimes they don't want to take control so much as they just want to help. And they're bumbling their way through it."

"I will not give them custody of Peter. I will not."

"No one asked you to—not even your parents. That's *your* fear." Nel sounded timid. She'd overstepped and could sense it. Still, Chandler knew that Nel didn't know why. She didn't know she'd hit a sore spot. An infected, oozing sore spot of absolute terror. Terror that was entirely different from that of stumbling into a dead body. It was the terror of losing. Of losing her health, and then losing her son, and then maybe . . . losing altogether, everything. If she asked for help, or took help, then not only would she be recognized but she'd also be thought of as a fraud. That was worse than staying hidden in the shadows, flying just under everyone's radar, and maintaining a level of success that kept people from asking too many questions.

Maybe she was shutting people out, even while she ached to be seen.

It was a wicked oxymoron. But wasn't that what life was?

CHAPTER
TWENTY-SIX

handler woke with renewed energy, and a little boy nestled into the crook of her back. She rolled over and dislodged Peter's arm from her waist. Studying his face, his rounded cheeks that would one day chisel out into a man's features, she wondered when the right time was to insist he sleep in his own room. What was healthy for a young boy? The safety and bond of his mother or the courage and boldness of his own room? It was probably way past time, but for now Chandler dismissed the thought. It was disconcerting enough to wake to the gray skies outside her window and the autumn rain that pelted against the glass panes. Ominous, and it didn't bode well for a good day.

There would be the update call with Jackson and Uncle Neal, when she would inform them the project had been stalled, with the police holding the depot hostage as a crime scene. She could work in her office at the costume house or maybe transfer her investment of time into that small building and what they could potentially do with it instead. But it was residential-sized, nothing that would yield much profit for Uncle Neal. Not to mention, it was haunted by a box-throwing spirit—if Lottie was to be believed.

Chandler felt someone looking at her and transferred her attention from the window to taking in the large brown eyes of her son.

"Momma!" He was always so wide awake the moment he opened his eyes. Even if they were still heavy with sleep and had the leftovers in the corners the Sandman had disposed of before taking his leave.

"Morning, Peter Pan." She tweaked his nose and hopped out of bed, fully clothed in her joggers, sports bra, and T-shirt.

Peter stretched his lanky arms and legs, his basketball shorts riding up and revealing the white skin and a dark tan line. He'd not inherited his naturally olive skin from her genes. Chandler pushed away the thought. She had accepted seven years ago that her transgressions meant she would never know Peter's father unless she asked for paternity tests. There were only two real possibilities. Maybe someday—if Peter asked. But she'd lost track of both. The college football player and the other guy who was destined for medical school. Truth be told, regardless of the athletic and intelligence prowess, Chandler knew her parents would never have truly approved of either guy anyway. Neither man had cared much about faith or character or even the welfare of others. Well, the future doctor did to a degree, but Chandler even then had realized his motives were based in the financial figure associated with a surgeon's salary more than the human soul that would be held at the tips of his fingers. Chandler had her strong suspicions, though, and that was why it knifed her every time Peter picked up a football.

It didn't matter. He was hers. All hers.

"Forever and always." Chandler dropped onto the edge of the bed, making it bounce and causing Peter to flop. He laughed.

"Do it again, Momma."

She obliged.

He laughed.

Chandler launched herself over her son and dug her fingers into his rib cage while blowing zoobers into his neck. The peals of laughter and shrieks drowned out her own personal angst for the moment, as well as the terrifying images of the skeleton and killer's lair that had taunted her the entire sleepless night.

"Okay, okay, Dude-face," she said and pulled back. Peter held his belly and made exaggerated gasping noises as he caught his breath. Delight twinkled in his eyes, and he gave her a toothless grin, his top two teeth missing.

"Tongue-tooter!" he shouted. They each made a game of coming up with silly names to inspire the other to laugh.

Chandler cast him a mock motherly glare. "Flame-fodder!" she countered.

"Bird-butt!" he yelled.

"Ooooooooookay, that's enough." Chandler urged the boy up and shooed him off to the bathroom.

She slipped her arms into a boyfriend-style cardigan and jogged down the stairs to the kitchen. She rounded the corner and—

"God have mercy!" Chandler yelped as she slipped to a halt, her bare feet sticking to the wood floor.

"You and Peter sure are loud in the morning."

Hank Titus sat at her table. Coffee was brewing. Leaning forward, elbows on the table, he glanced up at her. A newspaper was spread open before him, all of it looking as though he lived here and this was their morning ritual.

Chandler was aware that her mouth hung open and her eyes were bulging in stupefied bewilderment. "What? How?" She looked at the back door. It was locked and bolted shut, just as it had been when she'd gone to bed last night. "Did you break in?" Her voice rose an octave. She might kill him. Or worse. She wasn't sure.

"No." Hank rested his scruff-covered chin in his hand and ignored her as his eyes skimmed the paper. He held up his other hand, a key dangling from a ring looped over his index finger. "My uncle owns the place."

Incredulous, Chandler shot a glance up the stairs to make sure Peter wasn't coming down yet, and then she stalked over to the table. "So, you just let yourself in? How long have you been here?"

Hank dropped his hand with the key and turned the page of the paper. "Long enough to get through the sports section."

Chandler surged forward and snatched the paper out from

under him, sending the black-and-white pages floating to the floor. "How dare you!"

Tongue in cheek, Hank eyed her with not much expression on his face. Then he picked up the key and chucked it at her. "Here. Have it. I won't *break in* again." He stood, the chair scraping on the floor as he pushed it back.

Chandler bent and retrieved the key from the floor where it'd fallen. "Good." She curled her lip at him.

A laugh pealed behind her, and Margie entered the kitchen, her arms full with a box of doughnuts and a jug of milk. "Go easy on him!" She deposited the doughnuts onto the table. "He's just teasing. When I got here a few minutes ago, he was outside on his bike. I let him in."

Hank went to the coffeepot and pulled it out, pouring the fresh brew into the empty mug that sat waiting.

Chandler stared at his broad back that tapered in at the waist, and then she turned to Margie. "Oh." Her paltry acknowledgment was accompanied by a *clank* as she dropped Hank's key on the table. He'd goaded her. She'd succumbed.

Margie broke the seal on the box of pastries. "They're from the gas station, but boy are these things good!" She whipped one out and took a bite, her finger stuck through the hole in the middle of the sugar-glazed doughnut.

Chandler reached for one, and Margie batted her hand away with a stern but caring glare. "No. Not for you. You don't need this poison in your body. The doughnuts are for me and Peter— and, well, Hank."

"Do you always spoil your kids?" Chandler asked.

Hank shot her a quick look she couldn't interpret.

Margie chewed and nodded, her eyes widening. "Always." She mumbled around the mouthful, "Now. You survived the night. Both of you. Any word from the police on what happened yesterday?"

"I just woke up." Chandler now regretted not checking her

phone. Although it wasn't as if the police would be calling her with regular updates.

"No word," Hank growled. He had stuffed an entire doughnut in his mouth.

Gross.

Chandler pulled out a kitchen table chair and sat down. Thumping from upstairs told her Peter was already running paces with his Nitro Steel persona, chasing down imaginary bad guys like Rustman.

"Do they think it's Linda Pike?" Margie also pulled out a chair and plopped herself down.

"They'll have to do a DNA analysis." Chandler spoke authoritatively. She'd seen enough *Criminal Minds* to know that.

"It's her." Hank sniffed and ran his hand over his mouth, dislodging a crumb of sugar glaze.

Chandler jerked her head up to stare at him.

Margie paled. "It is?"

Hank nodded. He pushed off the table and stood, speaking as he did so. "There was a necklace hanging on the wall, along with some of the others. Denny ID'd it as Linda's."

"So the Watchman killed her?" Margie looked breathless, almost in awe.

Hank shook his head. "They think maybe he kept his souvenirs there, but whoever killed Linda was very much alive. And"—he glanced at Chandler—"whoever it was also knew more about the Watchman than anyone else in Bluff River. They knew where he hid his mementos."

"Someone quite devious and quite alive in 1983," Margie mumbled. Her body gave an inadvertent shiver. "Why would someone want to kill Linda? Because she was too close to the Watchman's things? She was always so intent on proving it wasn't their grandfather who killed all those women on the circus train route."

Hank shrugged. "Maybe. But then why would someone want to protect the truth about a serial killer long after he's dead?"

Chandler cleared her throat and eyed the tempting doughnuts. "It's really creepy that Linda was hidden in that boarded-up wall in the closet. How come no one ever found that place before?"

"So many questions," Margie breathed.

Hank moved to the coffeemaker and refilled his mug. The pot clattered as he slid it back onto its heating pad. Chandler almost asked him to pour her a cup, then frowned as a question raced through her mind.

"So, why *were* you outside my house this morning when Margie got here?"

Hank shot her a glance over his shoulder. He poured cream into his coffee. Chandler hadn't pegged him for froufrou in his joe, but there he was, stirring it like a gentleman in a men's-only club.

"Someone was outside last night."

"What?" Chandler stiffened. "Outside where?"

"Here." Hank took a slurp from the coffee, noisy and rattling as he sucked the liquid in through his lips. He tipped his chin up toward the window that overlooked the backyard. "They were hanging out there. Underneath the window on the west side."

Chandler froze. Her breath caught. It was the second bedroom window. The window to the room Peter would have been sleeping in had she not continued the habit of letting him curl up next to her. The habit she told no one about.

Hank turned. His green eyes slammed into hers. "I couldn't sleep. I was out for a run and came by just to check on the place. That's when I saw the guy. Or woman. Who knows?" He shrugged.

Chandler digested that bit of information. The idea of him just outside her cottage all night was either disconcerting or comforting. She wasn't sure which. She opened her mouth to speak, but Hank stopped her with a look.

"No, I didn't call the cops. They ran off. They didn't do anything. There wasn't anything to call the cops for."

Margie *tsk*ed and shook her head. "What *is* Bluff River coming to? I've never known this place to be anything but safe. Well, at least in the past twenty-or-so years. Why would anyone be snooping outside Peter's bedroom?"

Chandler exchanged glances with the worried nanny. She shivered. *Peter's bedroom*. She was thankful she hadn't tried to acclimate him to his own room. And, proper or not, there was no way she was going to now.

"I'm still going to call the cops, because—" Chandler was interrupted by the sound of Peter bounding down the steps. He ran into the kitchen, and a big grin split his face.

"Hey! It's *you*!"

Chandler knew Peter probably didn't remember Hank's name, even though they'd tossed a football back and forth.

"Yeah. It's me." Hank's face transformed as he returned Peter's smile. He lifted his mug. "Want some coffee, kid?"

Peter shot Chandler an exuberant look, then settled it on Hank. "Sure!"

"Wait a sec—" Chandler started, but Hank cut in before she could finish.

"It's just coffee, Chandler, not a beer."

"He's *my* son." Chandler felt every nerve bristle as Hank ignored her authority and poured Peter a cup of coffee. He even went so far as to open the freezer and pop some ice cubes out of the tray.

"Yeah, he's your son." Hank handed Peter the coffee. "But you drink coffee. Don't be duplicitous."

Margie's eyes widened, and a humorous smile touched her mouth. She rolled her lips tight so as not to laugh and waggled her brows at Chandler.

Chandler frowned. "I'm not duplicitous." She jumped from her chair and marched over to Hank, jerking his now-empty mug from his hand and slamming it on the counter.

Peter's eyes widened, even as he gulped at the cool coffee as though she'd rip it from his hands any second like she did with Hank.

Call it anxiety from the thought of someone creeping around

outside her house, or unsettled energy from yesterday's tussle with Linda Pike's skeleton, or maybe it was just outright fear. But, whatever the reason, Hank's independent action of usurping her role as parent was the last straw to her staying calm.

Hank towered over her, his frame nearly twice her size. His eyes narrowed. "We need to talk."

"I'll say," she hissed.

"Now," Hank added.

"Absolutely!" Chandler made no bones about it.

Hank stalked over to the door, wrapped his hand around the knob, and yanked it open.

Chandler gave Margie and Peter a stern look, intending to tell them to stay behind, but Margie's expression stopped her.

"Lovers' spat?" Margie teased. She waggled her eyebrows. "I'd have a lovers' spat with him, if I could."

Exasperated, a growl ripped from Chandler's throat as she started after Hank. She heard Margie behind her, "Do you need a refill on that coffee already, buddy?"

He leaned against his Harley—or maybe it was Denny's, or maybe they both owned them. Like uncle, like nephew. His arms were folded across his chest, and Chandler could see the corded muscles in his forearms, the veins that traced a maze along his inner arm and wrist, and the beaded bracelet he wore.

She stepped closer to him, her feet bare on the leaf-covered grass. The dew cooled the bottoms of her toes and reminded her it was fall, no longer summer, and the frost on the tips of the grass told her how foolish her emotional response had been.

Chandler hauled in an audible breath meant to calm herself. Control herself. Hank wasn't a threat—not really. He was just intimidating, presumptuous, and fell just short of understanding human boundaries. Like he'd never quite had any taught to him as a child.

She posed like a mirror image of him, only Chandler wrapped her arms around herself to ward off the morning chill.

"I suppose I should say thank you. If there was someone outside my house last night . . ."

Hank grunted. His green eyes glimmered and leveled on her. Truth be told, she'd rather have Hank outside standing guard all night than have to deal with an intruder. The very idea made her shiver.

"Lottie told me about your relation to the Watchman—Denny's relation. I had no idea he was Denny's grandfather." Chandler swallowed her nervousness as she called him out. She deserved honesty from Hank. Now more than ever. But there was that niggling in the back of her mind that poked at her to remember she needed to be sensitive too. This was a family with a sordid past, a traumatic disappearance, and now, more than likely, the confirmation of a violent murder.

Hank eyed her. His upper lip twitched.

Chandler shifted her feet. Why was she the one trying to eat humble pie? Sure, in a way, his family was the victim here, but he was a boorish—who said *boorish* anymore? Well, he was. A boorish oaf.

"You should have just told me. Told me you wanted to finish what Linda had started. That you wanted to find the truth once and for all as to whether their grandfather was actually the Watchman. It must be awful to be considered related to a serial killer."

"I'm not related," Hank grumbled out.

"But—Lottie said—"

"I was a foster kid."

Hank's admission stilled Chandler. And now she felt like even more of a heel. She stepped off the grass onto the sidewalk, hoping it was warmer on her feet.

"Uncle Denny isn't my uncle—not really. He took me in when I was sixteen."

Chandler waited, feeling her face soften.

Hank cleared his throat and looked down the street before half sitting on the Harley and crossing his feet at the ankles. He looked so casual, so undisturbed, but there was a storm brewing in his eyes. A hurricane of buried feelings.

"My mom was an addict. My dad wasn't in the picture. I went into foster care when I was eleven, and"—Hank's chuckle sounded cynical as it rumbled in his chest—"I wasn't the model foster kid."

Chandler met his smile hesitantly.

"Anyway, Denny took me in after I landed in juvie for a few months."

"Juvenile detention? What for?" Chandler asked, then bit her tongue.

Hank didn't seem to mind. A glimmer of humor twinkled in his eye, as if he enjoyed toying with her a bit and shocking her with his story. "Petty theft, vandalism, and I had marijuana on me."

"Small stuff." Chandler joked in order to cope with and to comprehend a life so different from her own. She could recall going to youth group on Wednesday nights at church, hanging out at the mall with her mom and friends on the weekends, her worst trouble breaking up with her boyfriend as a junior in high school and thinking the world had ended. Well, her worst trouble before college and Peter.

A thin smile stretched Hank's face and creased his cheeks. "It was my first jump into crime."

Chandler nodded, listening.

Hank shrugged. "I was never a good kid, Chandler. Denny tried to reform me, but it took him years. Took me a few years too. Behind bars. A preacher and an inmate Bible study got me on the straight and narrow, I guess."

Great. She had a Christian felon on her front lawn. What did that mean? Could he even vote now? Was he on some sort of blacklist with the authorities?

Chandler coughed to cover her frayed emotions. "So, why are you here now?"

Skip ahead—she didn't need the details. She didn't *want* the details. She just wanted him away from her house. She couldn't trust him. Didn't trust herself as she stood before him. Chandler had no intention of being like one of those airheaded women on that cable show where they all fell in love with men in prison and then were stunned when their lives unraveled after the men got out.

"I know what it's like to have people draw conclusions about you." His eyes deepened with knowing as he read Chandler's face. "I know what it's like when their conclusions are wrong."

There was a long, expectant pause.

A maple leaf detached from the tree limb above them and began its gentle descent to its wintery grave on the yard.

"Denny's grandfather didn't kill all those women. The Pikes don't deserve to have the reputation of a killer connected with their family. Linda felt that. Denny has tried to ignore it. I won't let them live with it—or die with it—hanging over their heads anymore."

"But who really cares?" Chandler argued weakly. "It was a century ago."

"You really want to stand there and tell me people forget the wrongs done them even after the calendar changes?"

No. She didn't.

The images of her parents' disappointment etched in every nuance of their bodies flashed before Chandler's eyes. The resignation in Uncle Neal's voice as he reluctantly agreed to give her the legal leave of absence for maternity purposes, even if she was only an intern at the time. But worst of all, her own disappointment. In herself.

"So you're here to set things right?" Chandler asked.

Hank nodded. "Or at least find the truth. If we don't like the truth, then—that's life. But at least we'll know for certain. It won't be the result of a prejudiced witch hunt."

"And Linda?" Chandler ventured.

Hank's expression remained the same. "I owe it to Denny to

find out what happened to her. He saved me. It's the least I can do to return the favor."

"But you can't save Linda or make right any injustice done to Denny's grandfather, not if he wasn't really the circus killer."

"Prob'ly not." Hank pushed off his Harley and straddled it, firing up the engine. The bike roared to life. "But the effort goes a long way." He speared her with a green-eyed stare. "Maybe I can even save you while I'm at it."

"I don't need saving." She didn't. She didn't even know why Hank would say something like that.

But for a moment, the biker's expression softened and everything about his countenance oozed understanding. Empathy.

Chandler shifted on her toes, less because of the cold ground and more because he made her nervous.

"We all need saving." He smiled just a bit. Just enough to make the creases at his eyes deepen. "It's the idea that we don't that makes us fools."

CHAPTER
TWENTY-SEVEN

PIPPA

Candlelight flickered and cast broad-fingered shadows on the wall of the library. Dark wood molding framed the walls, and all of them housed floor-to-ceiling bookshelves laden with volumes rarely read. Three wing-back chairs covered in ruby velvet made a welcoming circle around a table inlaid with various shades of wood patterned with intricate precision. The artistry was lost to Pippa as she rested a rounded keepsake box on the table. She moved the candle closer and wished she had the courage to just snap on the electric lights. But if her father saw them glowing down the hallway, he would investigate, and she really didn't want to answer any questions tonight.

A week. A whole week of afternoon visits to the circus. Soothing Lily, watching Ernie put salve on her cuts, and trying to breathe whenever Jake neared her. There was something about the sideways glances he gave her and their short conversations as she stroked the four-foot-tall baby. She was becoming familiar with him. His occasional mentions of his sister reinforced that Bridgette was never far from her brother's memory. It was as endearing as it was worrisome. If Bridgette was close to mind, then so was her killer. Jake had no intention of forgetting his sole purpose for being a part of the circus. To find him—the man with the hood—who had taken Bridgette's life. A few times, Pippa had caught Jake with the unfolded and worn drawing, staring deep into the Watchman's coal-sketched hollow eyes. Just this afternoon, she had rounded the corner and bumped into his arm, catching a glimpse herself of the hooded face she'd ached to see beneath.

Jake had jerked away from her, surprised by her presence. Then he had methodically folded the drawing to place it back in his pocket.

"If you find him," Pippa ventured, "what will you do?" She was afraid of the outcome. While part of her longed to guard the Watchman in the way she felt he had guarded her, a large part of her wrestled with fear that Jake's sister's sketch truly did condemn the very person Pippa had communed with via messages for so long. That tentative bond between them was threatened with severing if Jake Chapman was able to enact his vengeance for his sister. And then, if Bridgette's story was true, how was the Watchman even safe to be near? Which meant Pippa's quest to find the zebra toy and continue this game of chasing after him to uncover his identity and his relation to her was foolishness. Dangerous. Naïve.

Jake hadn't answered her. Not verbally. He'd just looked at her, his face overwhelmed by an expression she couldn't place. A hardness that warred with pain, fighting a weariness she saw etched in the corners of his eyes. Jake was tired. The quest for justice brought with it the draining force of anger. Of violation.

And yet, here she was. Tonight. Shoving back Jake and Bridgette's story and trying to believe they were not connected to her own. That the Watchman was truly her guardian, and that if she could only find the truth of her birth, the identities of her father and mother, and the roots of her place in the circus, that all would fall to rights. All would be well. Somehow. In some vague, inexplicable way.

Penn padded across the floor, her toenails clicking on the

polished wood until she met with the massive Oriental carpet that muffled her steps. She nosed Pippa's hand, and Pippa acknowledged her before returning her attention to the keepsake box. She ran her fingers across the satin roses, sewn and embroidered, then nestled onto the lid and attached with a few well-placed French knots. Though the lid's golden edging with its scrollwork hinted at riches inside, Pippa knew the truth. There were no riches in the box. Only memories from a day no one ever spoke about.

She opened the box that held the items left with her on the day she was, as a baby, abandoned on the doorstep of Ripley Manor. A familiar musty smell from lack of use met Pippa's nose. She wished the objects inside could speak. Then she wouldn't need the Watchman with his manipulative ways of enticing her with his secrets. But, while Richard and Victoria Ripley never hid her origins from her, they also never expounded on them.

She fingered the edge of a cotton ivory blanket, yellowed from nineteen years of age. Yet its tatted edges remained brilliant with lacy red loops and swirls.

"You were wrapped in that."

The blanket slipped from Pippa's hand back into the box. Her father stood in the doorway and turned the knob to switch on the electric lights. The light bounced off the glossy burnished wood of the library shelves and made the red tatting reflect like royalty.

Pippa reached for the blanket again. She couldn't look Richard Ripley in the eye. If she did, she would see the sternness on his handsome face, the firm set to his jaw, and the thick mass of peppered black hair that, even ruffled from sleep, made him imposing. She should never have been his daughter. She knew that. He did too.

Pippa shifted her position on the floor, very aware of her crippled leg as she drew it under her nightdress. Footsteps sounded across the wood floor, then silenced as her father's feet landed on the Asian rug, and finally the puff as his body settled on the ruby cushion of the nearby chair.

"Why did you take me in?" It was a question she'd wanted to ask many times before.

"Your mother." It was his only explanation, spoken without emotion. A simple explanation. Victoria Ripley had wanted a child. Pippa had been left for her.

She knew if she inquired further, Richard Ripley would withdraw from her. He had never shown much empathy or concern for her. His purpose was always Bonaventure Circus. The summers when he was so consumed by the circus's successful performances, Pippa hadn't even missed him. In fact, she had been relieved. A time of respite. Part of her even believed her mother felt the same way.

Pippa reached for a piece of paper, a note card, and lifted it from the box. She ran a finger across the words carved with a script that was a stark contrast to the paper's feminine attributes. While the ink had faded, it was still heavy enough to show a hand that had pressed harder than necessary. The loop in the *R* ran wide, the rest of the letters wavy, as if the writer's hand shook when penning them.

Remember us.

The writing looked masculine.

The words made her ache inside. Remember them. She was a part of them.

"Your defiance of late shows ungratefulness."

Her father's condemnatory statement hurt. More than she cared to admit. Pippa twisted her position and met her father's frank gaze. "Have you been honest with me? Do you really know who my parents were?"

Ripley remained expressionless. "You question my honesty." It was another statement, and it was spoken with censure.

Pippa braced herself.

"You have much to be grateful for." He leaned forward and rested his elbows on his knees, his gaze pinning her to the chair in which she sat. "There is no reason for you to be so discontent.

Don't think I'm oblivious to your motives for being with that elephant. Your mother may be superstitious and believe you to be disturbed, but I know. I know you seek more than you should." He buried his dark look into her soul. "You play with fire, daughter. If you trusted me, I could spare you that. *Forrest* could spare you that."

"If I trusted you?" She pushed the idea back on her father. He had mapped out her entire life, and when questioned as to the truth, he'd chosen to hide it instead. Of course she didn't trust him, and she was helpless to do anything about it. He cared for her out of obligation, out of acquiescence to his wife, and out of need to uphold good community standing.

Penn rested her nose on Pippa's knee. Pippa stroked her head and fingered the tip of Penn's ear. The sides of her newly bobbed hair tickled her chin.

"You have every need met. Every future need arranged. I've provided for you. Protected you. I don't know what you're searching for."

Hope? Love? A father who could be honest?

Pippa couldn't say those words. Not when hurt crowded out her voice. She had no desire to trust the man who had provided for her since birth. Providing and cherishing were two very separate things. What would it have been like to have tender moments as a little girl where she could have confided in him? Been reassured by him? Asked him about who she was or who God could help her become? Instead, she was reminded of every obligation she had toward Richard Ripley in return for how he had met their parental obligations to her.

Penn nudged her hand, sensing Pippa's angst. Pippa met the dog's commiserating gaze. Penn's warm nose tucked its way under Pippa's forearm.

Ripley pushed his palms against his knees and stood. "You've no idea what life could have been like for you if I'd left you to the circus. Or deposited you in a home for parentless children.

I took you in. *I* made sure you were educated. *I* have kept you from needing anything. There are many a young woman with a past like yours who have been forced into much more difficult circumstances. You, young lady, are not one of them."

Pippa stared at the note in her hand, her thumb flicking a corner.

"And Pippa?"

She looked up.

Ripley had risen from his chair and now stood in the double doorway of the library, his robe tied at his waist, spectacles perched on his Roman-straight nose.

"I wouldn't make a decision on your behalf without the Ripleys' welfare in mind. That should count for something."

CHAPTER
TWENTY–EIGHT

Pippa?"

She screamed, clapping her hand over her mouth, her shoulder banging into the wall. A flashlight with its large, round glow lifted as Forrest shined the light into Pippa's face.

"What'n heck are you doing here?" He took a few quick steps toward her. Stopped. Shot a look over his shoulder to the open door and the night outside. "It's almost midnight."

Pippa tried to collect herself, to calm her raw nerves. She sucked in a wobbly breath and glanced around the carriage house that stood just behind the Ripley house where everyone slept. Assumedly.

That she had determined to search here for the elusive zebra toy was beside the point. That Forrest was there, after midnight, was more the question.

"What are *you* doing here?" She wasn't sure if Forrest paled or if it was just the odd lighting from the flashlight mixed with a little moonlight.

He rested his hand on the bumper of her father's car. His flashlight swung in an arc around the open room with its vaulted ceiling, highlighting for a moment a carriage, tack, and other sundry items.

"I was—I misplaced a notebook. I thought I may have left it in your father's vehicle."

Pippa frowned. "And it was necessary to find it in the middle of the night?"

He seemed surprised at her questioning his judgment. Forrest squared his shoulders, the shadows making his eyes appear deeper set and his nose more angular. "There are financial records in the notebook. The last thing I need is for it to fall into the wrong hands—someone like Georgiana Farnsworth."

Pippa nodded. It was plausible and made sense. Just that morning, Georgiana had been picketing the circus again, this time more peaceably. Still, her presence remained a veiled threat nonetheless.

"And you? Why are you up at this hour, and in the carriage house, no less?" Forrest edged past her and moved to the doorway. He looked out into the blue-tinted night.

She had no intentions of explaining herself. Of explaining the Watchman's directives to find the zebra toy. His silence was evidence that he would reveal nothing until she did. An urgency was rising in her, even now, to find it. Somehow that toy had to be key to uncovering who she was—who the Watchman was—and any pure or incendiary motives.

"I—needed some fresh air." Her excuse sounded as pitiful as the look Forrest shot her.

"Fresh air? In the carriage house?" He spun and marched toward her until he was mere inches away. As he looked down his nose at her, Pippa could feel his breath on her face. "What are you hiding, Pippa?"

She drew back, surprise riddling her. "Hiding?"

Forrest lifted the flashlight to reveal her face to him. "Your insistence on cutting your hair, helping with the elephant, dallying with Chapman and, God forbid, his friends. It doesn't add up. It's not like you."

"His friends?" Pippa frowned.

"Benard. Patty Luchent. Clive. They're all of the circus, Pippa. You're better than they are."

"I am not," she whispered and shook her head, even though it made little difference.

Forrest leaned forward until his nose almost touched hers. His eyes burrowed his disapproval into her soul. "You are. You were rescued from that life—from those outcasts and misfits. Why must you attempt to become one of them again?"

"You're part owner of the circus itself!" Pippa couldn't help but argue, feeling the pressure of incredulity pressing into her. "What could you have against them?"

Forrest drew back and expelled a breath of disbelief. "I own them—I'm not one of them."

"Own them?" *Appalled* was too kind of a word to describe the emotion that pained her. "*Own* them?"

Forrest waved her away. "Not like that. They're our employees, yes, but merely that. They're not on our same level. They're a part of Bonaventure because they've nowhere else to go. Your father spared you that. Why return, Pippa? Why?"

He had moved back to the doorway, turning away from her. He grasped the doorframe and looked up at the moon. "I saw them this year. On the circuit. I followed their paths from city to city, and you know what?" Forrest spun and addressed her again. "No one sees them as *people*, Pippa. They are entertainment. Objects. Anomalies of life. Curiosities and queer and daredevilish. Not to mention, loose living. The liquor that flows when the lights are out. And you know as well as I do that some of the girls, like Patty, aren't morally upright!"

Pippa leaned back against her father's automobile, seeking its frame for support. Her weak leg shook, and she worried the hem of her sleeve's cuff as she watched Forrest and listened to him rail against the circus folk.

Forrest slapped the doorframe with his hand. "Why must you try to be one of them?"

Silence cut through them, separating them as thick as the night air that floated around their shoulders. Crickets chirruped outside the house, and a breeze chilled the air, sneaking through the doorway and penetrating Pippa's dress. She wrapped her arms around herself.

"I am one of them, Forrest."

"No." He took three long strides and grasped her shoulders, hauling her to himself. Pippa tried to pull back, but his grip was strong. "No. You are not. You never will be. I'll keep you safe from people like them. From people like Georgiana who want to slander us. You will walk the line between them, with me, and we will be better than your father ever was."

"What do you mean, Forrest?" She could barely breathe, let alone make sense of his words.

Forrest's expression darkened. His fingertips bit into her arms. "We will be better than your father."

"You're hurting me!" Pippa squirmed as she felt her skin begin to bruise beneath his grip.

Forrest dropped his hands as if she were fire and he'd been burned. He backed away, shaking his head. "You may go to the circus, you may tend that blasted elephant, you may even cavort with the likes of those who aren't meant for better things, but you—*you*, my Pippa—I won't let you fall."

He disappeared into the night. Taking with him any last remnant of peace that Pippa had hidden in her heart, and leaving behind more questions, more thoughts that were fast brewing into fear.

CHAPTER TWENTY-NINE

Did you hear?"

Chandler startled at her desk and jerked her head up, her messy bun tipping just a bit at the movement. She took in Cru Dobson's form as he poked his shoulders out the screen door of the costume house that he held open with his right hand.

"Hear what?" Explanation would be good before she gave her answer. She'd heard a lot of things already this morning. She'd heard Jackson go on a cold-and-collected rant that the discovery of a body in the depot wasn't just a delay on the project but a damnation of it. She'd heard her mom's same old message on her voicemail: "Give us a call. We're just checking in." To see how she'd failed again? Probably. She'd also heard thumping. Upstairs. In the haunted section of the still-disarrayed second floor. Patty Luchent? Lottie would say it was. But Chandler wasn't thrilled with the idea of her own personal poltergeist keeping her company. She'd been too chicken to go upstairs and see what had caused the sounds. A mouse or a bat probably, nothing nearly as dramatic as a lost spirit.

Cru stepped inside, and the screen door slammed behind him. Chandler jumped again.

His blue eyes flickered. "You okay?"

Chandler waved her hand at him and pushed her laptop a few inches away from her. "Yeah, yeah, I'm fine. What was I supposed to hear?"

Cru grabbed a chair and spun it on one leg, then dropped onto it, straddling it with his arms crossed over the back. "DNA came back on your skeleton."

"Not *my* skeleton." Chandler grimaced. She could still feel the smooth coldness of the bone, the stringy awfulness of the remaining hair on the skull. Like a Halloween prank come to life.

"It's Linda Pike," Cru announced. "The town is in an uproar. She's been missing for decades. Without even a hint and yet she was here the entire time."

Poor guy probably thought she'd rejoice in the confirmation like everyone else. The image of Denny's bearded Santa Claus face bending over her at the hospital crossed her memory, and tears burned behind her eyes. She looked away and made a pretense of straightening papers.

"That's—it's good they identified her."

Cru studied her, and his scrutiny made Chandler uncomfortable. She risked a sideways look at him, and he tipped his head, his brow furrowed. "This messes up your project with renovating the depot, doesn't it?"

Chandler nodded. "Sure. But I'm not complaining. I'm relieved for the Pike family." Hank's image flashed across her mind. *Even their foster kid*, she added mentally. Aloud, she finished, "It has to be a relief. Tragic, but a relief nonetheless."

Cru shifted in his chair and scratched his temple, his fingers ruffling his thick dark blond hair. He had a gentle face. A gentle way about him.

"Is this going to affect your tours?" Chandler realized the discovery of Linda Pike's body in the depot could sway the tour both ways. One, make it more intriguing to those so inclined to find murder exciting. Two, make it more distasteful, as the reality of a more recent death shocked any empathetic person's senses.

Cru shrugged. "I don't think so. We'll take the depot off the tour for now. I don't want to leave a bad taste in anyone's mouth. Mom wants to keep it on, says it shows an appreciation and a memorial for those who have passed. I think it's too soon, though. What do you think?"

His question snagged Chandler's attention. She hadn't expected him to want her input. She fumbled with a pencil on the desk. "Um, yeah. I get your mom's point, but I'm with you. It's way too soon."

"Right." Cru pressed his lips together and nodded. His eyes brightened. "Hey, would you care if we detoured and put this place on the list of stops? I mean, actually tour the inside?"

"The costume house?" Chandler squirmed. Why did she have to be the caretaker for the haunted places in Bluff River? The circus museum down the road had to have some of the same. Wasn't there that old elephant house? Surely there were the dead spirits of elephants haunting the insides of its yellow walls.

"Yeah," Cru affirmed. "We always need to switch up the ghost tour anyway, for repeat visitors. The costume house features Patty Luchent's ghost the same as the depot does. Her story doesn't change, and since no one knows exactly where she was murdered . . ." He frowned.

"What?" Chandler leaned forward.

Cru gave a quick shake of his head. "I dunno. I just had the random thought that it's strange how the depot seems to be a magnet for death."

It wasn't a new thought for Chandler. *Patty Luchent, Linda Pike . . .*

"Anyway"—Cru was still talking—"there's the whole angle of the Watchman too. He physically haunted the circus and depot grounds in the twenties. If that really was his hidden memorabilia in the depot, then who knows what else is tucked away here or on the grounds? He did roam the circus, you know?"

It was a statement whose tone implied a question. Cru was fishing. He wanted to know what she'd seen. The details the police had yet to make public.

Chandler recalled the locks of hair, the circus tokens, the cannibalized circus posters that hinted at some sadistic slaughter of the circus itself.

"What *is* the story of the Watchman?" she asked. Hank had told her snippets only, and now she wanted further clarity.

Cru gave his customary casual shrug. "The story has been capitalized on for years. But the nuts and bolts are that he murdered Patty Luchent in the autumn of 1928, and shortly after that, they caught him. He was sent to prison and eventually sentenced to life. Wisconsin didn't have the death penalty."

"I thought he was executed." Chandler recalled Hank's insinuation that the Watchman had been electrocuted.

Cru shook his head. "Nah. People wanted him to be. Especially after the rumors started circulating that he was responsible not only for Patty's death but also the deaths of several young women along the circus train circuit."

"He was Denny Pike's grandfather, right?" Chandler pressed, mostly to see if Hank's story stood up to popular opinion and Lottie's sensory feelings.

"Yeah. It's easy to trace. Go to any online ancestral site and it's right there. It's gotta suck, growing up the grandkid of a serial killer. I can't imagine people went easy on them. I know, even now, people talk about Denny. Whether it's genetic."

"Whether what's genetic?" Chandler frowned.

Cru shot her a sheepish smile. "Killing. Is being a killer genetic?"

Chandler snorted in disbelief. "Mental illness might be, but that by no means indicates someone would be a killer. In fact, I find it insulting."

"I didn't mean it that way." Cru was immediately apologetic.

"What about the news reports of the Watchman's trial?" Chandler chose to ignore the implications and instead flipped the pencil she'd been fumbling with. It launched over the desk and rolled until it hit the side of a glass candleholder.

"Nothing secretive about it. Plain and simple. They caught him, he was tied up with some scandal with the Ripleys' daughter—she was the one who originally knew him as the Watchman—and it all blew up."

"I don't know much about the Ripleys. I know they owned Bonaventure Circus and lived in that yellow mansion on the hill. The one that's now a bed-and-breakfast?"

"Yep." Cru coughed and cleared his throat. "But the Watchman almost did them in totally. I mean, things were already tenuous with Bonaventure in those days. People were starting to get in on the idea of animal abuse—much like they are today."

Chandler nodded. "I heard about that large circus in New York shutting down last year under allegations of elephant abuse."

Cru tapped the back of the chair he straddled. "The last of the big circuses. Sad, really. It's a legacy of entertainment, and for many it was their home when they couldn't find one elsewhere. Still. Long before the animal-rights activists gained a major voice, the Watchman almost shut this place down."

"How?" Chandler reached for the wayward pencil, more for something to do than anything else.

"Besides the string of murders? There was an *accident* on the grounds at the time. Some attributed it to a rally against the maltreatment of animals, but later many figured it was the Watchman himself. Deflecting attention off his murders. Destroying the circus from the inside."

A *thump* upstairs silenced them both.

Cru's eyes lifted toward the ceiling.

Chandler's pencil stilled in her hand.

Silence, and then a shuffling sound, like a box being pushed across the floor.

Chandler's stomach twisted into anxious knots, and she met Cru's eyes. He gave her a thin, knowing smile.

"Patty's not keen on this conversation," he stated.

Unnerved by the ghostly attributions above their heads, Chandler squeezed the pencil and it snapped in half. If Patty Luchent had an opinion, Chandler was beginning to share it. It was very tempting to run away, to stop, to turn all attention off the old story of the Watchman, of Patty, and of circus sabotage. Circuses were supposed to be entertaining and fun, vivid and lively. But this one? This was dark and thick with questions. Age-old questions that should have died with the Watchman but instead lived in his secret room in the closet, guarded for the last thirty years by a young woman whose disappearance was the last major crime to ever touch Bluff River.

The screen door slammed as Peter charged into the house, brandishing his paper towel roll turned toy laser gun. He waggled his brows at Chandler as he raced past, clomping up the stairs, some mission in mind fully taking precedence over eating.

Margie turned from where she was frying taco meat on the stove and rolled her eyes. "That boy!" she chuckled.

Chandler gave a little smile and nodded. Smiles felt rarer these days.

"Well," Margie said, wiping her hands on a dish towel and flicking the gauge on the stovetop to off, "I'll leave you two to your supper. I've got to run by the store and pick up some things before I head home." She paused and tilted her head, studying Chandler. "You gonna be okay?"

Chandler, sitting in a chair at the small kitchen table, looked up from where she'd been resting her chin in her hands. "I'll be fine." But she didn't bother to lift her head. She didn't have the energy. Every cell in her body was rebelling against the recent surges of adrenaline and the companionship of nervous energy.

Margie frowned and reached over to smooth back Chandler's hair in a motherly fashion. "Okay, then. But you call me if you need anything."

Chandler tossed her a reassuring smile. One that promised a phone call only in an extreme emergency. She'd no intentions of bothering Margie more than she already did. Her nanny had turned into friend and housekeeper. Chandler owed her a bonus at the end of the month.

With Margie gone and Peter's feet pounding on the floor overhead, Chandler lowered her arms and laid her head on them. Relishing the feel of her olive-green chunky sweater and buttery-soft leggings, the only thing she needed now was someone to come carry her to the couch and tuck her in with a movie and a bowl of popcorn. *North and South*, maybe, to satiate her need for period dramas. Or *John Wick*. Not particularly relaxing, but the violent extremism might make her own recent activities seem paltry and less frightening by comparison.

A knock on the back door startled Chandler. Her head shot up off its lazy position on her arms, and her vision collided with Hank's. He stood just outside, an odd smirk on his face. He dangled a key from his finger but spoke through the closed door, his baritone loud enough to wake the dead without even raising his voice.

"Uncle Denny sent me over to check on you."

Chandler pushed away from the table and stood, her sweater falling over her hips in a tunic style. Flipping the lock, she opened the door.

"Decided not to use your key?" was all she could think to say.

Hank shrugged. His hair was pulled back into one of those ridiculous man-buns at the back of his neck, but a strand of curly hair touched his brow. He was too rugged to be remotely pretty. Maybe one of the few men who could still successfully pull off the whole bearded-bun look.

When he offered no explanation for having a second key, Chandler stepped aside. "Come in."

He did and handed her the key. "Uncle Denny thought you might want my spare to give you peace of mind that I won't just let myself in."

"Oh." Chandler snatched the proffered key with a sheepish smile. She set it on the counter. "I didn't mean to—well, sorry I assumed that."

"I'm used to it." Hank must be. He was a felon. He wasn't a good guy. He wasn't the clean-cut, trustworthy male that came with high standards and deep values.

Or was he?

The window over the sink captured her attention. Like it was an escape, Chandler stared out at the fall foliage that made the evening seem brighter than usual, the warmth of the oranges and yellows with green undertones on leaves yet to give in to their inevitable death.

"Going out in a blaze of glory," Chandler muttered.

"What's that?" Hank stood beside her.

She could feel the heat from his body. Not the seductive type, but comforting. The kind that gave Chandler the sudden vision that Hank would be a good one to pick her up and tuck her in on the couch. She could even envision herself laying her head on a pillow propped against his lap while she fell asleep to the sounds of John Wick killing his ninja opponent, and maybe even the deep rumbling chuckle of Hank as he laughed appreciatively at the needless violence.

It was too domestic.

It was too close to the secret dream in her heart. The one that imitated the happy life of a married couple with a vibrant little boy. The one where proving herself wasn't necessary, where looking over her shoulder to be aware and alert was needless, and where—frankly—she could have a behemoth hero rescue her. Just once. And not forever. She could stand on her own. Really, she could.

"Heyyy." Hank caught her as Chandler swayed.

Her body was rebelling. Even the taco seasoning in the air from supper waiting on the stove made her stomach turn.

Chandler pushed off Hank. "I'm fine."

"Like heck you are."

He didn't pick her up like a hero, but he did take her by the elbow and walk her into the living room. Hank sat down on the couch and pulled her down next to him. Chandler avoided letting her exhausted impulse allow her to lean into him. But she could smell the spicy scent of his cologne, or deodorant, or whatever it was that was so inviting.

Chandler swayed again.

Hank's eyes widened a bit, then narrowed. "Do I need to call a doctor?"

Reason returned, and Chandler jerked away from practically initiating the realization of her imaginary wishes. "No. No, I just need some sleep."

"Denny figured you'd be a wreck. You've had one heck of a welcome to Bluff River," Hank muttered. He adjusted his position on the couch and then tugged Chandler into him. It was platonic, or it was meant to be, but Chandler suddenly didn't care what the definition was. She didn't care that Hank had a criminal record. She didn't care that not long ago she'd been snuggling with the dead skeleton of Linda Pike. She didn't even care that supper was growing cold.

Chandler swore she felt Hank press a kiss to the top of her head. A gentle, calming one. The sort that wasn't so much romantic as it was simply comforting.

"Go to sleep," he commanded in a deep-chested rumble.

"Peter . . ." Chandler mumbled but didn't fight the way her body was collapsing into Hank's.

"I've got him. He'll be fine."

They were small words. Six really. Yet they relieved Chandler of the necessity of being a 24/7 guardian. Her eyes closed, and she sensed her body giving in to the strains of bullying through her disease.

"Hank?" Chandler whispered into his shirt.

"Yeah?"

"I'm sorry." A tear escaped the corner of her eye, tracing a hot trail down her cheek and onto her neck.

"What for?"

"You shouldn't have to be here—helping me." She closed her eyes. "I-I usually don't need this much help."

Hank's hand settled on her shoulder and pulled her a bit closer as he shifted on the couch. The television snapped on, and Chandler sensed he had picked up the remote in his other hand, casual, unaffected. The strains of a sportscaster garbled in the background.

"I really am sorry," Chandler said as another tear escaped.

"Shut up." They were two words every Kindergarten teacher would reprimand their student for, but Hank's muttered words were so endearing, so dismissive of her guilt that Chandler allowed her tears to come unfettered. Allowed herself to feel. Allowed herself to believe that sometimes God brought peace in the most unusual and outside-the-norm ways.

CHAPTER THIRTY

She couldn't blame it on morbid curiosity. Something inside of Chandler wanted closure. Fast. Every piece of her had shifted this morning. This morning, when she'd awakened in her snuggled position on the couch, a blanket tucked around her. When the smell of coffee and bacon had reached her nose. When she'd risen and shuffled to the kitchen to witness Hank pouring Peter a cup of coffee. When she'd watched Hank toss a red grape into Peter's waiting mouth and then laugh when it bounced off Peter's nose instead. When she'd seen the hero worship on her son's face.

Chandler was no longer jealous of Hank. Instead, she longed. She longed for normalcy. That concept that she didn't have to fly solo. She even entertained Nel's admonition that maybe her parents were genuine in their desire to help, but just awkward in how they offered.

Hope. She'd awakened with hope, which spiraled all too quickly into resolution. The mystery of Linda Pike's murder, the ghostly activity at the costume house, the spirt of the Watchman, who hovered over every corner of Chandler's life since she'd arrived in Bluff River . . . it all needed to end.

Somehow, as Chandler watched the father-son-type domestic scene play out before her at breakfast, she sensed a renewed energy to fight. To monopolize on the lore around the old circus town. To move on and restore that crazy old train depot. To help

Denny find closure surrounding his sister's disappearance and now confirmed death.

There was something inside of Chandler's soul that told her the equation was simpler than it should be. As she watched Hank chug his coffee and ruffle Peter's hair, she wondered if the problem of trouble plus conflict plus heartache could be solved by dividing it with the acceptance of help. Trusting that people—that *God*—didn't expect nearly as much of her as she did of herself. That people like Jackson were small blips on the road of her life.

Whatever it was, Chandler had allowed herself to feel this morning. To really *feel*. To feel the peaceful calm of the little mock family as they ate bacon, threw grapes, and drank coffee. She'd relished the curl of Peter's lanky frame on her lap and his endearing "Momma" as he buried his face in her neck. She'd let herself enjoy watching Hank as the burly Sasquatch washed the breakfast dishes like he belonged here. A part of them. He didn't. But she could pretend, couldn't she? Just this once?

Now, having left Peter with a doting Margie, and sending Hank on his way with a casual and underwhelming "Thanks," she had gone to work. Returned to the costume house. To the silence of its empty rooms that seemed to inhale every other second with the breath of some secret, unseen life. Today, more than usual, Chandler thought she could feel a presence here. It was her imagination, she believed, but still. It was living, breathing history that demanded to be resolved. Except she didn't know how to help it—how to help Patty Luchent's life be put to rest. How to exonerate Denny Pike's grandfather from the label of killer and inmate who deserved death row. She didn't even know if she agreed with Hank's assessment that he should be exonerated. There was much evidence to show the killer existed, and history might be murky, but it didn't often lie.

Stepping out onto the porch of the costume house, Chandler gave the neighborhood a quick scan. The depot to the west, the animal houses in a row on the same side of the street as the costume house. The river behind them. Beyond the animal houses and menagerie barn stood a more modern brick structure. The circus itself—or at least the memorial to it.

She hurried down the porch steps and made her way to the museum. Across the river, she saw the massive wagon barn where many of the circus wagons were still stored. Being repaired and restored and then put on display. A Big Top tent was still erected, but the grounds were empty of the summer tourists, and she guessed the tent would be coming down soon, releasing its red-and-white-striped folds and leaving instead a gaping emptiness on the circus grounds. Up the hill, she noted several of the old Victorian houses that had kept watch over the circus since its early days, and the farmers' old feed mill that had been erected on railroad property back in the fifties, which was now its own vacant building. The city on this side was run down. No wonder tourists were beginning to forget about the circus of old, even the museum in its stead. The history was there, but the beauty outside the leftover circus structures had waned.

Could she truly hope that reviving the depot into a center for cute shops and specialty boutiques would even be possible? There had to be enough draw for tourists, even if it was a modified and dumbed-down version of the circus that existed during the summer. A few elephants, dogs, ponies were at least a memorial to the magnificence of the days of old. Zebras, camels, lions, tigers, pythons . . . none of those animals graced the grounds any longer, but the memory of them? It lingered and haunted every nuance. An empty shell filled with photographs behind displays, miniature models of the circus, and a few costumes propped behind plexiglass.

Chandler pulled on the modern glass door of the museum's main entrance. A wave of cool air from the A/C blasted in her face. Unnecessary with the temperatures comfortable in the low sixties. Still, it was Wisconsin, and the sixties brought with it humidity. A gift shop was set up to Chandler's right. Books and souvenirs greeted her. Clown masks, stuffed elephants, big red foam noses, and vintage reprinted circus postcards.

"Hello!" A rotund man poked his head out of an office tucked behind the ticket counter. His glasses perched on the tip of his nose, and his brown eyes were barely discernible between his bushy eyebrows and rather plump cheeks. "What can I help you with, miss?"

He clapped his hands on the counter, folding his fingers and leaning on his elbows.

Chandler wasn't sure. Not really. She needed to understand the circus. The circus past and the circus present. Its lure and its lore.

"I'd like to see the museum." She moved to the counter, tugging her wallet from her bag.

"You're Chandler Faulk, aren't you? Gal who's trying to restore the depot?"

"Umm, yes." She didn't know she was known by people around Bluff River.

"I'm Barry Sides. I've been working here since I was a kid. My dad used to be the ringmaster till he retired in '84."

Chandler smiled politely.

Barry waved her on. "You go ahead. I'm just glad you're here to help liven up this side of town. We sure need it." His expression fell. "Nowadays, people don't appreciate the circus."

"What do you mean?" She had to ask.

Barry tapped his temple with his finger. "Kids don't use this anymore. Their brains. Let them turn to mush with all those video games, and then the circus doesn't seem all that daring, you know? What's the big deal about a gal swinging from a trapeze when they can practically experience a real-life war zone on the TV?"

Chandler gave him a muted smile of empathy. He was right, after all. Physical phenomena were becoming less interesting in the wake of technology.

"And then there's the animal-rights people." Barry swore softly. "Been around since the turn of the century, but man, have they gotten loud. I'm not standing here saying every circus is innocent of animal abuse, but I can vouch for our trainers. They've always given the best care. Still, so many circuses are shutting down completely. Like the end of an era."

"Some would argue it's best for the animal to be in the wild."

Barry eyed her, assessing where Chandler stood on the issue. "It'd be better for the world to be perfect too," he retorted.

That was for sure. Chandler was careful to offer him a friendly expression. She adjusted her bag on her shoulder. "Well, I'm anxious to learn more about this amazing place."

Her statement seemed to win him over. Barry waved her through. "Go on ahead. There's another visitor in there, but for the most part, the place is yours. Always gets quiet around here after school starts back up."

Chandler nodded and gave Barry a little wave.

"Stop back and grab something from the gift shop on your way out!" he called after her. "If you got kids, there's some fun little trinkets."

"I will," she tossed over her shoulder. Peter would like something.

The double doors into the main part of the museum were shut. Chandler pushed on them and was instantly entranced by the room beyond. Its walls and floors and ceiling were all dark. Strategic lights hovered over display after display. The sound of lions roaring played subtly over the speakers, then shifted to the old metallic notes of the calliope.

She trailed down the path to the first display. Clowns. Chandler never really had an opinion on clowns. She wasn't terrified of them, but she was never particularly excited by them either. Still, the display was fascinating. A mannequin sat facing a makeup table. He was decked out in full hobo-clown garb and red wig, his face half painted and reflected in the mirror. Antique containers of face paints scattered across the tabletop. There was a red button to push outside the display, and Chandler did so. A man's booming voice began reciting facts about clowns, their history with the circus, the slapstick comedy that was the fashion back in the day, and even some interesting facts about modern-day clown colleges that still trained men and women in the art of clowning.

"Who knew," Chandler muttered. The thought crossed her mind that a clown made a great front for the Watchman. Who was Denny Pike's grandfather really? In her mind, he was the elusive Watchman, a killer who'd preyed on women. But he'd been a man too, whether disguised behind makeup, beneath a ringmaster's top hat, or maybe—

"I hate clowns."

Chandler spun and slapped her palm against Hank's arm in one frantic move. She glared at him. "If you sneak up on me one more time . . ."

The look he gave her was one of feigned innocence. "Hey, I'm just here to see the circus."

Chandler eyed him. "Mm-hmm."

"Come here." Hank grabbed her hand, and Chandler allowed it. She was still emotionally intoxicated from the night before.

She followed him to a display of black-and-white pictures, blown up and posted on foam backing. Cards beneath them were filled with text. They showed various scenes of the circus grounds, mud caked halfway up wagon wheels, with elephants hitched to the fronts and trying to pull them from the mire. Another of camels, and another with two zebras pulling a circus wagon with a few men in trousers and suspenders posing in front of it.

"Right there." Hank pointed to the photo and the men in the group.

Chandler leaned forward, squinting to make out a bearded man's features, blurry from the lack of camera quality. A cigar hung lazily from the corner of his mouth. His arms were crossed over his chest, muscular and corded. "He sort of resembles you," she observed.

"No connection." Hank shook his head. "I've no clue who that guy is."

"So why show me this picture?" Chandler tried to understand the importance.

"Notice the canvas sign in the background?"

It was faded. Hard to see. Chandler leaned forward and forgot about the plexiglass, bumping her forehead. "St. Louis?" she managed to make out.

"Yeah. It was taken on the circuit."

"I don't get it," Chandler admitted.

Hank stared at her as if waiting for her to remember.

It hit her with impact. Linda Pike's body. The locks of hair. The . . . Chandler gulped back the bile of the abhorrent memory.

"It's on one of the tokens we found in the Watchman's memorabilia."

Hank nodded. "Yeah. It said *St. Louis, 1928*."

"Same as the banner in this photograph."

"Sometime around when this photograph was taken, a woman was murdered in St. Louis."

"By the Watchman," Chandler mumbled.

"If all our deductions are right," Hank grunted in response.

"Who was she? The murdered woman?" Chandler couldn't look away from the old photograph with the nameless circus laborers and the cloth banner so proudly proclaiming the circus's appearance.

Hank cleared his throat. "We'd have to reference the St. Louis archives. Pinpoint murders during that stretch of time. But then who knows? If the woman wasn't well known, she may not have even been reported on. It'd probably be hard to figure out."

"But if the Watchman was a known serial killer, there would be records of crimes against women attributed to him."

Hank shoved his hands into his pockets, his burly shoulders hunching and his elbow brushing Chandler's sleeve. "I'm not great at researching. But I'd still like to figure this out. For Denny."

"We can." Chandler turned to study Hank's face. He was staring at the photograph, his expression bothered. Unsettled. "We will," she breathed and dared to reach out and squeeze Hank's forearm.

He looked at her, the dim lighting of the museum enhancing his deep-set eyes, his masculine features, and the troubled look that creased his brow. "Do you know what it was like to be Denny growing up?"

Chandler shook her head. She felt she should take her hand off Hank's arm, but he hadn't resisted her touch, and for some reason the heat of his skin against her palm was a connection she was unwilling to break.

Hank sniffed in a dry laugh. "Grandson of a local serial killer. People assumed he had a mutated gene or something. That he'd grow up with the same mental inclination to kill. Of course, I'm only going by what he told me of his school years, but the guy was a loner. Denny's whole family had to live with the stigma. He said when he was a little kid, someone burned 'killers' into the grass of their front yard. They never went to community events or Fourth of July parades. To Bluff River, Denny's family was the icon of murder. The blemish on the illustrious circus history they're so proud of. Not to mention, for years people had tried to get the state to execute his grandfather."

"You said they executed the wrong man?" Chandler pressed cautiously.

Hank tilted his head toward the circus display. "They fried his very existence, if not his life. Fried the entire family's reputation. From what Denny's showed me and from what I've been able to find, they didn't have a bulk of evidence that his grandfather was the Watchman. Patty Luchent was murdered, and all signs pointed in one direction, and by that time it was starting to get around that there was a repeat killer. They pinned it all on Denny's grandfather." Hank swore softly. "We just found more evidence than anyone back in the late twenties ever did." A pause and then Hank added, "So did Linda."

"And someone killed her for finding it." Chandler tightened her fingers around Hank's arm. He tugged his hand from his pocket, and the movement dislodged her grip. But her hand was soon encased in his large one.

"Which only proves there's more that's yet to be discovered." Hank squeezed Chandler's hand and finally looked at her. "Because if Denny and Linda's grandfather really *was* the Watchman, then who would have cared that Linda had stumbled onto his hoard of relics?"

Chandler's phone chose that moment to peal, the chords of "Eye of the Tiger" blasting through with the finesse of an eighties hair band. She fumbled through her bag for it, giving Hank a quick look of apology.

"Margie," she explained, then lifted the phone to her ear.

Margie's frantic cries were all Chandler could hear. She clutched the phone until her knuckles ached. "Margie, calm down. I don't understand—"

"It's Peter!"

"What about Peter?" Chandler stiffened and immediately began a quick hike toward the museum exit. She sensed Hank not far behind her.

"He's *gone*! Chandler, I can't find him anywhere!" Margie's voice caught in a sob. She cried more unintelligible words.

"Did you look outside?" Chandler knew Peter had made a hideaway of the rental's backyard toolshed.

Margie's high-pitched shouts were filled with panic, and Chandler held the phone from her ear. "The back door was open, Chandler—he didn't even put on his shoes! And his superhero costume is still in his room."

That didn't make sense. Peter had been wearing the homemade Nitro Steel costume all day, every day.

Chandler shoved the doors open and entered the well-lit main lobby. Barry looked up from something he was reading on the counter. Hank caught the doors before they slammed shut behind them.

"What about Buck? Is he missing?" Peter wouldn't have gone far without taking his stuffed baby deer he'd gotten when he was two.

Margie's reply made Chandler freeze. "Buck is here. Peter's shoes are here. He was in his boxer briefs, for pity's sake! The back-door lock was picked or something. It was open, and I'd kept it locked. Peter didn't just run off!"

Chandler could barely compute what Margie was implying. Peter was too responsible, too sensitive to unlock the back door and just leave on his own. Her little boy was always thinking of others, always worried others were sure of where he was. In many ways, he was too mature for his size-seven body, and yet there he was. A little man. *Her* little man.

"I should've known," Chandler muttered, ignoring Hank as he drew nearer, trying to assess what was happening.

Margie was still sobbing on the other end of the phone.

"Someone was snooping outside Peter's window the other night." Chandler looked up at Hank, panic beginning to grow in her chest like a vicious demon. "Someone was looking for him."

"But who? Who would want to—oh, I can't even say it!" Margie wailed.

Barry had come from around the counter and approached her. Hank leaned toward her.

"What's going on?" Hank demanded.

"I called the cops, Chandler," Margie sobbed. "Someone took Peter. I was in the kitchen baking cookies. How could they just take him from under my nose?" Her voice slid high into a wail again. "You've got to get home! The police are on their way."

Without saying goodbye, Chandler ended the call.

"Can I help with anything?" Barry interjected.

Hank ignored him and grasped Chandler's shoulders. "What happened?"

Chandler drew in a shivering breath and blew it out to will away the light-headed panic that had enveloped her. Adrenaline surged through her with vehemence.

"I need to go." Chandler shook off Hank's grip. She charged past him toward the entrance of the museum.

"Chandler!" Hank insisted.

Ignoring him, she slammed her palms against the metal bar that stretched across the glass door, releasing the latch. She didn't hesitate but rushed outside into the chilled autumn air.

"Chandler!" Hank's shout echoed through her, yet Chandler didn't pause. She didn't stop to explain. There was no explanation to be given. No reason why anyone would have absconded with her son, disappeared, vanished, and taken him away from her.

It was the culmination of her worst fear. That one day she would lose him. That he would be gone.

Peter. *Her* Peter Pan.

A nightmare that had come true.

CHAPTER
THIRTY-ONE

I am *not* waiting for twenty-four hours!" Chandler glared at the police detective who stood in her kitchen.

Margie had collapsed onto a kitchen chair. Hank had followed Chandler home on his bike and then trailed behind her into the house.

Chandler's chin shook as she pointed out the open back door. "My son has disappeared! He is seven. *Seven!* Where do you think he would just wander off to? There's nothing to wander off *to* in this town. And don't even get me started on the reputation you all have with people disappearing and *dying* every forty years or so!" She slammed her palm on the kitchen table.

Margie jumped, a tissue crumpled in her hand, damp with tears.

"I hate this town!" Chandler gritted through clenched teeth. She was biting back her own tears, her own burning need to tear Bluff River apart until she found Peter. God help the person who had taken her son. God help them, because when she got her hands on them—

"Chandler." Hank's voice was even, calm, and horribly annoying. His hands guided Chandler to a chair, and once she was seated, she realized her body was trembling violently.

The detective who'd introduced himself as Detective Pagiano, who'd patiently allowed her to release her anger, now squatted in front of her. His brown eyes were kind, his graying hair evidence he'd been on the force for many years. A small-town police force, Chandler reminded herself, where they had limited resources.

"I know this is extremely difficult," the detective began, "but I need you to think back and tell me if there's any place that Peter was excited about. Any place we may have somehow not thought of."

"He's seven," Chandler repeated, still glaring at the officer who really didn't deserve her fury. "He's not even from here. He doesn't know anything about this area." She whipped her head back and forth in denial. "I know my boy. He didn't just wander off on some excursion. Someone broke into the house, took him right from under Margie, and—"

"Oh my! I'm so, so sorry!" Margie's tears dripped onto her bosom and stained her yellow T-shirt.

"I don't blame you," Chandler quickly inserted, not far from hysterical tears herself. She swiveled her gaze back to the detective. "But I want my son found. Something isn't right! Hank saw someone prowling under Peter's window the other night! They have to be part of this equation!"

Hank nodded, affirming her words to the detective. "Yeah. It was around midnight."

"And you didn't report it?" Detective Pagiano inquired with a raised eyebrow.

"Nothing to report. They ran off when I came by. I couldn't tell if it was male or female, and whoever it was didn't vandalize anything. I didn't like it, but I can't report a bad feeling, can I?"

"All right." The detective blew out a breath of air, his goatee peppered with gray but his eyes as sharp as a younger man's. "I don't see what this would have to do with your recent discovery of Linda Pike's body and the serial killer's hideaway, but . . . I agree, there's been a string of weird events, and you've been associated with all of them, Ms. Faulk. Now, with your sighting of a possible prowler . . . you said it was under the boy's window?"

Chandler wrapped her arms around herself, suddenly cold. So very cold. "Yes. Only, he sleeps with me, so he wasn't in his bed."

"Okay." Detective Pagiano nodded. "Have you had any threats, any suspicious interactions with anyone recently?"

She shook her head. "Not anyone specific." She couldn't exactly accuse Patty Luchent's ghost in the upstairs of the costume house, could she?

"And the boy's father? Often these situations involve someone known by the child."

Chandler avoided Hank's eyes. "Peter doesn't know his dad. His dad doesn't even know Peter exists."

"And if he recently found out?" the detective asked.

Chandler squashed her mortification. "*I'm* not even entirely sure who his father is."

Detective Pagiano nodded without censure. "That's okay. It's not unusual. What about grandparents? Aunts, uncles? Anyone in your family you're estranged from or connected with because of the boy?"

The room began to grow fuzzy.

"Hold up." She heard Hank's deep baritone. Felt his hands on her arms. Margie was on her feet, running water, and a cold washcloth was soon pressed to Chandler's forehead.

Detective Pagiano waited patiently until Chandler's vision came back into focus. He must have seen her senses return, and she could feel the intense searching of his eyes.

"Anything. Anything at this point might be critical."

Chandler sucked in a shuddering breath. The adrenaline was activating every negative element of her disease. This. This was how she was going to fail her son. Right now, when he needed her most. Right now, when the situation was dire, she was going to go into seizures, a deep panic, not be able to breathe, shaking . . .

"Hey." Hank was at eye level with her, Detective Pagiano having backed away. "Chandler, look at me." His hand lightly slapped her face.

Chandler squeezed her eyes shut, then opened them.

Hank's rough features were etched with concern. He lifted his hand again to brush her cheek with his palm, but all Chandler saw was the rosary tattoo. Prayers. Pray. She needed to pray. Pray to God that Peter would be returned safe.

"Jackson," she muttered. Her eyes locked with Hank's green ones. She garnered strength in them. "My co-worker . . . he wants my position. Maybe he's behind this?"

Jackson would hate her forever for casting suspicion on him if he were innocent.

"What's Jackson's last name?" the detective inquired.

Chandler didn't break eye contact with Hank. "Nowitzki."

"Okay. Anyone else?" Again, the detective.

Chandler was desperate. Even in her soul, she couldn't see Jackson doing anything so devious. It would gain him nothing. Uncle Neal certainly was no threat. Her parents?

"My parents?" Chandler ventured a guess, and even as she did so it struck her as ludicrous.

"Are you estranged from them?" Detective Pagiano asked.

"No. Yes. Well, they weren't exactly pleased with me when I had Peter. They're always offering to take care of him for me. I—I've been a good mother, though."

"Yes, of course," the detective nodded.

Margie's comforting hand curled around Chandler's shoulder. "For sure you have!"

Hank nodded.

"I can't think of—of anyone else."

"It's okay, Ms. Faulk. This is all helpful." Detective Pagiano stood, his knees cracking. "We'll find your son."

Chandler broke her gaze with Hank and leveled a serious stare on the police officer. "You can't promise that."

The detective's eyes shadowed.

She knew what they were all thinking. Someone had told the same thing to Linda Pike's parents, and it had taken thirty years to find her dead, decomposed body.

Chandler heard the voices from the kitchen like echoes, faint and in the distance. She curled up on the couch, clutching Buck to her chest, the stuffed deer smelling like Peter. Who knew a child would have a distinct smell, and yet they did. She ached to bury her nose in his hair. To have his lanky arms and legs wrapped around her.

"They haven't found him?" The voice was distant. Vaguely familiar.

"No, Barry. But it was kind of you to stop by." Margie. Margie was fielding all the awkward, concerned calls and drop-ins. It must be Barry Sides from the circus. Nice man.

"If there's anything I can do . . ."

"Just pray, hon," Margie urged.

"Good thoughts, for sure. Will do."

The sound of the door closing.

Footsteps.

Chandler clutched Buck tighter and brought her knees up to her chest. The couch sank on the far end. She caught a whiff of Margie's perfume.

"Hon, I got a call from your mom."

Chandler didn't respond.

"They said they'd be on the first plane."

Chandler stiffened. "No. No, I don't want them here."

"I'm not sure you can stop them. They sounded determined."

Chandler whispered through a tight, tear-blocked throat. "I just want Peter back."

She bit her lip until it bled.

Margie left, and soon the couch dipped again.

"Hey, kiddo." Denny.

If anyone understood, it was Denny.

Chandler turned her tortured eyes onto him. His reflected her pain with a very stark knowing. He pulled on his beard, then tugged on the brim of his black leather cap. The familiar smell of cigarettes lingered around him, only instead of being off-putting, for a strange reason, Chandler drew comfort from it. Familiarity. Empathy.

"Hang in there. We're here for ya."

Thankful that he didn't make empty promises, Chandler nodded and swiped at the tear on her cheek.

Next were Lottie and Cru. They quietly set a plate of cookies down, and then Cru hovered over her for a moment before taking a cue from her silence and backing out of the room. She glanced at Lottie, whose blue eyes were blurred with tears.

"Oh, Chandler, I—this is awful."

Chandler couldn't respond. Of course it was awful. It was hell.

Lottie shifted her feet nervously. She wanted to say something, Chandler could tell. Chandler lifted her gaze with question, giving Lottie permission to speak.

"I know you may not agree with, or believe in, my gift. But if you want my help, I'm happy to try to see what happened to Peter."

Psychic. Were they the same as mediums who spoke to the dead? Chandler wasn't sure, and she didn't want to ask.

"Thank you." Chandler hoped her words would be taken as a polite decline of the woman's offer. She didn't want to dabble in something so unfamiliar. Jinx the search for her son. Make God mad that she was contacting a medium the same way King Saul had ticked God off in the Old Testament.

"It's fine." Lottie nodded. "Just—let me know if you change your mind."

And then she left.

Chandler wondered if she was wrong. What if God was dumping Lottie in her lap? What if she wasn't making use of the benefits given to her because of a childhood Sunday school lesson?

The couch sank again.

If one more person offered their condolences as though Peter was already—

Chandler was lifted from her seat and pulled into a hard body. Hank might be a man with a questionable past. An abandoned foster kid who'd dealt drugs and vandalized properties. He might have tattoos and long hair and look like a Sasquatch, but . . . Chandler buried her face in his chest. Hank saw her as no one else did. She didn't need to be spoken to—she needed someone to share with. To share the pain. To be seen.

He didn't say anything, but his lips moved against her temple. Not kisses or caresses, but as if he was praying . . . silently.

She should do that too, but she hadn't the strength. Maybe this was the gift God was giving her. Someone else's strength, when she simply had no more left within her.

She'd never done well with asking for or receiving help.

Soft footsteps and then Lottie returned and whispered to Hank over Chandler's form, "Margie ran home to let her dog out. She'll be back soon with something to eat. I picked up Peter's toys. That way Chandler won't trip over them when she heads to bed."

Bed? Chandler kept her eyes squeezed shut, yet the idea of sleep was laughable.

"Thanks." Hank's word vibrated in her chest.

"Tell her I put his superhero costume in the closet and his zebra toy in the toy bin."

"Okay," Hank said.

Chandler popped her head up. Instantly aware. "Zebra toy?"

Lottie seemed surprised at Chandler's sudden attention. She nodded hesitantly. "Yes. A vintage wooden one on wheels?"

Chandler shivered. "Peter doesn't *have* a zebra toy. I don't even know what you're talking about."

Lottie pulled back.

Hank stiffened. "A zebra toy?"

"Yes," Lottie nodded.

Chandler was very close to Hank's face. She could see his mind calculating in his eyes. "What is it?" She pulled away from him.

His brows created a deep v between his eyes. There was a fierceness in his expression. He didn't mince words. "Denny's grandfather— the Watchman—he was known to have left a zebra toy with the

Ripleys' daughter. Shortly before Patty Luchent was killed. Almost like a taunt."

Chandler stilled. "You're saying the *Watchman* took Peter?"

"Even *I* don't believe that." Lottie lowered herself onto the sofa on the other side of Chandler and rested a comforting hand on Chandler's knee.

"No. But there's a connection." Hank half pushed Chandler off his lap toward Lottie. He surged to his feet and grabbed for his phone and keys. "We found Linda in the Watchman's hideaway for all his sick souvenirs. Now a zebra toy is left behind, and Peter has disappeared? It's all connected. And someone is sending a message."

Lottie nodded. "Connected maybe, but still, it makes no sense."

"I'll be back." Hank charged from the room.

Chandler turned toward Lottie, helpless. She didn't know what to do, or say, or even how to calculate how all of this was inter-related—or if it even was.

"We will find Peter," Lottie attempted to reassure Chandler. But all Chandler could see, looking into her not-very-distant future, was the image of herself, alone, with only the memories of her sweet baby boy, and a very dead Linda Pike.

CHAPTER THIRTY-TWO

Georgiana Farnsworth can rot in—"

"Richard, please." Victoria Ripley bit off the end of her plea, choosing instead to bite into a forkful of her dinner. She cast her gaze toward her plate and looked surprised at her own speaking up.

Pippa forked at the boiled trout on her plate and nudged an asparagus stalk out of the way. Glancing up, she caught her own future husband's eye. His narrowed. He was suspicious of her, and she was of him. They'd not shared words alone since a few nights before in the carriage house. Pippa's feelings toward Forrest, while always platonic, now waffled between wary and wondering. Wary of his controlling declarations and wondering if he'd meant them with good or bad intentions. Regardless, she'd wasted time since searching for the elusive zebra toy. There were moments Pippa questioned whether even the Watchman was being honest with her regarding its importance. Or were they all merely playing games with her affections and emotions, devious and self-serving men that they all were?

Richard Ripley chewed and swallowed. He pointed his fork at his wife, unaffected by her blushed porcelain skin, upswept blue-black hair, and brilliant sapphire eyes. Equally as unaffected by her subservient role in their household.

"I will say as I please about Georgiana Farnsworth and her pathetic little band of plebeian females. The circus is my livelihood. It is my pride. I've no intention of letting her yellow-ribbon renegades spread more untruths."

"What has she done now?" Victoria Ripley's tone was long-suffering as she asked the very obviously required question in response.

Ripley's fork clanked against his plate as he reached for his wineglass. "She picketed my office outside the train depot. All afternoon she traipsed up and down the platform chanting lies. She's finally got her wish and rallied Bluff River on her side."

"Her supporters are growing." Forrest dabbed his upper lip with a napkin.

Pippa looked away. Any other man with different character traits and she'd find him handsome with an air of confident sophistication.

"I counted sixty-three people." Ripley spoke around a mouthful of potatoes.

Pippa noticed her mother wince at his manners, or lack thereof.

"And eighteen of them were men. If that woman somehow garners support from the empty-headed voting members of this community, I'll serve up Jake Chapman's head on a platter. And Ernie's. And, for that matter, my own!"

Pippa found her tongue, even as her mother cast her a warning look to stay silent. "Women have the vote now."

The following pause was thick with held-breath expectancy. Victoria's fork stopped, lofted midway to her mouth. Forrest's eyebrow rose, and he stared across the table at Pippa as though she'd taken leave of her senses.

Richard Ripley's sigh of controlled derision was audible. He set his wine goblet down and made exaggerated pretense of gripping the edge of the table. Looking down his aquiline nose, he addressed Pippa. "Our nation's most recent and most obvious error in judgment."

Pippa squirmed under his scrutiny. He held her stare for so long, the ensuing silence grew painfully uncomfortable. She finally nodded, even though her implied agreement was insincere. Once she'd acquiesced, Ripley continued to fixate on her, the superiority of his expression so poignant, so oppressive, it took everything in her not to flee the room.

Forrest cleared his throat, effectively rescuing her and breaking the awkward stillness. "Miss Farnsworth is aggravating, to be sure. However, Bonaventure Circus stands on years of good rapport. Especially since we're sponsoring the Autumn Bluff River Formal." He took a sip of his wine.

Ripley sneered at Forrest, as though his dead partner's son was foolishly not seeing something that he should. "It is a step we shouldn't be required to take to preserve our name. We shouldn't need to preserve our name at all."

Pippa didn't understand the look Forrest shot her before he focused again on his dinner.

Ripley continued, directing his attention to his wife. "As it stands, Victoria, your niece had better be finished with Georgiana Farnsworth. Pippa, since you're so devoted to the welfare of the circus and the elephant, I'll expect you at the Formal as well."

"But . . ." Dread coursed through Pippa. She hated the community's formal dance every autumn. Despised that she had to sit at the edge of the ballroom like an old-fashioned wallflower. Her leg forbade her to dance smoothly. And her social inadequacies made small talk and interaction uncomfortable at best.

She met her father's shrewd gaze. He was punishing her. Her presence at the Formal would do little to assist the reputation of the circus. It was something she didn't want to do, and Ripley simply wished her to suffer. Pippa avoided casting a pleading glance to her fiancé. She knew Forrest would do nothing to aid her cause.

"Must she, Richard?" Victoria interceded meekly on behalf of her daughter.

"She has to attend the Formal." Ripley's look communicated he'd brook no further argument. "It would look ridiculous not to have us all in attendance. It would undermine the picture of family unity as we support the circus and renew favor toward it. I will regale the community with stories from our summer tours, and Forrest?" He redirected his sternness. "You will as well. I realize you weren't with the circus during the bulk of the summer, but expect you to have many astounding tales to tell and leave our community spellbound with the representation we give to Bluff River as we travel throughout the nation."

"Of course." Forrest nodded.

A *bang* from the front foyer of the Ripley house made Pippa jump, and her hand hit the edge of the table, upsetting the water in her glass. She twisted in her chair as a bedraggled man burst into the dining room, followed by a visibly upset butler.

Ripley lunged to his feet. "What is the meaning of this?" he demanded.

"I'm sorry, sir. The man here just pushed past me . . ." Their butler heaved an affronted chest while he grappled for his next breath.

Pippa recognized the man, who twisted his cap in nervous energy. His face was mottled, white with dark patches of skin and a nose offset from his eyes. Benard the blacksmith offered a small smile of recognition, but she noted the urgency that oozed from his posture.

Forrest stood from the table, following Ripley's suit but at a much more controlled pace. "What's the matter, Benard?"

"It's one of the tents, sir—at the circus." Benard pointed out the window as if they could all look and see. "Someone tampered with the ropes. It collapsed!"

"Was anyone injured?" Victoria Ripley pressed her fingers to her lips.

"The lion trainer," Benard replied. "Not seriously, but he's cut up. He didn't have the cats in the tent. They're fine."

"It's that blasted Miss Farnsworth." Ripley threw his napkin on his plate.

His wife drew back. "Georgiana?"

Ripley leveled her with a glare. "Yes. *Georgiana.*"

"You really think she would stoop to sabotage?" Forrest was the only one who dared challenge Ripley now.

"Anyone is capable of anything." Ripley stormed from the room, a dreadful silence remaining in his wake.

Pippa stole a look at her betrothed. The steel set to Forrest's jaw and the lack of emotion or surprise on his face sent needling fingers of doubt through her. The unbidden question fluttered through her mind and collided with the doubts she'd been harboring since the night at the carriage house. He wouldn't possibly have orchestrated the collapse of the circus tent to cast blame on Georgiana, would he? It was evident he neither liked nor respected the woman, but to go to such devious lengths . . . Still, he had indicated his intention to protect the circus. To protect *her.* The idea that Forrest could perhaps be responsible suddenly didn't seem so preposterous. It would devastate Forrest just as much as her father if the circus was ruined because of one woman's fancy. Pippa was loath to think such things, even of Forrest, but somehow his connections and protectiveness toward the circus made it believable.

It was all spiraling, and Pippa nudged past Penn as the dog nosed behind her heels, loyal to a fault and unwilling to let her mistress creep through Ripley's study alone. It had to be here somewhere. Moonlight shafted through the window of her father's study and made the leather of his desk chair shine. He had yet to return from the catastrophe at the circus, while Forrest had already come and gone, weary and soiled from the mess. Someone had singed the ropes, he'd explained, perhaps using a hot blade. Either way, the tent had collapsed, and they were lucky no one had been seriously injured.

Such sabotage would keep her father away most of the night, she was sure of it.

Pippa ran her fingers along the inside of his desk drawers. A false bottom? A secret switch? Something that would trigger a reactionary door to reveal the hiding place of this elusive toy. Nothing. The drawers were organized and uncluttered. Her father's letter opener lay perpendicular to the drawer's sides, next to his ink pen and notepaper, also neatly arranged. Pippa shut the door with careful precision. If the articles inside were off-kilter, Richard Ripley would know someone had been snooping.

Every drawer, every nook, and every cranny in the study had been searched. Pippa flopped onto the leather chair, and Penn mimicked her actions by dropping to the floor with a grunt. Frustration stimulated Pippa's antsy leap back to her feet, slowed only by the weakness in her crippled leg that served to remind her of her own insecurities. She hobbled to the window in her father's study, positioned directly below her bedroom window, pushed back its curtain and swept her gaze over the back lawn of the Ripley house. This place, it was her home, and it was also her prison. Though the stately house should represent security, instead it made her restless.

The carriage house was the size of a two-story farmhouse but square like the manor with no gables or turrets. Its yellow siding dimmed in the night shadows, empty now as her father and driver had taken the motorcar to the circus. The brick driveway rounded between the buildings, creating an avenue, and curled beneath the covered archway where carriages could pick up and drop off worthy visitors.

Movement at the right-side pillar of the arch startled Pippa. She pushed the curtain back further and pressed her forehead against the windowpane. Pippa's breath caught in her throat. The shadow that stretched across the ground both slaughtered her worries and revived new ones.

The Watchman emerged from the darkness. He stood, legs apart, hands at his sides, head tilted back, fixated on the window. On her. She couldn't move. It was as if he drew her into the gaping dark holes in place of eyes in the burlap sack that cloaked his head. His hand lifted in a slight wave, as if in a worrying air of someone who watched her. Knew her. Waited for her.

Hesitation marked her breaths. They came quick but stuttered. Previously, Pippa would have rushed to meet him. Begged for him to stay. He had always been elusive, but now he stood there, waiting. Now her hesitation was marred by mistrust, by stories of Jake's murdered sister, and by the doubts that anyone was trustworthy.

If God would only speak. Speak aloud. Simply announce to her what she should do as He had the men of old. But He was silent. In His guidance. In His direction. In His caution.

Hang it all. Pippa whirled from the window. If she stayed under the arch, if she didn't come close, certainly she would be safe. She was at home. She would not leave her doorway.

Pippa closed the study door behind her as softly as she could so as not to send its echo up the stairs to awaken her mother. Her footsteps were muffled on the cream-and-navy carpet runner that raced ahead of her down the hallway toward the front entry. She reached the front door, her fingers fumbling with the locks. Penn panted next to her, anticipation of adventure in her eyes. With the door open, Penn slipped through first, but Pippa didn't follow. She watched Penn, who halted in the drive, sniffing the air. Her hackles weren't raised. She seemed calm and unworried.

Crickets chirruped in the nighttime silence. A breeze lifted her hair from her face. Pippa squinted into the night, into the archway.

"Hello?" Her whisper was hoarse. The crickets fell silent. All she could hear were the trees with their brittle and dying leaves blowing in the light wind.

"Hello?"

Nothing. Pippa wrapped her arms around her torso as a shiver from the autumn chill reached her bones. She looked to Penn. The dog was uninterested in the archway, the bushes, the pillar, or any of the surrounding structures. Penn padded to the edge of the drive and sniffed at the ground, then shook her body as if shaking off drops of water before trotting back to Pippa and the entry.

Pippa bit her lip. The Watchman was gone. Again.

She moved to retreat into the house when something caught her eye, something in the bushes. White. Fluttering. Pippa hurried forward and squinted her eyes to see through the darkness. She reached into the shrubbery, and her fingers closed around a handkerchief. Its edges were bordered in the same tatting as the blanket she had been wrapped in as a baby. A red flower was embroidered in the corner. The crunch of paper pinned to its back made Pippa turn the handkerchief over.

This was your mother's. Before she died, she wiped tears from her eyes. Tears for you. But she wasn't the only one who loved you. Have you found it yet? It will reveal my truth—will you bear it once you know?

Pippa ripped the note from its pin and held the handkerchief to her nose as she clenched the missive into a ball. Tears burned her eyes. Tears of anger that time had stolen away her mother, the woman who loved her. Tears of frustration that as much as she ached to know who her guardian was—truly was—she was also terrified of what he might imply. The vengeance in Jake's eyes as he spoke of his sister, the idea of a man willing to take the life of an innocent young woman while masked behind a veil of cowardice. And yet, here too was the one who had communicated with her for months now. Who she had seen in the shadows, asked after, worried her mother because of . . . and now he too revealed his own fear.

Will you bear it once you know?

Know what? And what must she bear? That he was a murderer? That he had slaughtered Jake's sister and yet harbored protection and love for Pippa? Or was he unrelated to Bridgette's death and simply Pippa's guardian? The one who knew more of who Pippa was than it seemed anyone else was willing to say. The one who knew her as a . . .

Pippa stopped, knowing where her heart of hearts was taking her. She shouldn't go there again. Shouldn't entertain the deepest dream that she'd protected for years. Her mother was dead. This she knew. This was clear from the moment she was able to conceptualize her unorthodox adoption. But her father? The one who should have protected her and stepped in to care for her. Where had he gone? What force of life had ripped him from her and, in his stead, entrusted Pippa to a man who clearly cared not for a daughter, but for an act of charity? For his livelihood, and perhaps for his childless wife.

She peered into the darkness. She could beg, she could demand. But her entreaties would only be met with silence. This she knew. While Richard Ripley demanded she live her life on his terms, so too did the Watchman demand she learn of his identity on his terms. Whether either man was truly her father or were both the masters of a game in which she was merely a piece they moved at their whim and fancy, Pippa knew she must choose which one she would let control her. And truth be told, neither of them made her feel safe.

CHAPTER
THIRTY-THREE

Clive looked up as Pippa entered Lily's stall. The elephant lifted her trunk and reached for Pippa. The recognition calmed Pippa's flustered wits from the night before. She would never admit to anyone that she had sat at her bedroom window for hours, straining to see through the darkness. She'd only been greeted by the sight of her father—Richard Ripley—returning home. He was disheveled, his jacket slung over his elbow, and even his shirt unbuttoned at the top. Odd, how different the man looked in the darkness. More vulnerable, maybe. Or perhaps just different. More of a man and less of a demonstrative authority figure. And what was her father like as a man? Pippa wondered. Then she'd recalled her mother's meekness when he was home, and Pippa realized he must be no more endearing as a husband than he was as a father. He was his own person and answered to no one. Not even his partner's son.

For a moment, in the wee hours of the morning, Pippa thought she might understand Forrest a little bit. He was grappling for control of something of which he truly had little. He could control only her—and then only when Ripley released her to Forrest in marriage.

The circus brought little solace, but now, as Pippa met the dewy, black-eyed gaze of Lily, a part of her calmed. It was the empathetic bond. They were both unwanted in their own ways. Both misfits in worlds they weren't born to live in.

Pippa reached in return and finger-kissed Lily's trunk. The baby elephant wrapped its trunk around her wrist and pulled her in. Pippa couldn't resist the smile that touched her lips, and she let the elephant mouth her hand. Clive's smile wrinkled the lines on his face. A wisp of gray hair stood on the top of his head. The familiar reediness of his voice soothed Pippa further.

"Pippa Ripley, you're that babe's favorite person."

"Hardly." But she knew it was true. That Lily had shifted toward improving was evident, both in the life in the calf's eyes and in the steadiness of her stance.

Pippa didn't know why Jake wasn't here. She'd seen Ernie out with the other elephants, walking them in their ring. He'd given her a nod of affirmation. He approved of her presence, but his face was serious. She'd seen Benard outside earlier, along with the man who was Jolly the clown, only sans his usual face paint. They too were stoic, almost sad. There was a pall over the circus. Ever since the tent had been sabotaged. It blew an ill wind, and they all sensed it.

Clive sat on a three-legged stool. He tipped his head and peered up at her. "Something's bothering you."

Pippa didn't respond for a moment, weighing her thoughts. She leaned against the wall.

"I have questions." She gauged Clive's reaction. He waited. "About my birth."

Clive nodded. He drummed his fingers on his knee. "I wish I could help give you answers, my dear."

Pippa responded with a shaky smile, understanding his ignorance toward her birth but wishing it were different. Clive had been one of the first people Pippa had asked questions of many months before. He had been with Bonaventure Circus for as long as she'd been alive. It made sense that Clive would know something. A hint, a clue, anything.

"You know I was ill the year you were born." Clive adjusted his position on the stool. "I've always struggled with my condition. I was in and out of the hospital then."

His trousers were hitched above his ankles, the stitching well mended, as they'd been tailored for his short stature. Pippa briefly wondered if Patty was responsible for the excellent seam work.

Lily's trunk pushed against her neck. Pippa stroked it as she moved it down until Lily curled it around her arm. "I know. I know you don't recall much from that time. I just—" She stopped.

"Spit it out, Pippa," Clive urged.

She gave a small laugh, knowing she would tell him. Knowing that Clive knew she would confide in him. She merely needed to find the words.

"My place isn't with the Ripleys. But my father can't see that. My place is here—at the circus. It always has been."

"Of course, your father won't support you. You want to find his replacement."

Pippa had never considered that. She edged closer to Lily and rested her palm on the elephant's cheek. "He has no fatherly instincts toward me."

Clive's expression was awash with disbelief. "I find that difficult to believe. He has cared for you since your birth. Fed you, clothed you, seen to your welfare, and even given you quite the amount of liberty in spite of how it may feel."

"He's arranged a marriage for me, he's told me what I can and cannot do, he's lied to me, hidden my past from me . . ." Yes. She met Clive's eyes with an unspoken challenge. He could say what he wanted, but she knew the other side. That she was Ripley's greatest regret in life.

"He was chosen to care for you by someone." Clive's argument pierced her.

"I was abandoned there as his responsibility. He owned the circus. He employed my dead mother—whoever she was." Pippa's retort stung her tongue, just as the truth of it stung her heart. "He may provide for me, may see to my future, but he is a stranger to me. I don't have fond memories of him as a daughter should. I don't really have memories of him at all. He is gone so often. The circus is demanding of his time, his passions, his . . ." Pippa dropped off. She didn't know where she was going with her thoughts.

Clive shook his head. "You have to believe it will work out for the best."

"God works all things together for good?" Pippa didn't mean to mock the Scriptures, but Clive's faith was sometimes exhaustingly positive.

Clive raised an eyebrow. "To them that love Him. Do you, Pippa?"

"Love God?" Pippa picked at her fingernail.

"Yes." Clive nodded.

She didn't respond. Loving God, as a father, was a difficult concept when she had no father with which to compare Him to, other than Richard Ripley and, perhaps, the Watchman. Did she wish to love God? Most certainly. But wishing and understanding how were two concepts that warred with each other. They were not easily reconciled.

"I want to," she finally conceded. "I want to believe He cares. That the crucifix stands for something bewilderingly heroic."

"It does," Clive was eager to reassure her.

Pippa smiled sadly. "No one has ever been bewilderingly heroic for me, Clive. And the ones who should have been specifically chose not to."

Clive didn't respond. How could he? She'd left him little room.

There was no holding back. Not now. Pippa rifled through her mother's dresser drawers and pushed aside undergarments, lace-edged handkerchiefs, and stockings. Nothing. No zebra toy. No clues to her birth, abandonment, or whatever circumstances drove it all in the first place.

Pippa slammed the drawer shut and leaned against the white bureau with its scalloped edge and tall mirror. She stared at her reflection. She looked harried, tired, and frantic. Pippa loosened her grip. She needed to calm down. To think. The last message had arrived. This time by a knock at the front door, much in the same way his original message had arrived when it all began two years prior.

Hurry.

The one word injected itself into her psyche like ink on the tattooed lady. The message was clear. Definitive. Even the Watchman felt it. Time was running out. The circus was in trouble, and with it the plausibility of their meeting.

Pippa opened the wardrobe doors and hesitated. A row of her mother's elegant dresses hung neatly, organized by color. A whiff of her perfume drifted into Pippa's senses. She vaguely remembered sitting on Victoria Ripley's lap as a child, her hand brushing back her hair, a melody hummed in her ear. That feeling of being cherished. It was a fleeting memory. Stuffed deep inside her. Pippa pushed it back down.

"What are you doing?"

Pippa yelped and spun, her breath catching in her throat. Franny. Her cousin stood in the doorway of the bedroom, curiosity etched onto her pretty face. Her calf-length dress had a beaded fringe, and she'd wrapped her long hair with pins and netting to make it look short. Short like Pippa's. Even Franny hadn't the audacity to bob her hair. Her brilliant eyes sparkled with interest.

"Are you snooping in Auntie's things?" Franny took another step into the room.

"Did you let yourself in?" Pippa inquired. She knew her father was gone, her mother at the Mulrooney mansion preparing for the upcoming Autumn Formal, somehow hoping to save face for the circus by putting forward her best foot.

"Of course not. I knocked. I was told everyone was out but you, and I insisted you'd be fine if I came upstairs. Your butler is so old-fashioned. Anyway, here I am! I needed company." She flounced onto the bed. "Georgiana hasn't any rallies today, and gosh, if it isn't so boring just sitting at home. What are you looking for?"

Pippa didn't answer but pushed her mother's dresses and parted them in the middle like circus tent flaps. If she found the toy, she would confront her parents and it would all come out, so there was no reason to shoo her cousin away.

"Can I help?"

Genuine, or driven by Franny's insatiable curiosity, Pippa didn't know. But she nodded.

"The more the merrier." Her uncharacteristic sarcasm didn't register with Franny, who drifted to her side like an ethereal angel of spontaneity.

Pippa pulled out hatboxes jammed in the back of the wardrobe and handed them to Franny.

"What am I looking for?" Franny stacked the boxes without opening them.

"A toy zebra."

Franny held a blue box Pippa handed her, a quizzical slant to her dark brow. "A toy zebra?" she repeated. "Whatever makes you want to find that?"

Pippa pulled herself from the innards of the wardrobe to cast her cousin a bewildered look. "You know of it?"

Franny shook her head. "No."

Pippa released her breath. She resumed her quest to dive for more boxes. "Open those." She waved her hand behind her toward the hatboxes Franny had stacked but not opened.

"Why do you need to find a silly old toy?" Franny fumbled with the lid of a hatbox.

Pippa pulled a yellow hatbox with her as she stood. "I just— want it."

"Because you think it will connect you to your birth family?" Franny slipped papers from the inside and revealed a hat.

Pippa didn't answer. Franny was more astute than she'd given her credit for.

Franny lifted a hat and hovered it over her head like a child playing dress-up. "Goodness, this hat is horrible." She dropped it back into its box. "I never understood that."

"Understood what?" Pippa opened the yellow box.

"Why you have this insatiable need to be at the circus. To know who you came from, or at least uncover why they gave you away."

Pippa didn't have the energy to respond to Franny's musing. She couldn't find the words to explain it anyway. Franny would never understand. How could she? She didn't know what it was like to be unnecessary. To be crippled. To be someone's unspoken and unwanted regret.

Franny moved on to her fourth box. She lifted the lid. "I always wished you could just be happy."

Pippa's chest constricted at her cousin's voice, which had lost its vivacious harmony and instead fell to a wistful melancholy. That her cousin had even considered her—well, it meant something. Pippa wasn't sure how to process the feeling that spread through her. She searched the yellow box instead. A velvet winter hat of blue and no toy.

"Is this it?" Perched in Franny's hand was a wooden zebra. The very sight of it made Pippa immobile. It had to be what she'd been looking for, and yet it was unassuming in its simplicity. Certainly this could not be a key to uncovering who she was or the identity of the Watchman. The zebra's hooves were carved onto a square base that had wooden wheels attached to the bottom. It was a pull-toy. Aged paint of white and black, the wheels red, and the base yellow.

Pippa couldn't reach for it. She couldn't move.

Franny ran a finger down the back of the zebra. "It's rather cute, though I've no idea why on earth you'd care about a silly toy like this." She turned it over. "Oh! There's an etching on it!"

Pippa waited of no choice of her own. Her body had paralyzed itself by the mere sight of the elusive and mysterious toy.

"That's odd." Franny lifted wide eyes and held the toy toward Pippa as if she wanted nothing to do with it.

Pippa didn't take it.

"It says 'I love you.'"

I love you . . .

Finally, Pippa reached for it. Her hand trembled. That wasn't at all what she had expected. Of course, she wasn't entirely sure *what* she had expected when she found the toy, but those three words? While full of potential depth and meaning, it wasn't his name, nor his identity, and certainly not something that would tell her anything unique about the Watchman.

"What have you done?" Richard Ripley's voice ripped through the room as his chiseled features twitched with suppressed emotion. The bedroom door was propped open, his hand gripping the doorframe as though, if he were to let go, he might launch himself at the toy.

"Oh, gosh!" Franny exclaimed. She dropped the zebra toy on the bed. "Gosh, Uncle Richard," she fumbled again.

"You, out." Richard Ripley moved into the room and pointed at his niece, then toward the hallway. Franny edged past her uncle, cast Pippa a lingering look, and closed the bedroom door behind her. The soft click of the latch echoed in the room, the few yards between Pippa and her father as wide as a chasm left empty by the past roars of floodwaters.

"What have you hoped to accomplish by ransacking your mother's private quarters?"

Pippa's chest clenched. An ache that had taken root as a child bubbled up inside her like a geyser that had long been ready to burst. "How could you hide this from me?"

She held the toy toward him, like an accusation, the evidence of a crime that had been committed against the heart of a little girl whose only dream was to be cherished. "You held this back from me. And Mother? Does she know about this toy?"

His glare ran her through like a sword into a mannequin. "How do *you* know about the toy?" Ripley yanked off his coat and tossed it on the bed. With a few quick steps, he crossed the floor and shut the wardrobe doors as if somehow it would shut out the past.

"Did she know?" Pippa pressed for an answer, refusing to

explain herself. There was no way she was going to even broach the subject of the Watchman with her father—least of all before she had even sorted him out.

Ripley raised an eyebrow. It was a formidable one, as eyebrows went, and it took everything in her power not to shrink back as it winged upward in a dark swoop of condescension. "I forbid you to—"

"To what?" Pippa interrupted, but her voice shook. "To find the truth in this godforsaken house?"

"God has never forsaken this house." Richard Ripley laughed scornfully. "*You* forsook it."

Pippa snatched the zebra toy from the bed and clutched it to her chest. "You can't make this my fault. You hid this from me. What else are you hiding from me?" She twisted the toy and held it toward him, the etching pointed in his direction. "*I love you.* This was from my family, wasn't it? My father?"

"*I* am your father!" Richard Ripley kicked at a hatbox and sent it sliding across the wood floor.

Pippa's hand dropped to her side, the toy with it. "You're—you're not. Not really."

Ripley marched toward her, and before she could react, he had grabbed her upper arm and pulled her toward him until Pippa's shoulder touched his chest. "That *toy* is a lie. What it says is a lie. *We* are your family."

"My family?" Pippa's voice trembled. The anguish was too deep and the wounds too open not to argue. She tugged her arm away, and he released her but with a meaningful slowness that exemplified his concealed power. Pippa paced away from him, stopped in front of the window of her mother's room, and stared out at the sky. Dusk was settling in, and with it large thunderclouds in the distance.

She turned. "You left me. Every summer. You've no desire to be a father." Her whisper sounded louder than if she had shouted it. Pippa gripped the zebra toy with both hands and lifted it to her mouth so her trembling lips could press against its cold wood.

She was loved.

She was loved.

She was loved.

"You never held me." Pippa grew in confidence, spurred on by Ripley's dark silence. "You hardly spoke to me. You left me for weeks. I became a castoff. Are you ashamed of me? My leg? Where I come from?"

"Stop." Ripley's voice was chilling. "You don't know what you speak of." His chin lowered, and he glared down his nose at her, striding toward Pippa until she backed into the window. He leaned down until he was eye to eye with her. "You will tell me how you found out about that toy."

"No." Her refusal was a trembling whisper.

"Tell me now!" Ripley's roar bounced off the bedroom walls and silenced Pippa, the piercing strength of it matching the thunderclap that rattled the crystal beads hanging from the lamp by the bed.

She shook her head, clasping the toy tighter to her chest. Rain began striking the windowpane, a tiny cadence of musical notes without order.

"You're a conceited little one, Pippa. You always have been. Never wanting to belong to us, and then accusing us of keeping you from your own." Ripley sneered at her, shaking his head in mock disbelief at Pippa's rebellion. "You *know* your mother lost children before you. Our family crypt holds no secrets there. When you were left on our doorstep with that toy, was I to tell my wife no? No, she couldn't take in a crippled waif whose parents were my own employees?"

Ripley snatched the toy from her hands and threw it against the wall. The square corner of its base dented the wallpaper scattered with pink roses, and the toy fell to the floor with a clatter.

"Then you know who my parents are?" It was all she had taken from what he'd said, but it was enough.

"No."

"Liar." Pippa whispered the accusation with every ounce of belief in her heart.

"I'm telling you the truth."

He wasn't. She could tell. She could read his face and see the deceit in his eyes, even as he refused to look away. She hurried to retrieve the zebra toy, but he stepped in her way.

"*I* am your father!" His shout was drowned by another crack of thunder.

"But I don't want you!" Tears choked her cry. Yet she didn't regret saying it. Didn't feel shame at the breaking of the truth from her lips.

Pippa swiped at her eyes. Her chin shook, her hands shook, her entire body quivered.

Richard Ripley marched to the bedroom door and yanked it open. His chest heaved as he leveled her with an expression burdened with unintelligible emotion.

"Then our feelings are mutual," he concluded.

The door slammed behind him.

CHAPTER THIRTY-FOUR

The zebra toy was on the table in a clear plastic evidence bag. Chandler eyed the old wooden toy, its paint so faded it was almost hard to tell its base had once been yellow. There was an engraving on its bottom. Words that might have been carved there, the mark of the toy maker perhaps, but scuffed so badly now it was impossible to read.

It had been forty-eight hours. *Forty-eight hours.*

Chandler sat in the police meeting room, scanning the myriad of evidence on the table before her. Hank stood beside her chair, Denny Pike on the other side.

Detective Pagiano stretched his arm in a swoop over it all. "This was all taken from the hidden space in the train depot where you found Ms. Pike's remains." He glanced at Denny. "My apologies."

Denny shook his head. "Don't. I long ago came to terms with the fact Linda was gone."

Detective Pagiano nodded. "I don't know if this will help, but if the toy was left behind by whoever took Peter, there may be a plausible connection we're missing between today's events and the story of the past."

Hank grunted.

The detective shot him a look. "Hey, I don't know much about the zebra toy, but Barry Sides down at the circus confirmed it was tied to the Watchman back in the day. He said it was used by the Watchman as a connection to who would have been his next victim had he not been stopped. Richard Ripley's own daughter was apparently targeted by the Watchman. Given that Ripley was the owner of Bonaventure Circus, and considering this toy was found with Peter's things, does any of the *other* paraphernalia here on this table ring any bells? Anything we can connect to today and tie to Peter's abductor?"

Chandler was going to be sick. She hadn't eaten much and she was paying for it now. It'd been all she could do to remember to take her medications, and that was only because Margie made sure she did. Uncle Neal had called several times, offered to fly over, but Chandler had refused. He tried to encourage her that she didn't need to worry about the project and that Jackson could handle everything until Peter was found. What would have once threatened her now didn't matter. She'd give it all away just to hold Peter, to touch her son, again.

Both Hank and Denny were eyeing the bagged items on the metal table. The locks of hair—hair from victims who had died a century before—now nameless and unremembered. The circus tokens, boasting of the glorious circus in each particular city while the Watchman harbored them away as mementos.

"Were them murdered girls along the rails like this Miss Ripley the Watchman had his eye on?" Denny inquired.

"You mean, in appearance?" The detective dipped his head in acknowledgment of Denny's theory. "Could be. I looked up some of the old records on the murders. There's not a lot that links the Watchman to each girl specifically. Just that he was in the towns with the circus when they wound up deceased. A lot of it seems like conjecture to me, to be honest. Certainly, they didn't have the means to solve crimes across the country like we do today."

"But what does any of this have to do with Peter?" Chandler couldn't help the frustration in her voice.

"None of this stuff brings anything to mind?" Detective Pagiano asked again.

"Nope," Denny muttered.

Hank shook his head.

Chandler gave the detective an exasperated look. "I'm from Detroit. What would I know?"

He coughed. Cleared his throat. "All right then. Let's try it from another angle. What did your sister, Linda, possibly have to do with the story of the Watchman?"

"It was a bit more than fifty years after he was caught that she went missing," Hank offered.

"Meaning?" the detective inquired.

"Well, the Watchman was already dead by then. Fried him."

"Actually," Detective Pagiano countered, "folks wanted him electrocuted, but he wasn't. Wisconsin hadn't adopted the death penalty."

"News to me." Denny pursed his lips. "My family always said the state fried the wrong man."

"Families don't always get the facts straight in all the emotion of the situation," Detective Pagiano supplied. "No offense."

"None taken." Denny gave a nod.

"So, your grandfather died in prison," Hank ventured.

"Must have," Denny replied.

Chandler frowned. "How were you born?" She didn't really care, but if it led them to Peter . . .

"Whaddya mean?" Denny creased his forehead.

"Well, if your grandfather, the Watchman, was in prison after he was found guilty of murdering Patty Luchent, then how did he have a child who could later have you?"

"Huh." Denny crossed his arms over his stomach, his leather vest creaking. "Never really thoughta that. They give prisoners conjugal visits back then?" He directed his question to the detective.

Detective Pagiano gave a slight laugh. "Maybe? Your—mother was his daughter, correct?"

"Yup." Denny nodded.

"I think if we do the math with birth dates, your mother," Pagiano continued, "had to have been born prior to his imprisonment."

"So, the Watchman—a serial killer—had a child with some woman?" Chandler tried to wrap her mind around the facts.

"My momma, Elsie, never knew her momma. She grew up in a children's home and always had the label hanging over her head of being the daughter of the Bluff River Killer, or the Watchman." Denny stroked his beard and sighed. "Heck, I've lived with it all my life. Never married 'cause no one would let me date their daughter." He gave a sad chuckle. "Guess they were scared I was like my grandfather. Labels are cruel things. And that was one of the reasons why I took you in." He looked at Hank. "Kids need more than a label on them. They need a place to belong, ya know? Not judged by priors."

Hank reached out and gripped his uncle's shoulder. Squeezed and dropped his hand.

"I still don't see how any of this is helping." Chandler bit her lip. She tasted blood. "Taking Peter doesn't help anyone's cause."

"No," Detective Pagiano agreed.

"Hold up now." Denny's expression shifted. He held his index finger in the air. "Wait a minute. In high school, Linda was part of a small history club. You know, one of them clubs girls throw together on their own?"

"Okay?" The detective pulled out a metal chair and deposited himself in it.

Denny did the same.

Hank remained standing.

Denny leaned forward on the table and folded his hands in front of him. "I remember now. Linda was happier than a lark she'd been included. Of course, most them gals were nerdy, but Linda—she didn't have many friends."

Chandler closed her eyes and prayed. Prayed for patience, for Peter. Prayed that God would come out of His hiding place and fight for her. Rescue Peter. Make something make sense.

"How is this important?" Detective Pagiano asked what they all were probably thinking.

Denny scrunched his face in thought. "Not sure exactly. But what if Linda talked them into helping her prove our grandfather wasn't the Watchman like my family has always claimed? And what if they stumbled on that hiding spot in the depot as young people? One of them gals didn't want word of it getting out, so they turned on Linda?"

"But who would that be?" Hank ventured. "Linda's the one who had the most to lose if it got out."

"Was she?" Denny swept his hand over the evidence bags. "What on this table confirms that our grandfather was the Watchman? Nothing. It's all from the victims. Nothing to identify the killer. But what if there *had* been something there? Something that proved Linda's theory and implicated one of the other girls' family trees? They might've tried to keep Linda quiet."

"It seems farfetched," Chandler muttered, toying with the fringe on her scarf. She would go out herself later and comb the streets. Break into houses if she had to.

"Crimes are usually farfetched," Detective Pagiano said. "If what Denny is theorizing is true, then you, Ms. Faulk, are another person who's gotten in the way and potentially outed the real killer's family."

"Who cares!" Chandler pushed off from the table and stood. She wobbled as blood rushed from her head and the room spun. She grabbed for the table, but Hank was there and held her steady. "Who cares about a circus train serial killer from the 1920s? It's a century later!"

"I care." Denny's quiet voice stunned her into silence. She met his sad eyes. His look in response was firm but gentle. "A person isn't that far removed from it when it's their grandpa who did the killing. Sure, some may glorify what happened or be all into the intrigue of it, or you can see it for what it really is. Sick. A sickness. And who else in the family could end up with the killing gene? If there is one. You know, those are the thoughts that go through a person's mind."

Chandler lowered herself back onto her chair.

The room was quiet for a long moment, and then the detective cleared his throat. "So, Mr. Pike, I think we need the names of the people in this little club with your sister. Maybe they know something."

Denny blew a puff of air from his lips. "Boy, you're testing my mem'ry. Lemme think . . . Judy Commings, but she died last year of cancer. Lottie Dobson was part of it. Go figure." He chuckled. "Oh! Barry Sides's sister, Barbara. She was in it too."

"Just those four? Linda, Judy, Lottie, and Barbara?" Hank prodded his uncle.

Denny looked up at him. His eyes shadowed. "Yeah. Barbara was pretty intense too."

"They were circus folk?" Detective Pagiano asked.

Denny nodded. "It practically runs in their veins."

"Where are you going?" Margie asked.

Chandler rammed her arms into her fleece jacket sleeves, ignoring Margie. She frantically hurried after Chandler, who stopped in the hallway and snatched up her scarf and hat from the bench where she'd tossed them earlier after returning from the police station.

Chandler tugged the stocking cap on her head, not caring that it made her look like an unpopped popcorn kernel. "I'm going to find Peter."

"Don't be stupid!" Margie slipped in front of Chandler, blocking the door. "You can't do anything more than what the police are already doing."

"I can add my eyes and ears to the search." Chandler's voice caught in her throat. "Margie, please. The next thing they'll be doing is putting grids together and hiking through fields to find his body." Tears burned her eyes. "I can't just sit here. I can't wait around and do nothing. He's my *son*!"

Margie hesitated, then reached for her coat. "Fine, but you're not going alone."

"No!" Chandler grasped Margie's arm.

Margie's hurt expression stung Chandler. She softened her grip. "I mean, if Peter comes home, someone needs to be here. For him."

A shadow fluttered through Margie's eyes. Chandler didn't want to interpret what it meant. That Margie believed Peter would never come home? Chandler bit the inside of her lip until she tasted blood. She couldn't unlock her worried stare from Margie's telling one. She didn't. She didn't believe Peter would come.

"He will come home, Margie." Chandler licked the blood away she'd drawn from the bite she'd barely felt. "He *will*."

She whipped the door open, then stumbled back. Cold shock warred with the adrenaline and the unexpected anger she was tempering toward Margie. Margie and her disbelief in Peter's well-being after only forty-eight hours!

A couple stood on the steps.

Chandler remained placid. Expressionless. She had to or she would react with all her pent-up emotion and become a raging lunatic. That wouldn't help Peter.

"Mom? Dad? What are you doing here?"

Her parents' exhausted faces gazed back at her.

"Oh, baby," her mother breathed.

Chandler's stomach curled. Curled in agony, in relief, and in struggle against the fact that her parents were here. They would find out everything! They would see her medications and supplements to combat her PTLDS on the counter in the kitchen. They would affirm that if she'd only let them raise Peter, none of this would have happened. They would butt in, tell her how to live her life, how to be a good mother to Peter . . .

Chandler clapped her hand over her mouth to prevent a sob that threatened to betray her. There was no being a mother to Peter . . . not if he remained missing. Like Linda Pike. Like Linda Pike had for decades!

Chandler stepped aside so her parents could come in. But she remained wordless.

Margie hurried forward, and Chandler's faith in her friend's support was renewed a little. "Come in, come in!" Margie ushered them into the hall. "I'm Margie. I'm Peter's nanny."

Her parents entered, offering smiles to Margie. Chandler's father extended his hand, and Margie took it.

"We're so grateful for how you've been here for Chandler," he choked, his eyes red-rimmed. "I'm Tom, and this is Sherry."

"Nice to meet you." Margie gave a warm hug to Sherry, who tried to capture Chandler's gaze.

Chandler left the entrance and hurried into the kitchen. She had to hide her medications. Had to remove all evidence of her inability to care for Peter. She grabbed a bottle of magnesium—not all that unusual considering it was a natural supplement—but one look at the dosage would indicate her body was sorely lacking. She hurried to collect her antidepressant, her antianxiety pills, her—

A hand closed over her wrist.

"Leave it there."

It was Dad.

Chandler turned and worked her mouth back and forth, willing away the tears. Willing away the distress. "I—I have a sinus infection and I—"

She could tell her dad wasn't buying it.

"Chandler, we know."

"Know what?" she replied glibly, sliding the pill bottles away so the labels were more difficult to read.

"Neal called me. He's been concerned. You've been overworking, trying too hard to outdo Jackson. He's seen through it. He told me you've had nothing to worry about, that your work is spectacular, and Jackson is no threat, but he also said you wouldn't believe him."

"Are you saying I'm paranoid?" Chandler wrapped her arms around herself. She didn't want this conversation right now.

Her mom stepped into the kitchen, followed by Margie. "No, baby. No. But you won't ask for help. You've shut us out, and you won't let us in. We want to help you!"

"I don't need—" She caught Margie's look and stopped. "I can support Peter on my own. You don't need to take care of him for me. And . . ." Her hand flew to her mouth as her words choked on tears. "What if he's dead? What if they killed my little boy?"

Her dad reached for her, but Chandler pulled away.

"We know you have Lyme." Mom stepped closer. "Nel's been worried about you, so she confided in us. You're pushing yourself too hard."

"Stop." Chandler shook her head. She waved them off. "I don't care. I don't care if I have a disease. I don't care if it kills me. I want my son home. I want my Peter Pan."

She spun and charged for the back door, yanking it open. Like a wayward and hurt child, Chandler plunged into the night for the safety of her car. Her parents behind, calling for her. Calling for her as they had done for seven years. And as she had done for seven years, Chandler ran away.

CHAPTER
THIRTY-FIVE

The Watchman.
The Watchman.
The Watchman sees all, knows all, is all.

At least that was how she felt as she drove, her lungs burning from her tears. Chandler didn't go far, her first stop foremost in her mind. Parking, Chandler hopped out, taking with her a flashlight, her phone, and pepper spray. Finding Peter was enough motivation to put herself in harm's way if needed, but she had no intention of being foolishly unprepared either. She had no idea who she was up against. Who was so devious as to involve a seven-year-old boy in their vendetta of—whatever it was!

She hurried up the sidewalk from her vehicle and looked around her. The streets were well lit, the nighttime almost beautiful in the quaint historic town of Bluff River.

What was it like to have run from the Watchman? The women he'd assaulted. What had he done to them? She didn't want to know. She only knew that years and years later, his ghost was still haunting them. Hidden in the shadows of Bonaventure Circus, laughing, mocking, and chasing girl after girl, woman after woman, generation after generation.

She fumbled with her key as she climbed the stairs to the porch of the costume house. Chandler glanced to the west and noted the depot was dark. A large, ominous silhouette against the skyline.

She never wanted to go there again. She would turn the entire project over to Jackson, gladly. Her position too. She'd take a job at McDonald's or become a cashier at Walmart. Those were adequate jobs. Honest jobs. Plus there were food stamps, government aid . . .

Chandler swore as she jammed her key into the lock. None of it mattered if Peter was dead. Why did her mind instantly go to the worst-case scenario? Had she seen one too many crime shows on TV? Maybe, but she'd watched enough documentaries to know that more than forty-eight hours missing was a bad omen. Her brain replayed every news broadcast she'd seen of people searching fields, of boats with divers dragging lakes, of backyards dug up and black garbage bags covering the remains.

Her mind was still in a struggle with Linda Pike, missing for all those years, then suddenly wrapping her bones around Chandler in a viselike embrace.

Remember me! her remains had demanded.

Peter's might one day do the same.

Chandler swore again. Then prayed. Prayed so hard that she didn't have words and hoped the Holy Spirit truly did intercede with groans that could not be understood by anyone but God. At one time, she might have scolded herself for swearing and praying simultaneously, but she was certain God understood and even empathized. He didn't expect perfection in prayer. He only expected prayer. Chandler hated that it could be her last recourse and only hope. But then prayer was supposed to be powerful . . . If only it had proven so in the past.

Flicking on a light, she surveyed the costume house. Patty Luchent had worked here once. Sewing costumes, flirting with passersby, smoking cigarettes maybe . . . before her life had been cut short. Cut down. Sucked from her. Chandler didn't know much about Patty Luchent, the legendary woman from the twenties. Who had she been? Why was she so important to Bluff River and Bonaventure Circus, when really all that seemed to matter was that she was the Watchman's last victim?

Still, Patty Luchent was a question mark. And one that might need answering in order to piece together who had abducted Peter. Who had put her son in the middle of an age-old haunting that refused to be laid to rest?

Chandler glanced at the stairs that led to the ghostly second story. Lottie or Cru would probably love to be here tonight. Inside the haunted house itself. Chandler wasn't even anxious. Let the poltergeist eat her alive.

She marched up the stairs, turning the lights on as she entered the spacious second floor. The boxes were still in disarray from the first day she'd arrived in Bluff River. For a moment, Chandler half expected to see Patty Luchent herself, perched on top of one of the crates. Glowing. Staring at her with hollow, black eyes. Speaking to her with the willowy whisper of a soul that wished only to terrorize and seek revenge for her own murderous end.

But the place was empty.

Chandler fumbled around the boxes. She wasn't sure what she was looking for. If Linda Pike and her friends had stumbled upon evidence that the Watchman wasn't who everyone thought he was, maybe some of it was here. Maybe some of it, somehow, would explain where Peter had been taken.

The boxes were filled with old magazines, musty and unread for decades. Another crate was full of mothballs and old blankets. Half of the boxes were empty. Chandler sneezed as dust entered her sinuses. She sniffed back angry tears.

Of course her parents would have shown up. Even though she'd told them not to.

Chandler rifled through a trunk. More magazines. *Time, Life, National Geographic* . . .

Acting as though they wanted to help. There was criticism in their eyes, though, or maybe it was her own self-inflicted sense of failure. She didn't know.

Another box. Old receipt books from the eighties.

A crate. A trunk. A banker's box of circus souvenirs.

Nothing.

Chandler sent a half-empty box flying across the room to match the vehemence with which Lottie claimed Patty Luchent's spirit had first tossed the boxes.

"What do you want?" Chandler yelled, letting the cry of agony rip from her throat, leaving it sore and tight. "Where did you take him?"

She fell to her knees, jeans doing little to pad her collapse. Tears burned her face, and Chandler pounded the floor with her fist. She didn't even know who she was screaming at. Certainly not a ghost. Not Patty. Not the Watchman. They were all dead. So was Linda Pike. It was just the remnants left behind, taunting, pretending they still lived when all that remained of them were souvenirs of an era long gone.

Souvenirs.

Like a whisper to her soul—one she determined to credit only to God and not a lost spirit—Chandler jerked her tear-filled eyes up to stare at a banker's box. The box itself wasn't remarkably old. Maybe from the nineties. But inside it?

She crawled to the box and flipped the lid off. Old brochures, some of them glossy, in bright yellows and reds and purples, splashing advertisements for the circus. Many were for the museum itself, in 1993 or 1988. She dug deeper and pulled out older pamphlets. In 1954, the circus seemed to be waning. The front of the brochure pictured only elephants and tigers. She fumbled even deeper and found old, yellowed black-and-white prints.

Bonaventure Circus Train

Returns to Bluff River, September 1928

The front of the one-page print was a sketch of a train with a fabulous circus wagon perched on a flatcar. Chandler flipped it over to read the listing of cities the circus had visited through the summer. Her eyes widened. *St. Louis* quickly met her eye, as did several of the other cities that matched the tokens in the serial killer's hideaway.

Chandler grappled for her phone in her back pocket. She dialed and Hank answered, his voice gruff. Maybe he'd been asleep, or maybe it was just him.

"The Watchman. He traveled with the circus. The circus train."

"I know," Hank said.

"But—did Denny's grandfather?"

"What do you mean?"

"You said that Denny's family—that Linda—wanted to disprove their grandfather's guilt. Do you know if he traveled with the train?"

"Yeah. He did."

Chandler ran her finger down the list of towns with Bluff River as the final stop. "Who else traveled with the train that summer of 1928?"

There was a long pause, and then Hank cleared his throat. "A crapload of employees."

Chandler nodded as though Hank could see her. She adjusted her legs until she was sitting, as Peter called it, "crisscross applesauce" on the hardwood floor. "Was there any employee who maybe just happened to travel occasionally, and happened to hit only the cities where women were killed?"

"What are you getting at?" Hank wasn't following, and she didn't blame him.

"Think about it. Of all the towns the train passed through, why was it only big, popular cities where the assaults took place? Why not a small town? Why not a no-name town? A serial killer with the circus had plenty of opportunity over the course of the summer, but his M.O. was to assault and kill only in cities."

"Ooookay? There's obscurity in large populations," Hank reasoned.

"But not in Bluff River!" Chandler shook the pamphlet in the air. "Bluff River is the circus's hometown, for criminy's sake! He's going to get a lot of attention by killing Patty. So why do it then in the circus hometown when he could stick to big cities?"

"You're thinking something specific. Spit it out." Hank wasn't one for mincing words.

Chandler slapped the advertisement down on the floor, her palm on top. "What if—what if Denny's grandfather *wasn't* the Watchman? What if . . . well, what if there were *two* killers? Think about it. Patty Luchent was found strangled with the mermaid necklace around her neck. The one you found in the depot. But the other necklaces weren't on the bodies—they were in the Watchman's loot from his kills. He didn't leave the necklaces behind with his victims; he took them as mementos. Whoever killed Patty . . . deviated from the Watchman's M.O. They killed Patty in a small town *and* they left the necklace behind with the body."

Hank didn't say anything for a long moment. Finally, Chandler heard him sniff and clear his throat. "Are you thinking someone from circus management took Patty's necklace after her body was removed from the costume house and stuffed it in their office in the depot?"

"It's a thought!" Chandler waved her hand, although the only one in the upper room to see it would be Patty's own ghost—if she was there.

"Then you're implying that Patty's murder only framed the serial killer we know as the Watchman, and whoever murdered Patty wasn't really the serial killer at all?"

"Yes!" Chandler nodded vehemently.

Hank didn't seem thrilled with the idea. "Then Denny's grand-father *was* a murderer."

"But only of one person! Patty Luchent. Not of a string of mur-ders." Chandler's conclusion brought with it a warped sense of celebration.

Hank wasn't sharing it. "And one murder is better than multiple?"

Chandler stilled. He was right. This wasn't good news. It made the story more complex, more sordid, and more intolerable. "It's better than having a propensity to kill, isn't it?" It was a weak offering.

Hank sighed into the phone. "Okay. So, say it was someone in circus management who was the serial killer, and Denny's grandfather only committed one murder for whatever motive and tried to pin it on the serial killer. Then you're implicating a circus higher-up, Chandler. Someone who would have visited only the major cities and not actually ridden the rails with the circus the entire summer."

"Like a Ripley. Or maybe one of the circus management staff?" Chandler knew it was outlandish, and she clenched the phone tighter. "If whoever took my son figured this out when Linda figured it out, and they wanted to keep it quiet . . . well, we stumbled on the same thing Linda did—assuming she was snooping around the old depot and found the hideaway. Who is still living who would care about keeping it quiet if the killer *was* a circus bigwig and not just a general laborer like Denny's grandfather?"

Hank grunted. "I don't know."

"But I'm not crazy, am I?"

"This whole flipping thing is crazy and confusing," he mumbled. "Lemme make a few calls."

"It's almost one a.m." Chandler tried not to crumple the old paper in her hand.

"Who cares." It wasn't a question. It was a silent declaration that Peter's life was at stake. This was more than the preservation of Denny's grandfather's legacy, or even a resolution to Linda Pike's murder. It was the life of a little boy. A little boy who pretended to be Nitro Steel, and who still believed he could fly.

CHAPTER
THIRTY-SIX

PIPPA

What are you doing here?" The wind chased away Jake's shout as he hopped over a deep rut in the road, the chilly air penetrating the thin cotton of his white shirt and blowing the shirttail flat against his back.

Pippa perched on the corner, arms wrapped around her body, her hair damp from the spitting rain. The length of it stuck to her face, bordering her chin, plastered and still cold from the wetness. Penn danced around her feet, and her whines carried through the darkness and storm.

She'd done it. She had left the house, her father shouting her name. Pippa didn't care anymore. It was her final act of breaking into her own freedom. But now that she was free—free of him and his controlling secrecy—she didn't know where to go except to her roots. And even those were elusive and maybe not even buried firmly in any soil to speak of.

"Pippa?" Jake bounded over another rut. He must have spotted her from his room in the guesthouse. She had been aimlessly standing at the corner, the rain pelting her face. She was free, though, and it was all she could think about at the moment. Free, without aid from anyone, not even the Watchman.

Yet she'd run from Ripley Manor into a different kind of prison. One that no level of independence could break her from. It was a lost sort of freedom, purposeless and confused.

Jake approached Pippa and bent to investigate her face. The night enveloped them as thunder crashed overhead.

"We need to get to shelter," he said.

Pippa shook her head, hugging her body tighter.

"Pippa, come on." Jake reached for her arm, and she jerked back. Away from him.

She felt him skim her body quickly and she read his mind. He was looking for bruises, for signs of assault. He was trying to interpret her lost expression in the darkness and fearing his nightmare had come true again. That she was his sister—battered from the Watchman's greedy hand. He was wrong. She wasn't. The Watchman had never hurt her. He had only watched over her. Guarded her. He only seemed to *care* for her! It didn't piece together with the image of a brutal murderer.

"I'm all right," Pippa assured Jake, barely audible above the wind.

"He didn't hurt you?" Jake half shouted back, rain whipping into his face.

"No. He—the Watchman . . ." She choked. Thunder cracked in unison with the reactive jerk of Pippa's body. The zebra toy her father had thrown against the wall, its etching of attachment, invaded her mind. "He loved me," she finished.

"*Who* loved you?" Jake's response was thunderous, not unlike the storm.

Moisture spit in their faces as a gust of wind flattened Pippa's dress against her legs. "The Watchman." And with that declaration came another. The one she'd wanted to believe for so long and now chose to cling to as truth. "He's my father."

Jake rubbed her upper arms. She was shivering, whether from cold or shock or both, she didn't know.

Concern and a growing fury etched themselves into the lines of his face. Droplets of rain dripped from his beard and his hair.

"Who is the Watchman?" he yelled as lightning flashed overhead. A steely set to his jaw told Pippa that his intent to know wasn't born out of concern for her own past, but for Bridgette's.

Pippa stuttered, trying to find an acceptable answer. "He's—the one. The one who's always watched out for me. You think he's a killer, but he's *not*! He's my father."

Jake tossed a glance over his shoulder at the guesthouse and the row of animal lodgings across the street. "Pippa, c'mon."

"No." Pippa pulled further away from him. "I found proof that my father loved me. Richard Ripley hid it from me. All these years!" She yelled over the wind and swiped at wet hair that slapped against her face. "He kept it to himself and refused to tell me. How could he do that? Keep me from my own father?" Pippa's shoulders lifted in a sob. "He always promised he was being honest. He *promised*. But he wasn't! He hid it from me. I'm not enough for him. I've never been enough!"

Jake jumped when lightning shot across the sky like a sword of iridescent fire. He palmed her cheeks and bent until their noses almost touched. The rain continued to lash them.

"Pippa, you're enough."

"No." Her head turned from side to side in denial. "I'm not."

Jake touched his forehead to hers. Lightning illuminated his face momentarily, and the rain stung her eyes.

"Listen to me!" He was shouting. The wind had increased into a constant gale. "You. Are. Enough!" He enunciated each word as if they were their own sentences.

As she stared at him, she felt his hands wrap around her arms, her gauzy dress sleeves wet, but his hands lighting her on fire.

"You're enough, Pippa. You've always been enough."

They burst through the doors of the horse barn, Penn on their heels. The rain chased them with thick drops laced with the fragile beginnings of ice. Jake pushed into her as momentum moved him forward. Pippa met the wall of the barn with her palms and spun just as Jake pressed against her. His hands braced on either side of her. His eyes drilled into hers, gray and turbulent like the storm outside. As if they could meld with hers and become one vision. The rain pelted the floor behind him. Lightning brightened the sky and emphasized the steady rise and fall of his chest. It matched hers. Moment for moment. Raindrop for raindrop. Warm in the cold, wrapping them in an intimate embrace. The dance of breaths, hers mingling with his. Even the horses were silent amid the violence of the storm and the calm within the shelter of the barn.

Jake's fingertips soothed her wet skin as he pushed a dripping strand of hair behind her ear. His eyes never released hers. They captured her with unspoken desperation, need, as if honesty would only wound the moment. He bent his head next to hers, his left arm still braced against the wall, his face against her cheek, rough and strong. His breath was warm against her cold ear, with the faint scent of tobacco and spice.

"What were you thinking? Out there? Coming to the circus in the storm?"

She wasn't thinking. She hadn't been thinking. Drenched in rain, beaten by the argument with her father, running, always running.

"I want to be free, Jake. I want to be seen, to be someone, to be needed and wanted," she whispered.

"You shouldn't be here," he said, his voice ragged.

Pippa could feel his mouth move against her hair. He nuzzled her temple, drawing in a deep breath as if he were memorizing her and fighting against the pull of her.

"This is where I came from." Pippa couldn't help it. Her hands traced paths up his chest, so thick, so strong.

He dipped his head to the base of her neck where it met her shoulder, bare from the scoop of her neckline. His lips kissed away a raindrop.

She trembled.

"It's not safe for you to be out alone." The words moved against her skin.

She didn't answer. Thunder rumbled and matched the erratic pace of her heartbeat.

"Then keep me safe. Please, keep me safe."

Everything inside of her crumbled. Into pieces of shattered heartbreak now scooped and held in Jake's palm. He drew her close until they could feel each other's heartbeat, in unison now.

Jake laid his palms on either side of her face. She felt rivulets of rain trace down her forehead from her drenched hair and dissolve as they met with the heat from his hands. He tilted her head and rested his forehead against hers.

"I won't let anyone hurt you," he rasped.

"I know." Pippa swept her eyes closed as he raised his mouth and pressed a kiss against the bridge of her nose, between her eyes. Tender. Hesitant. She wasn't his. She couldn't be his. They were so far apart, and yet tonight they were almost one as their embrace fused them into a unit.

He drew away only a millimeter, and then his lips touched the corner of her mouth, nudging, begging for her reciprocation.

And she did.

Pippa formed her lips into his. They tingled as they met, and she was no longer in control. He massaged her mouth, gentle, then desperate until his hand pressed against the back of her head and pulled her further into him. He claimed her mouth, made her his, for this moment. This wild, stormy, urgent moment when the forces that pulled them apart dissipated in the power of their emotion.

They sank in a fluid motion toward the straw-strewn floor, his mouth never stopping its caress. Jake pulled her into his arms. She sat in his embrace while the storm raged outside. Safe. And she fit there. Even as he withdrew to a chaste hold, her seated half in his lap, her back against his chest and his chin resting on her shoulder, they watched the raging storm outside. It had not subsided—*wasn't* subsiding. But for now, Pippa didn't care. She was seen. She was seen for being simply who she was. Pippa. No surname, no circus crown or gypsy rags. She was just Pippa. And he? He was just Jake. They were both lost souls crying to be heard and finally finding someone who would listen.

"I saw you and him last night."

Patty Luchent's appearance beside her on the walk was preceded by a whiff of cigarette smoke mixed with flowery perfume.

Pippa would have walked faster had her leg not prevented it. Her nerves were raw. Raw with emotions that ranged from shame to exhilaration. Penn trotted beside her, the only blissfully unaware creature at the moment. She smiled her dog-smile. Happy. Content, having spent a night in the warm horse barn.

"We didn't—" she started, but Patty's red-nailed hand gave a graceful wave.

"Oh, I know, doll." Patty grabbed hold of Pippa's arm. "Hey-a, slow down. Wasting your energy on walking fast isn't going to change anything. There's no shame in finding love."

Pippa jerked her head up to lock eyes with the pretty seamstress. Patty's bobbed hair was held tight by a band around her forehead. Her dangling earrings caught the morning sunlight on their platinum dangles.

"We didn't find love," Pippa corrected. Although, she had defied her father, and in the heat of the moment succumbed to Jake's caress like a wanton woman. Warmth spread over her cheeks.

"Listen here." Patty pulled Pippa off the walk to an iron bench that posed beneath a flaming orange maple tree. She pushed Pippa down and sat next to her. Patty's fingers fumbled with something in Pippa's hair, and she pulled out a piece of straw, flicking it to the grass. "It's all right to be your own woman. To make up your own mind and think for yourself."

Pippa ducked her head. She was sure she shouldn't say out loud what crossed her mind. That Patty's independence also came with a price. The rumors of her own waywardness, the guesthouse by the train depot, potential lovers, even the rumors she'd entertained Al Capone himself.

Patty chuckled, her smile spreading, all too knowing. "Ohh-hhh, yes. Well, my grandmother always used to say, 'If we were all good and flawless, then Jesus wasted His blood.'"

Pippa couldn't help but smile a bit at the comment. She lifted her eyes.

Patty took a long draw from her cigarette perched on the end of an elegant black holder. She gazed into the distance, at the circus buildings, the river behind them, and the rails beyond that. Her eyes shifted to the depot and rested on it.

"I'm getting out of here," she said.

"What do you mean?" Pippa tried to tamp down the night previous, the memory of Jake's kisses, the rain, the way his strength molded into her and infused her with confidence, and the way she awoke in the straw not far from Lily with Jake standing over them, a cigar in his mouth. He'd been watching the door, not them. Pippa had left in a flurry. Muttered words. Awkward embarrassment. If she was seen, her newfound free will would quickly turn into rumors like those that circulated around Patty Luchent.

"It's not good for me here. Not anymore." Patty blew a puff of smoke from her lips. "Funny how things can be seen as a spectacle, whether circus or soul, and yet the truth is never really seen."

She was being cryptic.

Pippa waited.

Patty dropped her gaze from the depot and offered Pippa a reassuring smile that reached the corners of her blue eyes. "There's a darkness here. At Bonaventure Circus. Jake knows it. He's experienced it. Lived it."

Pippa stilled.

"He's always had my back, you know? Mine and Benard's, even

Clive's. But even good fellas like him can't outdo the darkness. No matter how strong he thinks he is." Patty's kohl-lined eyes studied Pippa for a moment. "And it isn't always what you want it to be, darling. The circus is a place of illusions. Of mirrors that alter who we truly are. We may be a family—a community—but we also hide our secrets, even from each other."

Patty's face shadowed as she took a long draw from her cigarette. "Even I hide my own secrets. But," she continued, her voice brightening, "I'll be gone long before they catch up to me. I've got Georgiana to thank for that."

"Georgiana Farnsworth?" Pippa hadn't realized Patty would be associated with someone like Georgiana.

Patty gave another very knowing smile. "She's a misjudged soul too, you know. Her heart's in the right place, but she sees atrocities where there ain't none and doesn't see the real ones that hide away."

"Like what?" Her breath sounded wispy, even to her own ears. Pippa envied the confidence in Patty's shoulders as she drew in a deep breath and squared them, tapping the cigarette so the ash fell to the ground.

"All the bad and the ugly. Like I've been saying already, and I'm not talking about freaks and sideshows. You know, you've talked with Jake. His sister. The others."

"Others?" Pippa's throat tightened, like a hand was squeezing it. A bad omen. An imminent threat.

Patty's eyes narrowed, and again she studied Pippa for a long moment. "You really don't see it, do you? Big cities. Girls, power . . . aw, never mind, doll. You're better off being innocent. Georgiana is helping me get right with life. I'm going to leave Bluff River and this circus—*tonight*. While the Autumn Bluff River Formal is lording its fancies over us peons, I'll be on a train. I've told Georgiana what I know. She can handle the truth from there."

Another reassuring smile. Patty held them as treasures and bestowed them on Pippa like fairy dust.

"The truth?" Pippa echoed, feeling remarkably dim-witted.

"You just stay close to Jake, okay, darling?" Patty tucked a short strand of hair behind Pippa's ear in a sisterly gesture. "Sometimes heroes like him and Georgiana hide in plain sight and no one sees them for who they really are. They're our angels, sent to earth by God himself, I'd say."

Patty rose, her straight dress like a long sheath of gray over her thin body. But her face was brilliant with confidence. She looked down at Pippa. "Go home, Pippa. Go to the Formal and bid your life farewell. Then become what you were meant to be. Only don't do it here either. The circus and its dark corners can ruin a soul. You were saved from it once. Don't come back."

"But what if my family is here? Here at Bonaventure?" Pippa breathed.

"The truth?" Patty took a thoughtful draw from her cigarette. "The truth is that Bonaventure . . . it's not even a tiny bit of what you're expecting." She turned and started down the path away from Pippa, but then hesitated and looked over her shoulder. "Oh, and Pippa?"

"Yes?" Pippa had the strange desire to flee with Patty. To forsake it all, run to the depot, board the next train, and only look back to see the silhouette of her father in his office window on the depot's second floor. Watching her with no intention to chase after or to bring her back home.

"I know about the Watchman, Pippa."

Blood rushed to Pippa's head. Her eyes widened.

Patty gave her a firm nod. "Stay close to Jake, darling. Stay close." She kissed her fingertips, turned them toward Pippa, then proceeded down the walk toward the train depot and toward her new life.

Pippa wanted to rush after Patty. Grab her and make her tell her everything. But Pippa sensed it would be futile. Patty was finished with her. She'd given her goodbye before she left for parts unknown.

How she knew—and what she knew—Pippa couldn't reconcile.

But the way in which Patty gave direction convinced Pippa to follow through with her instructions. Because if Patty could break
away and start a new life, so too could Pippa.

The violin shuddered its haunting melody. Beautiful yet lonely.
The kind of lonely that mimicked Pippa's heartbeat. She had stood
in the face of her father tonight. Stunned him by hooking her
fingers around the elbow of a manure-shoveling circus laborer.
Infuriated him by shunning Forrest, an egotistical replica of her
father. Perhaps it had been foolhardy to request Jake meet her at
the dance and then use him to strike out at her father. But when
she had suggested it, Jake's hesitation was short-lived. They both
knew why. That moment in the barn had seared itself on them
both. From here on out, they were united.

And here she was, enveloped in her silk and sequins, diamond
tiara slid around her head, her strawberry-blond hair curled short
and against her face. Pippa had successfully ostracized herself
from her father, maybe for good. And her mother? Victoria Ripley slipped in and out from among the attendees, graceful, soft-
spoken, and always stealing hesitant glances at her husband. She
wanted his approval. She was what Pippa would have continued
to be were it not for people like Patty, Clive, and Jake. Recognizing
that Pippa was more than a player's piece on a game board. She
had value, and while not always strong enough to stand alone,
she was strong enough to stand nonetheless.

Pippa reached out and fingered a leaf on a potted palm, the
veranda behind her. A breeze drifted through the open doors and
chilled her shoulders.

Jake's breath was warm against her neck as he came up behind
her. His mouth flirted with her ear when he whispered, "Why
aren't you dancing?"

Moisture stuck in Pippa's throat. Maybe she should have clarified with Jake that coming to the dance didn't mean participating

in one. Her leg, twisted in all its ugliness, made dancing for her as mock-worthy as the bearded lady who bore the deprecating laughter of spectators summer after summer.

His nose touched her earlobe. He was bold. Brash even. Jake seemed to come alive with passion when challenged. That he had slicked his hair back from his handsome, broad forehead, trimmed his beard, and somehow encased his body in a tailored suit borrowed from the ringmaster stunned her, excited her, and terrified her all at the same time. Jake was powerful—when he wanted to be.

"I can't dance." Pippa's voice hitched.

"What a waste." His chuckle covered her skin in gooseflesh. Jake's hand pressed against the small of her back. Uncouth and inappropriate, but oh, so right. "Let me teach you."

She dared not look up to where she knew Forrest had rarely taken his eyes from her. She dared not look over her shoulder to see the brewing storm that was her father. Jake was so close, their lips were sure to tangle, and that would just be so wonderful and scandalous.

"Dancing can't be all that hard." His chuckle sent staccato rhythms and toyed with her heartbeat.

"I-I can't." Pippa's eyes burned. But oh, how she wanted to. Dance in his arms with the grace of Franny. Her cousin flitted in front of her, a swath of peacock blues and greens. Graceful. Beautiful. Natural-born to the family tree and exactly where Franny belonged.

Pippa sucked in a breath as Jake's arms slipped around her waist from behind. He pulled her close to his chest. Her shoulders brushed his torso. She could smell the fresh air that clung to his outdated evening coat. The palm plant stuffed into the corner with them hid their embrace, but barely.

Jake swayed to the left, pulling her with him. His arms tightened their grip at her waist. His lips played with her ear. "It's just like being in a boxing ring. Light on your feet. This way, then that."

Pippa nodded. Yes. Sway. She could sway.

"And then you duck a blow." Jake dipped her gently to the left, just enough to make it more of a dance than a dodge. "Then you come up for air."

He brought her upright. What air? She couldn't breathe.

Pippa's bad leg was shaking.

"Are you all right?" Jake didn't stop the intimate sway. He didn't remove his arms.

"I'm fine," Pippa lied. She wasn't fine. She was celebrating a romantic interlude so fragile that she was like Juliet, who cherished her moment with Romeo for fear it would be her last.

Yet here they were.

Jake's lips touched the base of her ear.

Pippa held her breath.

His mouth trailed to the crook between her neck and shoulder and rested there, unmoving. Cherishing. Daring. Challenging opposition.

And Pippa knew as her eyes lifted and locked with Forrest's that this moment would crumble around them into a thousand tiny pieces, irreparable. She let her eyes close. She would breathe deep of this moment. Before her past crashed into her uncertain future.

CHAPTER
THIRTY-SEVEN

Do you want to be the talk of the town in the *News Republic* tomorrow?" Forrest's scathing denunciation ripped into Pippa's already roiling conscience. His hand on her upper arm squeezed to the point of pinching her flesh. Pippa staggered next to him as he pulled her onto the veranda. She cast an anxious glance over her shoulder. Jake had not left her side for the past hour. He had seemed to defend her, and his demeanor challenged the men who'd previously oppressed her. A silent challenge. One that Forrest was fast to meet the instant Jake reluctantly left her side.

A few moments before, he had been summoned with the delivery of a message from the circus grounds. His eyes skimmed it, concern darkened them, and he crumpled the note in his palm.

"Did you know that Patty was leaving the circus?" he'd whispered in her ear.

Pippa looked up at him and couldn't hide the truth. "Yes." The look in his eyes stung a bit. She could see the affection he held for Patty. The loyalty. He'd jammed the message in his pocket. "I need to—Benard messaged me. I can't let Patty leave without—"

His stammering for an explanation told Pippa so much and so little at the same time. That Jake had looked out for Patty was no secret. He'd been doing it probably long before the night he'd left during Lily's birth to help her out of a scrape.

"Go." Pippa nodded. It wasn't fair to try to keep Jake.

"I at least need to check on something. I won't be long." With that, he had slipped away.

It was no surprise then that Forrest pounced the moment Jake left her alone. The dark brooding of his eyes and the rigid demeanor of his body told Pippa he would be Richard Ripley's voice tonight.

"Let me be." Pippa tried to shake off his hold.

Forrest released her only when she had backed against the stone banister. Light glowed from the ballroom and silhouetted Forrest's shoulders. Crickets chirruped from the yard below and matched the rapid beating of Pippa's heart.

Forrest's finger pointed toward the ballroom, his other hand propped on his waist. "I would have thought you of all people would know how important tonight is. To regain the good graces of this community. Instead you're cavorting in the corner with the brute who started it all. If you think that will go unnoticed, you're a fool."

Pippa should have been used to Forrest's sour insults by now. But she wasn't. She placed her hand over her chest and tried to calm herself. "We're over, Forrest."

She was breaking their engagement. It was both freeing and terrifying the moment the words escaped her lips.

"Don't be ridiculous. You *need* me."

"I don't, Forrest. Not anymore."

"I don't have time for this behavior, Pippa. Not with Miss Farnsworth here in attendance and ready to cause a rouse." Forrest shot a glance into the ballroom, as if Georgiana were about to set free a giant python. He jabbed his finger toward her chest but didn't touch her. "Reform your behavior at once."

"I've no behavior to reform." She straightened and glared at her intended.

Forrest harrumphed, scoffing. He stuck his hands in his pockets, and his jacket bunched up behind his arms. "The circus is in disarray since Georgiana's rallies and the sabotage on the tent. And it all started the night Jake Chapman decided to abandon the elephant calf. What else is his magic touch going to light on fire?"

She blushed.

His eyes darkened. "You are playing with that fire, aren't you, Pippa?"

"You don't know what you're talking about." Pippa turned her face to avoid Forrest.

"Don't you know who he is?" Forrest gripped her chin and forced her to face him.

Pippa whimpered. She twisted her neck to try to release his hold on her, but to no avail. His features were stern, intense and insistent. "I told you that *I* would take care of you. *I* would protect you. Stay away from Jake Chapman, and for all that is holy, stay away from the circus."

"Stay away from the circus?" Pippa winced as Forrest's fingers bit into her jawline. She felt claustrophobic in the circle of his arms.

"You don't understand, Pippa, and you shouldn't."

"No, Forrest." Pippa craned her neck to the left, and Forrest finally released her chin. "*You* don't understand. I belong there. It's where I was born, Forrest, and I can't get it out of my blood."

"Pippa!" Forrest dropped his voice to a deep hiss. "It's too dangerous. The tent ropes being tampered with and the tent collapsing was no accident. You can't insert yourself into a place like that. It's not for you."

"But I thought you believed Georgiana to be behind the tent catastrophe? Behind the chaos?"

Forrest shook his head. "Georgiana is a publicity issue. But I know better. There have been *other* incidents. *Accidents* that happen, and women—" He stopped abruptly. "There's a real threat here, Pippa, and I'm telling you that you need to stop this nonsense before you get hurt."

"You're talking about the Watchman, aren't you?" Pippa whispered. None of it was true. None of it made any sense.

Forrest's eyes darkened. "If you can't see all I've done to protect you, you're more blind and foolish than I ever thought you
were."

"No. *You're* the foolish one." Pippa's response rose from the
depths of her. Words she'd always wished to be brave enough to
say. Her tone was even, her confidence sure. "You were foolish to
ever think I could love you."

The slap from the back of Forrest's hand seemed to shock him
as much as it stung Pippa. His face whitened. Her hands flew up
to cup her cheeks, the skin beneath on fire from his smack.

"Pippa!" Forrest's apologetic cry rent the air between them.

"Get away from me!" Pippa swiped at the tears that came unbidden, even as she shrank back against the veranda's stone rail.
"Get away from me . . ."

Forrest's expression looked as shattered as she felt. There was
no loyalty where Pippa was concerned, and he had proven that
to her tonight.

The roar from the doorway crashed into the stunned silence
between them. Jake charged Forrest, having come out of nowhere,
apparently finished—or not having left yet—for whatever mission
he'd been on to pursue the departing Patty.

Pippa stumbled away from the men, and the moment she heard
the first shriek of a woman when Forrest and Jake toppled into the
ballroom, she ran. More screams. Men hollering at the clamor as
Jake and Forrest collided with the refreshment table. Goblets collapsed from their pyramid and shattered into pieces on the floor.

Georgiana Farnsworth froze in mid-stride with a sign she had
just hoisted to cause problems of her own: *End the Circus, End
the Abuse.*

Franny clutched her aunt Victoria Ripley's arm, and they both
held a free hand over their gaping mouths in horror at the spectacle.

Pippa ran. Or at least as much of a run as she could muster, with her leg throbbing and her feet unsteady. She pushed through the chaos and elbowed her way past men who stood like statues, frozen in awe at the sheer glory that was Jake Chapman, scrappy ring fighter.

She sucked in a sob as she rounded the corner into the entry-way. Pippa's flight was cut off by the abrupt slam into the body of Richard Ripley. He grappled for her, saving her from falling into a disgraced pile of silk and deformity.

A word. Any word of empathy, compassion, or even a bewildered question would have made Pippa pause. Instead, she saw the emptiness in his eyes.

"I . . ." Pippa couldn't even mutter her apology. She wasn't sorry. Or was she? Confusion and desperation saturated every ounce of her. She righted herself, and he stepped away. "Father, I . . ." She searched his face for something, anything, but could see he was done with her.

Pippa limped toward the door, one step for every tear that trailed down her cheeks. She burst onto the front steps. No longer did the pleasant, inviting sounds of musical strings reach her ears. Instead it was the clamor of men and women, the sound of glass shattering, as if the entire ball had broken into an all-out brawl.

There was only one place left she could run. Only one place that held even the slightest hope of bringing light into the chaos. It echoed in Pippa's heart, over and over again. Three words. One promise.

I love you.

She would find him tonight. She would search for the Watch-man, tell him she understood his pain, and see her birth father's face for the first time. She would believe in him, like no one had believed in her. Believe that he wasn't the man Jake sought. Believe that he'd been misjudged and mistreated just as she had always been. Perhaps she was being foolish. Rushing headlong into danger. Unwise and even stupid. But there was nothing left to hold her back. Nothing but the brawling elephant trainer who had vowed to enact justice on the very man Pippa wished to find salvation from.

The shadows of the train depot drew Pippa as she made her way toward the circus grounds. Maybe she could see Patty just one more time. Infuse herself with the contagious enthusiasm Patty possessed for believing that life could be better. She passed the hotel where the circus staff lived and slept. It was quiet. A few windows were lit, maybe Clive's, maybe Benard's . . . definitely not Jake's.

A train whistled in the distance. The stars stared down but didn't twinkle. They were afraid to look, to watch from their perch in the sky and see the drama unfolding beneath. At least that was what skittered through Pippa's mind as she took note of them.

The river cut through the circus grounds, its sparkling water reflecting the moon. The tent that had collapsed left an empty void on the skyline, but the row of animal buildings was there. Lily was there. Slowly strengthening, slowly regaining her health. It was a strange paradigm, the ruined tent and the renewal of Lily. Like darkness warring with light, despair with hope. What was the circus really but a façade for them all? A pretend place of wonder when behind its beautiful and celebratory cover were hurting hearts, broken people, and wanderers who had nowhere else to go.

The whistle sounded in the distance again, only this time nearer.

Pippa limped forward. A thud from inside the costume house snagged her attention. Down the row of animal houses was the answering ice-sharp chirrup of a peacock.

Then she heard a shuffling from the far corner of the costume house. "Hello?" Pippa craned her neck to peer into the darkness. "Is someone there?"

Silence.

Pippa tiptoed into the shadows, each step hesitant, each accompanied by misgivings.

"He took my sister—strangled breath from Bridgette—and she wasn't the only one."

Another footstep into the blackness of the night drowned out the memory of Jake's recounting of his sister's murder.

"If it weren't for Jake, I'd be a mess. He was there for me when— well, when others weren't."

Another footstep, the echoes of Patty's musings only solidifying the potential of Jake's credibility and claim that the Watchman was not who Pippa hoped he was.

"Remember, what to us seem like God's biggest errors, to Him they are His largest promises."

She stumbled, and Pippa palmed the porch rail of the costume house to catch herself. Clive's voice filled her thoughts, and the faith he held that she never truly understood.

The river that cut through the grounds filled the void as its waters hummed a melancholy tune, rippling over rocks and debris in its path. She stepped onto the bottom porch step of the house.

Another shuffling sound.

Pippa whirled around as if someone stood behind her. No one. She rubbed her bare arms, conscious of the fact she wore neither cape nor shawl. The chill of the night emphasized her growing unease. The grounds were so empty tonight.

"There are things you shouldn't know."

Forrest.

"I love you."

The Watchman.

She should go home.

"You came." The words ripped through her as they were delivered behind her left ear.

Pippa started and jerked around. She stared into the gaping black holes of the hood. Eyes blinked in the caverns, but she could see nothing else.

She stumbled back, her heel hitting the step, and her left foot lifting to balance on the step above it. Her height on the stairs made her almost eye to eye with him.

The Watchman stood silent. Trousers, plain shirt, hands at his sides. No definable features, and the burlap sack that doubled as a hood was tied around his throat with a red bandanna.

"Did you find it?" he asked. His voice was muffled by the hood.

Pippa couldn't find her voice. It was far more terrifying separated by only a few feet. She nodded. Yes, she had found the zebra toy. But its message of love was perverted by the sinister appearance of the hooded man up close.

She moved up another step, and he held up a hand. "Don't be frightened! I've waited—for an eternity for you to know."

"H-how did you know I was here?" Pippa searched to identify him by his voice, his stance, anything. There were vague recollections of having heard his voice before, but she couldn't place it.

The Watchman tipped his head to the side as if the answer was obvious. "I've always watched you. Since you were born. Since I left the zebra with you as a baby so you would know." He took a half step forward. "You were always meant for me. I've watched over you, just as I promised your mother."

Visions of the joy in reuniting with her birth father were becoming clouded with uneasiness. Pippa retreated another step.

The Watchman followed. "I was hasty to meet you here the night Lily was hurt."

He knew of Lily. He was no stranger to the circus.

"I realized after, when I saw you with them—with those men. I needed to know you understood how I felt before we met. I needed to know you felt the same way about me. That you loved me too."

Pippa bit at her fingernail.

"Do you?" he asked, wrapping his fingers around the stair railing.

Pippa's feet found the porch floor. "Do I what?" she whispered.

"Love me," he replied simply.

She tried to see through his hood, to see if there was any hint of emotion in his eyes, but they were empty. It was night. He was hidden.

"Women are fickle, you know. And they are liars." He tilted his head, assessing her. "All these years, you—you've been honest. Vulnerable."

"The letters." Pippa could see the box of them on her desk at home. Short missives. Cryptic. About his undying devotion. Explanation of his shame.

He lifted a hand to touch her, then hesitated. "I've waited. Those letters were the beginning of meeting you again. The zebra toy was my promise to you when you were yet a baby that I would be back."

"Who are you?" A cold gust penetrated the silk of her dress and swept across the exposed skin of her neckline and arms.

She could see his eyes blink behind the shroud.

"You don't know?"

Pippa shook her head. "I don't know you."

The Watchman stiffened. He was visibly stunned. "I thought you would understand when you saw the toy."

Pippa grappled to hold on to something, to steady her shaking legs. But there was nothing except empty porch covered in darkness. The answering silence was taut with the Watchman's obvious torment. He stepped to the side, then back, his shoes clomping on the step. He wrung his hands, and his knuckles popped.

"All these years? The letters? I held you as a baby. Your mother— she was like my own. She took me in when no one else would. And she made me promise—*promise* that I would watch over you. And I have."

Yes. He had. But not in the way she imagined a father would. Her hopes collapsed with the realization. The stunning power of the fact that his body was erect, lithe, and young. His voice that of a man's minus the quivering of age. He was not her father. He was not what Pippa had conjured in her dreams—a lost guardian who merely wished to reunite with her, to claim parentage, to finally bring her home to the circus.

Pippa looked up the street. It was empty. Dark. Even the animals had grown silent. The only sound was the rippling water of the river. Jake's story of the Watchman and Bridgette seemed more real now. More plausible. Her own foolishness stark in the context of the moment.

The Watchman's breath sounded hollow. "When your mother died, they tossed you aside, just like they did me."

"Like they did you?" Dread continued to grow inside her.

The Watchman's voice was sharp. That voice. She *knew* it, but she couldn't identify it.

"I tried," he went on, an undertone of desperation in his words. "I tried to love someone else, but they—they only lied to me. It was you, Pippa. It's always been you."

The need in the Watchman's voice had lowered the tone a notch. Threatening.

Pippa didn't answer. She couldn't. She reached behind her. Fumbling, her fingers finally meeting up with the cold handle of the costume house screen door.

"Don't you love me?" the Watchman repeated, tilting his head to the left as if seeking to read her soul.

Pippa swallowed. No. He wasn't her father. He wasn't anybody but a lost boy in a grown man's body who was obsessed with knowing her. Her insides chilled. He had stalked her, for years, and she had opened her heart to him—to the man she thought was someone else entirely.

"No." The whispered word of rejection escaped her mouth.

The Watchman's hands shot out, and he yanked her to himself. "Don't tell me that!" He shook her.

Pippa's cry for help clung to her lips as she was swallowed up by the black voids in his hood. She lost her grip on the screen door and it banged back against its frame. Pippa twisted. She had to break free.

"Why are you doing this?"

The Watchman dragged her back until she was pressed against his chest. In quick steps, he pushed her face forward against the rough screen of the door, its frame digging into her waist. "You've always been mine. Your mother gave you to *me*, not to be left on the Ripleys' doorstep!"

His hand crawled up to her throat. He shoved her into the door. "Patty—she wasn't you. Not my Pippa."

Nausea roiled in Pippa's stomach. *Patty!* Had she survived an assault herself? Had she hidden the horrible secret behind her smile, her cigarettes, and her rough faith?

The Watchman's fingers spread across her cheek. His breath was hot in her face. Chilling eyes, almost shimmering, stared out from their tombs.

"Please, let me go." Pippa struggled against his hold, but he was too strong.

The Watchman's mouth pushed against her ear, separated only by the shroud over his head. Its rough burlap scratched her face. "I was going to take care of you. But I can't. Not if you don't love me."

He dragged her with him as he whipped open the screen door. The scream that tore from her throat was loud enough to awaken the elephants. Pippa struggled to break his hold on her. A trumpet sounded. *Please. Make noise. Awaken someone. Ernie. Anyone.* But what if this *was* Ernie?

Pippa clawed at the mask.

He slapped her away. His hands bruised her as he manhandled her against him. The Watchman twisted the doorknob and flung open the costume house door. He forced Pippa in front of him and then spun her so she faced the inside.

"We were meant to be together. *She* lied to me. She didn't tell me about the baby." The Watchman crooned into her ear with the devotion of an obsessed and jilted lover.

"Who? What baby?"

His words sickened her, as did his intent as he shoved her into

343

the blackness of the costume house. "Say you're mine, Pippa. Say it." His breath was hot in her ear.

"I-I can't." Her fingernails dug into his arms, clawing, scratching, but it didn't seem to bother him. He pushed her farther into the room. Pippa tripped on her bad leg and fell to the floor, her knees connecting hard with the floorboards.

The Watchman straddled her, his hands closing around her throat. Squeezing. She clawed at them. Breathe. She needed to breathe.

"Say you're mine," he insisted, then lifted her head and banged it back against the floor.

As blackness drifted over her vision, Pippa looked up. She saw bare feet hanging above her. Swaying. Like a silent dance with death. A limp hand dangled, and Pippa heard the creak of a rope as the body swayed. Then she recognized it.

Patty.

Patty hung above her, dead, her head tilted above the noose of a rope. Just shy of meeting her train, of finding new hope.

Pippa's scream gargled in her throat as the Watchman's hands dug into her larynx. Out of the corner of her eye she saw movement behind him, and a small body leapt from the ground, launching toward the Watchman. The stature was unmistakable, his expression one of fierce protection and determination. His chance of survival against the brute who straddled her, improbable.

"Clive." Pippa's gasp was choked. "No!"

CHAPTER THIRTY-EIGHT

CHANDLER

Chandler snatched the pamphlet with the listing of cities where the circus train had stopped, and she almost tripped over her shoes as she clambered down the stairs. She'd ended her call with Hank, but when she reached the bottom of the steps, she swiped the screen until she found the number she intended to call next.

His voice was groggy when he answered.

"Cru?" Chandler didn't wait for him to respond. "Who would have traveled with the circus in 1928? Someone who might also have connections at the depot?"

"Chandler?" She could picture Cru squinting at the clock, seeing it was one in the morning and deeming her crazy. She didn't care.

Peter was out there. Alone. Crying. She knew he was crying. Her sensitive soul of a little boy. Chandler forced her thoughts to the puzzle at hand. If she could solve it, if she could piece together the connections, maybe she could find who wanted her to stop digging in the first place. Who hadn't wanted her to find Linda, and who had taken Peter for no good reason than sick revenge or trying to distract her?

"Cru, think. Was there anyone in history tied to both the train station and the circus?"

She heard rustling. Bedsprings creaking. Finally, "Okay, yeah, I dunno, Chandler. My mom might know. Why? What's this got to do with any—?"

"I'm at my office. I'm trying to . . ." No. She didn't have time to explain. "Never mind. I'll call your mom. I know it's late but—"

"It's fine. Call her. I'll throw on some clothes and meet you there. You shouldn't be alone."

Chandler hesitated as she hung up on Cru. She shook her thoughts clear and punched Lottie's number. A few seconds later, another sleepy voice answered, but then Lottie was instantly aware once Chandler explained and inquired with her questions.

Lottie cleared her throat on the other end, obviously wracking her brain trying to recall all the subtle historical details she might know.

"There were a few offices in the depot the Ripleys used—circus management offices. I don't know exactly who all worked there, though."

Anxious excitement mounted within Chandler. She slumped onto her chair and bounced her knee up and down. "Someone important. Someone who may have met the circus at various points on its summer tour."

The air was quiet for a few seconds, followed by Lottie's hesitant voice. "Ripley?"

Chandler straightened.

"The owner, Richard Ripley," Lottie suggested. "He would have worked out of those offices. He would have had the finances to meet up with his circus occasionally."

Chandler had no care for the whys or even if he was a plausible suspect. She barreled forward with her line of reasoning. "Who is still alive who might be related to the Ripleys? Someone who didn't like Linda Pike snooping around the depot, trying to clear her grandfather's name? Someone who didn't like that I found the Watchman's hideaway and wants to shut down any further findings?"

Lottie clicked her tongue. "I'm thinking. No one in Linda Pike's close circle of friends. I was one of them and—and, no, none of us. Sure, some of us had relations in the circus, but that's not uncommon in Bluff River. But related directly to the Ripleys? I can't think of anyone left here who is."

"The Ripleys couldn't have just disappeared into oblivion," Chandler argued.

"Well, no, but they aren't around Bluff River anymore. At least Richard Ripley's line. His daughter died years ago, somewhere in North Carolina, I believe. All his descendants are down South now."

Desperation flooded Chandler. "Think, Lottie, think." *Use your blasted insight if you have to!* she wanted to yell.

"Oh!" Lottie's voice rose over the phone. "No. No, never mind." She dismissed just as fast whatever she'd been thinking.

"What?" Chandler insisted. "Anything, even something little, might help!"

Lottie's breath shook on the other end. "I remember—well, the Ripleys *did* have extended family in Bluff River way back when. There was a niece who was quite vocal against the circus. In fact, she used to hobnob with my grandmother, who truly hated the circus for penning up its animals."

Chandler tapped her fingers on the desk, waiting impatiently as Lottie started pulling the pieces together.

"My grandmother Farnsworth was a spitfire. She pulled Richard Ripley's niece, Franny, into her cause to picket the circus. I remember her telling me about it. She said she knew stuff about the circus that would make folks' heads spin. But for whatever reason—out of deference maybe, people she knew?—she didn't say much about the matter. She *was* a friend of Patty Luchent, though. That's how I know so much about Patty. Grandma Farnsworth was going to help Patty leave town, right before Patty died. She'd helped Patty a year prior with placing her daughter in a home, kept it rather secretive, and—"

"Patty Luchent had a baby?" Chandler interrupted.

"Yes. At least that's what my grandmother said. No one ever knew for sure. If she was telling the truth—which she did like to exaggerate things—then Denny Pike's mother was Patty Luchent's daughter and the Watchman's offspring. Still . . . that's off the subject. Grandmother Farnsworth's protégé was Franny Ripley. She was Ripley's niece. Another little flutter bug of a gal for her day, I guess. I'm not sure what happened to her, but she settled in Bluff River until she died."

"So, her offspring would be direct descendants of circus family?" Chandler concluded.

"Mm-hmm . . ." Lottie said, her voice growing quiet.

"Who's her offspring?" Chandler pressed.

"Chandler, I'm sure—it can't be—" Lottie argued weakly.

"Lottie." Chandler heard the sharp command in her voice.

Lottie must have too. She sighed over the phone and finally muttered, "Margie. Margie is Franny Ripley's descendant."

The phone slipped from Chandler's hand and collided with the floor of the costume house.

PIPPA

From the darkness and through the fog of pain, Pippa woke. She was no longer in the costume house. No longer on the floor beneath Patty's lifeless body that dangled from the rafters. Damp grass lay beneath her. She'd been pulled from the house. Or carried maybe? Dragged. At least that was how her body felt. Pippa moaned, trying to clear her mind as she lifted herself from the ground.

"Clive!" Her scream brought clarity rushing back in. He lay a few feet from her, his body bruised, but it was evident he had tried to get her from the house to help of some sort. If he had bested the Watchman, he was nowhere to be seen. Clive was unresponsive.

Pippa scrambled on all fours to his side.

"Clive!" She shook his shoulder. There was a small moan to indicate life, but other than that, he remained silent. She hooked her arms beneath Clive's shoulders and dragged him. The man was short, stocky, and his head lolled to the side as if he were dead.

Pippa laid him down and turned. She looked up as lantern lights hanging from the side of a motorcar lit the street. Scurrying to her feet, ignoring the pain in her battered body, she stumbled toward the road, waving her arms.

She didn't expect to see—and for the moment, didn't care—Forrest and Jake both alighting from the car. Their suit coats were gone, their shirts torn and bloodied from their scrape. Forrest was sporting a swollen lip and a massive black eye. Jake appeared ruffled, with a split on his cheekbone and dried blood on his cheek.

"It's Clive!" Pippa wasted no time. "You've got to help him! He's been hurt!"

Forrest lurched past her, and Jake followed but stopped at Pippa.

He gripped her arms, bending to search her face and body for injuries. "Are you all right?"

She nodded, and a sob caught in her throat. "The Watchman—tried to kill me, Jake. And Patty—"

"What about Patty?" Jake's face had gone pale in the moonlight.

"She's dead. She's in the costume house." Pippa felt like she might vomit.

"Jake!" Forrest's commanding voice eliminated the opportunity to grieve further. Jake pushed past Pippa and raced toward Forrest and Clive. He dropped to his knees and felt for the dwarf's pulse.

"It's erratic, but he's alive."

"He looks bad. Get him to my car," Forrest directed Jake, who nodded.

"Pippa . . ." he began.

But she couldn't look at him. She was frozen. Staring through the darkness toward a suspicious form in the shadows. "It's him," she whispered, and tremors started in her body. A violent shaking, fear and the knowledge that yards away stood the man she'd once believed held the hope for her future. It was the Watchman. His body half hidden by the edge of the costume house, but the outline of his masked face was visible in the moonlight. He was watching. Watching his handiwork.

Jake sprang from the ground beside Clive and sprinted for the corner of the building. The Watchman saw Jake running toward him, and he spun, racing toward the river and the train yard beyond it. There was intent in Jake's movements.

"Jake!" Pippa screamed. Not to stop him, but for no other reason than utter gut-wrenching fear that he would kill the Watchman. Kill him as Patty had predicted and have blood stain his hands that he could never wash off.

"Pippa!" Forrest's voice followed her as she chased after Jake as much as her bad leg allowed her.

Jake sprang forward, his arms encircling the Watchman and tackling him to the ground. They collapsed and rolled on the grass. Jake grunted as he flipped the Watchman onto his back and pressed his forearm against the man's neck.

"You son of a—" Jake's words were muffled as he brought his fist into the Watchman's face.

The Watchman clawed at Jake's arm with his good hand.

"What did you do?" Jake shouted in his hooded face.

Another strike, this time accompanied by Jake's knee in the Watchman's gut.

He was going to pummel the man to death.

"Jake!" Pippa shouted and flung herself forward. Forrest caught her arm, but she ripped from his grasp.

"Pippa, leave him!" Forrest commanded.

She met the whites of his eyes with her own fearful glance. Forrest shook his head, his hair askew. The moonlight made his eyes look deep-set and frantic.

"We need to take care of Clive."

Jake was shouting in conjunction with more assaults on the Watchman.

Pippa waved at Forrest. "Go. Take Clive to the hospital." She ran from him, her feet pounding across the yard, her ankle twisting as her bad leg refused to cooperate. She sprawled on the earth only to have Forrest haul her back up. Tearing herself from his grip, she screamed at Jake.

Jake was inches from the Watchman's covered face. His eyes were wild as his hands wrapped around the neck of the one who had murdered Bridgette. Taken his sister and ruined the last year of Jake's life as he sought to find this man. To bring him to justice—while not lawful—one that would end in termination.

"Tell me who you are!" Pippa cried, dropping to her knees beside them as Jake pushed the man against the ground.

The man flung his head back and forth.

"Tell her!" Jake resumed the pressure, and the man coughed through his mask.

A half sob, half laugh pushed through the hood. "I didn't mean to hurt anyone. Not like him. I'm not *him*! I just—needed Pippa!"

Pippa's fingers tangled with the knot in the bandanna around the Watchman's neck. She could tell he was crying beneath his covering. Fight drained from the Watchman, but not from Jake.

Finally, Pippa slipped the knot loose. She yanked off the bandanna, and the hood released. Now was the time. The time she would see the man who had terrorized Jake's sister. Who had murdered Patty and seriously injured Clive. Who had planted in Pippa false dreams that had faded into oblivion.

She reached out and tore the hood from the man's face.

CHANDLER

Chandler snatched her keys from the desk with such force, they went flying out of her hand and skidded across the floor. She dived after and grabbed them, charging from the costume house, the screen door slamming behind her. As she sprinted for her car, another pulled up against the curb.

Cru.

He rolled down the window. "Where're you going?"

"Home!" she yelled and yanked open his passenger door without asking. Chandler was shaking. She'd be lucky not to pass out. "I need to call the police. It's Margie."

"*Margie!*" Cru drew back, staring at Chandler incredulously.

"Go, go, *go!*" Chandler pounded on the dashboard.

Cru shifted into drive and hit the gas, the tires squealing as he pulled away from the curb.

Taking out her phone, Chandler punched in 911. "Detective Pagiano was working the case," she explained. "I think it's my nanny. My nanny took my son!"

Cru kept ping-ponging glances between Chandler and the road.

She ended the call. "They're dispatching units."

Cru shook his head. "Why does Margie have anything to do with Peter?"

"Because she was home alone with him and had the opportunity to make it look like however she wanted it to. She's a Ripley by bloodline. We did the same thing Linda Pike did and stumbled into the entire sordid history of the Ripley family. Hank was right. It wasn't—*it couldn't have been*—the Watchman who killed all those women. Maybe he murdered Patty, maybe because she'd had his kid and given it away, but not the others. That was all Ripley. It *had* to be Ripley!"

"You know you're not making any sense and sound completely

irrational, don't you?" Cru offered her an apologetic wince, then turned the corner toward the rental cottage.

"Since when is crime rational?" Chandler retorted.

The car screeched to a stop in front of the house, and Chandler bolted from it, Cru yelling after her from the driver's side. She bounded up the stairs and burst into the house.

"Chandler!" Her mom, Sherry, clutched at her throat as Chandler barged into the kitchen.

"Where is she?"

"Who?" Sherry swallowed, catching her breath from her fright, her plaid pajamas dark against her pale expression.

"Margie! Where is Margie? Did she go home?" Chandler demanded, marching past her mother into the living room.

Tom, her dad, hurried down the stairs, his hair tousled as though he'd been trying to sleep but couldn't. "What's going on?"

Sirens in the distance alerted him.

"Did they find Peter?" Tom demanded, following Chandler from the living room into the small bathroom just off the hall.

Chandler whipped back the shower curtain as if Margie would, for some reason, be hiding there.

"Where is Margie?" she insisted again.

Tom gripped her by the shoulders, but Chandler shook him off. "Leave me alone, Dad. I need to find Margie. I need to find my son."

"Chandler!"

Her father's voice was sharp. It pierced her growing panic and sent a wave of shock through her. Eyes wide, she stared at him.

"Listen to me!" Tom was stern but loving, his expression gentle around the eyes. "Stop for a second. Pull yourself together. Panicking isn't going to help anything, and you need to think straight."

Chandler didn't respond. She couldn't. He might be right. She hated to admit it, but he might be right.

Tom continued, "Let us help you. Yes, we were disappointed with the choices you made back then, but that's all in the past now. I don't care anymore and neither does your mom. Together, we have Peter. Please, Chandler, let us in! Let us share with you. Stop hiding from us."

Stop hiding . . .

The words shattered Chandler. Had she projected her own feelings about herself onto them? Had *she* pushed *them* away? In her desperation to prove herself, had she truly gone into hiding?

It didn't matter now. Peter did. And only Peter.

"Honey." It was Mom. She wrapped her arms around Chandler from behind. "Baby, the police just got here. They found Margie. They said other cops arrested Margie across town at her apartment. She's swearing she had nothing to do with it, but they found evidence that Peter was in her house."

Chandler broke free of her parents and ran to the living room. Cru was standing, bewildered, in the center of the room.

"Ma'am." A policewoman stepped in front of Chandler. "Ma'am, I need you to stop." She held her palms out toward Chandler, who skidded to a halt.

"Chandler!" Mom cried from behind her.

Chandler skimmed the officer's face. The eyes that squinted as if afraid to look directly at Chandler. Worry and restless angst carved into every curve of the policewoman's face. Numbness filled Chandler, rushing through her like a wave of cold reality. Along with it came the memory of Linda Pike's body. Her dead bones hidden for years. She thought of Margie, working in her home. Caring for her, caring for Peter, all the while those same hands had hidden a dead woman in the train depot. That same mind that had baked them cookies had also boarded up Linda Pike's corpse, hoping it would never be found.

Chandler's eyes locked with the officer's.

If Margie had killed once . . .

"No." Chandler shook her head back and forth. "No, no, no . . ."

CHAPTER
THIRTY-NINE

PIPPA

Pippa was unprepared for the face below her. Unprepared to see his mottled skin, his haunted eyes, and the familiarity of his expression. Jake's knees dug into the man's side, his forearm pressing into his chest. His breaths were labored.

"Why?" The question tore from his throat. The pain of his friend's betrayal knifed across Jake's face.

Benard twisted his deformed face away from them. Tears stained his cheeks and glistened in the moonlight.

Jake rammed his hands against Benard's chest and he sat back, still straddling the man. His own knuckles were bloody from pummeling Benard, but now his vengeance was stilled for a moment. Stilled by the shock that it was his friend beneath him.

"Why, Benard?" Jake choked out. He shook his head in stunned disbelief. "I've—helped you. You and Patty both. *Why?*" Jake's face was inches from Benard's. "You took everything from my sister."

"Your sister?" Benard shook his head. "I don't know who you're talking about, Jake." His eyes lifted to Pippa. "It's you. It's only been you."

Jake's lip curled, and he shoved his thumb and fingers beneath

Benard's chin. He would make the man face him. Make him answer for his deeds. "What about Patty?"

Benard blinked. A jealous glint sparked in his weeping eyes. "Patty—I tried. I thought maybe if I couldn't have Pippa, I'd be happy with Patty. But . . . Jake, she got rid of our kid! You know she did! Just like *he* got rid of Pippa, and I had no choice with either of them. Pippa or my newborn girl. Why would Patty do that? Give her away? And—Pippa—" He looked back at her, and she was torn between utter repulsion and hatred. "You've always been mine."

"Pippa's, not yours!" Jake kneed him.

Benard grunted and gave a half laugh. "I've watched Pippa grow up. I held her as a baby when I was thirteen. I saw her leg. I saw him leave her on the Ripleys' doorstep, and I vowed—I vowed I would never leave her."

"Who left her?"

"Her father. Clive!" Benard's grunted exclamation weakened Jake's grip.

Pippa fell backward. Her breath was stolen from her, almost as if Jake himself had leveled a fist to her gut.

Jake nearly lost his hold on Benard, but then recovered. He pushed Benard harder against the ground. "What are you saying?"

Benard flung his head to the side to free himself from Jake's clutches. "Clive's wife was like my own mother. When she died, he couldn't take care of Pippa. You've seen him. The world doesn't take people like us seriously! A short man with a normal-sized daughter? He took her to Ripley, and I left a toy with her. I told her then I loved her. I vowed I'd take care of her."

Jake dragged Benard up from the ground, scrambling to his feet alongside of him. He pushed his face into Benard's and shook him. Hard. "What about Bridgette? What about my sister?"

Benard's smile was both coherent and unfriendly. He snorted, blood running from his nose. "He stole my idea. The hood. He stole my idea and wore it. But I didn't kill those girls. I didn't kill them, Jake."

Jake's jaw twitched with hardly concealed fury. His knuckles were white as his fingers curled into Benard's shirt, pulling the man into him. "You killed Patty," he gritted into Benard's face.

Benard looked confused. "Well, yeah, Jake." His tone was pleading, as though Jake was dumb and should understand. "She got rid of our baby girl. I couldn't let it happen again. Not after Pippa."

Jake gave another shake, spit out another curse, but Pippa heard no more. She was stunned. Trembling. Everything she'd thought she surmised as truth was a lie. Clive. Her father. All this time . . . Pippa's gaze fell to the empty hood on the ground. It had hidden more than a man obsessed with what he felt belonged to him. It had hidden the secrets of her birth, and with it the stunning reality that her father had always been inches away.

CHANDLER

It looked like it might rain. Dawn was creeping over the horizon, yet all Chandler could do was sit on the front porch of her rental and stare vacantly up the quiet street. Leaves danced softly down as they dislodged from their summer homes on branches turning bare. Omens of winter, cold and solemn.

A teal chenille blanket lowered over Chandler's shoulders. Her mom eased onto the porch swing next to her and pushed a hot thermos of tea into Chandler's hands.

They'll find him was often the typical, expected phrase spoken at times like this. Instead, Mom simply leaned against Chandler and whispered, "I haven't stopped praying."

"I don't have any more words to pray." Chandler's voice was dull. Even to her own ears.

"Your father just got off the phone with the police," Mom

informed her. "Apparently, Margie has confessed. At least to killing that other woman."

"Then they should find out where Peter is." Chandler leaned forward, her elbows on her knees, her face in her palms. "Margie. Why?" she whispered. Lifting her head, she met her mom's direct gaze. "What if Margie doesn't tell them where Peter is? What if—?"

"Shh." Her mom reached out and ran her hand over Chandler's back in a calming gesture. "We can't go there, Chandler. Not yet."

Lottie Dobson stepped onto the porch, the screen door slamming behind her with the exclamation point that all was not yet well.

"Margie." Lottie eased into a porch chair with a sigh. "I never saw that one coming. But you were right, Chandler. She was trying to save herself—to save her reputation."

Mom patted Chandler's knee.

"Which is bull-pucky," Lottie scoffed. "The fact is, Margie saw what Bluff River did to Denny and to Linda. They wore that brand of being offspring of a serial killer like a tattoo that passed itself down from generation to generation." She blew a puff of air and it lifted her graying blond bangs off her forehead. "Margie is a coward. A *coward*. She can't stand the idea that someone would look sideways at her for the rest of her life, just like they did to the Pike kids. Bloodline of a serial killer. No. She wouldn't want that. Not Margie."

Chandler didn't really care that the women were both talking to each other over her head. She was too numb, too disembodied to respond or to move.

"So, we think this Ripley fellow who founded Bonaventure Circus *was* actually the Watchman?" Mom asked.

Lottie nodded but not without a shrug of question. "Cru was chatting it up with one of the detectives a few minutes ago. I guess, when they examined the evidence found in the room Chandler and Hank uncovered, they found the initials R.R. etched into each circus token. For Richard Ripley, they figure. And checking records, they confirmed that space was his office."

"How awful," Mom breathed.

Lottie nodded. "The worst thing? It's really not substantial enough evidence to formally change history. Two initials? Who really can know what was the truth? The Watchman—Benard, Denny Pike's grandfather, or Richard Ripley? We'll probably never know for certain."

"But they thought they knew back then, didn't they?" Mom shifted in her chair. Chandler could sense her concerned assessment. They were keeping her busy, keeping her mind preoccupied with anything but the silence in the outcome of Peter's fate.

Lottie gave a sad nod. "They did. Benard spent his entire life behind bars. Honestly? He *did* confess to killing Patty Luchent, and God knows what else he did to people. So, he was in no way innocent. Just maybe not of the Watchman's string of killings. Which man wore the mask of the killer? Maybe both."

Mom picked her fingernails. It was a nervous gesture, and one Chandler recognized because she'd adopted it herself.

A light rain began to fall. The fresh smell mingled with the dying leaves.

Chandler pushed off the porch swing, feeling the eyes of both women on her back. She wanted to stand in the rain. It's what Peter would have done. She walked down the porch steps and stood on the sidewalk, raindrops dotting her face and running down her neck.

Peter would have laughed. He would have shot a toy gun. He would have done a half cartwheel and claimed it was worthy of the Olympics.

He would have . . .

She spotted Hank in the distance. The rain was coming down harder now, yet his form was undeniable as his bike rumbled near. He'd been making calls. *Making calls* while her world had crumbled around her! But, as she saw him coming toward her, a huge part of her wanted to collapse into his arms. To know that she could be herself and he would let her. That he of all people understood the complexity of life, of errors, of being unseen, of being swept aside.

Chandler stilled as Hank pulled closer. His broad shoulders were outlined against the gray morning. His hair hung around his shoulders in unruly curls, and his chiseled face was scarred and tough, squinting into the rain.

Hank parked the bike and, as he swung his leg over, reached behind him. Her knees gave out, and Chandler collapsed to the walk with a cry.

Mom and Lottie barreled down the porch at Chandler's cry, her father and Cru not far behind as they exited the house.

But it was Hank Chandler's attention was focused on. It was the little boy whose arms he disentangled from his waist when he lifted him off the bike.

"Momma!" Peter's word tripped out of his mouth just as his feet tripped over themselves.

Hank righted the boy and urged him toward her.

When Peter's little body slammed into her, Chandler knew it would be hours before she'd let him go. Maybe years. Maybe never. She rocked him back and forth, both of them weeping. Her mom and dad fell to their knees beside them, embracing them, and Lottie kept repeating, "I didn't sense this. I had no idea!"

Cru shook Hank's hand. "Where was he?"

"In a warehouse Margie rents. After I hung up with you, Chandler, I did some calling around and was able to make the connections. It started to fall into place in my mind. I checked into Margie's background. It was easy to find any properties she was linked to. I'm guessing the cops weren't far behind in figuring it out. I let them know I had Peter on my way here, but I wasn't keeping the kid from his mom any longer."

Hank reached out and ruffled her hair as the others embraced her and Peter. Chandler tilted her chin up, and he trailed his fingers lightly down her cheek and then withdrew his hand.

"Thank you," she mouthed.

He nodded.

It was inadequate. It was less than Hank deserved. But he had seen her. He'd recognized her limitations and never diminished her. And yet when she needed him to fight for her, he had.

"Momma?" Peter drew back, and as he did so, everyone else did too.

"Yes, buddy?" She pushed his hair back. Checking him over. He was fine. Well fed even. Clean. Just tired-looking, and still wearing only boxer-briefs. "What is it, Peter Pan?" Chandler asked, pressing her lips to his cheek.

He thumbed over his shoulder at Hank. "Can he stay?" Eyes wide. Tears brimming like pools over his chocolate-brown orbs. "Margie told me I didn't need to be scared, but I was. Till Hank came. Momma, I don't want Hank to go!"

Chandler tugged Peter back into her arms. She met Hank's eyes. He gave her a slight nod.

"Yes, Peter. Hank can stay," she answered.

Hank squatted beside them and reached out his broad hand, encompassing Peter's shuddering shoulder. "I'm not going anywhere, kid."

"You're sort of like a superhero," Peter said and took a shuddering breath.

Hank met her eyes.

"He sure is," Chandler whispered back.

PIPPA

It was chaos that ensued. Ernie swooped out of nowhere, accompanied by Jolly the clown and two other menagerie workers. They pulled Jake off Benard. He wrestled against Ernie, desperation and anger emanating from every strained muscle.

"Back off, Jake!" Ernie pulled, and Jake's heels dragged across the ground. Jolly held Jake by an arm. The menagerie workers made short work of containing the battered Benard, who crumpled into a mess on the ground.

Pippa backed away, the night embracing the horrors it held with all the wicked blackness that should go with it. The canvas of a tent flap whipped in the wind, snapping its echo in the night. The sounds of the animals in their houses and barns started to filter into her conscience, and with it the startling reality of Patty's dangling form in the costume house.

With a suppressed cry, Pippa whirled from the madness in front of her and stumbled back toward the house. Motorcars had begun to line the street. Policemen, curious onlookers, and who knew who else. People were beginning to mill about, questioning the bedlam that had awoken the area to its shock and confusion.

She pushed past a policeman who was jogging toward Ernie and Jake and blowing a whistle that would have woken the dead. Pippa tripped. The dead. No. It wouldn't wake the dead. Oh, that the whistle would somehow startle life back into Patty!

Stumbling up the porch steps, Pippa was reaching for the doorknob when a voice stopped her.

"You're taking her necklace off her neck? You sick, sick wretch. I know what you did before this, and now you want a memento from Patty? Did you kill her too, or are you just borrowing from someone else's depravity?"

Pippa slid to the floor of the porch, scooting up to the door to listen but slinking behind the frame so as not to be seen.

Georgiana Farnsworth? In the costume house? Surely, she wasn't speaking to Patty's hanging corpse!

"You revel in power and death, don't you?" Georgiana's footsteps were distinct on the floor. A definite click of her heels against the hardwood.

Then a man's muffled response, followed by, "Your accusations are appalling. Just like all your others."

Pippa huddled closer to the house as she heard the man's steps near the door. But he didn't speak. Only Georgiana did, her voice strident with accusation.

"Patty told me everything. She told me who you really are. And you'll let that man outside bear your crimes?"

A low laugh, then, "What crimes?"

Georgiana's own laugh followed. Scoffing but brilliantly assertive. "I will let them know the truth. You will never lay another hand on a woman again. You will never be allowed to abuse your power."

The door began to open.

Pippa startled, her foot striking a potted plant at the edge of the step and sending it careening down to the sidewalk.

There was a shout.

Then Georgiana cried out.

Pippa clambered down the steps, following the trajectory of the now-broken pot. Tripping toward the assembly gathering, toward the police, toward the line of faces she could no longer make out. Her vision blurred as she stumbled forward. Strong arms grasped her and held her upright.

"Get a doctor!" A shout echoed in her ears.

"Georgiana—help . . . her." Pippa collapsed, her body violently shivering with the effects of the night. She noticed the mustached face of the policeman holding her. She took in the swirling lights from lanterns and flashlights as more men arrived, shouting commands, a siren, and then the trumpet of an elephant from down the row.

But it was Jake who captured the last bit of her consciousness. His resigned expression. His weary frame as it marched slowly beside Ernie and followed Benard, who was flanked by two officers.

"It's over," he mouthed.

Maybe. Maybe it was, Pippa thought as she descended into blackness. If one could call this night any sort of resolution.

She tried to break from her thoughts and tell the policeman that Georgiana might need help. That the real Watchman—the real serial killer—might very well yet need arresting. Instead, she slipped into oblivion, the second trumpet of the elephant echoing in her ears.

CHAPTER FORTY

CHANDLER

Margie stared at her. She was a different woman. Her eyes were void of the life, of the laughter, she had brought to their house. Chandler eased into a chair opposite the woman clothed in orange, her hands cuffed to the table.

It was easy to know what to ask. And Chandler did so without hesitation. "Why?"

Margie blinked but didn't answer. Finally, she drew in a shuddering breath—whether due to regret or shame, Chandler was sure she'd never know—and said, "I-I couldn't, Chandler. I couldn't let my kids be known as the bloodline of the Watchman. Of the Bluff River Killer."

"So, you took *my* child instead?" Chandler brushed at a tear that both irritated her for its presence and shocked her for the fact she actually cared a tiny bit about Margie, even in this moment.

Margie's face transformed, her own tears barely concealed. She bit her lip and blew quick breaths from her nose. Her chin mottled as it shook. "Chandler, I—my kids are coming home from their dad's! I couldn't have you exposing what I'd hid for so many years."

"Linda," Chandler stated.

Margie nodded, casting a glance at the officer in the corner and at her lawyer, who sat a few feet away. She'd agreed to talk to Chandler and agreed to be honest. She'd already signed her confession. Guilty. Now she could only hope for leniency. She tapped her thumbs together, the cuffs rattling against the table. "It wasn't ever supposed to happen."

"It never is," Chandler couldn't help but insert. She crossed her arms over her chest, waiting.

Margie cleared her throat. "Linda was so—she was so bent on clearing her grandfather's name. She was sick of being ridiculed and assumed to be trouble due to his awful legacy. The day we went to the depot, it was just me and her. I didn't think she'd find anything, let alone connect the Watchman to *my* family! It was a complete shock to us both."

"You found the memorabilia he'd hid in the closet, didn't you?"

Margie nodded again, her expression sheepish, her lips pale. "At first, we were both excited. It was what we'd been looking for. But then Linda noticed the initials on the tokens. She started putting together that the office in the depot was Ripley's. She concocted the theory that maybe *he* was the killer and not her grandfather."

Margie stopped. She glanced at her lawyer, who gave a small nod. She reverted her stare to her hands. "I argued. *We* argued. It was an accident really. I don't even know why I—there was an old hammer lying in the corner. I grabbed it. I hit Linda and then . . ." Margie sniffed. "Then it was over. She just lay there. And all I could think to do was to put her with the Watchman's things. We'd only pulled off a few boards. It was easy to put them back. Easy to hide Linda."

"The police said you even helped in the search for Linda," Chandler said. It was odd to think of Margie as a cold-blooded killer. Odder to think of her having the stamina to cover it up for decades.

"Yes." Margie tried to reach for Chandler, but the handcuffs attached to the table stopped the journey of her hands. Chandler drew back. "Chandler, please." A tear trickled down her cheek. "My kids are the most important thing to me, and I won't have them wear the title of a serial killer's relations, even if it's not direct in line."

"But, to involve Peter?" Chandler shook her head in disbelief. "He's as innocent as they are."

"I know." More tears wetted Margie's face. "I know, I *know*! But you and Hank were getting close and you weren't even looking that hard. It was coming so easy for you. When you found Linda, I—I panicked. I'd taken the zebra toy with me to your house that day. I was going to tell you some story about how it was Linda's and she'd given it to me when we were kids and on and on. I was going to try to steer you in a different direction. But then you *found* Linda! I was too late."

"So, you traumatized my son in order to get me to stop looking into Linda's murder?"

It was so basic. So simply basic that Chandler wanted to laugh at the same time she wanted to throw herself across the table and throttle Margie.

"Is . . . is Peter okay?" Margie bit her lip again. Her upper lip was wet with moisture from her nose, and her cheeks were blotched red from crying.

Chandler stared at her. A pathetic form of humanity, captured by her own need to hide, to hide who she was and what she'd done. To hide to protect her children's future. In the end, Margie had ruined lives. She had concocted a story of what-ifs and could-be's that had never actually happened. The roundabout relation to Richard Ripley—the Watchman—and Margie was certain her children, even a further generation removed, would bear the scars of Ripley's sins.

Maybe Margie was right. Maybe it would have happened. But at least . . . at least she could have shared the burden with Denny and Linda—even Hank. At least they would all have been alive and able to write a new future for themselves, to draw on the strength of the family that circus history claimed was once a close-knit community.

"Is he all right?" Margie pressed.

Chandler didn't answer. Instead, she bent for her purse and

drew it up over her shoulder. She nodded her thanks to Margie's lawyer and caught the eye of the officer in the corner, who moved forward to lead Chandler from the room.

At the doorway, Chandler turned to address Margie. "If you had only asked for help, Margie . . ." Chandler gave a sigh of defeat with every ounce of truth in her words. "I would have been there for you."

PIPPA

He was dead.

Richard Ripley had been found in the costume house, a pair of scissors lodged in his back, with Patty Luchent hanging above him like the ultimate scene of horror.

Pippa and her mother, Victoria, sat side by side on the settee. People had come and gone through the parlor, offering their condolences, expressing their shock, and asking questions. So many questions.

Why?

Have they found who killed him?

What reason have the police uncovered?

There were no answers, but deep inside, Pippa remembered Georgiana's proclamation that she would expose the Watchman. She recalled the familiar voices and then the scuffle that had begun when Pippa had careened down the steps and lost her own senses in the madness.

There were certain facts that lined up all too coincidentally. Her father often visited the circus throughout the summer at its various stops. He had been in St. Louis, where Jake's sister, Bridgette, had been murdered. He was cold, calculating, and oppressive toward her and her mother.

Yet there was also nothing to say any of that wasn't pure co-incidence. And to tarnish the Ripley name and leave her mother in ruins . . .

Pippa was used to being quiet. She had been that way all her life. Richard Ripley had taught her as much. She had a feeling she wouldn't be alone in her silence this time. That Georgiana Farnsworth would temper her voice going forward, knowing more than she would admit. Someone had to have shoved the scissors into Richard Ripley . . . the circus would remain a place of secrets. The questionable kind. The kind that even if told, would still have inquiry circling around them. Answers they would never be able to firmly resolve.

Pippa felt her mother's gloved hand come to rest on top of hers. She met Victoria's gaze. The beautiful lines of her mother's face were marred by weariness that came with planning a funeral, laying to rest a spouse, and sifting through the effects of what they left behind. Forrest had been helpful. Very quick to step into the role of executor for Bonaventure Circus. He would be honest and careful with her mother, Pippa knew. Even so, he would never be anything more to her than her father's partner.

Had Forrest suspected her father? Was that why he'd been hell-bent on protecting her? Perhaps. Either way, protecting her from the Watchman—whoever he was—was Forrest's excuse for why he and Jake had finally ceased their fisticuffs at the Autumn Formal. That at the last possible moment they'd joined forces and arrived at the circus together. They were not comrades by any means. Only united by the mere fact that Pippa's mother had cried for them to stop and for someone to go after her daughter. Now Forrest seemed remarkably defensive of Georgiana. A bewildering turn of opin-ion. That they seemed connected somehow was an avenue Pippa didn't wish to explore further. That Forrest might share Georgiana's secrets, might know more than he was willing to admit . . .

It was unforgivable from any angle, and Pippa had no desire to try to sift through it and find more truth. She was already overwhelmed with the truths that had been revealed. Of Benard. Of—God help her—Clive! Pippa had yet to face her birth father. Word had come that he would make it. The hospital was confident of this. But what lies had Clive told her all these years? Feigning ignorance and illness to excuse his knowledge of who Pippa was?

"Pippa?"

She lifted her eyes to Victoria Ripley. The woman's fingers wrapped around hers, and Pippa dropped her gaze to them. It was the first time, in a very long time, that she recalled her mother touching her gently.

"I am so sorry," Victoria whispered. Her eyes glistened with unshed tears.

Pippa was unsure of what Victoria meant. "For what?"

Victoria's breath was shaky, and she looked up to the ceiling for a long moment before giving an answer. "He tolerated you because of me, Pippa. I couldn't—I tried to protect you from him. But, in doing so, I pulled far away from you."

Pippa squeezed her mother's hand. "He never hurt me." Good heavens, did his own wife suspect him too?

Victoria nodded. "Yes. He was a hard man to love, Pippa. But he did allow me you."

Pippa stilled at the words.

Victoria's soft smile burrowed its way into Pippa's soul. "I wanted a child . . . so badly. I begged him. I begged him to let me keep you. I've always seen you, Pippa. You've always been just a heartbeat away from mine. But your father—he was a jealous man. I couldn't allow him to resent you more than he already did, by showering my affections on you. On you, my lovely, my beautiful daughter."

A tear escaped Pippa's eye. She wasn't sure how to curl herself around the words Victoria spoke. Around the admission that her mother had hidden so much more from her than she'd realized. That, after all this time, she had been remarkably and loyally loved by her mother, who had sacrificed for Pippa's own sake.

That neither of them would miss Richard Ripley was not a relief, nor did it bring peace. That he had wedged between them for years, that he had commanded and lorded his strength over their bond and effectively stained it brought an agony for which Pippa was unprepared. The lost years, the lost memories, the not knowing that she was, after all, wanted. By someone.

Victoria shifted on the settee and faced Pippa. She ran her hands down the length of Pippa's black chiffon sleeves, then cupped Pippa's face with her hand. "No more, my dear. I have prayed for this day. Not this outcome, but this day, for years. I knew God would bring you to me in time. I had only to remain patient and trust that He could work where others couldn't. That He could overcome what we all made so dreadfully wrong."

Pippa leaned into her mother's hand. "How is it you think God cares about us so?"

Her question was honest. Achingly so. If she retraced her life, she saw only lies, desperation, loneliness, and yet now her mother saw rescue, hope, and fruition to long hours of beseeching a higher Power.

Victoria's lips thinned in a solemn smile. She reached down and took Pippa's hands in hers. "How is it you think that God doesn't? When you could have been orphaned, instead you became mine. When you could have been hurt, instead your father merely commanded you. When you could have been scoffed at and mocked, instead you became respected and admired. He has taken back His justice and is making right His plan, in spite of what man intended."

Pippa nodded, though she didn't say more. She couldn't say more. For while Victoria's words made sense and offered a kind of comfort she hadn't expected, they also left her with the blatant question that had yet to be answered.

How could her father, Clive, love God so much, and his daughter so little?

CHAPTER
FORTY-ONE

She would finally face Clive. But not the little man of the circus whom Pippa knew. She would face her father. Pippa paused outside the door of Clive's room at the small Bluff River Hospital. The smells of medicines and antiseptics mixed with the familiar tang of cigar and spice.

Jake gave her a short nod. "Go."

Pippa paused, her gaze roving his face. Bruised, he looked down at her. Jake smiled then. A lazy smile, his unlit cigar drooping in the corner of his mouth.

"I'll be here. Waiting."

"Are you all right?" Pippa whispered, her words thick with meaning. Bridgette. Closure to Jake's sister's assault.

There was so much wickedness. It was hard to know if evil had been silenced or simply arrested for the moment. She supposed evil would always lurk in the shadows, unrepentant, in its own hiding of sorts.

Jake bent and pressed his lips to her forehead. A long, lingering kiss of weary understanding. "I will be," he said. But there was struggle in his face that told her it would not be resolved with the imprisonment of Benard or the ceasing of the work of the Watchman. Another kiss, this time to Pippa's temple. "If justice were simple," he added, "we wouldn't struggle with closure. I'm not sure I'll ever have it, to be honest. If Ernie hadn't pulled me off Benard, I—" Jake paused, choked—"well, I guess I got to leave God something to do, and instead I need to make a fresh start."

"Patty doesn't get her fresh start." Tears burned Pippa's eyes.

"No." Jake's forehead rested against hers. "But we do." He stepped away and tipped his head toward the door. "This moment isn't for me. I need to check on Lily—Ernie said she's going to be all right."

"Is Georgiana . . . ?" Pippa's question was left hanging between them. Jake didn't know what Pippa had overheard that night. Regardless, Pippa was still worried that Georgiana would take advantage of the current weakness of the circus and capitalize on her cause.

"Georgiana has been quiet." Jake ran his fingers through his hair, thoroughly mussing it and giving him a rakish appearance. "She would be a fool to go after Bonaventure now. In the wake of your father's death, there is much community sympathy for your loss. Forrest will—he'll capitalize on that, and Bonaventure will ride the rails again next summer. With Lily."

Pippa gave in to her impulse, embracing him and breathing deep of his scent. Pulling back, she whispered, "Thank you."

"Of course," he replied, then gave his customary shrug.

"I need to go now."

Jake looked past her to Clive's hospital door. Then he locked eyes with her. "It's not easy to protect the ones we love, Pippa. We all fight for them in our own way. Don't be too quick to judge the avenues by which we do so. We are only human."

Pippa pushed open the door.

The room was white. From the ceiling to the floor. The bed looked empty until her eyes rested on its midpoint, where Clive's feet poked up beneath the blankets. His eyes were closed, outlined by black bruises. Stitches lined the side of his head, and his arm rested in a cast.

Pippa sucked in a shuddered breath. Clive. He had known—all these years as she'd grown up before his eyes—that she was his daughter. He knew she searched for him. Why hadn't he confessed he was her father?

Clive's eyes fluttered open, as far as they could beneath the swelling of his eyelids. He reached out his good hand. "Pippa . . ." His voice sounded raw. She didn't move. She couldn't. "I'm sorry." While he said the words, Pippa struggled to accept them.

"Why didn't you tell me?"

Clive pulled his hand back. "Sit."

There was nowhere to sit but in the chair by his side. Pippa took it but moved it back a few inches so she was out of his reach. Clive turned his head on his pillow.

"I made a grievous error." Clive swallowed. It seemed laborious, as if it pained him. "You were that error."

Pippa pulled at a thread on the lace cuff of her sleeve. Those words smarted.

Clive corrected himself. "*Leaving* you was my error."

"Why did you?" The words forced their way through Pippa's throat. "Was it my leg? You didn't want a deformed child?"

Clive's eyebrows drew together, and he slammed his palm on the bed. "Look at me! Do you think I would judge your malady?"

His passion stunned Pippa. She slumped in the chair and looked at him. Clive struggled to sit up, pillows dropping behind his back as he did so.

"It was a miracle your mother loved me. She was beautiful. She was . . . *normal*, at least as most men would consider it. When she had you, I held you in my arms and I didn't see your leg. No. I saw that you were *perfect*."

As Clive ground out the words, Pippa met his eyes, staring intently now at her father. She had never been described that way before.

Clive shifted toward her. His wince made him stop, yet he continued his confession. "There I was. Widowed. A dwarf. A circus sideshow, and my baby girl was an average human being. I knew she would grow up to be beautiful like her mother who'd died giving birth to her child." Clive reached out as if to touch her, then drew back his hand. "I couldn't keep you. Raise you in my world? Allow you to be ridiculed because of who I am? Who wants his child to have to bear that sort of title? To have society wave the banner over her head that she is different somehow?"

Clive waved his good arm down the short length of his body. His words choked. He coughed. His mouth pursed, and his eyes speared Pippa in her seat.

"I couldn't face the truth that you might grow up to be ashamed of me. Embarrassed by who I am. That you are the daughter of the circus dwarf. I lost sight of who God had created me to be, and of what beauty God could bring from the daughter He'd given me.

"I met with Richard Ripley. I knew that he and his wife were childless. He agreed to take you, but I asked to make it appear as if you'd been abandoned. That way, you couldn't find me. You wouldn't know my shame. But now you do. And as it turns out, my shame is not my height, or the proportion of my limbs, or my face. My shame is that I gave you away."

Pippa focused on her cuff, pulled some more on the thread, and unraveled another delicate loop of lace. It was a distraction, helping to keep her feelings at bay. She couldn't look at Clive at the moment. "Why didn't you tell me when I asked? When you knew I was looking for you? And how did you not know that Benard—that he was watching me all these years, with you right beside him?"

"Oh, Benard." Closing his eyes, Clive lay his head back on his pillow. "I didn't know about Benard. He hid it well. I only knew that he grieved for you, just as I had. I didn't even realize he had followed me the day I left you at the Ripleys, that he had known where you went. I just knew you were fragile, and if I told you I was your father, it would only confuse and hurt you. I had to protect you. I did so with my silence. I was wrong. My silence was always my way of trying to protect you."

"You *were* wrong." Pippa swiped at her tears. "I would never have been ashamed of you."

"Benard was a child when he joined the small circus band we were with at the time." Clive opened his eyes again. "For a while he was like our son, more so your mother's. She loved him. And when you were born, he helped me care for you the few days after your mother died. He shared my grief.

"After I left you at the Ripley house, Benard and I grew apart. I was drowning in my grief. I didn't realize that he was too. I didn't know he'd slipped a toy in your basket when you were a baby and I left you. I didn't know he'd spoken with your mother in the hours after you were born, before she slipped away from us. I had no idea he'd vowed to watch over you or developed a bond with you as a baby, which would later become a sick sort of obsession with him. Benard was gentle, loyal. But he was broken, and it turned him into a wicked man."

Pippa watched Clive's throat work. Benard's duplicity, his acts of violence had wounded Clive far worse than he'd injured her. Clive loved Benard, she could see it. A part of her was jealous for the fatherly love he'd bestowed on someone on whom it was wasted when she had longed for this her entire life.

When Clive spoke again, Pippa raised her head and met his earnest gaze.

"Please forgive me. You were . . . *are* loved, Pippa. Very, very much."

Pippa stared into her birth father's eyes and saw in them the very pain she had carried. The rejection she assumed had followed her entire existence. Pippa thought of Jake, of his past. She saw Richard Ripley's hard face. She thought of Forrest, his tendency toward arrogance, but also the protectiveness he'd shown her. Of Franny and her desire to be accepted by Pippa. Even Georgiana Farnsworth and her campaign to bring awareness to the abused and unloved—and maybe her own secrets she would carry with her for years to come.

"Come here." Clive reached out his hand. Pippa rose, the lace cuff a long ball of thread in her hand. She dropped it and laid her head on her father's small chest.

"I forgive you," she whispered through her tears.

Clive's hand stroked her head, the way a father tended his daughter. Loving. Protective. He had been willing to give his life for her. He had given his entire life for her.

"You are a gift, Pippa Ripley." Clive's words breathed through her heart into her soul. "And I've never lost sight of you."

CHAPTER
FORTY-TWO

CHANDLER

She had removed herself from the group gathered in the backyard around the picnic table, and now Chandler stared out the window, watching them all. Cru stood over the grill, flipping hamburgers, his hoodie sweatshirt spotted with grease that must have spit from the meat. Lottie and her mom sat opposite each other, hands holding mugs of hot apple cider. Lottie threw her head back and laughed at something Mom said. They seemed to get along well. Sure, they had their differences of faith and foundation, but that didn't eliminate the beauty of kindness.

Chandler's dad raked a pile of leaves, and as fast as he piled them, Peter launched into the pile, throwing the leaves into the air like confetti. Denny sat in a lawn chair a bit away from the group, balancing a bottle of beer he'd smuggled in to the "very prohibition-style picnic" and sucked on his cigarette. There was contentment on his face, but Chandler saw sadness there too. The police had finally released Linda's remains for burial, and a memorial service was planned for the following week.

Movement beside her caught Chandler's attention.

Hank.

He had a mug of coffee in his hand. His jeans were loose and his feet bare in leather flip-flops. He wore a T-shirt proudly boasting the name of a local gas station.

"Aren't you cold?" Chandler tossed at him, glancing at his brawny bare arms.

"Me?" Hank winked and took a gulp of his coffee. "Nah."

"My uncle signed off on the renovation proposal for the depot." Chandler hadn't told anyone that yet. Hadn't mentioned either that Jackson had been assigned to a different project.

"Great." Hank nodded. "It'd be nice not to have the place torn down."

Chandler drew in a deep breath, fixing her eyes on Peter as he rolled in the leaves. "I just hope everything that happened there—well, that it's not a deterrent for some people. Lottie often told me it's hard to sell a home if someone was murdered in it, just because of superstitions."

Hank shrugged. "But this isn't a house. And, unfortunately, I think the history behind it might lend toward *more* interest. People get excited about morbid stuff like that."

Chandler turned and eyed him. "How *did* the depot door get unlocked the night of the ghost tour? And the screams . . . was that really Patty Luchent?"

Hank raised his brows and gave her a squinty grin. "I'm a felon, remember? I can think of all sorts of ways someone could have unlocked the padlock and gotten the door open."

Chandler stuck her tongue out at him. "That's not an answer."

Hank chuckled. "I think the likely answer to the question is that your contractor who visited did in fact leave the door unlocked—just like we'd questioned."

"I'm still curious, though," she ventured. "I mean, how Patty Luchent's necklace made its way into the secret drawer in that desk. And what the heck has been making all that noise upstairs in the costume house and tossing boxes around."

"I doubt we'll ever know about the necklace. Maybe the killer removed it and secreted it away? Maybe someone else hid it to protect the Ripley name? As for the noises . . ." Hank gave her a side-eye scrunch of his face. "Maybe it's Patty? Just like Cru and Lottie say?"

Chandler's shoulders dropped and she stared at Hank. "You really believe in ghosts?"

He smiled. "It's sorta fun."

"I think it's probably a squirrel. Or a bat or something," Chandler concluded.

Hank's arm draped over her shoulder as he dropped a kiss on her temple. "I didn't know squirrels could toss boxes."

"Oh, shut up!" Chandler laughed and slapped his arm.

Hank ducked and gave her a glare. "Hey, watch the coffee!"

"I don't believe in ghosts," Chandler repeated with conviction. She didn't.

"That's fine. Don't then." Hank winked. "But if you ever see cigarette ashes upstairs, well, then you'll know it was Patty for sure."

Chandler's eyes widened. "What?"

"She smoked. Lottie says every now and then people see little piles of ashes at the depot or the costume house."

"Knock it off!" Chandler laughed again. She could tell Hank was toying with her now. Teasing, having fun in trying to creep her out.

"Well, I do know about the screams on the ghost tour," Hank offered.

Chandler waited.

"Cru admitted that was all part of the ghost-tour ruse. They'd hidden a small outdoor sound system, and all he had to do was push play on his remote. The screams broadcast through the well-hidden speakers, which get people all worked up and freaked. In fact, he was the one in the depot the night we met. He'd squeezed in that side window like I'd thought might have happened. He needed to check one of the Bluetooth speakers he'd stashed inside. Lottie saw the light and didn't know it was Cru or she'd have never called the cops. He feels a bit stupid about it all."

Chandler leaned into Hank, resting her head against his arm. "Go figure. It sure scared the life out of me."

"Yeah. Cru said they're going to get rid of that part in the future."

"Good riddance. He'll be lucky I can give my uncle a good word on his behalf and spare him trespassing charges. I know Cru's intentions weren't to harm anyone or anything." Chandler looked up at Hank then, and he dropped his green gaze on her. "Thank you, Hank," she whispered.

He smiled, and it reached his eyes. It made the corners crease and his severe features soften. "You're gonna make it." Hank lifted his mug to take another casual sip. "You've got people who want to help you. So does Peter. I know it's going to be tough on him, working through the aftereffects of Margie, but you'll make it. You're not alone."

Chandler looked out the window again. At Lottie and Cru. At her parents. At Denny. Then she looked back at Hank. "I have my tribe, don't I?" she breathed in a thankful whisper.

Hank dropped another kiss on the top of her head. "The best families are made of broken people." Another kiss on her temple. "Because we get each other. We see each other."

"I think that's what God intended." Chandler raised up on her tiptoes and returned Hank's gift of kisses with one of her own. A little one. For now. Maybe later she'd have more gumption to stake her claim more seriously. For now, she was content. She had come out of hiding. She had received help. She hadn't lost but had only gained.

And that was the beauty of being seen.

Pippa sat on a barrel, her legs dangling, her dress hiked above her calves. She wasn't worried that her twisted leg showed. In a way, she was proud of it. She was proud to be where she belonged. In the circus, watching Ernie lead Lily around the elephant-house ring, her father, Clive, leaning against the wall next to her, with Jake on the other side. Ernie tapped Lily on the rump with his prod. A light tap. One the calf responded to as she took another step forward.

Pippa leaned into Jake. Closing her eyes, she listened. She listened to the sounds of the elephants, the commands of Ernie, the distant whistle of the train, and the voices of laborers outside the elephant house preparing the circus grounds for winter. She drew in a deep breath, letting the pungent scents fill her. Of coal fumes from the furnace that heated the house, straw and manure, of crisp autumn, of Jake's cigar, and of Clive's aftershave. She let her eyes see into herself. Into the person she was becoming. A daughter of the circus. A woman with a purpose.

And in her heart echoed the voice of Patty Luchent.

"We were all meant to be . . . Providence places you there . . . who knew God had one of me up His sleeve?"

Who indeed?

Pippa reached out and scratched Penn's nose as her dog came up beside them.

It was a peaceful thing. The knowing. The knowing that she had never truly been unseen. She had only been lost. And even in that lostness she had been given direction. Maybe Clive's faith and her mother's hope for the future were founded on One more capable and more invested in her than Pippa had realized. Maybe it was worth pursuing faith. For in the pursuing, one must come out of hiding and run toward grace. Because it was only grace that would ever truly save.

Pippa opened her eyes. She drank in the sight of Lily, the now-unbroken elephant calf. Her tail whipping back and forth, her ears flapping as if she were a bird taking flight. The elephant turned her head, searching, and her dark eyes met Pippa's. Lily's trunk lifted as if in a wave, and her mouth stretched into a smile.

No. Life was far from perfect. The circus celebrated that. And while some believed that it only mocked it, Pippa knew better. She knew deeper. She knew, in her soul, that they found communion under the circus banner. And they would rescue each other, because that's what family did.

AUTHOR'S NOTE

The circus has always been a part of my heart and my childhood. Even though I'm an adult and "home" changes with moves and relocations, growing up in the shadow of the Ringling brothers' wintering grounds made the glory of the circus more real to me than if I had merely read about it in a history book. I remember riding the elephants, I remember the endless circles ridden on the merry-go-round, the pumping cadence of the calliope, the roar of the tigers, and the sight of elephants in the river bathing.

Running around the circus ring, under the Big Top, as a circus clown is a feat I'll never forget. The stone-etched elephants carved into old walls around town. Circus murals painted and faded on old buildings. The theater, the circus wagons, the red and gold and purple and silver. Royal colors. A celebration.

But the circus also has a darker side to it. One of mockery, of judgment, the diminishing of humanity, and in some circumstances the actual abuse of man and beast. It only proves that while beauty can be tainted by the prowess of a wicked nature, it can still be a glimpse into the talent and magnificence of God and His creation.

In the end, I think the circus discovered something too many of us turned into a sideshow. What some mocked, some embraced, what some saw as entertainment, some made a family. The people, the animals, the aura that is the circus . . . it's beautiful. It is our history. It should always be preserved.

For more information, visit: https://www.circusworldbara boo.org/.

QUESTIONS
FOR DISCUSSION

1. The circus was a foundational form of entertainment in the United States starting in the last half of the nineteenth century. When you think of the circus, what images come to mind?

2. Chandler tries hard to disguise her struggles with her autoimmune disorder for fear it will hijack the perception she is a capable female in both the workplace and as a mother. How have personal health shortcomings impacted your self-confidence? What about others you know who suffer with health issues that threaten to compromise their view of themselves?

3. When Chandler meets Hank Titus, she draws conclusions about his trustworthiness based on his appearance and his lack of cultural etiquette. What parallels do you see regarding Chandler's fear that others will judge her based on stereotype? What other stereotypes can shape our perspective of other people?

4. Pippa Ripley embarks on a journey, going from being a submissive, nonvocal daughter to finding her own path and independence. In what ways can women be independent and submissive simultaneously?

5. Much of Chandler's and Pippa's struggles are rooted in the fear of their being seen for who they really are. What has held you back from allowing people to know the *real* you? What are some of your greatest fears about being truly seen by others?

6. Georgiana Farnsworth approaches the controversial subject of animal rights as it relates to the circus and entertainment-based animal performances. What do you believe is the appropriate position on the inclusion of animals in entertainment?

7. The Watchman's motivation was one of possessiveness, while the other serial killer's motives were based on a need to dominate and control women. What was the difference between the Watchman's possessive nature and the nature of the serial killer?

8. How has your faith affected your sense of self-worth and how you view others? How does a relationship with Jesus Christ change your perspective when you learn of others' struggles?

ACKNOWLEDGMENTS

A huge thank-you to the archives and the museum of Circus World in Baraboo, Wisconsin. What a fabulous place that should always be remembered as the home of the Greatest Show on Earth!

Thank you to my bestie, Julie Anderson, for helping me research, for lending me her Pupper Ice as the model for Penn, and for educating me about the plight of, and highly misunderstood, pit bull. Another creature sorely understated for their loyalty, their caregiving, and a history of nannying that shows how much these animals can truly love.

Massive thanks to my own personal Peter Pan, who helped me dream up Nitro Steel and Rustman. Who was super-duper important in making this book happen. Who makes this momma-heart turn into a momma-bear when it comes to her little boy. I love you, Peter Pan!

Thanks to Tracee Chu, who once again makes the Acknowledgments for her lending a hand in helping me think through the story. It was her idea to give Chandler a health issue. It was her idea to push me to look deeper into my own struggle with Lyme disease and to summon the courage to bring awareness to an underestimated condition that can no longer be ignored.

Rich and Steve at the Coffee Bean Connection, your liquid

heaven fueled this novel into being. You are both swell, and I thank the Lord He brought you into my life. May He touch the deepest recesses of your hearts.

Thanks to my parents. Both sets. Who love on the kiddos and me by giving of themselves. To my mom-in-law, who makes me diet-approved desserts and lets me sleep every Sunday in her recliner so I have the energy to work and write during the week. To my mom, who tucks me in when I'm not doing well and insists I take a nap at ten in the morning.

Special thanks to Joanne Bischof. We compared circus stories years ago, both of us wanting our stories to see the published page. While Jake is certainly no Charlie—be still my heart!—I'm so thankful our dreams have seen fruition and the circus runs thick in our imaginations to this day.

Darren Hornby, my longtime co-worker, and now the ringmaster of the entire circus town's chamber. I'm so proud of you, my friend, and I'm so thankful for the years we have shared a mutual adoration of all things Ringling Bros. Circus.

Chandler Carlson, who's my living proof that *Chandler* is most assuredly a feminine name! Thanks for letting me borrow it, my friend.

As always, I cannot forget my illustrious agent, Janet Grant, my team at Bethany House, the numerous other writers who pour their lives into mine: Anne Love, Laurie Tomlinson, Halee Matthews (who edited the early drafts of this book more times than I can count), Sarah Varland, Natalie Walters, Colleen Coble, Dani Pettrey, and Christen Krumm. YOU all are my tribe.

Finally, to my Cap'n Hook and my CoCo. You're the other half of Peter Pan and me, and together we make quite a force.

To you, my readers . . . always, *always* know you were born with a purpose. That you are not hidden. That you are seen. That you will be fought for by the One who breathed you into being.

Jaime Jo Wright, the author of five novels, is winner of the Christy, Daphne du Maurier, Carol, and INSPY Awards. She's also the *Publishers Weekly* and ECPA bestselling author of three novellas. Jaime works as a human resources director in Wisconsin, where she lives with her husband and two children. To learn more, visit her at jaimewrightbooks.com.

Sign Up for Jaime's Newsletter

Keep up to date with Jaime's news on book releases and events by signing up for her email list at jaimewrightbooks.com.

More from Jaime Jo Wright

Mystery begins to follow Aggie Dunkirk when she exhumes the past's secrets and uncovers a crime her eccentric grandmother has been obsessing over. Decades earlier, after discovering her sister's body in the attic, Imogene Grayson is determined to obtain justice. Two women, separated by time, vow to find answers . . . no matter the cost.

Echoes among the Stones

BETHANYHOUSE

 Stay up to date on your favorite books and authors with our free e-newsletters. Sign up today at bethanyhouse.com.

 facebook.com/bethanyhousepublishers @bethanyhousefiction

 Free exclusive resources for your book group at bethanyhouseopenbook.com

You May Also Like . . .

A century apart, two women seek their mothers in Pleasant Valley, Wisconsin. In 1908, Thea's search leads her to an insane asylum with dark secrets. In modern-day Wisconsin, Heidi Lane answers the call of a mother battling dementia. Both confront the legendary curse of Misty Wayfair—and are entangled in a web of danger that entwines them across time.

The Curse of Misty Wayfair by Jaime Jo Wright
jaimewrightbooks.com

Annalise knows painful memories hover beneath the pleasant façade of Gossamer Grove. But she is shocked when she inherits documents that reveal mysterious murders from a century ago. In this dual-time romantic suspense novel, two women, separated by a hundred years, must uncover the secrets within the borders of their town before it's too late.

The Reckoning at Gossamer Pond by Jaime Jo Wright
jaimewrightbooks.com

Fleeing a stalker, Kaine Prescott purchases an old house with a dark history: a century earlier, an unidentified woman was found dead on the grounds. As Kaine tries to settle down, she learns the story of her ancestor Ivy Thorpe, who, with the help of a man from her past, tried to uncover the truth about the death.

The House on Foster Hill by Jaime Jo Wright
jaimewrightbooks.com

BETHANYHOUSE

More from Bethany House

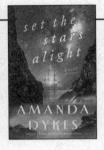

Reeling from the loss of her parents, Lucie Clairmont discovers an artifact under the floorboards of their London flat, leading her to an old seaside estate. Aided by her childhood friend Dashel, a renowned forensic astronomer, they start to unravel a history of heartbreak, sacrifice, and love begun 200 years prior—one that may offer the healing each seeks.

Set the Stars Alight by Amanda Dykes
amandadykes.com

Determined to uphold her father's legacy, newly graduated Nora Shipley joins an entomology research expedition to India to prove herself in the field. In this spellbinding new land, Nora is faced with impossible choices—between saving a young Indian girl and saving her career, and between what she's always thought she wanted and the man she's come to love.

A Mosaic of Wings by Kimberly Duffy
kimberlyduffy.com

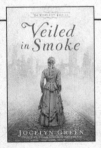

As Chicago's Great Fire destroys their bookshop, Meg and Sylvie Townsend make a harrowing escape from the flames with the help of reporter Nate Pierce. But the trouble doesn't end there—their father is committed to an asylum after being accused of murder, and they must prove his innocence before the asylum truly drives him mad.

Veiled in Smoke by Jocelyn Green
THE WINDY CITY SAGA #1
jocelyngreen.com

◊ BETHANYHOUSE